Below Bartle Frere

C.R. Cummings

Also By
CHRISTOPHER CUMMINGS

Below Bartle Frere

C.R. Cummings

DoctorZed
Publishing
www.doctorzed.com

This 3rd edition Published 2023 by DoctorZed Publishing

DoctorZed Publishing books may be ordered through booksellers or by contacting:

DoctorZed Publishing
10 Vista Ave
Skye, South Australia 5072
www.doctorzed.com

ISBN: 978-0-6456384-1-7 (hc)
ISBN: 978-0-6456384-2-4 (sc)
ISBN: 978-0-6456384-3-1 (ebk)

National Library of Australia Cataloguing-in-Publication entry

Author: Cummings, C. R., author.

Title: Below Bartle Frere / Christopher Cummings.

ISBN: 9780645638417 (hardcover)

Target Audience: For young adults.

Subjects: Adventure stories, Australian.

Military cadets--Queensland--Fiction.

Cover image Gold Nuggets © Vitaly Korovin | Dreamstime.com
Cover design © Scott Zarcinas

DoctorZed Publishing rev. date: 24/02/2023

Respectful Thanks
To

The late Mr Les Pearson—*Silver Wolf*
Leader of the 4th Cairns Scout Troop,
who introduced me to hiking in the Mulgrave Valley,
Below Bartle Frere.

Chapter 1

KYLIE

Saturday, 12th December, a sunny summer day, as twelve-year-old Kylie looked through the front windscreen of the car. A dozen kilometres ahead bulked the huge mass of Mt Bartle Frere. Seen from the northwest as the car passed Lamins Hill, the massive bulk of the mountain appeared to fill the whole windscreen.

Highest mountain in Queensland, Kylie reminded herself, knowing that she did so every time she saw it.

Unusually for this time of year the entire mountain was visible, standing up like a giant dark blue cut-out against a clear blue sky. During December, which was the start of the 'wet season' in North Queensland, the mountain was more often than not wreathed in clouds and rain.

The car, driven by Kylie's mother, Mrs Cynthia Kirk, turned left on to a side road at the top of Lamins Hill and proceeded at a slower pace along a gravel road with open fields on the left and a thick belt of tropical rain forest on the right. In the back sat Kylie's two friends: Margaret Lake and Allison Nichols.

Margaret was the same age as Kylie. She also had the same colouring of hair and eyes: brown. There the similarity ended. Where Kylie was slim and had a dancer's grace Margaret was chubby and rounder; although not round in the places she wanted to be. Their skin also marked them apart. Margaret had pale skin liberally sprinkled with freckles whereas Kylie's complexion was a smooth 'peaches and cream'. Allison was the oldest of the three and had just turned 13. She had sparkling hazel eyes, brown hair with tints of gold in it and was just beginning to blossom into the curves of young womanhood.

The car turned right and went down a long, open ridge with dairy farms on both sides. Soon after passing a farmhouse it crossed a tiny bridge, passing through a wall of jungle in a tunnel formed by the overhanging trees, to emerge on a long upslope with more open fields on both sides. Dozens of dairy cattle dotted the lush green pastures.

Margaret clapped her hands with delight. "Isn't it pretty!" she said.

Allison nodded. "It looks more like England than Australia," she added.

Kylie smiled. "I think it is the prettiest part of North Queensland. I just love all the greens."

She gazed out and sniffed the fresh country air. Everywhere she looked was another shade of green: light green of the pastures, bright green of individual trees, darker patches of rainforest.

Margaret pointed. "Look at all those black and white cows. They look just like toys on a model farm," she said.

"Frisians," Allison added knowledgeably.

Kylie became excited. Not far now. "We are almost at the farm," she said. "It is just up the hill here."

She wriggled in her seat. Visiting her grandmother was always a pleasure, doubly so because she loved the farm with all its animals and its little adventures. This visit promised to be even more enjoyable as it was to be for three weeks. Usually they just drove up for a day, or a weekend.

It was the first day of the school holidays, which was an added source of pleasure. All three girls went to the same school in Cairns and were in the same Guide Troop. Margaret and Allison were staying for the first ten days and the thought of that made Kylie squirm with anticipation.

"You will really like it on the farm," she said. "It is ever so interesting. There is always something to do."

Allison nodded. "I hope so. Is it much further? I'm sick of sitting in this car."

They had been driving for two hours, having left Cairns at 9am. They had driven up to Mareeba first, to drop in on Kylie's other Grandmother, her father's mum. From there they had driven south via Atherton and Malanda to the south-eastern edge of the 'Tablelands', that upland area of lush green farms set amidst encircling jungle covered ranges.

"We are nearly there now, just over the hill," Kylie replied.

The car slowed near the crest of the hill. There was more rain forest on the right. At the end of the patch of jungle was a road junction. Mrs Kirk turned the car right along the side road. Kylie leaned forward, eager for her first glimpse of the farmhouse. The low hilltop on the left was part of the property. The road wound over the low crest and down to the left, the jungle still walling them in on the right. Ahead the country opened out on the left, giving glimpses of rolling fields and clumps of trees.

Buildings became visible on the left of the road.

"That's the milking shed down there," Kylie said, pointing ahead.

The car slowed even more as the road was rough gravel. At the bend above the milking shed another large shed stood beside a dirt track which went off to the left along the side of the hill. Mrs Kirk turned onto the track, which was of hard packed, red basalt soil, and drove past the shed. This was typical of all such structures on farms; constructed of galvanized steel, open at the front and full of tractors, farm machinery, assorted tools and accumulated odds and ends which 'might come in handy one day'.

Just past the shed the track ended on a flat area of lawn at the front of a house. The house was built on the hill slope and looked out over the valley and hills beyond to the jungle covered slopes of Bartle Frere.

"Here we are!" squeaked Kylie, quite unnecessarily.

Mrs Kirk stopped the car on the lawn just past the concrete driveway which led into the garage on the left side of the house.

As soon as the car had stopped moving Kylie opened the door, scrambled out and ran across the lawn. The front door was open and she took the three steps up to the concrete patio in a single bound before entering the house. She experienced mild disappointment that 'Gran' had not come out to meet them.

Probably busy and didn't hear the car, she told herself as she went in through the vestibule.

All the time her eyes were busy noting the tiny details which were so much a part of a visit to the farm: the lovely old, varnished wood side table with the telephone and notebook on it, the old kerosene lamps from the days before electricity, the paintings of country scenes on the wall, and fine crochet work on the side table.

As she reached the kitchen Kylie called out, "Gran! We are here."

In her mind had been a desire not to alarm the old lady by suddenly rushing in but as she entered the dining room Kylie stopped in stunned surprise. On a chair in the lounge room sat Gran- and she was bound hand and foot by rope- and gagged!

Even as Kylie's astonished gaze took this in she experienced a rush of pure fear which gripped her spine and the back of her head like fingers of ice. Her mouth dropped open in amazement and disbelief. Standing beside Gran was a man. That he was not a welcome visitor was instantly obvious as he wore a stocking mask and looked very agitated.

Kylie opened her mouth to scream but the man spoke first. "Not a sound girlie or the old biddie gets hurt."

Kylie snapped her mouth shut with an audible snap, her mind racing. What was going on? Who was this man? How to rescue Gran? How to warn the others not to come in? Even now she could hear their voices at the front of the house.

Her eyes took in the fact that all the cupboards had been opened and their contents strewn on the floor. *A burglar!* she thought, then revised this when she heard noises downstairs in the basement. *Two of them.*

Blazing anger surged to replace surprise and fear. *These animals have tied Gran up!* A series of rapid impressions crystallised to action. The man did not appear to be armed and also gave the appearance of being surprised and unsure. He was a thin, dark-haired youth. His age was hard to assess but she guessed at late teens or early twenties. His most notable characteristic was a mouth curled into a sneer.

"Let Gran go!" Kylie cried angrily, then turned to shout, "Mum! Don't come in. Go and find Uncle Bill. There are..."

She got no further. With a snarl of rage the man hurled himself across the room at her. She tried to dodge but ran into the wall. Simultaneous with this the man struck her; a hard, stinging blow to the face. Kylie reeled away and twisted to dodge another blow. Dimly she was aware of her mother calling out and of Margaret running forward to hit at the man.

Another blow landed, sending Kylie's senses reeling. Screams rang out, her own included. Kylie broke free and ran into the corridor, colliding with another wall as she did. At that moment a second man appeared at the top of the internal stairs which led up from the basement. Like his companion, the second man's face was masked by a woman's stocking pulled over his head. It gave him a frightening, deformed appearance. He was a solid brute, wearing soiled and worn denim jacket and jeans. Gloves covered both hands.

Kylie tried to turn but was not quick enough. The man punched her hard in the head, knocking her down. Even before she had fallen to the floor the man had pushed past her into the lounge room. There were more screams and a strangled sob.

For a moment Kylie was too stunned to move. She lay with her vision blurred and her face numb. Through her mind raced nightmare images of rape and murder. She tried to get up, but the second man's voice stilled her. She could not see him as she lay in the corridor, but he was obviously near Gran.

The man's voice sounded shockingly loud. "Stop the noise and sit down or I will cut the old ladies throat!" he snarled.

There were muffled gasps and sobs, but the others went silent. The man snapped at them, "Sit over there in the corner, all of you. Move! 'Donk' see if there are any more outside."

Kylie lay still and squinted through her hair as the man called 'Donk' walked past her feet to the front door. After a quick look he walked back.

"No-one there," he said.

"Good. Find some more rope so we can tie them up," the solid man ordered.

Kylie felt her heart beat rapidly as the man walked back to near her feet. To her relief he turned the other way and went through the side door into the garage. The solid man began to question her mother and the others: who were they? Why were they here? Was anyone else expected?

Hope surged in Kylie's heart. *He's forgotten me. I can get away while they are busy,* she thought. But away to where? To get Uncle Bill, Gran's son who worked the farm now Grandad was dead. But where was Uncle Bill?

Then another idea came to her. She was lying next to the door to Grandad's room. *Grandad always kept a loaded shotgun behind his door for snakes. I wonder if it is still there?* Grandad had been dead for three years now but on their last visit in October his room had appeared quite undisturbed. Gran had obviously just left it as it was when he was alive.

Poor old dear! Kylie thought. *She misses him terribly still.*

With these inconsequential thoughts she silently eased herself to her feet and tiptoed to the doorway. The door was open, and a glance showed that the intruders had been in there already as the floor was strewn with a mess of Grandad's clothes and papers. As quietly as she could, Kylie slipped into the room and looked behind the door.

Yes! The gun was still there. An old single-barrelled shot shotgun with a long barrel and a stock of wood that was black with age. With trembling fingers she picked it up. For a moment her vision blurred, and she had to lean on the wall to steady herself. Her breathing came rapidly, and she could taste blood on her cut lip.

For a moment Kylie held the gun, her mind in a turmoil of indecision.

She sensed that a ghastly tragedy was possibly only seconds away. Part of her hesitation was over the gun itself. Was it loaded? Dimly she remembered an argument between Gran and Grandad about having loaded guns in the house and she thought Gran had said not only was it dangerous it was against the law. Kylie had fired it once, recollections of the colossal bang flooding vividly through her mind. She bit her lip, unsure how to open the gun to check.

"If only Graham or Alex were here. They would know what to do," she muttered. Alex and Graham were her older brothers; but Alex was at sea with their father and Graham was at an army cadet promotion course down near Townsville.

With sudden resolve she gripped the gun and went out into the corridor. As she arrived in the lounge room the thin man named Donk came through the doorway from the garage. He stopped in surprise and dropped the rope he was carrying. Out of the corner of her eye Kylie saw the second man, the blonde brute who had knocked her down. He was standing in front of the others, who huddled along the wall beside Gran.

Kylie pointed the gun at him. "Put your hands up or I will shoot!"

Donk did as he was told, his mouth sagging open, making his face in the stocking mask even more hideous. The solid brute did not. He turned and growled.

"Don't be stupid little girl. Put the gun down before you kill someone," he snarled.

"No. Put your hands up," Kylie countered. The two men were standing at right angles to her so she could only point the gun at one at a time. She wavered uncertainly between the two, finally settling on the solid one as the more dangerous.

He took a step forward so that he was only about three paces from her. "You wouldn't be game to shoot," he sneered. "So give me the gun before you do something you will regret."

"Stop!" Kylie cried, her voice rising in near panic as the man took another step forward. Her stomach churned so that she felt nauseous. *Could I shoot?* she wondered. She aimed the barrel at the man's stomach.

He licked his lips but still did not raise his hands. Kylie was dimly aware of the look of horror on her mother's face. The solid brute sneered again. "It probably isn't even loaded. And even if it is it isn't cocked."

Cocked! Kylie glanced down to check and, even as she did, knew that she had been tricked and cursed herself. Before she could react, the man moved with speed and strength that was truly stunning. He pounced forward, sweeping the barrel up with one arm and smashing her in the face with his other fist.

Kylie reeled back from the blow, desperately clinging to the gun. Another blow made her see stars and she felt herself falling. Even before she hit the floor, she experienced the bitter feeling of failure and defeat. The gun was wrenched from her hands. The solid man hammered the gun down, driving the butt into her chest.

Kylie felt a wave of fierce pain and heard shouts and screams. Donk yelled loudly, "Christ Almighty Burg! Don't kill her!"

The beating abruptly stopped but the screaming and shouting went on. Through eyes that were rapidly closing Kylie glimpsed Margaret grappling with the man, kicking, and scratching at him. He swore foully and lashed at her with his free hand, knocking her down as well. Allison took her place, but her attack was only half-hearted and she was easily held off. Mrs Kirk waded in, throwing a China vase which burst on the wall behind the man.

The solid man swung the gun to strike at Kylie's mother. She warded the blow off with her arm and stepped back. Allison was grabbed by Donk. She screamed and tried to bite him as she struggled. Margaret sprang to her feet and reached for another vase from the cabinet beside her. The solid brute swung the gun in a vicious swipe. Margaret managed to duck just in time. Before she could move away the brute had her in his grip.

By then Kylie's head had cleared. Sheer terror now drove her to act. *These men might kill us all. I must get help.*

A glance showed that both of the men were struggling with Allison and Margaret. Seeing her chance Kylie fled along the corridor and down the internal stairs. Behind her she heard a shout, warning her that she had been observed. At the bottom of the stairs was a short corridor leading to a side door. She fled through this, out onto the back lawn.

Ahead of her was a downhill run of a hundred metres of rough pasture to the milking shed, obstructed by two fences. From inside the house behind her came loud yells and screams. She heard the brute shout, "Get after her Donk, you bloody drongo!"

Fear lent Kylie strength. She fled.

Chapter 2

WHO? WHY?

At the bottom corner of the lawn was a gate. Kylie did not pause to open it. Despite her throbbing head and misting vision she vaulted it with all the skill and ease resulting from years of Gymnastics and Ballet. As she landed, she glanced back. Still no sign of the men.

With frequent glances over her shoulder she fled down the slope towards the milking shed, all the while hoping to see Uncle Bill; or even one of the dogs. When she was about halfway the thin man appeared at the side door of the house and set off after her. Another spasm of fear clutched at Kylie's heart and she let out a sob.

There was another fence ahead, bordering the muddy lane around the hillside along which the cows came for their twice daily milking. This fence was all barbed wire and steel pickets and the gate was a wire gate. Although she wore shorts and not a skirt Kylie knew it was too risky. No jumping this one. Instead she threw herself on the ground, oblivious of mud and wet manure and scrambled under the bottom strand.

By the time she regained her feet on the other side the thin man was over the first gate. He was yelling angrily at her; horrible threats and swear words. From the house behind him the other man was also yelling, although Kylie could not make out what he was saying.

She dashed across the small concrete-floored holding yard. With a gasp of relief she reached the open exit door of the milking shed. The interior was in darkness, but the layout was familiar to her and she found there was enough natural light for her not to trip or collide with things.

"Uncle Bill! Uncle Bill!" she cried, her voice a cross between a croak and a sob.

There was no answer. A glance showed her the milking area was empty. Driven by mounting desperation she wrenched open the door beside her and fled into the room which contained the huge stainless steel storage tanks and the pumping machinery. No-one there either. Her heart turned over with sick realization that the milking shed was not a sanctuary.

Kylie did not stay for more than a second. Biting her lip at the dilemma and at the growing pains in her chest and side she dashed out the far door and along the driveway to the gravel road beyond. Ahead of her was a belt of rainforest through which the road cut its way. Somewhere beyond that was another farm: the Griersons. She had only been there once. How far was it? She could only guess, perhaps a kilometre or more.

Can I run that far? she wondered, feeling rapidly growing weakness as she ran out of breath and energy. "Have to," she decided. "Anyway, if I can't keep running, I will take to the jungle and hide."

With that resolve she turned left and headed down the road, rejecting the uphill option back towards Lamins Hill. As before she frequently glanced back, worry gnawing at her.

What if I reach the next farm and there is no-one there? she thought.

The rainforest closed in on both sides, dark and damp and gloomy. Its familiar odour of rotting vegetation made her wrinkle her nose in distaste. She did not really like the jungle at all. Now she kept glancing at it, seeing it simultaneously as a dark and menacing tangle which could hide all manner of horrors, and as a possible refuge.

There was movement back at the milking shed, and distant shouting. Kylie looked over her shoulder. It was the thin man: Donk. He had come out onto the road. Once again, an agonised sob escaped her, for she was nearly at the end of her wind. A sharp 'stitch' had begun to bite into her right side and her breath was coming in hot gasps.

The only good thing was that the man appeared to be no closer. Kylie forced herself to keep running. There was a bend about a hundred metres ahead. *If I can reach that I can take to the jungle and he won't know which side I have gone into,* she reasoned. The road was no help. It was poorly graded and in places was muddy and soft from the morning dew.

Another glance back made her gasp with relief. Donk had stopped and turned back towards the house. *He's given up!* she thought incredulously. It seemed too good to be true.

As soon as it was plain that he really had given up the chase Kylie slowed to a jog, then to a fast walk. By then sweat was coursing down her face and into her eyes and she was gasping for breath. She pressed on as fast as she could force herself to go, her body and face a mass of pains and aching numbness.

She rounded the curve and the view changed. A hundred metres ahead sunlight shone on a grassy hillside on the right. Driven by anxiety about her mother and friends she forced herself to jog along to this. The other farm was only a few hundred metres past that. As fast as she could Kylie made her way to the open country. The road curved left at that point. A dirt farm track went off up the slope to her right. Ahead of her loomed a jungle covered shoulder of Bartle Frere, rising from behind the cluster of buildings on a low ridge.

Three painful minutes of running and walking brought her to the entrance to the farm. Kylie had always admired the place from afar, it being clearly visible from Gran's. The house was a gracious old dwelling set amidst fruit trees and gardens. The road led into a tree-lined enclosure with the house on the left and the other farm buildings on the right.

As she turned in through the gate Kylie looked anxiously back across the valley to Gran's. The house sat there on the green hillside as it always had, but there was no sign of any movement.

Oh God! I hope I'm in time, she thought, biting her lip in anxiety.

And there was Mrs Grierson! Kylie let out a cry of relief. A grey-haired woman dressed in a work shirt, knee length tartan skirt and rubber 'gum' boots, was standing in the entrance to the shed on her right, her eyebrows raised in astonishment.

"Mrs... Mrs Grier... son..." Puff! Puff! "Mrs Grierson, help!" Kylie croaked. She staggered to a halt facing the woman, whose expression had now changed to concern.

"What is it little girl? Why, I know you. You are one of Mrs Feltham's grand kids aren't you?"

Kylie nodded, too puffed to answer for a moment. As soon as she had recovered a fraction she gasped, "Men! Two men. They are holding Gran and Mum and Margaret as prisoners. Phone the police, quick!"

"Men! Prisoners! Good heavens! What ever is going on?"

Mrs Grierson glanced fearfully towards Gran's house, then put her arm around Kylie's shoulders and led her towards the house. "Are you alright little girl? Did they do anything to you?"

Kylie was considerably nettled to be referred to as a little girl and she answered with some heat. "No. They just hit me a bit. Quick, call the police!"

Mrs Grierson called out. To Kylie's added relief Mr Grierson appeared from another shed and came hurrying over. Like his wife he was grey haired but had a look of such solid dependability that she felt immensely re-assured. She allowed herself to be led inside but would not accept any doctoring. As quickly and coherently as she could she blurted out her story and again insisted that they call the police.

Mr Grierson looked out the window. "And you say one of them was chasing you?"

"Yes, but he gave up," Kylie replied.

"Hmmm." Mr Grierson muttered as he went into the next room. He returned with a double-barrel shotgun. It looked new and gleamed with oil and good care. The farmer checked it quickly and Kylie had no doubt he both could, and would, use it if need be. The sight of him loading and cocking the gun made her stomach turn over at the realization of how fearsomely real the situation actually was. Terrible things could happen, things which she sensed she would then carry in her memory for the rest of her life. It was very sobering.

By then Mrs Grierson had phoned the Malanda Police station. To Kylie's frustration the story had to be retold to an incredulous sergeant. Several questions were directed at her, and she fumed with impatience.

"Oh please hurry! They've got Gran and Mum and my friends tied up."

"And you say they have a shotgun?" the policeman asked.

"Yes."

"Thanks. Now, give the phone to Mr Grierson please," he ordered. Kylie did as she was told and moved to look out of the kitchen window towards Gran's.

Even as she focused her eyes, she saw two figures running up the hill behind the farmhouse. "There they are! Look! They are running away. Oh quick!" she cried.

Even as the Grierson's joined her the two men went from view through a hedge of tall weeds along a fence line near the top of the low hill.

Mr Grierson grunted, then said, "They are leaving all right. I'll bet they've got a vehicle just over the hill on the other road." He relayed the information to the police and was again instructed not to go back to Gran's farm.

Kylie was indignant. "Oh poo to that! They have gone," she cried. "Come on. They might have hurt someone."

"You stay here girlie," Mr Grierson ordered. Kylie barely heard him. She ran to the door and down the garden path with the Griersons following.

As she reached the yard Mr Grierson called to her and pointed to a mud spattered, green Land Rover. "Be quicker and easier if we drive."

Kylie saw the sense in that and climbed in. Mr Grierson told his wife to drive. "I'll go in the back so I can use the gun if need be," he explained.

That was an even more sobering thought. Mrs Grierson did as she was told and they set off. During the drive back through the belt of rain forest Kylie was on the edge of her seat from anxiety and impatience. At any moment she feared they would meet one or both the men. However, nothing happened and they rounded the bend near the milking shed.

A hundred metres from the shed, on the edge of the jungle, Mr Grierson banged on the roof and told his wife to stop.

"That's far enough. I will walk forward to the milking shed. You turn the Rover round in case we need to do a quick getaway," he instructed.

Kylie went to get out but both adults firmly forbad it. Reluctantly she sat while the vehicle did a three-point turn in the road. Only then was she allowed to get out, so as to be able to look back towards the house, which was just visible beyond the milking shed.

Mr Grierson walked cautiously forward, keeping near the edge of the jungle, his gun at the ready and his wife biting her knuckles. As he approached the milking shed a figure appeared running down the road from the machinery shed near the house. Kylie let out a little cry of relief.

"It's Margaret. She's got free."

Without waiting for permission Kylie ran forwards to meet her. Mr Grierson stepped out to intercept Margaret, giving her a bad fright for a moment. As Kylie ran up to her Margaret cried out, "They've gone. Quick, call the police."

"Done that," Mr Grierson replied. "Do they need an ambulance? Is anyone hurt?"

"Not too badly," Margaret replied. She came to a panting standstill and touched her own cheek where a livid bruise showed. "Oh I'm so glad you are safe," she said to Kylie.

The girls embraced, and Kylie hugged her friend. She could feel their hearts beating and knew she was on the edge of breaking down herself.

Mr Grierson interrupted. "Can you use the phone at the house?"

"No. We tried, but the men tore out the wire," Margaret replied.

Mr Grierson ran back to the waiting vehicle, spoke quickly to his wife, then returned to the girls. The Land Rover started up and accelerated back towards the Grierson's farm.

"I've sent Mavis to use our phone," he explained. "Alright, let's go up to the house."

The three walked along the road past the milking shed and up to the turn-off at the machinery shed. As they reached it a vehicle came around the crest of the hill from the direction of Lamins Hill. It was a white utility driven by Uncle Bill. Kylie cried with relief.

Uncle Bill was her mother's brother. He was a solid man in his early forties and had a ruddy, cheerful face and thinning fair hair. He looked at them with astonishment.

"Hello there. Hunting, are we?" he asked.

Even as he said it his eyes took in the condition of Kylie's clothes and battered face and the smile died on his face.

Kylie gestured towards the house. "Two men. They attacked us."

Instantly, concern and anger flared on Uncle Bill's face. "What happened?"

"Tell you as we go. Quick! Up to the house," Kylie replied.

Uncle Bill needed no urging. He accelerated along the side track and braked to a halt at the garage door. Before the other three, who had broken into a run, were even past the end of the machinery shed he had vanished inside the house. Two dogs were left chained in the back.

Kylie rushed in ahead of the other two, to be met by her anxious mother who embraced her and cried with relief.

"Oh you poor dear! Are you alright? Oh I was so worried when you ran off," Mrs Kirk cried.

Gran hobbled over and clasped Kylie, tears coursing down her cheeks. "Oh Kylie dear! That was the bravest thing I have ever seen. You were just wonderful. But oh, I was so frightened that you would be really be hurt," she said.

"I was scared too Gran," Kylie replied, hugging the loving grey head to her own. "Are you alright? Did they hurt you?"

"No, not really dearie. But they certainly gave me a terrible fright."

After a minute Kylie released her trembling Grandmother. She had spied Allison seated on the lounge looking very pale and drawn. She went to her and took her hand.

"Are you alright Allie?"

Allison nodded. "Yes, I'm fine. How are you?"

The question made Kylie realise just how much she hurt. "Bit battered and bruised," she said.

Uncle Bill and Mrs Kirk now took control. Uncle Bill insisted they go out onto the back veranda. "Don't touch anything. The police will want to search for fingerprints," he explained.

"Oh fiddlesticks to that," Mrs Kirk snapped. "I need the First Aid kit and these girls need to lie down. Bill, you help Mum to her room. You girls go to the veranda and lie down. Allison, would you please make tea for us like a good girl?"

Only when she lowered herself onto the couch did Kylie realise just how badly she needed to do so. Reaction set in swiftly and she began to shiver and tremble. Her mother quickly wiped her face and her legs and arms, helped by Margaret, who insisted she was alright.

A cup of strong, sweat tea helped to calm her. While they were drinking this there was the sound of vehicles and Uncle Bill went out to investigate. He came back in with two policemen and a paramedic.

The sergeant introduced himself, but Kylie did not catch his name. He was nice enough, but she was irritated at having to repeat the whole story again. By then Mrs Grierson had also joined them. The sergeant made notes in his notebook and sent the young constable who had come with him out to use the car radio several times.

"You say the two men ran off up the hill behind the house?" he asked.

"Yes. Mr Grierson thought they might have had a vehicle parked there," Kylie replied.

At that Mrs Kirk interrupted. "I'm sure they did. One of them had a mobile phone on his belt and it rang while he was tying us up. He answered it at once, then ran out the back yelling to his mate that someone was coming and they had better get out. After that he swore at us and ran off out the front. That was the last we saw of them."

Uncle Bill rubbed his chin. "Come to think of it, I passed a brown Toyota Land Cruiser coming from this direction just after I crossed the creek. It had two men in it and was really boring along. That might have been them."

"Could have been," the sergeant agreed. "Can you remember what the men looked like, or its number?"

"Fair go! They just looked like a couple of men," Uncle Bill said.

A sudden chill gripped Kylie's skull, then moved to her stomach, making her feel sick again. "There must have been three of them," she said softly.

"What's that?" Uncle Bill asked.

"There must have been three of them," Kylie repeated. "Don't you see? If someone rang the two here on a mobile phone, then that person was watching the road, a lookout. When he saw Uncle Bill coming, he rang up and warned them."

The sergeant looked sceptical. "Then why didn't he ring up to warn them about you? You claim you surprised them."

Kylie shook her head. "I don't know," she said, feeling foolish.

Uncle Bill frowned. "Where could he have been watching from anyway?" he said. "I didn't see any vehicle parked beside the road."

Mrs Kirk looked at him. "There are a few old tracks leading off into the jungle aren't there?" she suggested.

Uncle Bill nodded. "Yes, there are," he conceded. He rubbed his chin thoughtfully. "I will have a look for tyre tracks as soon as I get a chance. In fact I will go up to the top of the hill now and see where these mongrels parked their vehicle."

"You take care sir," the sergeant said. "Go with him constable."

Uncle Bill stood up to leave. "I'll take the dogs," he added.

As he turned another sickening thought came to Kylie. "I know why the lookout didn't phone when we came along; he knows you by sight and was watching for you."

Uncle Bill turned back to face her and bit his lip. "That's a worrying thought. But it makes sense. So it is someone who knows me."

"Oh Bill! But why?" Mrs Kirk cried.

Uncle Bill shook his head. "I have no idea. I can't imagine what they wanted. There is nothing of value here, not that would justify their actions."

Mrs Kirk frowned. "Well they obviously thought there was because they nearly tore the place apart searching." She turned to Gran. "What were they looking for, Gran? Did they say?"

Gran rubbed her arms and muttered to herself for a moment, then replied, "They said they wanted the treasure map."

"Treasure map!" they echoed.

Chapter 3

WHAT MAP?

For several seconds Gran was the focus of a circle of incredulous faces. "Treasure map! What treasure?" Mrs Kirk cried.

Gran looked uncomfortable as though she regretted having spoken. Her eyes flicked to the sergeant, then to Mrs Kirk. She gestured irritably then answered, "Oh there isn't one as far as I know. It is just that old story that has been in the family for generations about the gold mine that your grandfather is supposed to have found in the jungle way back in the nineteen thirties."

Uncle Bill knelt close to her. "The one he called 'The Jeweller's Shop'?"

Gran sniffed and nodded. "Yes, that's the one. Only he didn't call it that. The story is that he cried out just before he died; that he had found a jeweller's shop."

"Is there a map Gran?" Kylie asked, her heart quickening with interest.

Gran shook her head. "Not that I know of," she replied. "I only wish there was. We need a treasure right at this moment." Her eyes met Uncle Bill's and he gave a wry smile.

Uncle Bill shrugged. "The farm's in a bit of financial trouble right at this moment," he explained. "I borrowed heavily to install that new stainless steel storage vat and to build up the herd. If I can't pay it back the bank will foreclose on the loan."

Kylie felt as though she had been hit again. "Does that mean the bank would own the farm?"

Uncle Bill nodded sadly. "Yes. They would sell it."

Kylie was appalled. She looked anxiously from Uncle Bill to her mother's shocked face. All her life the farm had been a constant; a place of love and happiness. Her mother and Uncle Bill had been born here, and it had been their childhood home. To lose it would be a terrible blow.

"Oh we mustn't let that happen. We must find the treasure!" she cried.

Gran smiled but shook her head. "I wish we could; but I'm afraid there isn't one. Heaven knows, enough people have looked for that goldmine over the years."

"Where is it?" Kylie asked.

Gran gestured out the window towards Bartle Frere. "Somewhere out there in the jungle."

Kylie looked out at the tangle of rainforest which extended out to the east below Bartle Frere. Ridge after jungle covered ridge, then the crestline which marked the Mulgrave Valley, and beyond that the massive bulk of the Bellenden Ker Range. Thousands of square kilometres of the thickest jungle in North Queensland. Her heart sank.

"So there isn't a map?"

Gran again shook her head sadly. "Not that I have ever heard of."

Mrs Kirk looked annoyed. "So why were these men looking for one?" she asked angrily.

Uncle Bill grimaced. "Obviously someone has a different version of the story," he suggested.

Another thought crossed Kylie's mind. "These men must be locals then, to know about this story. How many people might know about it?"

Gran smiled again and so did Mrs Kirk. Gran said, "Hundreds of people probably. It has been a family legend for over sixty years now and there have been at least half a dozen expeditions to look for the thing over the years. Why, the Reid brothers went at least five times that I know of."

"Who are they?" Kylie asked.

"Who, the Reid brothers?" Gran said. "Bruce Reid married young Violet, my sister Violet's daughter."

Kylie tried to sort that out in her mind. She dimly knew she had other uncles and cousins but had not met many of them and had taken little notice of them. She said lamely, "So other relations know about the gold mine?"

Gran nodded. "Heavens yes! My brother Joshua has a real tribe of kids and they all know about it."

Kylie looked so disappointed that her mother hugged her and Gran said gently, "Cheer up Kylie-bub. It is not the end of the world. It is just an old story."

"Maybe. But someone believes it enough to come and rob you and bash us," Kylie replied fiercely.

"And we will catch them," the sergeant said.

"How? They were wearing gloves," Kylie replied.

"There can't be too many young men nicknamed 'Donk' and 'Burg' on the Tablelands," the sergeant replied. "Now, we had better get on with our search and you ladies had better get to hospital for a check-up."

"Oh I'm alright," Kylie replied.

Mrs Kirk intervened firmly. "You had better have a doctor check you over. You look a bit of a wreck; and Gran is definitely going in for a check too."

"Oh piffle!" Gran expostulated. "I'm as right as rain."

But they overruled her as well. Uncle Bill went off with the constable up the hill to where the water reservoir was while Mrs Kirk and Allison collected things for the trip to hospital. By then Kylie felt very sore and her face was one throbbing mass. As she collected a bag, she saw herself in a mirror and hardly recognised herself. There was a huge bruise on one cheek and around the other eye and her lip was swollen and marked with a painful scab. Her ribs felt very sore and there were bruises and scratches on her body, arms, and legs.

At the insistence of her mother and of the paramedics she was loaded into the ambulance with Gran. Mrs Kirk put the other two girls into her own car and followed as the ambulance drove off. It was nearly an hour's drive to the hospital in Atherton. By the time they arrived Kylie was feeling very sick and sore.

The hospital was another irritating ordeal. Kylie was X-rayed to check her ribs for fractures, then examined by a doctor. He wanted to keep her in overnight for observation, but she insisted she was alright. Gran had suffered little more than a bad fright and some bruising where the ropes had bound her. She also refused to be admitted.

It was nearly dark by then. While Kylie had been in being seen to her mother had phoned their father, then Allison's parents, to inform them before they heard about it from the news media. After Kylie came out Mrs Kirk helped Gran out to the car. Kylie was supported by Margaret and Allison.

"Do you girls want to go back to the farm?" she asked as they settled in their seats.

Kylie was appalled at the thought that the holiday might end before it had even begun. "Yes of course Mum! We can't leave Gran now," she replied.

Margaret nodded agreement. "Yes please. We do Mrs Kirk."

"You too Allison? I can drive you home if you want?"

"I want to stay Mrs Kirk," Allison replied.

"Good. Your parents say you can stay if you want to. I must apologize though. We don't usually have that sort of trouble at the farm," Mrs Kirk replied.

At that Gran snorted. "You can say that again! It is the worst thing that has happened to me in sixty years!"

Mrs Kirk looked at her watch. "We have to wait for Bill. He won't be finished the milking yet. Let's find a cafe and have some food."

They were squeezed into the car, the three girls in the back, and drove down to the main street. Kylie did not want to go into the cafe because of her bruises so her mother brought her some food which she ate in the car. Margaret and Allison stayed with her. It was dark by the time they finished. Mrs Kirk drove them back to the hospital and they sat in the waiting room.

Here they were pestered by a reporter, but Mrs Kirk was very firm and sent him away, refusing to allow Gran or the girls to be interviewed or photographed. During this exchange Kylie sat with her head down, resting on Margaret's shoulder. Reaction was setting in and she was very glad her best friend was there to give comfort.

By the time Uncle Bill arrived Kylie felt feverish and so sore she half wished she could just drop off to sleep there and then. Uncle Bill took Gran out to his car and the girls climbed into Mrs Kirk's. Mrs Kirk fussed with cushions and a rug to get Kylie comfortable. She did not object. She now felt really sick.

On the drive back to the farm Kylie dozed fitfully. When she was awake she puzzled over the vicious attack and its motives. She also felt quite scared at the thought of someone watching them as they drove around. It made the darkness even more scary.

Back at the farm she was hurried to bed. The place had been cleaned up by then, presumably by Uncle Bill. The three girls were bunked down on a mattress on the floor of the big room downstairs at the side. There were two windows which opened out onto the lawn, but these were locked. Mrs Kirk pulled the curtains to give more privacy.

Margaret and Allison were wonderful. They brought Kylie hot Milo to drink and fussed over her. When they had cleaned their teeth and settled themselves Kylie went upstairs to Gran's room. Her mother sat there beside the bed. Gran was sound asleep.

"Is Gran alright mum?"

"Yes. She's sleeping peacefully. Now you get to bed dear."

"Yes Mum. Oh Mum! I hope she is alright."

"She will be. She is tough. So are you," her mother replied. She reached out and drew Kylie to her, hugging her tight. "You were very brave. But please don't do anything like that again. You could have been very badly hurt."

"Yes Mum," Kylie replied. She hugged her mother until her bruises hurt. Then she eased herself back. "Mum, do you think there really is a treasure?"

Mrs Kirk shook her head. "Not in the way you think. I suppose Grandad, your Great Grandad that is, definitely discovered some gold out there in the jungle, but it would be impossible to find it now."

For a moment Kylie pondered the problems of prospecting in thick tropical rainforest. "I suppose so. But I'd like to try."

Her mother smiled and kissed her forehead. "Yes. Now get to bed. We will worry about it tomorrow."

Mrs Kirk took her hand and led her downstairs to where Margaret and Allison were snuggled in under the sheets.

"Goodnight girls. Sleep well, and don't get up too early."

Allison looked anxious. "Mrs Kirk, what if those men come back during the night?" she asked.

Mrs Kirk frowned, then smiled. "Uncle Bill has locked the house and has his gun. Don't worry. It will be alright. Now go to sleep."

She turned off the lights and went back upstairs. There was silence for a minute, then Kylie said quietly. "Sorry about all the drama. I thought we were just coming here to milk cows."

"Speak for yourself!" Allison replied. "I came for a nice holiday thank you. You can do any milking that needs to be done."

Kylie laughed and tried to think of a smart answer. Instead, her laugh changed to sobs and she was crying. "Oh I was so scared this afternoon!"

"So was I," Margaret replied. She also began to cry and moved to put her arms around Kylie. The two girls clung together.

Allison put her arms around both and soothed them. "You were both very brave."

Kylie shrugged and eased herself free. She reached for a handkerchief, wiped her eyes and blew her nose. "I was so angry when I saw Gran tied up."

"I would have been too, if it had been my Nanna," Margaret said.

"Do you really think we will be safe tonight?" Allison asked, glancing anxiously at the curtained windows.

For a few minutes the girls discussed the events of the afternoon. Margaret gave a sigh and pulled her quilt close around her. "I wish Graham was here. I would feel safer then."

Kylie snorted and managed a laugh. "You just wish he was snuggled up with you. I don't know what you see in that big brother of mine."

"He would keep us safe," Margaret replied.

For a moment Kylie contemplated her two older brothers. It was true. She wished either of them was there. Both were very 'masculine', strong types. Alex was 16 and very down to earth and practical. Graham was 14 and was inclined to be very romantic but was very fit. Margaret had been in love with Graham for years. It was a somewhat one-sided relationship as Graham experienced frequent 'crushes' on other girls, to Kylie's annoyance and Margaret's distress.

Yes, I wish they were here, Kylie thought. But Alex was at sea with their father who was a ship's captain. He was somewhere off the coast of Cape York Peninsula. Graham was on his army cadet promotion course. She was terribly fond of both of them, but Graham was her favourite. She pictured his grinning, freckled face, the blue eyes smiling as he plotted the next adventure.

"Graham would probably march up and down on guard all night," she said.

Margaret nodded. "That would be nice. I would feel safe then."

Kylie snorted. "If you two keep carrying on the way you were earlier in the year you won't be safe at all. You will be in real trouble," she replied.

Allison's face lit up with interest. "What were they doing?" she asked.

"Playing 'mummies and daddies'," Kylie replied with a laugh.

"Humpf!" Margaret snorted in embarrassment. "We were not. Anyway, I don't mind if Graham gets me into trouble."

"Oh Margaret! You are only twelve. How can you talk like that?" Allison cried.

For the next half hour the girls discussed boys and babies and what adult life might be like. During this Kylie slipped quietly off to sleep.

Several times during the night Kylie stirred restlessly. She woke to find the sun well up. When she went to get up she cried in pain. It felt as though every bone and muscle in her upper body and arms was sore. She lay back and carefully flexed and eased the cramps and aches. Her head felt dizzy and her muscles seemed very weak.

Her mother appeared with Margaret in tow. "How are you dear?"

"A bit sore, Mummy."

"Then you just lie there. Margaret will bring you some breakfast."

Kylie looked around. "Where's Allison?"

"Went with Uncle Bill to help with the milking," Mrs Kirk replied.

"Milking!" Kylie cried. Allison was a real 'girlie girl' and she couldn't imagine her getting her hands dirty. She winced as a sharp pain lanced through her head. She lay back and Margaret went off to bring her a warm drink while her mother felt her temperature and pulse.

"I think you had better take it very easy today young miss."

"Yes Mum."

Kylie felt so worn and sore that she made no protest. After eating and a visit to the shower and toilet she returned to bed, dropping off to sleep almost at once.

It was several hours before she woke again. To her surprise and pleasure she found Gran sitting in a chair beside her. She was quietly knitting but put this down when she saw Kylie was awake.

"How do you feel now little Miss Amazon?"

"Better, Gran. A bit sore," Kylie replied.

That was not entirely true as when she went to sit up a sharp pain stabbed through her chest and her face felt numb. She ran her tongue over the scab on her split lip. Forcing a grin to hide the pain she got up and went to put her arms around Gran.

"What about you Gran? Are you hurt?"

"No dearie. I just got a bad fright. I tell you what, if those horrible men come back, they'll get what for! I'll be ready for them next time."

She indicated 'Scottie', the Border collie, who now lay in the corridor. Scottie met her eyes, lifted his head and wagged his tail before walking in to lick Kylie's hand. She greeted the dog enthusiastically, rumpling his ears and patting his coat.

Mrs Kirk came down the stairs. "Oh, you are awake. Come up both of you. It is morning teatime."

Kylie helped Gran out of her chair and up the stairs. They seated themselves on the back veranda. As she lowered herself into the chair Kylie winced and bit her lip. She saw her mother frown, so she shook her head. "I'm okay Mum, truly. It is just a few bruises."

Voices outside drew her attention and she saw Uncle Bill, Margaret and Allison walking up the track from the milking shed, 'Bluey' the second dog trotting along with them. Allison wore old clothes and knee length rubber 'gum' boots.

"Look at Allie. Has she been working?" Kylie asked in surprise.

Mrs Kirk laughed. "Yes. She and Margaret got up at five o'clock and went down to help. Allison's been there ever since. Bill tells me she has now been well trained in the art of milking."

Kylie shook her head in disbelief. "Hard to imagine. She usually avoids all work and hates to get her hands dirty."

Mrs Kirk laughed. "Well, she's been a big help; and so has Margaret." She stood up and leaned out the window. "Hurry up you lot. Tea is ready."

The others hurried up, coming in via the downstairs door. On the way they divested themselves of gum boots and gloves and washed their hands. After enquiries as to how Gran and Kylie were, they seated themselves.

Uncle Bill accepted a large cup of tea and a buttered scone. "Young Allison here has been wonderful. She moved that herd of cows like a veteran... Hello! Who's this coming I wonder?"

This last as the sound of a car coming up the drive reached them. Uncle Bill stood up and walked to the front door. Kylie sipped her tea and took a bite out of a biscuit. There was the sound of voices and Uncle Bill said, "Why yes. Good to see you. Nice of you to drop in. Come in. You are just in time for a cuppa."

There were footsteps and three people appeared in the kitchen door; a middle-aged woman who looked vaguely familiar; a young woman of about twenty who was obviously the woman's daughter, and a young man in his late teens.

Gosh, he's handsome! Kylie thought, taking in the square face, fair hair, blue eyes and broad shoulders.

Gran's face lit up. "Oh, hello Violet. Come in. Find a chair."

Introductions followed. Kylie learned that the woman was her 'Aunty' Violet; and that the other two were her children and therefore Kylie's second cousins. The young woman's name was Annabelle, and the handsome young man was Bert. They were the Reid family.

"Are you alright, Grace?" Aunty Violet asked anxiously. "We were just driving over to Theo's when we heard about it on the radio, so we came straight here."

Gran assured them she was. The interest then shifted to Kylie, whose injuries were clearly visible. The story had to be told again. Kylie felt very self-conscious and busied herself with drinking another cup of tea. She was acutely aware of searching looks from Bert.

He is nice, she decided, giving a shy smile, which he returned. She tried to guess at his age and decided he was about twenty. *Too old for me I suppose,* she thought wistfully.

Bert turned to Gran and asked, "Are you sure there isn't a treasure map Gran? I was always told there was one."

Gran shook her head. "Never seen or heard of one. Your version of the story must be different."

"What is the story, Gran?" Kylie asked.

"I told you that last night," Gran replied.

"Only the outline. What is the full story?" Kylie asked.

Gran made a face. "Oh heavens! It will take an hour to tell."

Aunty Violet nodded encouragingly, "That's alright, Grace. We've got an hour. Please tell us."

Gran looked from one to the other, then nodded. "Oh alright. But another cup of tea first."

Kylie felt a surge of excitement. "Oh thank you, Gran!"

Chapter 4

FAMILY HISTORY

Gran settled herself more comfortably and took a sip from her teacup. "Well now, to explain this I will have to go back in time and cover a bit of family history."

Kylie nodded and smiled. "Go on Gran. I would like to hear."

Gran smiled at her, then looked out the window. There was a moments silence as her eyes took on a misty, faraway look. Then she turned back to the waiting group. "This is a bit complicated," she explained. "I had better start as far back as I can. That would be with your Great, Great, Great, Great Grandfather."

"Heavens! That is a long way back!" Margaret cried.

Gran smiled again. "To you maybe. It seems like yesterday to me. Anyway, to begin. In 1880 Hector Pike migrated from England to Australia. He came to North Queensland to look for gold. From memory he went to the newly discovered field down at Goldsborough in the Mulgrave Valley. He must have found some gold because he bought the farm near Malanda and married Rose Till in 1885. They had eight children I think, but from memory only five of them survived."

Margaret looked horrified. "Only five. How awful. What happened Mrs Feltham?"

"Oh you young people don't realise how good you have it. In those days all sorts of things killed children, particularly in the bush: diseases we don't even worry about anymore; and things like appendicitis and septicaemia, infections from small injuries. You look around an old cemetery some time and see how many young children are buried in them."

"How sad," Allison said. She looked at Bert, who met her eyes and nodded sympathetically. Kylie noted this and felt a sharp little stab of irritation.

Gran agreed then continued. "Her son Daniel married Evelyn Bunt and they had five children too. One was my dad, Hector, and another was Herbert. Now Herbert Pike is your grandad, Violet."

Aunty Violet nodded. "Yes, I know that. His son Theodore married my mum, who is your sister."

Kylie frowned. "But wouldn't that make them relations?"

"Yes, they were cousins," Aunty Violet replied.

"But... but isn't that wrong?" Kylie asked. She was vaguely aware that there were certain relationships which were illegal. She wanted to know but was worried she might be intruding into a sensitive family area.

Gran answered her. "They were first cousins. It caused a few murmurs at the time I remember but it worked out very well in the end." She smiled at Aunty Violet, who smiled back.

Kylie wasn't the only one puzzled. Margaret asked, "But isn't that against the law; for cousins to marry?"

"No it isn't. People frown on it a bit because too much in-breeding within a family is a bad thing," Gran replied.

Kylie nodded and felt a bit embarrassed. She roughly knew what Gran was talking about and was very conscious of Bert's presence. She glanced at him; only to see that he was smiling at Allison, who was returning the smile. Nettled more than she wanted to admit Kylie turned back to Gran. "Wait a minute Gran. I need to draw all this on a piece of paper, to get a family tree. I am losing track of all these relations."

Gran laughed. "I lost track of half of them years ago, and good thing too. Some of them weren't the sort of people you'd want to know."

Kylie's mother chided her. "Now Gran! Keep the family skeletons in the closet."

They all laughed and there was a pause while Kylie found pencil and paper. More tea and biscuits were served and Kylie settled herself at the table and asked Gran to go back over the first part of the story. To help her understand she drew small circles for the females and little squares for the males, adding dates where these could be remembered.

"So Daniel Pike and Evelyn had five children?" Kylie checked. She drew a line down from where a circle and a square were drawn interlocked. From this she drew a line horizontally across the page with five stems downwards.

Gran nodded. "First a girl named Charlotte. She was born about 1900, I think. She went off south and married a baker at Dubbo in New South Wales. Never heard any more about her since. Then there was your Great Grandad Hector. He was born in 1908. His brother Herbert was born in the next year, 1909, then young Daniel in 1910 and last of all a girl, Emily, in 1912."

Kylie quickly added the details to her diagram. Gran went on, "Emily married Frank Joyce, a really nice man who was a carrier in Herberton. I think her family still live around there. Young Daniel was killed in a sawmill accident in 1929. I know that because it was the week my older brother Joshua was born. Have you got all that dearie?"

"Yes Gran."

"Good. Now, Grandad Hector; 'Grumps' as he was nicknamed, married Emma Croswell in the summer of that same year. Emma's people were bankers in Cairns and very respectable. They weren't happy about the marriage I know because dad was unemployed at the time. The Great Depression had just begun you see and there were a terrible lot of men out of work."

Kylie had heard about the Great Depression at school but only had a vague idea what it had all been about. Gran now talked for some time about the thousands of unemployed men and how they tramped around the country looking for work. "It was a real bad time," she said. "Dad was unable to find any work and nor could Hector so the two brothers went bush to go gold prospecting. They went searching for their granddad's old mine."

Bert nodded. "That was the one called the 'Sweat and Tears', wasn't it?" he asked. "Up here near Boonjee?"

"Yes, it was. They must have found a bit of gold for they somehow made ends meet and dad managed to buy a farm. That was the farm over at Churinga Flat at the base of Bartle Frere. It was the year I was born, 1930. But dad wasn't much of a farmer, and he had the gold bug real bad. He kept wandering off into the jungle to search and left mum and a hired hand to work the farm. Hector usually went with him but by then he had taken out a tin mining lease out beyond Irvinebank and was helping run the Malanda farm."

"Then dad made his discovery. He came staggering out of the jungle, sick as a dog with scrub typhus and dumped a bag full of nuggets on the kitchen table and boasted that he'd discovered the jeweller's shop. Then he collapsed and they rushed him to hospital. He lived for another week I'm told. Remember I was only a one-year-old baby at the time so this is all hearsay from mum. I gather he never regained consciousness but did a lot of babbling and raving in his fever about the gold he had found and how it would make us all rich. Then he died. Poor Mum!"

Gran stopped and stared out the window for a while. Then she sighed and went on. "Poor mum. She was expecting Violet by then. It was terrible hard for her but she managed somehow. She had Vi and worked the farm and raised us kids. Her parents wanted her to come back to live in Cairns, but she loved it here. She was a grand woman, true as steel and with a character as strong as could be."

Kylie nodded. She just remembered her great grandmother as a frail little lady who had sat here on the veranda looking out at the cows. "What happened then Gran?" she asked, as much to break the silence as anything.

"Well, Josh grew up and worked the farm, but he had the gold bug too and kept going off to look for the famous 'Jeweller's Shop'. He drifted away and settled up near Cooktown where he still is. I married Stanley in 1951. He grew up on this farm and had courted me for years. We went to school together." She paused and smiled at the memory. "There is a photo of us somewhere, six kids all on one horse riding off for school. Anyhow we married and we had four kids, all born here on the farm. They are your Aunty Tarah, Aunty Jennifer, Uncle Bill and your mum."

Kylie nodded and smiled at her mother, loving her deeply.

"And I had to marry a sailor," Mrs Kirk said with a smile.

"Yes, well, I did warn you," Gran reminded.

It was obviously an old argument as Mrs Kirk quickly diverted the story. "Your mum was married the same year wasn't she Violet?"

Aunty Violet nodded. "Yes. 1951. She married Hector's son Theodore. I was born in 1953 and my brothers Brian and Arthur two years apart after that. They were mad about the famous gold discovery too and went looking for it several times."

"So did your husband didn't he?" Gran asked.

"Yes. He and his brother. They went at least three times but all they ever found were lots of leeches and ticks." She smiled at the memory and Kylie shuddered. She hated leeches.

"Your husband's name is Bruce isn't it Aunty Violet?" she asked, drawing a square to overlap Aunty Violet's circle.

"Yes. And his brother is Vince."

"And how many kids did you have Aunty Violet?" Kylie asked.

"Three. Annabelle and Bert here, and Victor."

"What years were they born?" Kylie asked, her pencil poised over the diagram but her eyes meeting Bert's.

"Annabelle in 1977, Victor in 1979, and Bert in 1981," Aunty Violet replied.

Kylie pencilled the dates on the page, then studied the diagram. She made a face. "I was hoping we could work out who might be the person responsible for attacking Gran by working out who else knows about the treasure, but you were right Gran. If all these people knew about it and told their kids, it is dozens."

Gran laughed and so did Aunty Violet. "More like hundreds!" Aunty Violet said. "The whole Reid clan know about it. It must be the worst kept secret in history."

Kylie bit her lip and sighed. "It is a pity there isn't a treasure map. Uncle Bill could save the farm then."

"Well there isn't. So that all there is," Gran said.

The conversation shifted to farm expenses. Soon after that Aunty Violet looked at her watch. "We had better be going. Bert has to help with the milking."

They all stood up. Kylie spent a moment adding details to her diagram, then helped Gran to settle more comfortably. The others all walked out to the front. Kylie followed and was just in time to wave to Bert as he climbed into the driver's seat of a blue station wagon.

As the car drove off, they all waved goodbye.

"Isn't Bert nice?" Kylie said to Margaret.

"Yes, he is," Margaret replied. "I wish he was my cousin."

"He is only seventeen," Kylie added. She had done the sum when she had learned his birth date.

"Yes, I know," Allison replied. "He told me."

For a moment Kylie was surprised and a little hurt. When had Allison found time to talk to Bert? It must have been in the few minutes when they had walked to the front of the house. She was surprised how she felt about it.

I'm being silly, she thought. *He is too old for me, and for Allison.* But she did not find this convincing. Allison was 13; only four years younger.

They went back inside. Mrs Kirk looked at the clock and exclaimed, "Good heavens! It is lunch time. We've been chattering for hours."

Lunch was organized. Kylie did not really feel hungry, but her mother made her sit and eat. By then she was feeling quite stiff and sore again and her cracked lip made it hard to eat. As soon as she had finished her mother told her to clean her teeth and go and lie down. This she did, without protest. The other girls came down and lay with her. Allison was soon asleep.

"She was up early to help with the cows," Margaret explained.

Soon after that Kylie also slipped into sleep. She slept for nearly three hours and woke feeling refreshed but stiff. Her ribs and cheek were still sore and her lip cracked again as soon as she smiled.

Allison was the cause of this. She was standing at the door in old clothes and gumboots. "Awake, are we? Come up and have some afternoon tea sleepy head."

"Have you been out?" Kylie asked.

"Been looking for a cow that Uncle Bill thinks has calved down near the back creek," Allison explained.

Kylie was amazed. She could not picture Allison walking around the farm amid the mud and manure, but she was smiling and seemed to be enjoying herself. With a groan and a grin Kylie hoisted herself up and washed her face. She then made her way upstairs to join the others.

Afternoon tea was a pleasant break with hot tea and fresh, buttered scones covered with honey. They sat on the back veranda and happily talked. Kylie felt more rested and relaxed and began to enjoy the peace and sense of purpose that always came to her when on the farm.

When they finished afternoon tea Uncle Bill asked who wanted to help check the level in the reservoir. "I can show you where those men parked their car too," he added.

That got Kylie's interest. She pulled on gum boots and went out with her mother, Uncle Bill and her two friends. They walked up the overgrown track to the top of the low hill behind the farm. The track was just two wheel ruts in knee high grass and Kylie disliked walking along it intensely for fear of snakes but Uncle Bill went first with the dogs.

"There was a school here in the old days," Uncle Bill explained to Margaret and Allison. "The building was over there and this was the horse paddock." He pointed out the line of the old fence and the trees which once stood in front of the now vanished building. In its place on the crown of the hill was a large concrete water tank. As always Kylie was amazed by the sheer beauty of the scenery. From the crest of the hill they had almost a three-hundred-and-sixty-degree view. The massive bulk of Bartle Frere loomed over nearly half of this. Off to the west were glorious vistas of rolling farmland dotted with dairy cows, backed in the far distance by the blue line of mountains marking the other side of the Tablelands.

"It is absolutely the prettiest view I have ever seen," Allison enthused. "It reminds me of England."

"Have you been to England?" Uncle Bill asked.

Allison nodded. "I was born there. We have only been in Australia four years."

"Do you like it here?"

"Love it," Allison answered. She smiled at Kylie and Margaret, and they smiled back. Kylie felt a surge of affection for her friends.

For a few minutes she just stood and drank in the view and sniffed the fresh mountain air. It was all so pretty and clean. *How could such a horrible thing happen in such a nice place?* she wondered.

Uncle Bill checked the level of the water, then led them over to where two wheel tracks showed in the long grass.

"The men parked their vehicle here, just over the crest and out of sight of the road," he explained.

Once again, Kylie puzzled over what had motivated the men to come to the farm. The question nagged at her so much that she re-opened the topic when they re-joined Gran in the kitchen.

"I know that dozens of people must know about this lost gold mine, but from what you have said Gran no-one has looked for it for years?"

Gran nodded. "That's right. It must be twenty years. The last time I remember anyone actually looking for it was when Bruce Reid and his brother went off. That must have been in the mid-1970s; just after he married Violet."

Kylie frowned. "So why has someone suddenly started looking for it now? When did you last hear someone talk about it, Gran?"

Gran knitted her brows, then nodded her head. "Why, only a week ago now that I come to think of it. I took it into my head to sort out all Stan's papers which have been stored in the cellar. When I started to unpack them, I found several boxes of stuff that my mum must have put away, diaries and things belonging to my dad, Grandad Hector."

Kylie felt her pulse quicken. It had been Grandad Hector who had discovered the gold mine! "What were they Gran? Did they tell you about the gold?"

Gran shook her head. "Not that I saw, but then I didn't really read them." She then stopped and shook her head, frowned and went on. "Yes, now I remember. I mentioned finding them when I was at my weekly Mother's Union meeting at Malanda just last Tuesday. Someone asked if there was a treasure map and I said no, but I wish there was, and we all laughed."

"Who asked that Gran? Who was at the meeting?" Kylie asked. "One of them might have told those men."

For a moment Gran looked horrified. "Oh dear me no! I have known them all for years. They are dear friends."

"But someone said something to someone," Kylie persisted. "Who was there Gran?"

Gran hesitated again and looked slightly annoyed and upset. For a moment Kylie feared she had offended her and that she would refuse to discuss the topic but when Mrs Kirk also urged her she reluctantly named the people present.

"There were only seven of us. Myself, Mrs Philp, Mrs English, Miss Woods, the teacher; that snooty-nosed busy-body Mrs Tomlinson, Mrs Carlow and Aunty Violet."

Mrs Kirk asked gently, "Which one made the comment about the treasure map Mum, can you remember?"

"Of course I can! I haven't lost my marbles y'know! Why I can still remember quite clearly all that horrible business leading up to World War Two. Of course I can remember. It was Mrs English. But I've known her for fifty years and I'm sure she had nothing to do with the attack."

"No mum. But she might have mentioned it to someone else who got the story a bit wrong," Mrs Kirk suggested.

Gran nodded. "You could be right."

Kylie felt slightly sick. It was awful to think that there were horrible men out there who were a threat to them. "Oh I wish the police would catch them!" she cried. "Then we could all relax."

Uncle Bill heaved himself out of his chair. "No we couldn't. The cows would still have to be rounded up and milked. Who is going to come and help?"

The three girls all stood and went out to help. Kylie usually enjoyed bringing the cows in but this time she was still sore and distracted. She kept wondering who and how the story of the treasure map had been spread. From time to time she looked anxiously at the trees along the creek line and the wall of jungle beyond the road, wondering if anyone was even now watching. The thought made her feel slightly sick and quite robbed her of enjoyment. She noted that Uncle Bill carried his shotgun, something he rarely did, and the sight comforted her.

As she walked back behind the herd of dairy cattle, Kylie looked out over the ridges towards the east. Into her mind crept a thought which rapidly crystallised into a resolve.

The gold mine is somewhere out there. I'm going to try to find it! Then Uncle Bill and Gran won't lose the farm.

Chapter 5

DUSTY PAGES

Milking took up all the rest of the afternoon. For three hours Kylie helped the others at the milking shed. Because of her 'injuries' she was given the job of moving the cattle in and out. Margaret was detailed to clean the cow's udders and to spray their teats after milking. Allison, to Kylie's amazement, actually joined Uncle Bill in the process of attaching the suction caps, ensuring the milk was flowing and then removing the milkers from the cattle.

Kylie had always disliked the dirtier side of milking and was still a bit afraid of the cows, but Allison appeared to take to the task like a duck to water. She worked down in the concrete pit between two rows of cows, just behind their back legs, where she cheerfully washed, fed, adjusted, and milked. She leaned in under the cows and talked to them as though she had been doing it all her life. Even when wet manure splattered down and splashed on her she just laughed, wiped her face and kept on working.

Amazing! Kylie thought. She laughed, half with amusement, and half from embarrassed disgust, as a cow voided urine which splashed into Allison's hair. Allison just grinned and slapped the cow on the rump, then went on working. Kylie was glad to be given the task of feeding the new calves, a task at which Margaret helped her. Margaret was also a natural at this, talking softly to the calves, which nuzzled and pushed; their big, liquid eyes showing curiosity and fear at the same time.

By the time the milking was done it was dark. As they made their way up to the house Kylie felt quite worn out and stiff. It was a relief to have a hot bath and to change into clean clothes. Dinner followed, a happy meal with roast beef and potatoes with lashings of gravy.

After the meal Kylie went to the kitchen to help with the washing up but Margaret and Allison shooed her away. "You talk to your Gran. You should still be in bed," Margaret said.

Meekly but thankfully Kylie did as she was told. She settled herself in the sitting room beside Gran and poured another cup of tea. After chatting for a few minutes she plucked up the courage to ask the question that had been forming in her mind for hours.

"Gran, would you mind if I looked through all the old papers of Grandad's that you were talking about earlier?"

Gran looked over her glasses and smiled. "Of course not. But I fear you will find most of them very boring. I think most are just old bills and those sorts of things."

"Where are they Gran?"

"In the cellar under the stairs," Gran replied. "But don't try to get them out now. It is not very well lit and there are a few Redback spiders down there. It is very dusty too. You look in the morning."

"Oh it will be alright," Kylie replied, eager to begin the treasure hunt.

Her mother overheard this and also overruled her. "No! Bed for you young miss. You can look tomorrow."

Kylie protested, but her mother was not to be swayed. Kylie kissed Gran goodnight and was sent down to tuck herself in. By the time Allison and Margaret joined her she was already half asleep and when she did drop off it was to sleep soundly all night through.

Once again, she woke to find herself alone in the bed. A check of the clock showed it to be nearly 7:00am. On going upstairs, she learned from her mother, who was just starting to cook breakfast, that Allison had gone out at 4am again with Uncle Bill to help with the cows and that Margaret had also gone down to help with the morning milking. That made Kylie feel guilty, and she at once suggested she go down to help as well. Her mother shook her head and pointed out the window.

"They are nearly finished; only a dozen cows to go. You can join in tomorrow. How do you feel today?"

"Much better thanks mum," Kylie replied. She tested her muscles and ribs gingerly and was relieved to find that most of the soreness was gone, although her lip still split as she talked.

Over breakfast they discussed the plans for the day. Mrs Kirk was firm. "It looks like rain this afternoon. I think we should go for a short walk this morning down to the creek. Then you can rest after lunch. Kylie still hasn't recovered fully, I am sure."

So during the morning they walked over the next ridge along a cow path down to the main creek. Uncle Bill and the dogs led the way and Kylie felt quite safe. The creek was a delight, a crystal-clear brook murmuring over stones through a belt of jungle. Tiny fish flitted through the deeper pools and a tortoise was seen slipping out of sight under a log. Huge butterflies with brilliant blue and black wings fluttered in the bars of sunlight which penetrated the trees.

On returning to the farmhouse for morning tea they discovered the Griersons were visiting. They enquired anxiously how everyone was and asked if they could help in any way. When Mrs Grierson commented on how brave she had been Kylie blushed at the praise.

While they were talking a car was heard in the driveway. Uncle Bill went out to look. He returned with the police sergeant. The sight of him made Kylie's heart turn over with anxiety.

The sergeant smiled reassuringly. "Good news. We have arrested two men for the attack. They are in custody in Atherton now."

"Oh thank God!" Mrs Kirk gasped.

"Who are they?" Kylie asked.

"Two youths from Malanda," the sergeant replied. "Carl Limburger, nicknamed 'Burg'. He is the solid, fair-haired one; and Gerald Lucas, nicknamed 'Donk'- because he works with car engines all the time. He is the thin, dark-haired one with acne."

The names meant nothing to Kylie. Her mother shook her head and so did Gran. "Never heard of either of them. Are they locals?"

"Yes, Mrs Feltham, they are. Both born and bred here. Once we asked a few questions it was easy to track them by their nicknames."

Kylie was puzzled. "So how did they hear about this treasure map?"

"Alleged treasure map," Gran corrected. "Probably one of the ladies who was at the meeting mentioned it in their hearing; or to one of their sons who told them. As I said the story of the 'Jeweller's Shop' is hardly the greatest secret of the century in this part of the world."

"I suppose so," Kylie agreed.

"What will happen to them now?" Mrs Kirk asked.

The sergeant made a face. "They will front the magistrate tomorrow and he will set a trial date. You will have to give evidence at that."

The idea of having to appear in court and of facing the horrible men came as a sickening shock to Kylie. "But they will go to jail, won't they?"

The sergeant made another face. "Maybe. I wouldn't want to bet on it. We are opposing bail because of the assault, but they could be out again until the trial."

Kylie was horrified. The thought of the two men being free made her feel even sicker. "But they could come back and get us!" she cried.

The sergeant shook his head. "They could, but you can be sure the bail conditions will include a restraining order to stay away from you. They would be mad to do anything else. It would make their case ten times worse."

Kylie wasn't reassured. Nor was Mrs Kirk. "You will let us know if they are let out on bail, won't you?" she asked.

The sergeant promised to do so. He was offered tea and sat with them for a while, then took his leave. The Griersons left soon after, adding a warm invitation for the girls to come over to their farm anytime.

Uncle Bill stood up. "Well, I'm off to check that pump down in the bottom dam. Who wants to come?"

The girls all said they would come, although Kylie really itched to start searching through the old papers. Hats and boots were donned and they set off in the old ute.

It turned out to be an unpleasant experience. First they saw a snake- a red-bellied black which slid off into the long grass. Then they found a new-born calf drowned in the pond behind the earth dam. Uncle Bill made a grimace and told the girls to go away, but Allison insisted on helping. The body was fished out and dragged up onto the bank for removal. Uncle Bill then examined the pump. After a while he straightened up.

"As I suspected. I will have to take this up to the workshop and strip it down."

"Will it be easy to repair?" Allison asked.

Uncle Bill shook his head. "No. It's an old pump and I will probably have to pull it apart and even make a replacement part for it."

"Can't you just buy a new one?" Allison asked.

Again Uncle Bill shook his head. "I'd love to, but we can't afford one. So, it's got to be this one fixed, or we are out of water by tomorrow."

When Kylie heard this, she felt a stab of deep anxiety. If Uncle Bill could not afford to even replace a small pump then things must be bad indeed. *We must find that goldmine,* she told herself.

As they drove back to the house her mind turned this idea into a fierce resolve. On arrival she sought out her Gran. To her relief the others made no comment and assumed she was still not well after her bashing.

She found Gran asleep in her armchair. Rather than disturb her, Kylie asked her mother if she could look at the old papers in the cellar. Mrs Kirk nodded and again cautioned her to watch out for spiders. Taking a torch Kylie made her way downstairs. The door to the cellar was in under the stairs and the entrance was being used as a broom cupboard, which explained why the men had not found it. Moving the mops and brooms aside she looked in, found a light switch, turned it on, and went in.

The cellar was a room about 4 metres square with two posts in the centre. The walls were made of rough concrete and were lined with boxes and suitcases. The air was dry and musty, and everything was covered in a layer of fine dust.

First Kylie checked in and around the boxes for spiders and snakes. Satisfied there were none she began searching, opening boxes to look at the contents. It quickly became apparent to her that she was facing a daunting task. There were over a dozen cardboard cartons stuffed with papers and books, plus nine suitcases in various states of disintegration.

Oh well, nothing for it but to start, she told herself.

With a grimace she dusted the top of a carton and pulled the lid open. Movement inside made her snatch her hand away, but it was only silverfish. She made a face and started to lift papers out to look at them. They were bundles of old bills and bank statements and were addressed to her grandfather, Stan.

The most interesting thing about them was that most were in the old money: pounds, shillings, and pence. It took Kylie a moment to recognise the symbols. The actual values meant very little to her.

Money was worth a lot more then, I think, she mused.

That entire carton was the same. It was no real help to her at all. She moved it to the other side of the room and went to another. This was more interesting and contained bundles of letters and several large envelopes and an old photo album. The album was made of black cloth and contained hundreds of tiny black and white photos, now yellowed with age.

Blowing the dust from the cover Kylie moved over under the light and turned the pages. The photos were obviously of her relatives. That much was obvious from the family resemblance. To her annoyance few of them had any caption. She tried to guess at who the people were, and even when.

"Must be a long time ago, judging by the clothes," she muttered.

Noises of people walking around overhead decided her. "Mum might know who they all are; or Gran."

Taking the photo album, Kylie made her way upstairs to find afternoon tea in progress. Uncle Bill, Allison, and Margaret were back. Kylie was informed that the offending pump was now in the workshop and the dead calf 'disposed of'. She did not want to know how. Gran was now awake and she smiled as Kylie joined them.

"Look what I found Gran. I hope you don't mind me looking."

Gran laughed. "Not at all, dearie. Go for your life. You won't unearth any family skeletons in that lot. We are a terribly boring and proper crowd the Felthams; and the Pikes too. I will come down and help you later. I have a better idea where things are."

"Thanks Gran. Do you know who all these people are?" Kylie asked, opening the album.

Gran picked up her glasses and peered at the page Kylie had opened at. "Oh dear me! Oh, I think that is your Great Uncle Herbert. That is definitely my mother, Emma, beside him."

They all craned to look. Kylie turned the page. It was covered with more tiny photos showing men in working clothes standing around tree trunks and felled trees with an antique looking motor truck in the background. 'Boar Pocket – 1929' read the caption.

Gran shook her head. "Sorry. I don't know any of them. That one might be young Daniel who was killed in the sawmill accident." She pointed to a fine-looking young man in boots, trousers and singlet, holding an axe.

"What a shame," Margaret murmured. "He was very good looking."

Kylie turned a page. There was a photo of five children, all dressed up, the boys wearing ties and the girls in long white frocks and sun bonnets. Next to it was a photo of the same four children but this time the boys were in sailor suits and the girls held large union jacks. 'Empire Day – 1916' read the caption.

"Those must old Daniel's children," Gran said. "This will be Charlotte, then my dad, Hector, then Herbert, Young Daniel and Emily, the baby."

Kylie peered at the photo, fascinated. These were her flesh and blood ancestors. It was eerie to see the resemblance. Margaret thought so too, commenting, "Look at that girl. She is the spitting image of you, Kylie."

"I never spit, thank you," Kylie said, then laughed.

It was true. She was amazed. There were more photos on the next page of the same children, with a pet dog; playing with a toy pedal car; and with a pet cockatoo. The boys all wore long shorts with braces over white shirts with no collars on them and the girl's frocks were all below the knee and very frilly.

Kylie turned another page. A large photo of a bride took up one side and two others, both showing six children sitting on an old horse, the other. Gran smiled and pointed with pride.

"That was my mother, Emma, on her wedding day."

"She was very pretty Gran," Kylie commented.

"Yes, she was. And that was the photo I told you about of us kids on the horse on our way to school. That is me in the middle with my arms around Stanley. That is Stanley's sister Melba behind me, then his brother Noel and little Violet hanging on for dear life at the back. Josh is the boy at the front."

Kylie stared at her grandmother's photo with fascination. None of the children wore shoes and only three of them wore hats. She could not have recognised any without Gran. She turned more pages, revealing various family events: weddings, picnics and so on.

Gran shook her head and sucked her teeth with annoyance. "I wish I could remember who all these people were."

"You should have written on the back of all the photos, Mum," Mrs Kirk said.

It was obviously a discussion they had had before as Gran answered very shortly. "Well we didn't! We had to work hard in those days."

In her annoyance she quickly turned the page, to reveal a dozen photos of people swimming, sailing, lying on the beach ('Brampton Island – 1936' it read) and riding horses.

"Yes, lots of work," Mrs Kirk said with a grin.

"Oh poo to you!" Gran replied. She quickly turned the page. Out onto the table fell a loose photo. It was very old, a stiff, posed wedding photo of a severe looking man with a huge 'walrus' moustache and his hand gripping his lapel, standing beside a seated lady in a high-necked and lacy wedding dress.

"Oh heavens! That is Great, Great, Great Grandad Hector and Rose Till," Gran said.

"When was that Gran?" Kylie asked.

"Oh dear! When did I say they were married? About 1885 I think," Gran replied.

More pages were turned, showing photos of handsome young men in army uniform. "World War Two," Gran said, naming various great uncles. Then she turned another page and there was a full size, colour tinted photo of a bridal couple.

"That is my wedding," Gran explained.

Kylie gazed at it with rapt attention. "Gran! You were a beautiful bride!" she exclaimed.

Gran coloured and smiled. "Thank you my dear. And so will you be."

Then it was Kylie's turn to blush. The others laughed. Afternoon tea proceeded and more photos were studied. To Kylie's regret Gran could not remember who or where many of the photos were taken.

I will make sure I write on the back of all my photos, she silently vowed, well aware she had taken hundreds and never written on any.

Uncle Bill stood up. "Well, back to work for me. See you girls at four please."

"Yes, Uncle Bill," Kylie replied absently.

Allison went out with Uncle Bill but Margaret remained. She helped Mrs Kirk clean up while Kylie helped Gran down the stairs and into the cellar. She fetched a chair, then she set to work, helped by her mother and Margaret, to sort the boxes of old papers.

For over an hour they shifted, sorted and dusted. Margaret looked at her watch. "Time we went to help with the milking."

"Yes," Kylie agreed. "Just one more box." She opened the box, wrinkled her nose in distaste at the scuttle of cockroaches, and lifted out an old, leather-bound notebook.

"That is what you are after," Gran said. "That is one of Grandad Hector's diaries."

Kylie felt a thrill of discovery. She opened the book and scanned it. The pages were brown with age and the writing was all old-fashioned running writing done with a fountain pen. And there, right at the page she had opened up at, was a sketch map with the words 'Goldmine' on it. She gasped and felt an even more intense thrill. Goldmine! She showed it to the others, pointing to the word.

"Maybe there is a treasure map after all?" she gasped excitedly.

Chapter 6

RELATIONS

Gold! The mystique and thrill of the word made Kylie's heart skip a beat, then hammer faster.

Maybe there really is a lost goldmine? she thought. *And I will find it!*

Until milking time she tried to read the spidery writing in the faded ink. It was hard going but she began to get used to it before being called away by Margaret to help with the cows. Reluctantly she placed the old diary on the side table and went to help.

Milking time went faster this time as the girls all settled to doing particular tasks; and as they developed skills and routine. It was still tiring however and all were glad to walk back up to the house on dusk for a hot bath and change of clothes.

After tea, while the others settled to watch TV, Kylie sat in the kitchen and continued to read the old diary. She found it fascinating but very frustrating. There were numerous references to people and places but Kylie had no idea where these were.

During a commercial break her mother came into the kitchen for a drink. "How is it going dear?" she asked.

"Slow, and very irritating," Kylie replied. "I don't know where any of these places are. For example, Great Grandad keeps mentioning the 'Just in Time' mine, and Warramine Creek. Do you know where they are?"

Mrs Kirk shook her head. "No idea. All the mines had long been abandoned by the time I was a girl. You must ask Gran."

Kylie did this but Gran also shook her head. "Sorry dearie. I've heard of some of these places but in my day the women were expected to stay at home; and even when we did visit, we didn't use a map. We just went along for the ride."

Kylie made a face to show what she thought of men in 'The Good Old Days'. "Would there be a map to show where they were?"

"Sure to be, but not in this house I wouldn't think. Better ask Bill."

Kylie turned to Uncle Bill. He scratched his chin then said, "There would be detailed maps in the Mining Warden's records. They had to register all claims and mines accurately as a condition of their licence; still do for that matter."

"Licence!" Allison cried. "Did they have to buy one?"

"Pay a tax to the government for the privilege you mean!" Uncle Bill replied with a short laugh. "Of course they did. Governments knew how to make money even then. The price of the 'Miner's Right' was one of the main causes of the famous Eureka Stockade uprising."

Allison flushed. "Oh yes. I remember hearing about that in school. That wasn't in North Queensland, was it?"

"No. Victoria; and back in the 1860s," Uncle Bill replied.

Kylie cut in impatiently, "Where would these Mining Warden's records be kept?"

"They used to be in Herberton, but I think I heard something about them being removed or destroyed," Uncle Bill replied.

"Herberton! Why Herberton?" Kylie asked. She had been to Herberton several times and her impression of it was only of a sleepy little town nestled in a valley in the mountains.

Uncle Bill raised his eyes. "Herberton used to be the main town in the region back then."

Kylie turned to her mother. "Could we go to Herberton tomorrow?"

Mrs Kirk shook her head. "Slow down young lady. Herberton is a couple of hours drive."

"But mum, I can't find the goldmine without maps to help me understand these diaries," Kylie replied.

"Oh, you are going to find the lost goldmine, are you?" Mrs Kirk replied mildly.

Kylie flushed, but stubbornly raised her nose. "Yes, I am. We are going to save the farm for Gran and Uncle Bill."

"Good for you!" Uncle Bill replied. "I wish you luck."

"I mean it Uncle Bill. You don't have to laugh at me," Kylie replied.

"I wasn't laughing at you Ky. I would like to find it too. But..."

"But you think it is impossible?"

Uncle Bill made a wry face. "Yes. Plenty of men who knew a lot more about gold prospecting and jungle bashing than us have looked hard and failed."

"But they didn't have Grandad Hector's diaries and notes," Kylie replied, holding up the book.

"You might be right," Uncle Bill replied. "Maybe a trip to Herberton would be worth the time. I need to go to Atherton tomorrow anyway to see about repairing the suction pumps."

"Oh dear! Are the pumps breaking down again?" Gran asked. The anxious catch in her voice snatched at Kylie's heart and strengthened her resolve to find the goldmine.

Uncle Bill nodded. "They are starting to give trouble. I will get them seen to before they actually do break down."

So a plan was developed for a trip to Atherton, via Herberton, the next day. Kylie went to bed feeling tired but happy. Definite progress had been made. She drifted off to sleep imagining finding the old goldmine and of how the farm would be saved.

Next morning she was up with the others at 4am to help with the milking. It was cool and misty outside, the grass wet with dew but the sky was clear and by the time they had finished the sun was well up and the mist had evaporated. Over breakfast Kylie again raised the idea of going to Herberton.

Mrs Kirk nodded. "Yes we will go. But we won't all fit in my car. Are you taking your ute Bill?"

Bill swallowed some coffee. "Yes I need to. The pump won't fit in your car. Mum can come with me."

"Is anyone staying here?" Kylie asked.

"No," Bill replied.

"But what if those men come back?" Kylie asked.

"What if they do? We are not leaving one of you girls here on her own, not even with Gran," Mrs Kirk replied.

"But we need to guard the place in case they do come," Kylie replied.

Uncle Bill chuckled, then said, "Pass the toast. They are supposed to be in jail. Anyway, the farm has got by for a hundred years without being guarded night and day."

"But what if the men aren't in jail? What if they have been let out on bail?" Kylie asked, her face wrinkled into a frown.

"The sergeant said he would tell us," Uncle Bill replied calmly, buttering his toast.

"He might have forgotten," Kylie persisted.

"So what? What if they do come back?" Mrs Kirk said.

"They might take the old papers," Kylie replied.

"Then take them with you. Now eat up and stop talking silly nonsense," Mrs Kirk said.

By 9am they were ready and climbed into the two vehicles. As suggested Kylie had the old diary tucked into her bag. The route they took led them through Malanda and then up past Bromfield Swamp to the Kennedy Highway, then via Mt Hypipamee to Herberton.

Herberton was a sharp disappointment. They were informed that the Mining Records had long since been removed, to Archives 'down south,' (the man did not know where).

"You might find a few books on the subject though," he added.

"Which books?" Kylie asked.

"Try Bolton: '*A Thousand Miles Away*', for a general overview; then read Frank Dempsey's book: '*Old Mining Towns of North Queensland*'. It is pretty good; and easy to read. So is '*Angor to Zilmanton*'. Also, if you can find a copy, there is a book called '*Gold and Ghosts*' by de Havilland. I seem to remember it was very detailed," the man replied.

Mrs Kirk produced a notebook and wrote these down. They then went back to their car and drove to Atherton. Kylie immediately went in search of bookshops and was again disappointed. The lady there had heard of the books but none were in stock. Kylie was informed that '*A Thousand Miles Away*' was an old book and almost certainly long out of print. The lady advised trying the library.

As neither Mrs Kirk, nor Kylie were residents they could not borrow, but to Kylie's delight the library had a copy of both '*A Thousand Miles Away*' and '*Old Mining Towns of North Queensland*'. Uncle Bill was called in and was able to enrol himself as a borrower so they could take the books out.

After lunch at a cafe they set out to return to the farm. This time they drove to Malanda by the shortest route. As they drove through the rolling open country Mrs Kirk pointed to a farm ahead on the right. "That is Aunty Violet's place there."

That got Kylie's interest. She looked up from reading one of the books and studied the place. As she looked a man came into view from a shed and bent over a tractor.

Allison let out a little cry. "That looks like Bert."

"Yes, it does. Oh Mum, can we please call in and say hello," Kylie asked, her heart suddenly beating faster.

Mrs Kirk's eyebrows shot up but she only said, "We have to be back in time for the milking."

"Oh Mum, that's not till four o'clock. Please!"

Mrs Kirk glanced at her watch. "Alright, but only for half an hour."

She slowed the car and turned it up a gravel side road towards the farm. As they got closer, the man at the tractor straightened up and turned to look their way. Kylie felt a stab of disappointment.

"That's not Bert."

"No," Mrs Kirk agreed, "It is his big brother, Victor."

The car was stopped and they all climbed out. Victor came over to meet them. He was a solid, unsmiling version of his brother. His head was wider and his mouth had a twist to it which Kylie could not decide was a sneer or a smile.

Victor greeted them civilly enough and pointed to the house. "Mum is inside. Excuse me while I finish fixing this blasted tractor." He turned back to the machine.

The group made their way to the house and were warmly greeted by Aunty Violet. She showed them in and seated them on the side veranda. Cups of tea were produced and they began to chat.

As they did, Bert appeared from behind a shed. He wore only boots and jeans, a battered old felt hat adorning his head. Over his shoulder was a steel pipe. A dog trotted beside him. As soon as he saw them, his face split into a cheerful grin.

Kylie again felt her heart quicken. Her eyes took in his well tanned and muscular body. Having two big brothers she was used to seeing males without their shirts on but she was also aware that she found Bert's well-muscled arms and chest unusually disturbing and attractive.

He greeted them and flopped into a chair. The dog went from one to the other sniffing and wagging his tail. Bert laughed and clicked his fingers. "Here 'Bluey', down boy."

"Oh he's alright," Allison replied brightly, giving Bert a big smile.

Kylie noted this and knew she was feeling jealousy. For her it was an unusual emotion. *I must be growing up,* she thought. She had never taken much notice of males before, considering her brothers and their friends as 'silly boys'.

A few minutes later, Victor joined them. Bert stood up. "Would you like to see the farm?" he asked, his eyes shifting from Kylie to Allison.

"Yes please," they chorused.

The whole group stood and wandered down off the veranda. Kylie wanted to be with Bert but found herself and Margaret being shown the chicken run by Aunty Violet. There were dozens of tiny fluffy chicks and Margaret was delighted. Next they looked at new born calves and a beautiful chestnut horse.

"Only for riding," Aunty Violet explained, "Not a work horse."

The horse was admired and stroked. Only then did Kylie realise that both Allison and Bert were not with them. She looked around and felt a sharp stab of annoyance to see them both walking side by side along beside a field full of Frisians.

Being taken to see the pigs did nothing to improve Kylie's frame of mind. She kept looking towards where Bert and Allison had vanished from sight. *I'm being silly,* she told herself, *Allie is too young for Bert.*

But in her heart she knew she wanted to be with him. She felt quite cast down when Bert and Allison reappeared. As they walked towards them, he said something which made Allison laugh. The way her eyes met his and sparkled did nothing to restore Kylie's equanimity. In spite of that, she was sorry when her mother insisted they had to be going.

"See you again," Bert said, his eyes fixed on Allison this time. She smiled back and nodded.

As they drove off, she kept twisting around in her seat to wave. "Isn't he a dream?" she said.

Kylie could only shrug and feel upset, although she pretended she wasn't interested.

Back at the farm Kylie wanted to lie down and read at once but it was milking time and the girls changed and went out to help bring in the cows and then with the milking. By the time Kylie was able to get back to the books it was nearly 8pm and she felt so tired she made no real objection to going to bed when her mother ordered it.

The dream was exciting and arousing. Bert was holding her and gently caressing her back. It was sending shivers through her and making her feel warm in a way she knew was naughty. She wasn't quite sure, because no boy had ever actually held her like that; but it was what she imagined... "Huh? What?"

Kylie sat up and blinked. She found herself staring into Margaret's eyes. The light was on.

"Wake up. Time to get in the cows," Margaret said. "And it's raining."

Kylie shivered again and wished she could sink back into the warmth of sleep, and into Bert's exciting embrace. What would it really be like? With a groan she climbed out of bed and began to dress. The sound of rain caused her to make a face to which Allison returned a cheerful grin. That caused Kylie to remember Allison and Bert together the previous day. Kylie experienced a rush of emotions she was quite amazed by.

Mrs Kirk appeared. "Wear a pullover, you girls," she called.

"Pullover! This is summer, and the tropics," Allison replied.

"It might be, but you are nearly a thousand metres above sea level. This is the Tablelands don't forget," Mrs Kirk called back.

So the girls dressed themselves warmly before making their way upstairs for a cup of hot cocoa. Uncle Bill joined them and they went out into the night.

Outside it was cold and dark. The girls were rugged up in pullovers and raincoats, hats and gum boots. Walking to bring in the cows was a wet and muddy experience which Kylie did not enjoy. Luckily the cows had been placed in the paddock closest to the milking shed so they did not have too far to go.

As they walked back up to the house in the grey dawn after finishing the milking, Kylie shivered more and hunched herself against the chill of a stiff breeze which came whipping over the treetops. She looked around and saw that all of the upper slopes of Bartle Frere were hidden in a solid overcast. Showers and drizzle completed a gloomy picture, cloaking the other ridges and mountains. A hot breakfast of sausages and fried eggs washed down by hot tea was a pleasant relief.

Because of the rain the morning was mostly spent indoors. Allison went off with Uncle Bill to work in the machinery shed on fixing some machine. Margaret read and helped Mrs Kirk in the kitchen, chattering happily. Kylie snuggled into an armchair in the lounge beside the fireplace, where a cheery little fire crackled, and read the book on Old Mining Towns.

It was something of a revelation to her, all the pioneering and gold digging which had gone on and she found it fascinating. Lunch time came around and with it the sun. The clouds rolled away and water from the last shower trickled and dripped off the roof.

Over lunch Margaret asked, "What are we doing this afternoon?"

"I want to finish reading this book," Kylie replied.

To this Allison objected strongly. "I didn't come here just to sit around. Uncle Bill says there are platypuses in the creek. I'd like to see one. Let's go and look."

Reluctantly Kylie agreed. She had once glimpsed a platypus as it dived in. "We have to be very quiet and might have to wait for a long time," she cautioned.

"That's okay. We can take afternoon tea with us," Allison replied.

So an expedition was organized. The girls changed into old clothes, collected biscuits and hats and set off. Kylie slipped the books into her shoulder bag and happily followed. The farm track over the next hill and down to the creek was muddy and slippery and Kylie was thankful more than once for the rubber gum boots she wore.

The girls made their way to a section of the creek which flowed through rainforest. Here they settled themselves behind trees to watch a small pool below a set of rapids, using their folded raincoats to sit on. Once in place Kylie extracted her book and began to read; ignoring Allison's frown.

Uncle Bill's voice calling in the cows ended the vigil with no platypus sighted. The girls made their way up to help with the milking. As they walked back behind the cows more dark rain clouds came sweeping in from the southeast, blotting out the view of Bartle Frere again. The girls reached the milking shed in time but the rain which deluged down made milking a cold and muddy operation. To Kylie's annoyance even this did not dampen Allison's high spirits.

That evening, Kylie again immersed herself in the books. The others sat at the kitchen table and played Monopoly. As Kylie read on, she was excited to find a place mentioned in the old diary: Warramine Creek.

"I wish we had a map," she said aloud, shaking her head in annoyance.

"Well, we haven't got one, sorry," Mrs Kirk replied.

"Could we get one in Atherton?" Kylie asked, looking at Uncle Bill.

He nodded. "Should be able to, at the Land's Department offices. They sell maps there."

"Could we go to Atherton tomorrow?" Kylie asked.

Mrs Kirk frowned. "Fair go Ky-bub. We can't go driving about for a couple of hours every time you want something for your wild goose chase."

"Oh Mum! It's not," Kylie replied. "It's just that all these places are mentioned in both the old diary and in this book and I've got no idea where they are so it is no help at all. Someone must know where they are; this 'Perseverance' Mine; and all these other mines: the 'King of the Ranges'; the 'Rose of Shamrock', 'Cody's Claim', and so on."

Gran looked up from her book and peered over her glasses. "Plenty of people know where they are. Stan's people still have their farm right near Warramine Creek. It is just over there somewhere." She indicated the next ridge to the east. "And the Reids would know where they all are. As I said the Reid brothers went looking for the famous 'Jewellers Shop' half a dozen times and they had maps. I saw them looking at them."

"Who? Bert and... and... and Victor?" Kylie asked.

Gran shook her head. "No, not the boys. Their father Bruce, and his brothers Brian and Dennis. Back in the Seventies."

Allison's eyes lit up. "Perhaps we could ask them for the loan of a map?"

"Yes," Kylie agreed, her heart fluttering. "Could we go over to the Reid's Farm to see them? Please mum. It's not nearly as far as Atherton."

Both Uncle Bill and Mrs Kirk laughed aloud. "Not that much different," Uncle Bill replied.

"Please mum," Kylie wheedled.

"Are you sure it is to look at old maps you want to go there?" Mrs Kirk asked.

Kylie blushed crimson, knew it, and blushed even more. "Of course. May we, please?"

"I will think about it," Mrs Kirk replied.

Allison looked up. "If it is raining tomorrow we won't be able to do anything here," she put in.

Mrs Kirk looked at her and smiled. "Yes," she said slowly. "Alright. We will see what the weather is like tomorrow. If there is rain we will go visiting."

"Oh thank you Mum!" Kylie cried.

"Steady on. I said if there is rain."

"Yes Mum. Come on rain, fall!" Kylie called.

They all laughed. Mrs Kirk stood up. "Time you girls were in bed. Come on. Milo time."

Chapter 7

LESSONS IN LIFE

There was no rain. The dawn sky was clear and clean. Bartle Frere stood up against it like a massive piece of stage scenery. Kylie walked along in the semi-darkness shooing the cows towards the milking shed and thinking pleasant thoughts about Bert. She was mildly surprised at herself as she had rarely considered boys as anything other than grubby and often disgusting creatures who played silly games.

Thoughts of boys returned to her when she stood in the shower later. As the warm water soothed her sore muscles, she checked the bruises. Most had gone but there was still a large discolouration which showed with a sickly greenish tinge on her chest. That was from the whack by the gun butt. Kylie gently massaged it, noting that the bruise extended right from one nipple to the other.

It was the sight of them that got her thinking about boys. She knew that she was starting to develop breasts and was both fascinated and excited by the prospect. From talking to her friends and from overhearing her brothers and their friends she knew that boys were particularly interested in breasts and that boys liked to see them and play with them.

She was aware that Allison's were bigger and had already noted, with some annoyance, how Bert had looked at them, with evident approval. In a surge of jealous emotion she studied herself and fantasized about what the future might bring.

At that moment Allison banged on the door. "Come on Kylie! Hurry up! You'll dissolve; and I'm getting cold!"

Kylie finished her shower and hurried to dress, now hot and ashamed of the thoughts she had been entertaining. Fresh and scrubbed she went out to help prepare breakfast.

Over toast and marmalade her mother asked, "What are your plans for today girls?"

"Can we go over to the Reid's like we said please mum," Kylie asked.

Mrs Kirk considered this for a time, then nodded. "After lunch. What will we do this morning?"

"What is there to do?" Margaret asked.

"I will be cleaning the house," Mrs Kirk replied. "And there is a Christmas tree to put up."

"Oh yes please! May we decorate it please?" Margaret asked, her eyes sparkling with delight.

"Of course," Mrs Kirk replied.

After breakfast Kylie opted to do the washing up, then helped to dust and vacuum the lounge room. Allison and Margaret went off with Uncle Bill to cut the tree. They returned half an hour later with a sapling cut from the edge of a field. Uncle Bill brought in a large bucket which he had carefully cleaned. The tree was placed upright in this and then wedged and held in place by stones from the garden. Christmas paper was then draped around the bucket to hide it.

The Christmas tree was placed in the corner of the lounge room beside the old fireplace. Several cardboard cartons were extracted from a cupboard. These contained decorations which were taken out and sorted. Kylie laid out a row of coloured balls and tinsel flowers. As she did, she noted that many were broken, or had no hooks on the back. She felt a twinge of disappointment. The decorations were obviously old and had seen many Christmases. Unwilling to hurt Gran's feelings she said nothing but went on sorting, trying to find enough undamaged ones.

Not so Allison. She said, "These are very old, Mrs Feltham. Most of them are broken." She held up a tattered tinsel streamer which looked very ragged.

Gran nodded. "Yes dear. They have been used for many years," she replied. "I suppose it's time we bought some new ones."

"What with?" Uncle Bill asked. He was seated in his armchair beside Gran. Kylie saw his face twist into a bitter smile. The sight stabbed her to the heart.

Poor Old Uncle Bill! He can't even afford to buy new Christmas decorations! To her it was an appalling thought. *I must find that gold mine!* she told herself.

Margaret said, "May we buy you some new ones, as a present for giving us such a wonderful holiday?"

Gran coloured with embarrassment, then nodded. "That is very kind of you, dear. I would like that. But don't spend too much money."

"We won't, Mrs Feltham," Margaret said.

Allison turned from trying to drape the tattered tinsel around the tree. "We could go to town to buy them."

"To town!" Uncle Bill snorted. "That's all you girls want to do!"

"All girls do Bill, you know that," Mrs Kirk said with a smile.

"We could drop in on the Reids on the way," Allison added.

Mrs Kirk laughed aloud. "Yes, we could. As I said, we will go after lunch, but I will phone Violet to make sure she is home."

Mrs Kirk stood up and walked towards the phone. As she did, it rang, giving her a fright as she had been about to pick it up.

"Hello, Feltham Farm. Who? Oh yes sergeant."

The police! Kylie thought. *I hope it isn't bad news.*

But it was. Mrs Kirk said, "Yes, I see. Thank you for telling us. Goodbye." Then she put down the phone and turned to face them. "That was the police sergeant in Malanda. He says that the two men have been released on bail. The court case will probably be in mid-March. He will inform us of the dates."

Kylie was horrified on both counts. "Oh Mum! What if they come back here?"

Mrs Kirk shook her head and replied, "They are not likely to. The sergeant said they had been specifically warned not to come near any of us or they will face more charges. I don't think they will."

Kylie nodded, but in her heart she was scared and she knew it. Resentment that two strangers could so spoil their Christmas welled up in her heart and that made her feel guilty as she was not normally like that.

Later, when the tree had been decorated as well as the available decorations allowed, Kylie sat next to her mother having morning tea. The old diary was open on the table in front of her. As she sat staring out the window Uncle Bill went past with the two dogs. He was on his way down to the bottom paddock.

"Mum."

"Yes dear?"

"Why has Uncle Bill never married? He's a nice man."

Mrs Kirk glanced at her brother and a look of sadness settled on her face. When she did not immediately answer, Kylie voiced her thoughts, "Doesn't he like girls?"

Mrs Kirk shook her head. "Yes, he does. No, you see that farm away over there, the one beyond that line of pine trees?" She pointed to a distant cluster of buildings. Kylie nodded. Mrs Kirk then explained, "When he was young, he was madly in love with the daughter of the family who own it. Jane her name was. For years they were inseparable, and everyone just assumed they would be married. They even became engaged. Then one day Bill discovered her with another man doing something that was wrong."

Kylie's mind raced. She guessed what it was her mother was hinting at, the suspicion confirmed because her mother's cheeks and neck had tinged red with embarrassment. Mrs Kirk went on, "Jane just laughed and threw his engagement ring back at him, then went off. But she didn't marry that man either. She ran off with a salesman and we never saw her again. Bill was very hurt."

A wave of sadness and sympathy engulfed Kylie. *Poor Uncle Bill!*

"How could anyone do that sort of thing?" she asked, anger at Jane's actions becoming stronger by the minute.

Mrs Kirk shook her head sadly, "Because people are sometimes driven by strong emotions. You will understand when you get older."

"Didn't Uncle Bill ever fall in love again?" Kylie asked.

"I think his heart was broken. Worse, his trust in women had been broken. Oh Kylie dear, he is such a good man, straight and true. I wish he would meet a nice woman and get married. He would make a wonderful father."

Kylie pondered the nature of humanity in sadness and anger for a while. Her mother moved to refill the teapot and plainly did not want to discuss the topic further, so Kylie lowered her head to continue reading the old diary.

She was deeply immersed in this when Margaret came puffing up the back yard.

"Kylie, come and see. A cow is having a calf!"

Kylie wasn't sure that she really wanted to see that but Margaret was insistent. Mrs Kirk encouraged her. "Go and watch dear. It will be educational, if nothing else."

Feeling mixed emotions, not least embarrassment, Kylie put the diary aside and went to pull on her gum boots. She walked with Margaret down to a clump of trees near an old tumbledown shed. Allison was there, crouching to watch.

The cow was almost finished, and Kylie was just in time to see the calf actually slide out onto the ground. She found the sight both fascinating and disgusting. The calf was all covered in a sort of bluish membrane which was coated in blood and mucous.

"I wonder if that hurt much," Allison commented. "Mum says it really hurts to have a baby."

Kylie had seen videos of babies being born and she accepted the idea of being a mother herself sometime in the future, but she wasn't sure how she really felt about it. She was both amused and shocked by Margaret's next comment.

"My mum says it is more fun making babies than having them."

With that she giggled. Kylie did too, mostly from embarrassment. She had seen one of those sorts of videos too, at a friend's house. She also had two older brothers and from accidentally seeing them and from comments her friends had made she had a good idea of what life might be like. Some of it sounded quite disgusting and unpleasant but she assumed that if she was really in love things would just happen naturally.

It was all very worrying, but also very exciting. But not the sight of the cow licking the mucous and membrane from the calf's head. Kylie felt quite sick. "I think that is revolting," she said.

Allison shrugged. "Only natural," she commented.

Kylie watched the cow lick more of the blood and mucous off. The calf was lying on the dirt and grass and that made her feel even more nauseous.

Margaret said, "I wonder what it will be like to have a baby?"

Allison looked up at her. "It will hurt. Like trying to shit a watermelon mum said," she replied.

"I think I will like trying to make one though," Margaret giggled.

Kylie was shocked as well as amused. "Margaret! Don't you and Graham do anything naughty. You are too young."

And I don't want him to get into trouble either, she thought. She dimly knew there were laws about how old a person had to be to be allowed to do things like that.

Allison then shocked and peeved her more by saying, "I would like to make love to Bert."

"Allie! You are too young. Besides, he could go to jail," Kylie replied. She was astonished how strongly she felt about it.

Allison laughed. "Only if someone found out. I wouldn't tell."

Kylie was even more shocked. Worse, she knew she was being a hypocrite and was jealous. She struggled for an answer but was saved by Margaret who said, "If you got pregnant you would be found out."

Allison sneered. "I wouldn't. I'd be careful. We will take precautions."

Will! Kylie thought in hurt dismay, her mind grappling with how people 'took precautions' so as not to have babies when they had sex. It was all very adult and scary, and she felt sick with worry and annoyed at her own jealousy.

By this time the cow had licked the calf all over and the calf had its eyes open and was moving its legs. The eyes were huge, shining orbs which looked so appealing that Kylie's disgust ebbed. The cow nuzzled the calf in to her udder and it began to suck.

"It will be alright now," Allison said.

She was still watching with evident fascination. Kylie stayed for a while but then wandered back up to the house, her mind, and emotions in a confused whirl. She found it a relief to settle back to reading the old diary.

She noted that she was near the end of the writing. Before she had gone down to see the calf being born she had read that Hector had left home to try to find more gold. She resumed reading and was soon absorbed. She turned the page and read:

> - 11 March 1932 - Went down the track to the 'Erin'. Not feeling well. Tough going in the wet. Ask for work at the 'Erin'. No luck. Spend the night at Frank's.
>
> - 12 March - Prospecting up the side gullies off Nugget Creek. Rain.
>
> - 13 March - Prospecting up Nugget Creek above Frank's. A few 'shows'
>
> - 14 March - sick
>
> - 15 March - Prospecting. Found some dust but not enough to pay any bills!
>
> - 16 March - Prospecting. Found one tiny nugget the size of a Number 4 shot.

- 17 March - Prospecting. Found a few specs of colour. Food almost gone.

- 18 March - Frank very sick. Shot a scrub turkey. Took it over and cooked it for him. He is a cheerful coot, even when he is down. He has the gold bug bad; is convinced that there is a major reef somewhere up Nugget Creek.

- 19 March - Heavy rain. Search up Nugget Creek from Frank's claim. Found a few grains. Don't think I am finding even enough to be equal to the dole. Worry about Emma and the kids.

- 20 March - Prospecting. Found a few more grains. Maybe Frank is right? He is still very sick. Killed a big scrub python and made a stew for Frank.

- 21 March - Find a tick on myself. Maybe that is what made me sick. Frank is so sick I persuade him to go to see the doctor. Heavy rain.

- 22 March - Heavy rain. Take Frank down to Doc Ward's at Goldsborough. Have trouble crossing the creeks which are flooded. Takes all day.

- 23 March - At Goldsborough. Ask for work at the saddlers and from Jess Blake (carter) but no luck. This Depression is a hard time for working people. Walk back up to my camp. Takes all day in the rain.

- 24 March - Tidy up Frank's camp. Feel very sick. Back to my own camp but too ill to do any more.

- 24 March - Sick as a dog.

- 25 March - Ditto

- 26 March - Ted Phillips from the 'Bright Smile' dropped in and asked me over for lunch. They have just had a good strike and are celebrating. Go down to join them but can't eat much. They are good chaps.

- 27 March - Rain but stops by midday. Prospect further up Nugget Creek. Feel sick but make the effort as my food is almost all gone.

- 28 March - I have found it! I have found the 'Jeweller's Shop'! Nuggets the size of marbles just lying on the stream bed and gold dust trapped in the rock crevices, just waiting to be scooped up! Nearby is a rock face just studded with gold like plums in a pudding. Pegged a claim, then picked up all I could. Collected twelve jars of gold. Too heavy to carry so I have hidden them under a rock overhang twenty five paces upstream. Take only one jar as a sample. Back to camp feeling so sick I can hardly walk. Write a letter to Herbert with instructions on how to find the claim in case anything happens to me.

-29 March - Pack up. To the 'Erin' and mail the letter. Don't tell anyone. Just tell them I am off home for a rest and to get more food. Take the Christmas Creek track but can hardly get up the hill. Spend the night on the track in heavy rain.

- 30 March - Very sick but manage to make it home. Thank God! Give Emma the gold and send Billy Thorpe to register the claim. To bed. Very sick. Emma is a good wife.

The diary abruptly finished. As she was reading the page Kylie had been gripped by mounting excitement. Now the enormity of the tragedy swamped her. *Poor Grandad Hector! Poor Emma. Just as he found the gold he is struck down by fever. Oh how sad!*

But he did find gold! Excitedly Kylie re-read the account of the discovery. *There is a gold mine. And I will find it to save the farm,* she vowed.

The image of her ancestor struggling through the dark, wet jungle filled her mind, to be succeeded by the images of her Great Grandmother struggling to run a farm and raise four children. *Or was it only three?* That sent her back to her notes.

Only three: Joshua, Grace and Violet. Grace is Gran and Violet was Aunty Violet's mum, she reminded herself.

But how to find the gold? That sent Kylie back to re-read the page of the diary a third time.

"Ah yes! Here it is. He says: Write a letter to Herbert with instructions on how to find the claim in case anything happens to me. And here, on the next day: Pack up. To the 'Erin' and mail the letter. A letter! To Herbert. Who was Herbert?"

A check of the family tree showed that Herbert was Hector's brother; and that he was also Aunty Violet's grandfather. She remembered the discussion about cousins marrying.

Holding the diary Kylie ran into the kitchen where her mother and Gran were preparing lunch. "Mum! Mum! I have found the story about Great Grandad finding the 'Jeweller's Shop'. And he wrote a letter to his brother Herbert with instructions on how to find it."

Her mother and Gran both read the diary. Gran finished first. For a moment she stared into the distance, her face very thoughtful. Then she said, "A letter. I wonder if Herbert ever got it?"

"He was Aunty Violet's grandad, wasn't he?" Kylie asked.

"Yes dear."

"Then maybe Aunty Violet knows something about the letter?" Kylie suggested.

"Possibly. I think the Reid boys had some information," Gran replied.

"We can ask them this afternoon," Kylie said.

She was now gripped by intense excitement. A letter! And it would be the key to the riddle!

Chapter 8

THE LETTER

During the drive to the Reid's Kylie fidgeted with excitement. She also felt the gnawing of the worm of jealousy and that bothered her conscience. The cause of the jealousy was Allison's clothing. Allison had worn tight, white shorts which showed off her legs to very good advantage. And they were nice legs, Kylie had to concede, smooth and well-proportioned and a honey-gold colour. Worse still, Allison had opted to wear a short, loose, yellow cloth top which left her navel and midriff bare.

That the arrangement was effective was immediately apparent on arrival at the Reid's. Both Bert and Victor ran their eyes up and down Allison, while barely glancing at Kylie or Margaret. Kylie had worn jeans and a white cotton shirt and thought she must look very plain by comparison.

Mrs Reid welcomed them and showed them into the lounge room. A Christmas tree had sprouted there since the last visit and Annabelle was busy decorating it. The sight reminded Kylie they needed to buy more decorations for Gran's house.

The guests were seated and welcomed. Kylie wanted to be next to Bert but found herself outmanoeuvred and was too shy to push in. So she ended on the other side of the room beside her mother. To her chagrin Allison ended up beside Bert. To add to Kylie's annoyance Bert then began an animated conversation with Allison, ignoring everyone else. Mr Reid appeared, a bluff, weather-beaten man in his forties. He was so obviously Bert and Victor's father that Kylie had to smile. Tea, coffee and cakes were produced and they settled to polite conversation.

Allison mentioned to Bert that they had watched the calf being born the day before. Bert nodded and said, "That's interesting. We had a sow drop a litter yesterday."

"What dropped what?" Margaret interjected.

"A sow, a female pig, dropped a litter. That means it had baby pigs," Bert replied.

"Piglets, you mean," Kylie added.

Bert turned and met her eyes, then smiled. "Yes, you are right, piglets." He then turned to Allison and asked, "Would you like to see them?"

"Oh yes please!" Allison replied.

Kylie could not help herself. "Can we come too?" she asked.

A look of annoyance crossed Bert's face, causing Kylie to regret her request, but he replied with a smile, "Of course."

Kylie noted a tiny frown on Allison's brow. *She wants to get him away on their own,* she deduced. Another spasm of hurt and jealousy stabbed through her.

To deflect this she changed the conversation by saying, "I've been reading Grandad Hector's diary. He did find the gold."

That brought the other conversations to a halt. Both Aunty Violet and Victor swung to look at her with interest. Aunty Violet said, "Are you sure? My dad and his brothers went looking for that famous gold mine half a dozen times and found nothing. They gave up in disgust in the end, deciding it was just the ramblings of a delirious man in the grip of a fever."

"Well it wasn't, Aunty Violet," Kylie replied. "Grandad Hector did find gold. He wrote it all in his diary. I've got it here." She reached down into her bag and pulled out the diary. The others stared at the old book in fascinated interest. Kylie flipped the diary open at her bookmark and said, "Only I don't think it was a gold mine. He didn't actually dig any tunnels or anything. He just found the exposed gold reef. I'll read it to you."

The others sat in silence as she read the last page of the diary.

"Gold nuggets just lying in the creek bed!" Bert said in awe.

"And gold dust in the rock crevices just waiting to be scooped up!" Margaret added.

"And gold sticking out of the rock like raisins in a plum pudding," Victor breathed.

Kylie nodded, then said, "It says here that Grandad Hector wrote a letter to his brother Herbert with instructions on how to find the gold, in case anything happened to him." She read the actual paragraph, including the part on the next day about posting the letter. "So, if he posted the letter, did Herbert ever get it? Is there and old letter?" she asked.

Aunty Violet frowned, then shook her head. "Oh I don't think so."

At that Bert sat up and turned from Allison. "Yes, there is Mum. You know, the one in that old jewel box of Grandma's."

Again Aunty Violet frowned and appeared to think hard. Kylie also noticed Victor purse his lips and give a slight shake to his head. If it was a warning, Bert did not see it, or heed it. He stood up, "I know where the letter is. I'll get it."

Aunty Violet put up her hand, then hesitated, "Oh... Oh... Oh yes, dear. I think I know the one you mean."

Bert left the room and a brittle silence settled. Kylie had the distinct impression that Aunty Violet was not happy. Victor certainly wasn't. To keep the conversation moving Kylie said, "This diary is fascinating. Would you like to read it?"

"Thank you dear, yes," Aunty Violet replied. She took the offered book and settled to read the page.

Kylie smiled nervously, then said, "It is a bit hard to follow without a map. There are lots of places mentioned but nobody seems to know where they are."

As she said this Bert came back into the room. He was smiling and had an old brown envelope in his hand. "Here is the letter. It was right on top of that pile in the old wooden case. I knew I'd seen it about recently."

Mrs Kirk now spoke, "Oh please keep it to yourself if you want. I know your family has often looked for the famous 'Jeweller's Shop' and we don't want to pry into your family secrets. Kylie just has a bit of a bee in her bonnet about it."

Kylie blushed, "I just want to help Uncle Bill keep the farm. If he can't get money the bank will take it off him," she explained.

Uncle Bill gave a short laugh and shrugged. "It will be alright. We will make out somehow."

Bert smiled and walked over to Kylie, holding the letter out, "That's great, Kylie. Here, you have it. We don't need a gold mine. We are doing very well here."

"Oh thank you," Kylie said.

She took the letter and found her hands were trembling slightly. She extracted the single sheet of paper from the tattered envelope, noting the old Penny stamp with the picture of one of the King Georges on the front as she did.

It was the letter. Her heart leapt the moment she saw the date: 28th March 1932.

"This is it! Look, it is dated the same day as the diary says; and it is headed Nugget Creek." With her heart fluttering with excitement she read down the letter. It was a detailed description of how to find the gold. Having read it once she looked up, her eyes shining. "This is it alright. Listen. Hector says: Dear Bert, that must be Herbert, I have found the 'Jeweller's Shop'! It is the richest find I have ever seen. I have collected samples and stored them nearby as I am too weak to carry much. I am on my way home now but am very sick. Just in case something happens to me here are the details on how to find the place. Use the same method as we used in school."

There followed a detailed list which Kylie read one by one, "One: From the Erin Mine go South; Two: Don't cross the main stream; Three: Turn right at the 'Bright Smile'; Four: Don't cross Nugget Creek; Five: Turn left at Frank's Claim; Six: Go downhill to the mossy rocks; Seven: Take the left fork; Eight: Second Creek; Nine: Downstream 50 paces."

The last part of the letter read, "I am real sick and fear I have scrub typhus. Please take care of Emma and the kids if I don't make it and make sure they get their share. God be with you, your loving brother, Hector."

On the margins of the letter were pencilled: 'Where is Frank's Claim? Which creek is Nugget Creek? Where is the 'Bright Smile?' These same questions obviously crossed everyone's mind. Uncle Bill said, "Well, all we need to do is work out which creek is Nugget Creek and we should be able to find the place."

Aunty Violet shook her head, "I doubt it. Dad and his brother Bruce spent weeks searching several creeks from end to end. I even went once."

"Maybe a flood caused a landslide which covered it up?" Margaret suggested.

Aunty Violet again shook her head. "Maybe. The problem was in working out which creek was called Nugget Creek."

"Wouldn't it be on the map?" Allison asked.

"There are several Nugget Creeks scattered around the region," Bert answered. "And I don't doubt there are a hundred more in Australia. But these were local names that did not always make it onto the official map."

"But the mines would have," Mrs Kirk said. "Don't all mining leases have to be registered and accurately marked."

"Yes, they do," Uncle Bill replied. "So, if we start at the Erin Mine then we should be able to work out which creek it is."

Again Aunty Violet shook her head; "I'm not so sure. That is what dad did, and he tried for years."

"What about the mine called 'The Bright Smile'?" Kylie asked. "Is it on the map?"

Bert turned to Victor. "Get us that old map of yours Vic and we will have a look."

For an instant Kylie thought Victor was going to refuse, but he shrugged and went out of the room. Kylie again read the letter and the talk became animated about gold mining. When Victor returned he had a stiff parchment map which he spread on the coffee table. They crowded around to study it. Victor pointed. "This is the old family farm at Warramine Creek, and here is your place Mrs Feltham. Now, there were three main goldfields in that area. There was the Towalla Goldfield but it is too far south. Then there is this belt of mines which extends across the top ends of all these creeks from Wiandra Creek to Coopooroo Creek. The Boonjee Goldfield is its name."

Allison ran her ginger across the map. "They are all in a line. Why is that?" she asked.

"Because they are on the edge of the basalt country. The Atherton Tablelands were formed by volcanic activity and the lava flows formed a layer on top of the auriferous rock. That is where the underlying rocks have been exposed by erosion," Victor explained.

"The what rocks?" Kylie asked.

"Auriferous. Gold bearing rocks. Where the actual gold reefs are," Victor explained. He then pointed further north. "There was another cluster of claims here, just east of your farm in the Swipers Flat and Churinga Flat areas. That is where we think the Jeweller's Shop is. See, here is the 'Pride of Erin' mine."

He placed his finger on the map. Kylie looked eagerly at it. Her eyes scanned around. "There is Christmas Creek!" she said excitedly.

"Is the 'Bright Smile' shown?" Margaret asked.

Kylie looked hard but she could not find it. Dozens of other names were marked, and she read some of them out aloud, "The 'Union', the 'Blarney Stone', that's Irish isn't it? The 'Just in Time'; the 'Astronomer'; the 'Caledonia'. That is Irish too isn't it?"

"No, Scottish," Gran corrected. "Caledonia is the old Roman name for Scotland. Ireland is Hibernia."

"No 'Bright Smile' though," Allison said.

"Only yours," Bert replied.

Kylie glanced up sharply, just in time to see Bert smile at Allison, who blushed and smiled back. A sharp stab of jealousy lanced through Kylie. Margaret glanced from Allison to Bert and giggled.

Hiding her hurt with an effort Kylie turned to Victor. "Can we have a copy of the map please?" she asked.

Victor answered, "Take a while to copy."

Bert shook his head. "No it won't. We can photocopy at the Newsagents. Be done in a few minutes."

"Have to go to town to do that," Victor replied sourly.

"We were going anyway," Kylie replied.

Kylie held up the letter. "Could we also get a photocopy of this too?"

This time Victor actually scowled. Kylie thought he was going to say no but Bert cut in, "Of course. We've had the bloody thing for seventy years and haven't been able to find the gold. You can have a go. Just give us our fair share when you find it."

Kylie smiled her thanks. Victor said, "What about giving us a copy of the diary in return?"

"That's fair," Gran said.

"Let's go then," Bert said.

"Hang on. We only just got here," Uncle Bill said.

"I will drive the girls to town then," Bert said. That was news to Kylie. She knew Bert was seventeen, but it had not occurred to her that he might have a driver's licence.

Mr Reid nodded. "That's a good idea," he said.

Aunty Violet looked doubtful. "You drive carefully Bert," she warned.

"I will Mum. Who wants to come?" Bert replied. He stood up and looked at Allison.

Allison stood up, smiling. Kylie joined her and so did Margaret. "Don't be long you children," Mrs Kirk cautioned. "You only have an hour and we must start back for milking."

"Milking!" Margaret said as they walked out onto the side veranda. "I don't think I could stand living on dairy farm. You would never be free; always tied to milking times dawn and dusk."

"I could be," Allison answered.

"It's not that bad," Bert replied. "Besides, there are contract milkers who look after the herd if you have to go away for a while; or if you need a holiday."

"You'd have to pay them though?" Allison asked as they reached the car.

Bert nodded. "Sure. Nothing in life is free," he replied. He stood and opened the front passenger door for Allison and she slid in. Kylie and Margaret were left to open the rear doors themselves. That put Kylie in a bad mood, seeing Bert beside Allison in the front. She knew this was unfair and just jealousy. She also had doubts about whether she wasn't just fickle herself. For years she had had a crush on Peter Bronsky, Graham's best friend. Peter was on the same army cadet promotion course as Graham and she had hoped to see him when he returned.

It only took a few minutes to drive into Malanda. The quiet little town had its usual sleepy air. "I love this place," Allison said. "I come from London and this is heaven compared to that."

Kylie gave her another sharp look. *Is she just saying that? Or are they serious hints?*

As they stood in the Newsagents photocopying Allison asked Bert, "Is it true, that your farm is doing well?"

"Yes, it is," Bert replied. "In fact mum and dad are going to buy the old farm next to ours and will give it to me on my twenty first birthday."

"Oh isn't that wonderful! You are so lucky," Allison gushed.

Kylie watched unhappily, aware of hurt in her heart. *Is she a scheming 'gold digger' or what?* she thought. Then she regretted it and tried to forgive Allison. *After all Bert is very handsome.*

Margaret searched the shelves for Christmas decorations but was quite disappointed. The range was very limited and not what they were looking for. "All sold out dearie, sorry," the lady explained.

"We will look in Atherton next time we go there," Kylie said.

Half an hour later they were back in the car on their way back to the farm. Once again, Allison sat in the front with Bert. Kylie pretended to study the map as they drove along. In this she was more successful than she meant as she became absorbed by her search for the gold mine.

Back at the Reid's farm they had more afternoon tea, then went to look at the piglets before setting off home. On the way Mrs Kirk said, "I don't think Cousin Victor was very happy with you, Kylie."

"No. I suppose he wanted to keep the letter and the map secret so he could find the gold mine and keep it all for himself."

"Oh that's a bit unfair," Allison protested. "They don't need money that much."

"Maybe not," Mrs Kirk said. "But gold does funny things to people."

"If he does find it he should share. That's what Grandad Hector wanted," Kylie said.

"And you do the same," Mrs Kirk replied.

However, that evening after tea, when Kylie had spread the map on the table to study it, Uncle Bill made a comment which thoroughly depressed her. "From the look of it that gold mine of yours is slap in the middle of the 'Wet Tropics World Heritage Area'. Even if you find it you won't be allowed to mine it. So you may as well stop wasting your time."

That was very depressing to Kylie but she did not give up that easily. "We need a modern map that has the boundaries on it then."

"You can get that from the Land Resources people in Atherton," Uncle Bill said.

"Can we go tomorrow?" Kylie asked.

"Fair go!" Mrs Kirk cried. "We have been driving almost every day."

"But Mrs Kirk we need to buy the Christmas decorations, and I need some more presents," Margaret said.

"Oh alright," Mrs Kirk relented, only to laugh when Gran added that they would all have to drive to Malanda on Sunday to go to church anyway.

It was only as Kylie was lying down to sleep that another thought came to her. She sat up and said to Allison and Margaret, "Grandad Hector wrote that he hid some gold near the claim. Even if we can't do any mining we might be able to find that. It should be worth something."

At breakfast next morning Uncle Bill confirmed that it would be. "Gold is worth about $1,000 US dollars an ounce at the moment, so a dozen jam jars full of it would be worth a lot."

"How much is an ounce?" Margaret asked.

"About a twenty-cent piece," Uncle Bill replied.

That was music to Kylie's ears. She went into an excited daydream about finding the glass jars full of gold. She re-read the letter and the diary and pored over the map. She even went and found an old glass jar and filled it with sand, then weighed it, doing the conversion from grams to ounces. The total amazed her.

"That would be about $15,000 in one glass jar!" she said. She whistled in amazement.

"And that is Yankee dollars," Uncle Bill reminded.

"What's the difference?" Kylie asked.

"Look in the newspaper under exchange rates," Uncle Bill explained.

Life certainly is complicated! Kylie thought.

She had to have Exchange Rates explained to her and found it hard to accept that people actually bought money, and that it could be sold for more than it was purchased for; or vice-versa; or that the value could change from day to day.

"It's not fair!" she cried.

"Maybe not, but that is how the real world works," Uncle Bill said.

Kylie found the section in the newspaper and did the calculation. "Australian Dollars are worth eighty-three cents US today," she said. Her calculator came into use. "That is fifteen thousand divide eighty three. Is that right?"

Uncle Bill nodded. Kylie pushed the buttons and gasped. "That would be... Oh no. They are cents. Hang on. That would be eighteen thousand and seventy-two dollars. Would that be any help, Uncle Bill?"

"It certainly would," Uncle Bill replied.

"That is only one jar," Margaret reminded Kylie. "The diary mentions a dozen."

Kylie multiplied the sum by 12 and gasped. "Two hundred and sixteen thousand, eight hundred and sixty-four dollars! That couldn't be right!"

"Yes, it could," Uncle Bill agreed. "That is why people go looking for gold."

"Would that save the farm?" Kylie asked.

"Yes, easily," Uncle Bill replied.

"After we have given half to the Reids," Kylie added.

"Still be enough," Uncle Bill replied. "But I don't like your chances. Others have looked before, you know, and they were experienced jungle prospectors."

"We will find it," Kylie insisted stubbornly.

She wasn't sure how, but she was determined. She took herself off to the back veranda to re-read the diary and to plan the search.

Chapter 9

ON THE FARM

Kylie and her mother were carefully pruning the rose bush in the garden at the side of the house when Margaret's scream sounded. The scream was one of pure terror, followed by shrieks and sobs. It came from inside the house.

Kylie sprang to her feet, heart pounding. *The men!* she thought. *And Uncle Bill and the dogs are off down the creek somewhere!*

Before she had thought what she was doing she had picked up the pinking shears and started running. Mrs Kirk scrambled to her feet and followed.

"Kylie, be careful!" Mrs Kirk cried.

By the time Kylie had reached the side door the screams had stopped and been replaced by cries and then even by laughter. Kylie raced in through the door confused but ready to fight. She skidded to a halt in the hallway when she saw Margaret lying on the floor of the passageway, struggling to pull up her shorts and knickers, which were around her knees. Allison and Gran were standing in the passageway and were both convulsed with laughter.

"What? What happened?" Kylie cried, still holding the shears in front of her as a weapon.

Margaret was red in the face with a mixture of embarrassment and anger. She had obviously received a bad fright, but her face now registered both annoyance and the beginnings of a grin.

"Frog," Allison explained. "A big green frog in the dunny. It jumped on Marg's bum and gave her a fright."

Margaret hauled her pants up and rolled over to stand up. "It was awful!" she said. "I got such a fright. I had just sat down and relaxed and this huge, cold, slimy thing sprang out and clamped onto my bottom. I..." She suddenly burst into tears.

Allison continued to laugh but both Gran and Kylie moved to comfort Margaret. "There, there dearie," Gran said. "You'll get worse frights than that in life."

Margaret sobbed uncontrollably for a minute, then said between sniffles, "I hope not. I nearly had a heart attack!"

Kylie hugged her and patted her back. She was sorry for Margaret but also inclined to laugh with relief as her own fright subsided. They all moved to peer into the toilet. The frog was now crouched in the corner and he was huge.

Allison looked down and chuckled. "Looks like the frog got a fright too," she said. Then she laughed again.

Kylie shook her head while suppressing a grin. "Wouldn't you if you saw an enormous bum suddenly point at you?" she said.

Margaret wailed and said, "I haven't got an enormous bum!" She began to cry again.

Kylie felt awful. "I didn't mean that Marg. I meant it would look big to a small thing like a frog."

"It's not a small thing! Look at the size of it!" Margaret wailed.

"He is big," Mrs Kirk said. "Now, who's going to pick him up and put him outside?"

There were no volunteers for that. Luckily the barking of dogs and the pounding of running boots announced the arrival of a very worried Uncle Bill. "What's happened? I heard one of the girls scream from right down at the bottom paddock."

When Mrs Kirk explained and indicated the frog Uncle Bill put his head back and bellowed with laughter, which put Margaret into tears again. Uncle Bill then shooed the dogs back out and went into the toilet. After several attempts he at last grabbed the frog. The girls all backed out into the lounge room. Uncle Bill walked out, holding the frog. As he passed Kylie he suddenly thrust it at her.

Kylie sprang back and shrieked. Uncle Bill laughed and Gran snorted, "Silly boy! Take it outside!"

Uncle Bill chuckled. "Yes, Mum. Could have been worse, it might have been a red back spider."

As Uncle Bill went out the door, Mrs Kirk said, "And you girls take note; a girl has to kiss a lot of toads before she finds a prince!"

Gran laughed, "I told you that!"

"And you were right, Mum," Mrs Kirk replied.

"What do you mean Mrs Kirk?" Margaret asked. She was now only heaving an occasional sob and her eyes were dry.

"That there are lots of men in the world but most of them are no good and only want one thing from a girl. You have to be very careful and have to search hard to find a good one."

Kylie giggled. "You hear that, Margaret? They only want one thing, so you stop kissing Graham in dark corners."

Margaret flamed bright red. "I don't!"

Mrs Kirk stepped forward. "That will do girls. Now, I think a cup of tea is called for after that," she said with a smile.

Kylie knew that her mother had caught Graham in the bath with Margaret the previous year, but she also knew that her mother approved of Margaret as the right sort of girl for Graham.

If only the oaf would realise it!

But it wasn't Kylie she caught kissing a boy in a dark corner later that morning. It was Allison. When the garden had been weeded and pruned Mrs Kirk went in to prepare lunch. Kylie sat reading while Margaret sat beside Gran who was teaching her to crochet.

Mrs Kirk came to the doorway. "Kylie, go and find Allison and tell her lunch is ready," she said. "I saw her go down towards the milking shed a while ago."

Kylie went to the milking shed with Scottie trotting alongside her. She was feeling very relaxed and happy. The holiday was working out and she was excited at the prospect of finding the gold mine. She hummed as she walked down the road. Outside the milking shed was a white utility but she took no notice of that. Uncle Bill drove a white utility.

Still humming happily, she walked into the storage room at the far side of the milking shed and came to a shocked standstill. In the corner, in a passionate embrace, were Allison and Bert. They were kissing and Bert was holding her very close. As soon as they saw her, they stopped and let each other go. Bert snatched his hands away and went brick red with embarrassment.

So did Kylie. For a moment she could only stand and gape in shocked surprise, before the hurt of jealousy flooded in. "Sorry!" she blurted out. "Lunch is ready."

With that she turned and fled. Within ten paces tears had sprung to her eyes and she found she was breathing hard, and her hands had bunched into tight little balls. As she walked rapidly back up the road, she told herself not to be silly; that it was none of her business.

It's not as though Bert has ever indicated that he likes me. So he's not cheating or anything.

But it was small consolation to hurt vanity and pride. Kylie knew she was jealous and that she wanted Bert to do things like that to her. "He is so good looking!" she told herself. Then she sobbed and more tears came. Knowing that her tears would be noticed, she stopped in the machinery shed to dry them and to calm down.

A new problem then arose: how to react to Allison? *I don't want to spoil the holiday by being bitchy; and besides, she hasn't done anything deliberately to hurt me. I haven't told her I like Bert. Be sensible.*

A few minutes later, she heard Bert's utility start up. He drove off back towards town and Allison came walking up the road looking worried and a bit agitated. Kylie stepped out onto the road and waited for her.

"Sorry, I didn't mean to spring you like that."

Allison shrugged, then giggled. "That's alright."

Another worrying thought crossed Kylie's mind, "Did you know he was coming over?"

"I spoke to him on the phone," Allison replied.

He must really like her to drive all that way, Kylie mused. She replied seriously, "Please be careful Allison. Don't do anything silly. You are too young. And please let my mum know. She is responsible for you."

Allison had the good grace to blush and bite her lip. "Sorry. I never thought of that. Oh he's wonderful! I'm in love!"

That made Kylie jealous again, but, perversely she was also glad. It was wonderful to see Allison's happiness. Taking control of her own emotions with an effort Kylie managed a smile and walked on towards the house.

That afternoon they went to Atherton on the shopping expedition. Kylie took the time to go to the Land Resources office to buy a map. She found they were more expensive than she had expected, and also that there were several to choose from. She finally bought two, a Parish Land Survey map, and an Army Topographic Map of the sort her brother Graham used for bushwalking.

He can use it if it is no good, she decided.

After that she went to the Post Office to post a letter to the Mines Department, asking for information about any leases or claims registered by Grandad Hector. She was now losing heart about ever finding the old gold mine, but a stubborn streak in her character kept her working at it.

Then it was Christmas shopping. Kylie loved that. She helped Margaret choose more Christmas decorations, then bought more presents for family and friends.

While she was browsing in a bookshop Kylie received a pleasant surprise. Into the shop walked Roger Dunning. Roger was a cheerful, tubby boy who was one of Graham's best friends and a member of his 'Hiking Team'.

"Hi Roger! What are you doing in Atherton?" she asked.

"Spending part of the holidays with my Aunty," Roger replied. "She lives here. What are you doing?"

"Same. Staying at my Gran's farm over near Bartle Frere," Kylie replied.

"Have you climbed it yet?" Roger asked with a grin.

"No, and I'm not going to, at least not in the wet season," Kylie said. She had been told that winter was the best time to climb the mountain, otherwise the chances were that clouds would obscure the view.

Roger laughed. "Graham will drag you up it when he gets back!"

"Fat chance!" Kylie replied, then realised that wasn't the best comment to make to Roger, who was chubby and quite sensitive to comments about his weight.

"When does he get back from his cadet camp?" Roger asked.

"Three days' time, on Monday," Kylie replied.

"What are you doing then? Are you going back to Cairns for Christmas?" Roger asked.

Kylie shook her head. "No, we are spending Christmas at Gran's," she replied. Then, knowing Graham would tell his friend anyway, she said, "We are going to find a gold mine."

Roger snorted, "Goldmine! Get real. There hasn't been any gold found around here for a hundred years."

"There has so!" Kylie replied indignantly. She proceeded to describe the story of the 'Jeweller's Shop' to Roger. While she was doing this Margaret joined them. She knew Roger well and exchanged greetings.

When Kylie had finished Roger said, "In the jungle?" He made a face when Kylie nodded. "I suppose Graham will rope us all in to help find this bloody thing."

Both Kylie and Margaret laughed, and Kylie nodded. They gossiped for a while longer, then went their separate ways. The girls returned to the car laden with parcels and bundles. As they loaded them in Margaret nudged Kylie.

"Look!"

It was Allison. She was walking slowly along the footpath, hand in hand with Bert. She looked blissfully happy and was smiling up at him. He was talking animatedly to her and was loaded with shopping. Once again, Kylie felt the sharp claws of jealousy but also knew she was glad that Allison was enjoying her holiday.

I wish I was in love! she thought wistfully.

Margaret was obviously thinking the same thing as she said, "Only three more days before Graham gets home."

And I hope the stupid lout doesn't break your heart! Kylie thought. She was very fond of her brother but knew from experience that he was an absolute fool for a pretty face.

Bert gave them all a cheerful greeting. Mrs Kirk frowned but said nothing. When it was time to go Bert and Allison stood holding hands till the last possible minute, staring deep into each other's eyes.

"Isn't it sweet!" Margaret whispered.

"Humm," Mrs Kirk murmured. "As long they are only holding hands."

"Oh Mum!" Kylie said, but she coloured with knowledge of what the pair had been doing in the milking shed.

"Come on Allison," Mrs Kirk called. "Goodbye Bert."

Allison climbed in, blew Bert a kiss, then sat back with a sigh as the car moved off. "Oh he's wonderful. I'm in love."

"And you are too young," Mrs Kirk said. "You remember that Bert is a lot older than you."

"Only four years older Mrs Kirk," Allison replied.

"He's still a male, so don't do anything silly," Mrs Kirk said. "And please ask before you arrange to meet him."

"Yes Mrs Kirk, sorry," Allison said. But she didn't sound sorry and she smiled all the way back to the farm.

The shopping expedition returned home and unloaded. Mysterious parcels were swiftly spirited inside and hidden in cupboards. Then the girls set to work to put up the new decorations. Kylie was feeling very happy by the time they had completed the task but her spirits were dampened somewhat when she showed Uncle Bill the maps she had bought.

The Parish Survey Map was just black and white and showed only the creeks, the surveyed boundaries of all the land allotments and the vague outline of the mountains. The farm was easy to find but no mines were marked, only the words STATE FOREST. This was confirmed when they compared it with the Army Map. This showed that almost the entire area they were interested in around Swipers Flat and along the western edge of the escarpment above the Mulgrave valley was State Forest.

"That means it will all now be part of the Wet Tropics World Heritage Area," Uncle Bill said. "No-one will be allowed to do any mining in there."

That was a blow, but Kylie wasn't ready to give up yet. "Maybe we could just find those samples in the glass jars. That wouldn't be mining," she said.

"You are clutching at straws now girl," Uncle Bill said. "Forget about the mine. I will find a way to pay the bills."

But in her heart Kylie did not want to give up. "I will find it anyway, just out of curiosity," she said.

Uncle Bert eyed her with admiration. "You don't give up easily, do you?"

"No, not if I think it is important," Kylie replied.

"Good for you. Then I will help if I can. Now, are you girls too worn out from shopping or can you still help with the milking?"

Milking followed, after which the girls went back to the house for a bath. Allison was first in the bath. Margaret went in as soon as she had finished. Almost immediately there was a shriek and Margaret cried out, "Oh! Oh! Another frog!"

She came backing out of the bathroom with only a towel held over her front. Kylie ran to help her, then called out, "No Uncle Bill! Margaret isn't dressed."

Margaret realised her back was exposed and struggled to wrap the towel around her. Allison and Mrs Kirk arrived as she at last managed this. Margaret pointed into the bathroom. Kylie put her head around the door and saw a large green frog sitting on the end of the bathtub near the taps. She turned to Allison and said, "Heavens Allie, he must have been there when you were having your bath."

But Allison was convulsed with laughter and could not answer. That made Kylie suspicious, and she went into the bathroom and had a closer look at the frog, then reached forward and picked it up.

"Oh Allie, you rotter! That was a cruel trick to play on Margaret! Where did you get it?" She held the rubber frog up for all to see.

"In town. I didn't buy it. I told Bert about this morning, and he saw it in Toyworld and bought it for me," Allison replied. "Sorry Marg."

Margaret had been on the edge of tears but her mood changed to anger, then to a grin as Kylie was unable to keep a straight face. Even Mrs Kirk and Gran joined in. "It looked so real! I got a real shock," Margaret said.

A mischievous idea crossed Kylie's mind. "I will give it to Graham, and he will get to see you rushing out of the bath in the nuddy then," she said.

Allison laughed and added, "I didn't think he needed any frogs to help him in that from what I'd heard."

Margaret looked embarrassed and hurt. Mrs Kirk reached over and took the toy frog from Kylie. "That is enough of that talk. And I will take that, thanks. No more of this nonsense please."

Margaret went back into the bathroom and the others returned to what they were doing. In Kylie's case this was matching the three maps together and trying to puzzle out where the mine might be.

Later the three girls lay side by side in bed and talked quietly about boys, and about what they were going to do for the rest of the holidays. They were all aware that the holiday was nearly over.

"Home for Christmas in two days," Margaret said sadly.

"Don't you want to go?" Kylie asked.

"Yes, but I want to stay up here too," Margaret replied.

"What if Graham was in Cairns and not here," Kylie teased.

"Oh poo to you!" Margaret replied.

All three girls laughed and snuggled down into their bedclothes. Allison then said, "I want to stay up here too. Do think your parents might let me come back after Christmas?"

Kylie propped herself up on one elbow to look at her. "Are you really that keen on Bert?"

82

Allison nodded and hugged her pillow. "I think he is the most wonderful man I've ever met."

For a few minutes they discussed Bert's good points, then Allison repeated her request. "So, do you think I could come and stay for a bit longer after Christmas?"

"I suppose so. What will your parents say?" Kylie asked.

"They will let me. They were happy enough to get rid of me this time," Allison replied. There was just a touch of bitterness in her voice. This made Kylie suspect that all was not well in the Nichols' household, which made her sad.

Margaret now made the same request. "I'd like to come back for a few days too. I'm sure mum and dad won't mind."

"You just want to be with Graham," Kylie replied.

"Yes, I do," Margaret replied. "I think he is the most wonderful man in the world."

Seeing the sparkle in Margaret's eyes made Kylie very sad because Graham hardly noticed her and spent most of his time chasing pretty girls his own age. *It is so unfair!* she thought. *Margaret is only two years younger than him, yet he thinks she is just a baby because she is only in Year 7; yet Bert is happy to chase Allie who is four years younger.* Then another thought came to her which cheered her up a lot. *Margaret and I will both be at High School this year. So maybe he will treat her better.*

Graham had just finished Year 9 and was going into 10 while Kylie and Margaret were to start Year 8 in a few weeks. The girls discussed this for a while before drifting off to sleep.

Chapter 10

GRAHAM

Saturday passed without incident. Kylie spent a lot of time minding the young calves and reading. All the girls helped with the chores and the milking. That evening the subject of the girls returning for a few days after Christmas was broached over dinner.

Mrs Kirk eyed them for a minute then said, "Well I know why Margaret wants to come back, but what is your reason, Allison?"

Allison hesitated for a second, then said, "I want to see more of Bert."

"Not too much more I hope!" Kylie quipped.

"That will do, Kylie," Mrs Kirk replied, but she smiled. "Well, at least you are honest Allison. I have to say I think you are far too young to be interested in boys and I think your parents had better be appraised of the true reason for this. Don't go giving them a lot of eyewash about the lovely scenery and the brisk country air."

"Oh Mrs Kirk, that is all true as well. We have had a wonderful time here," Allison replied.

Mrs Kirk looked at Gran who shrugged and smiled. "You are only young once. Make hay while the sun shines children. Of course you are welcome to stay. All we ask is that you help with the work."

"Oh yes, Mrs Feltham!" Margaret cried happily.

"Hold on young miss," Mrs Kirk said. "You have to ask your own parents yet." Then she looked thoughtful. "I don't know where you will all sleep though."

"Put the boys out in the barn," Allison suggested.

Uncle Bill chortled. "We haven't got a barn," he commented.

"They can camp out in the yard in tents," Kylie said. "They are cadets and should be used to that sort of thing."

"Boys? I thought only Graham was coming," Gran said. "Isn't Alex at sea with his dad?"

"Yes, Mum," Mrs Kirk said. She looked quizzically at Kylie.

Kylie shrugged and said, "As soon as Graham hears about this gold mine, we are going to find he will rope in all his mates to help."

Mrs Kirk looked thoughtful. What Kylie had said was so obviously true she wondered why she hadn't considered it. "That could be four of them. Now where will we fit them in?"

Later Mrs Kirk spoke on the telephone to Margaret's parents and then to Allison's. After hearing both girls explain the true reasons for wanting to stay she again spoke to the parents again. When the girls heard her giving assurances to look after them, they grinned at each other, knowing they had won.

Mrs Kirk put the phone down and turned to them. "That is alright then. Now, let's organize the details of when and where."

Thus it was three very happy girls who went to sleep that night.

The following morning they all helped with the milking, then washed and changed and went with Uncle Bill and Gran to church in Malanda. After church they dropped in on the Reid's on the way home.

Allison could hardly wait to run over to Bert to tell him she was allowed to come back after Christmas. Watching her radiantly happy face from a distance Kylie was struck by a pang of concern.

Oh I hope she doesn't get her heart broken!

That Bert was pleased was obvious. Without thinking about it he took both of Allison's hands and grinned at her. Only the presence of the adults stopped the pair from embracing. Victor gave a sneer and a shrug and walked off to work on his pickup truck.

And poo to you too! Kylie thought. *Sour puss!*

By arrangement they all stayed at the Reid's for lunch. Allison sat next to Bert and everyone seemed to accept this as normal. *They are now an item,* Kylie concluded. With a wistful sigh she wished she could meet 'Mr Right'. *Then I will have that satisfying status with my peers!* she fantasized, imagining their faces with jealous looks all over them.

While they ate, Mr Reid asked, "Have you found that gold mine yet you kids?"

"Not yet, Mr Reid," Kylie replied.

Mr Reid laughed and pointed his fork at Victor and Bert. "Then you'd better hurry up. This pair have started talking about finding it. And bloody good luck to you! Me and me brothers went out seven times, for weeks at a time, looking for the bloody thing. And all we found was bloody jungle; and lots of leeches and ticks."

They all laughed and then listened to Mr Reid's accounts of searching for the missing gold mine. "Lot of baloney I reckon. You won't find any bloody thing; and like as not you'll get scrub typhus and die like old Uncle Hector."

That thought sent a shiver through Kylie. "What is scrub typhus?" she asked.

"A fever. You get it from the bite of a tiny mite," Mr Reid explained.

"A mite! What is that?" Kylie asked.

Mr Reid looked at her to see if she was pulling his leg, then shook his head and explained. "A tiny insect, about the size of a pin head. They look like tiny ticks, reddish in colour. They live in the fur of the warm-blooded animals in the jungle, and in the leaf mould. You need to take care you don't get them on you."

The thought of dying from the bite of an insect so small you could hardly see it made Kylie feel sick. Suddenly she wasn't so keen to go searching the jungle. Nor, obviously, at least judging by her face, was Allison.

After lunch they sat and talked for a while. Bert and Allison went off 'to see the pigs', or so they said. Margaret stifled a giggle at this excuse and the adults seemed not to even notice. Kylie still felt jealous, but more because she didn't have a boyfriend, than for Bert in particular. That set her thinking about Peter. Would he come to help Graham?

Do I like him like that anyway? she wondered.

That evening in bed the three girls exchanged confidences and discussed their plans for after Christmas.

"It's been a beaut holiday," Allison said.

"Only because of Bert," Kylie suggested.

"Yes," Allison replied dreamily.

"So, did you really go and see the pigs?" Kylie asked.

"Piglets. Yes, we did," Allison answered.

Margaret sat up. "Did he kiss you?" she asked, her eyes alive with interest.

Allison nodded and hugged her pillow dreamily. "Yes, he did. And he told me he loved me. He is very happy we are coming back up after Christmas."

Margaret sighed. "Graham comes home tomorrow. Oh I wish I was staying to see him," she said.

"You'll see plenty of him," Kylie replied, trying to console her.

"It sounds like she has already seen all of him," Allison added, her face dimpling into a mischievous grin.

Margaret poked her tongue at her but wasn't upset. She grinned and nodded. "He looks real good with nothing on."

"Margaret!" Kylie said.

Allison's eyes lit up with interest. "Did you two really have a bath together?"

Margaret went very red. "Oh that was years ago! We were only little then," she cried. She then giggled and blushed with embarrassment. "Anyway, we were talking about you and Bert. What's he like?"

"He gets very passionate," Allison replied. "And he certainly gets horny when we kiss. I can feel it."

"Allison!" Kylie cried, both interested and shocked.

Allison went red but just made a face. "Well, he is a male after all. You should know what they are like Kylie. You've got two brothers."

Kylie nodded. She did know, having accidentally seen her brothers at different times. Now she wondered whether she liked males at all. The idea of males doing things to her made her feel quite anxious and disgusted but she also sensed that if she was in love it would all just happen naturally.

For a while the girls discussed males and what they liked- or didn't like. Kylie found it fascinating but embarrassing and she was glad when the subject was dropped. They settled down to sleep.

Monday morning dawned with the girls tense with emotion. For Margaret there was the excited anticipation of seeing Graham; for Allison the unhappiness of being separated from Bert for a week; and for Kylie a mixture of emotions. She was sorry her friends were going, yet glad Graham was arriving.

Things will be different now, she thought. *Graham will want to get straight out into the jungle to find the gold mine. I wonder if Mum will allow it?*

After milking and breakfast the girls tidied up and then packed. Margaret was almost hopping with excitement while Allison walked around with a long face. Then it was time for farewells. Bert drove over to say goodbye and Allison and they had a passionate twenty minutes at the side of the machinery shed. When they emerged at Kylie's call Allison was weeping and Bert was trying to console her.

Gran snorted. "Stop your tears up, missie! Heavens above! Anyone would think it was he going off to the wars, not you going home for Christmas!"

"But I love him!" Allison sobbed.

"Fine, and if he loves you then a week apart will be a good thing. It will allow you both a bit of breathing space to cool down and to think things out. Now don't be silly. You are far too young for any of that nonsense," Gran said.

Allison dried her tears but obviously wasn't convinced. Margaret gave Gran a hug and thanked her. "See you in the New Year, Mrs Feltham."

"I look forward to it dearie," Gran replied.

At last the girls and their luggage were loaded. Mrs Kirk kissed Gran. "See you tomorrow, Mum."

"Drive carefully. Goodbye girls!"

The car was reversed and turned around, then they set off for Cairns. It was ten o'clock by then and Mrs Kirk was worried that the cadets might arrive before they did.

"They left camp at seven this morning," she reminded.

This time they drove down the Gillies Highway into the Mulgrave Valley and via Gordonvale. Kylie did not enjoy that. She disliked the winding road with its hundreds of sharp curves and the steep drop over the edge. By the time they reached the bottom, after 16 kilometres of almost continual curves, she felt quite car sick.

From Little Mulgrave, at the bottom of the range, they drove east along the Mulgrave Valley through country Kylie thought was the prettiest in the whole of Australia. She commented on this and Allison agreed. At Gordonvale they turned left onto the Bruce Highway and sped into Cairns in a mad rush of traffic which was in stark contrast to the quiet country roads they had just left.

It was nearly midday by the time they reached Cairns. First they dropped Allison at her home. Margaret had pleaded to be allowed to stay to meet Graham and this was agreed to. That made the next port of call the army depot.

They had timed it well as the army coach had just arrived a few minutes earlier and the cadets were busy unloading their gear. Kylie stood watching from the fence, with Margaret beside her, hopping from one foot to the other in her eagerness.

"There he is!" Margaret cried, pointing to the uniformed throng busy unloading kitbags and ports.

Kylie glimpsed Peter first, then his friend Stephen, and finally Graham. Peter's mother was there as well, and Mrs Kirk went to talk to her while they waited. Once all the gear was unloaded the cadets were lined up on parade and their OC, Captain Conkey, spoke briefly to them. They were then dismissed.

A happy group of boys and girls streamed towards the gate with their gear. Peter arrived first. That set Kylie's heart going as he smiled at her and said hello. Peter had bright brown eyes and dark hair and was slightly taller than Graham. He was also quieter and more thoughtful.

Peter's mother gave him a hug and a kiss. "How did it go?" she asked as he nodded to his little brother Paul.

"Okay. Graham did well. He came fourth out of one hundred and twenty on the Corporals Course," he explained.

Kylie's mother had been listening and she now smiled. "Oh good," she said.

Kylie knew her mother wasn't keen on the idea of Graham becoming a soldier, not that being a volunteer cadet gave him any obligation to do so, but she was also aware that the Army Cadets had been a major factor in stabilizing Graham's delinquent behaviour. Earlier in the year Graham had always been in trouble at school; and there had been stories about him and girls doing things they should not have been doing at their age. Becoming a cadet seemed to have given him some focus in life and he had steadied down a lot.

Graham struggled through the throng to join them. He dumped his kitbag and hugged his mother, then Kylie. Last of all he leaned forward and gave Margaret a peck on the cheek. Kylie knew that Margaret was just dying to be given a hug but she could not hint at this without annoying Graham. She stood back and admired her brother.

I can see why girls like him, she decided. *He's a good looking boy.*

Graham was well built, with broad shoulders and well muscled arms. He had fair hair and brilliant blue eyes set in a cheerful, freckled face.

Mrs Bronsky said to him, "Peter tells us you came fourth out of one hundred and twenty. Well done."

"Thanks Mrs Bronsky; but Pete is too modest. He came first."

Kylie cried out in delight. "Oh Peter! You didn't!"

Peter nodded. On an impulse Kylie rushed over and hugged him. "Oh well done!"

Peter was plainly pleased, but also embarrassed. Graham said, "Fair go sis!" Kylie stepped back and met Margaret's eye. Margaret was obviously itching to give Graham a hug but was too shy.

Their other friend, Stephen Bell, a pale skinned, black haired boy with glasses, came over to say hello.

"Where did you come Stephen?" Mrs Kirk asked.

"Only seventh Mrs Kirk," Stephen replied.

"Only seventh. I like your modesty. You boys have obviously done very well," Mrs Kirk replied, beaming at them. The boys were so often at each other's houses they were almost treated as part of the family.

"Not only the boys. Gwen Copeland came fifth," Graham added. That started Kylie worrying. Gwen Copeland was a very attractive blonde in Peter's class.

"Well, we'd better be going," Peter said, bending to pick up his gear.

"Yeah, see you after I come back from the farm," Graham replied.

Kylie interrupted. "What are you doing for the rest of the holidays Peter?"

Peter shrugged. "Nothing much. Christmas, I suppose. And if Graham comes down from the Tablelands we might go sailing, or maybe on a hike."

"How would you like to help us find a gold mine?" Kylie asked.

"Gold mine?" the three boys chorused.

"Yes, a gold mine," Kylie replied.

Graham snorted, "This isn't that old family legend about the famous 'Jeweller's Shop' is it?"

"Yes, it is. And we've found Grandad Hector's diary and an old letter which tells us where it is," Kylie replied.

That got their interest. "Tell us more," Peter asked.

Kylie shook her head. "No. You have to go home. Your mother is waiting," she teased.

"Kylie!"

"I will if you promise to come up to the farm for a week to help us find it," Kylie replied.

Peter looked at his mother and raised an eyebrow. "When?"

"After Christmas," Kylie replied.

Mrs Bronsky sighed and nodded. She knew her son and his friends. Peter smiled. "I'd love to. We will be in touch. I take it the wonder instrument invented by Mr Alexander Graham Bell in the late nineteenth century, I refer to the telephone, has been connected to that part of the world?"

Kylie's face dimpled into a grin. "You know it has. So ring us up."

"I will," Peter promised.

"Then let's get going," Graham said. "I'm starving, and I will need a good feed before I head off into the trackless jungle to find the gold."

He gave Margaret a smile as he said this which Kylie knew would send her hopes soaring. *Oh I hope he falls in love with Margaret!* she thought.

They loaded the car and climbed in. Kylie made sure that Graham ended up in the back beside Margaret. Graham spoiled this by absent-mindedly dumping his kitbag on the seat between them, but Margaret still looked happy- in an anxious sort of way.

Margaret was dropped off at her home next. She was on the edge of tears by then and was trembling slightly. It was obvious to Kylie that she did not want to leave them.

"See you next week," Kylie said.

Margaret nodded and bit her lip. "Yes," she croaked. Then a tear did trickle out. To save the situation Mrs Kirk let in the clutch and drove off, calling a cheery goodbye as she did.

"What's wrong with Margaret?" Graham asked.

Oh you stupid boy! Kylie thought. "She's had a really good time and is sad it is over," she said. "And she likes you and was glad to see you."

"Oh. I see," Graham replied, but he sounded slightly mystified.

They drove to their own home, which was closed up for the holidays. The car was unloaded and the house opened up. Kylie was sent to the shop to buy milk and bread while Mrs Kirk bundled washing into the washing machine. Graham changed out of his uniform and went to check on his model ships.

They ate a 'Take-away' meal for dinner as they were returning to the farm the next day and the fridge was almost empty. As they ate Graham happily chattered away about his promotion course. "It was great," he said. "Very hard; thirteen periods a day. We were on the go from dawn to dusk, but we learned a lot."

"What did you do?" Kylie asked.

"Learnt how to teach lessons; and we did lots of practice at that: teaching each other," Graham explained.

"What did you teach?"

"Lots of drill and weapon training, and some fieldcraft," Graham explained.

"That sounds a bit boring," Kylie replied.

"Oh we did other things as well. We learned First Aid and how to use radios and lots of navigation. I found that a bit boring though. And we learned how to plan patrols and to give Verbal Orders."

"I thought all orders were verbal," Kylie commented.

"No. This is a specific process to pass on orders and information so that nothing is forgotten or missed out. There are written orders as well," Graham explained.

"When do you get promoted?" Mrs Kirk asked.

"At the start of cadets next year," Graham answered. "Cadet Under-Officer Grenfell wants me as a section commander in Two Platoon."

"Is that what you want?" Mrs Kirk asked.

"Yes Mum."

"Good. Now eat up and get packed."

Graham turned to Kylie. "Tell me about the gold mine. If we are going to look for it I will need to take my hiking gear."

Kylie recounted the story. When she mentioned the thugs and their bashing and bullying of Gran Graham's face darkened with anger. "Bastards! They will regret it if I catch them!"

"Graham! Don't use language like that at home please," Mrs Kirk reproved. "And don't you dare go looking for trouble. They are much bigger and older than you. The police have dealt with it."

"Yes Mum. Go on Kylie."

Kylie completed her account, and it was obvious that Graham's imagination had been gripped by the idea of finding the gold. "Can we go and look, Mum?"

Mrs Kirk made a face. "It's dangerous in the jungle. You could get lost."

"Oh Mum! Fair go. Pete and I have been in the jungle lots of times. We won't get lost. And even if we do we will just walk back out of it."

"How? How will you know which way to go?" Mrs Kirk asked.

"With a compass. Pete's got a good one," Graham replied.

"What if you get separated?" Mrs Kirk persisted.

"Then I just walk downhill and follow the creeks out of the jungle," Graham replied. "The North Queensland jungle isn't that big. If you walk down a creek you will come to some joker's farm after a while."

Mrs Kirk knew this was true but she did not give up. "What about snakes, and wild pigs, and ticks?"

"I've been bitten by a snake Mum. That doesn't worry me. And the pigs aren't that bad. When did you ever hear of anyone actually being killed by wild pigs?"

Mrs Kirk had to admit she could not remember a single incident in twenty or thirty years, so she said, "Don't forget the diseases and poisonous plants. And you could get bitten by those mites and die of scrub typhus like Grandad Hector."

Graham nodded gravely at that. "Yes. We would need to be properly dressed and use plenty of 'Anti Mite'. I will take all my hiking gear."

Mrs Kirk sighed and knew it was no use trying to stop the search going ahead. Graham reinforced this by saying, "Anyway Mum, you always reckon we are safer out in the bush than wandering around in town."

"I don't know. There are a lot of creepy types lurking in the bush now: drug growers and bird smugglers and so on."

"We will be alright Mum. Can Pete and Steve come to stay on the farm for a while to help us?"

Mrs Kirk nodded. "If they like," she replied.

"Oh good. I'll give them a call to ask if they are allowed. And Roger."

"Roger is in Atherton at his Aunty's," Kylie put in. "I saw him there the other day."

"Thanks. I will ask them," Graham said.

He left the table and went to the phone to call his friends. Kylie helped her mother clean up, humming with happiness while she did. *Now we will find the gold mine,* she told herself.

She felt very confident. She also smiled about her Christmas present to Graham.

Chapter 11

CHRISTMAS

The following morning the family went shopping for Christmas presents. Kylie had purchased all hers but Graham had not. She insisted that Margaret come along as well. Mrs Kirk happily colluded in this plan, and they picked Margaret up on the way. Kylie knew that Margaret had bought Graham a present but wasn't sure if he was going to buy her one. Just to be sure, knowing how disappointed she would be if he did not, she got him aside and asked him.

Graham shrugged and said, "I've thought about it."

"She will be very hurt if you don't," Kylie replied.

"Maybe, but if I am too nice to her she will never give up. She thinks she owns me now," Graham replied.

"Oh Graham she does not!" Kylie said. "She just likes you a lot; but I can't imagine why. You can be really dumb and horrible at times."

Graham was obviously stung but equally he obviously felt he should do something. After a moment he replied, "I wouldn't know what to buy her. It's hard to buy presents for girls."

"Oh it is not!" Kylie cried. "Listen, we will walk along and talk about things we would like and you can take note, then later on double back and buy something she says she likes."

Graham sniffed and shrugged and made no reply, but that was the strategy they followed. In that way Graham bought Margaret a crochet set with needles and coloured threads, and a bright yellow cotton top that she had admired. He drew the line at buying her a necklace she liked. It wasn't the cost.

"If I start buying her jewellery, she will think we are engaged or something!" he commented.

After lunch they returned Margaret to her home, happily clutching her new presents but sad that she wasn't going to be with them for Christmas.

As she stood on the footpath outside her home Margaret looked at Graham and gave a wistful smile. Then she met Kylie's eyes. "See you next week. Merry Christmas!" she said.

Mrs Kirk then drove Kylie and Graham back up to the farm. Once again, she went via the Gillies Highway, although Kylie didn't want her to go that way. Graham didn't mind. As they wound up the mountainside he kept exclaiming about the view. A third of the way up the highway went past a clearing on the right. A sign informed them that it was the start of: ROBSONS TRACK

"It's an old pioneer track," Graham said. "Silver Wolf told us about it. I must walk it one day."

The track obviously went from the bottom of the valley right to the top of the range. Kylie knew that Graham often climbed such mountains on his hikes with Peter so wasn't surprised.

Graham pointed to the left along the valley. "That is Mt Bartle Frere at the end of the valley; the big one on the right of that saddle," he explained. He did so much bushwalking and travelling that he knew the names of all the mountains. There were times Kylie found him a bit boastful.

"I know," she replied. "The farm is just up on top of the Tablelands to the right of that."

The place she was talking about was still twenty kilometres away and invisible because of intervening mountains but Graham nodded.

By road it was more like forty kilometres as they had to go up onto the Atherton Tablelands, then west to Lake Eacham, then south past North Johnston. After that it was a fairly straight run south through beautiful rolling country. Mostly this was dairy farms but there were still patches of the original rainforest and various clumps of pines and other trees which had been planted.

Arrival at the farm included the usual happy greetings. Graham loved his Gran and she always treated him as her little favourite. Uncle Bill shook his hand and said, "How was your army camp?"

"Good Uncle Bill. I'm going to be promoted to corporal."

Uncle Bill grinned. "That's good. You won't have to scrub the dunnies anymore then. You can tell some other bugger to do it," he replied.

"Were you ever in the army Uncle Bill?" Graham asked.

Uncle Bill nodded. "Oh, only part-time in the CMF; the Citizens Military Forces. What they call the Army Reserve now. I spent six years in the good old 51st Battalion. Got to be a sergeant. That was a good twenty years ago though."

Graham was impressed and showed it. Over afternoon tea he plied Uncle Bill with questions. Uncle Bill happily talked about his army experiences. Mrs Kirk encouraged this and later Kylie overheard her say to Gran, "I'm so glad Graham has joined the army cadets. He was turning into a real juvenile delinquent before. I was at my wits end. He was always in trouble at school and was even getting into trouble with the police. Since he has been in the Cadets, he has become a different person. He is still mischievous and pretty wild, but now he has a focus and he is trying very hard to get promoted. He is even doing some of his schoolwork."

Kylie knew all of that. She had watched Graham going off the rails with some concern. She had even caught him with a girl from his class under the house one afternoon. They hadn't actually been doing anything, but they had looked so guilty she just knew what they had been up to.

And poor Margaret was so hurt, she remembered. Then she smiled. *They were probably doing just what Margaret wants to do with Graham!*

Milking followed. Graham cheerfully joined in. It was a task they had always done when they visited the farm. Uncle Bill was always glad of the help and that made the children happier. By the time they finished it was dark. They made their way back up to the farmhouse to hot showers and a large tea.

After tea, over the washing up, which Graham always did, he said to Kylie, who had the tea towel, "So tell me about this gold mine."

While they worked Kylie went over the story again. Afterwards she took out the maps, diary and photocopy of the letter and sat with Graham while he carefully read it all. It was transparently obvious that he was seized by the idea of finding the gold.

Kylie said, "I want to find the gold so Uncle Bill can save the farm."

"Save the farm! Why? What is wrong?" Graham asked.

"Uncle Bill owes the bank a lot of money and he says that if he can't pay them then the bank will take the farm off him," Kylie explained.

"Lose the farm!" Graham was aghast. "Oh we can't let that happen. We must find the gold."

Fired now by a fierce resolve he bent back to studying the maps and documents. Kylie also re-read all of it. She took a few more notes and they studied the maps carefully. Mrs Kirk had to order them to bed.

"You will be too tired to enjoy tomorrow otherwise."

So off to bed they went, Kylie now in the spare bedroom upstairs and Graham on the mattress in the basement.

They were up at 4am next morning to round up the cows. Graham was slow to start as he was still tired from the exertions of his cadet camp but despite that he did his fair share. When told that Allison had even done the milking he was astounded.

"That's hard to imagine," he said. "I can only picture her complaining she would break a fingernail or mess her hair up."

"Oh Graham, she's not as bad as that," Kylie replied. "In fact, since she fell in love with Bert she has really changed."

Graham was sceptical about that but not really interested. He was more interested in finding the gold mine. After breakfast he re-read the old diary. Then he went off on his own to explore the farm. This was so typical of him that nobody even commented. Kylie worked in the kitchen with Gran, learning to make pumpkin scones. From time to time she would see Graham in the distance as he walked slowly along, his eyes noting everything.

At morning teatime Graham returned. "There's a sick calf down the far end of that paddock over there," he said, pointing out the window.

"Oh no!" Kylie cried. She knew it would be the one she had seen born a few days before.

It was. They walked down with Uncle Bill after morning tea and found the calf lying in the grass beside a patch of wild raspberries. The mother stood helplessly nearby. The calf had a large, weeping wound in its hind leg and could not stand.

"Cut himself on something," Uncle Bill said after examining the wound. "Barbed wire or an old bit of iron maybe."

"He looks very sick," Kylie said. "Can you fix him."

Uncle Bill stood up and sadly shook his head. "Her. She needs a vet and the right medicine. That might save her."

For a minute Kylie did not understand. Then she asked, "Are you going to call the vet Uncle Bill?"

Uncle Bill shook his head again and avoided meeting her eyes. "I'd like to lass, but I can't afford it."

"Uncle Bill! Do you mean you are just going to let her die?" Kylie asked. She was appalled, both at the thought of the calf dying and of the fact that Uncle Bill was too poor even to pay the vet.

"Sorry, yes. We will have to let nature take its course," Uncle Bill replied. His mouth set in a hard line and Kylie was even more shocked by the bitter tone in his voice.

"Oh Uncle Bill! We can't. I will pay for it," Kylie cried.

"You don't know how much it will cost lass. It is expensive. I'm sorry. I wish I could do it but I can't. Be kindest if I shot the poor little bugger and put her out of her misery."

Kylie was even more upset at that idea. She knelt and stroked the sick calf and began to cry. The calf looked up at her with big soft eyes and tried to lick her hand. The calf was shaking, and her tongue was dry and puffed up so that it looked unnaturally large.

Graham now said, "But Uncle Bill, surely it is good economics to spend money to keep the herd healthy."

Uncle Bill rounded on him and shouted, "Yes, it is! Don't tell me my job boy! I would save the calf if I had the money. And it's a her not a him, so worth saving!"

Graham bit his lip and went very silent. Kylie was even more upset. She had never seen Uncle Bill angry. Never in her whole life had he shouted at either of them. She looked away and burst into tears.

Uncle Bill was instantly contrite. "I'm sorry kids. I didn't mean to lose my temper. It's just that things have been getting on top of me lately."

Kylie looked up, full of pity for the big, bluff man. "It's alright Uncle Bill. We will find Grandad Hector's gold and then you will be Ok again."

Graham nodded. "Yes, we will. And please, can we help pay for the vet. I'd like to help. I've got some money saved up and it would make a nice Christmas present to you."

For a moment Kylie thought Uncle Bill would refuse, but then he met her eyes and nodded. His own eyes then watered and he bit his lip and walked quickly away. Kylie gently stroked the calf's head and then looked up at Graham.

"Thanks for that. You can be wonderful when you try."

It was Graham's turn to be embarrassed. "Let's make sure we find that gold. Come on, let's go and organize the vet."

Later, after the vet had been, the children had a word to their mother. She said she already knew of their offer and was delighted. "That was very good of you kids. I will help you pay, so cheer up. Now come and help me weed the vegetable garden."

"Aw Mum! It's Christmas," Graham replied.

"I know that, but the weeds don't. Come on. We can have it done before afternoon milking."

"We want to go and find the gold mine," Graham replied.

"Well you can't. There isn't time before Christmas; and you are not going on your own. It is with a properly prepared group, or not at all. You will have to wait till Peter and Stephen arrive."

"And Roger too Mum. Can we see him tomorrow when we go to town?"

Thursday was Christmas Eve and a trip to Atherton had been organized to obtain the last-minute items everyone had forgotten.

"Yes, you can, now start weeding."

It was a very tired Graham who went early to bed that night. Kylie did a last check on the sick calf with Uncle Bill and her mother. The calf and its mother had been moved to an old shed in the home paddock. The shed was open on one side but was dry and gave shelter from the wind, so Kylie felt happier when she went to bed. She went to bed praying the calf would not die. It reminded her of the time her pet puppy 'Bounce' had died.

I wish the pets were here, she thought.

The family dog, 'Skipper', had been placed in a kennel for the holidays as Uncle Bill did not want her on the farm. On a previous visit Skip had chased the cattle and fought with his dogs. It was a sober and sad little girl who went to sleep, her head full of images of Uncle Bill losing the farm and of the calf dying.

Thursday found them up and milking before the sun. The routine of the farm claimed them, even though it was Christmas Eve. While Graham was rounding up the milkers Kylie and Uncle Bill went to check on the calf. She was still alive but obviously very sick. Kylie was given a milk bottle to feed her while Graham and Uncle Bill did the milking. After breakfast she checked on the calf again and was heartened by her progress. She was still too weak to stand but sucked greedily at the milk bottle when it was held in her mouth.

On the drive into town they stopped at the Reid's farm to drop off some Christmas presents. Aunty Violet and Annabelle were there, and Kylie was instantly peeved at how Graham reacted to Annabelle. He smiled and then openly flirted with her. *Poor Margaret,* she thought.

Mr Reid and Bert appeared from the machinery shed. Kylie felt her heart leap and she wished, yet again, that Bert liked her instead of Allison. Bert was introduced to Graham. The two boys shook hands but neither then spoke to the other.

"Where's Victor?" Mrs Kirk asked.

"Went to town," Aunty Violet replied.

Later, as they climbed into the car Kylie said to Graham. "Isn't Bert nice?"

Graham just shrugged, then said, "I like Annabelle."

Kylie bit her lip. *Oh dear!* she thought. *I'll have to make sure we don't visit the Reid's too often.*

They drove on via Malanda. As they drove along the main street Kylie pointed out the window. "There's cousin Victor." She saw that Victor was talking to a tall, thin young man of about his own age. The man had straggly, long hair and a wispy beard.

In Atherton they went first to Roger's Aunt's. Roger was very pleased to see Graham and the two boys agreed to walk to the shopping centre while Kylie went with Gran and her mother.

As the two boys walked along Roger asked how the cadet camp had been. Graham told him all about it, becoming very enthusiastic. "It was great," he concluded. "What about you? What have you been up to?"

Roger rolled his eyes. "Boring! All I seem to do is sit around; or I get dragged to visit more relations. And they all have gardens that have to be inspected in great detail. I mean, they are lovely gardens, but a man can only take so much. Now, what's this about an expedition?"

"We are going to try to find an old goldmine," Graham replied.

Roger nodded and sniffed. "Oh yeah? I heard Kylie mutter something about it. Do you reckon it is for real?"

"Yes, I do," Graham replied. "We've got Grandad Hector's old diary and also a copy of a letter that he wrote to his brother giving him details of exactly how to find the gold mine."

"So how come no-one has already found the mine?" Roger asked.

Graham shrugged. He wasn't sure and the thought had niggled at him too. "Don't know, but we will find it."

"Who is we?" Roger asked.

"Pete, Steve, you and me and the girls," Graham replied.

"Which girls?" Roger asked. He did not sound enthusiastic about it.

"Kylie and her friends," Graham replied. "Do you think you will be allowed to come?"

"Only if there is an adult with us," Roger replied.

That was a problem. Graham resolved it by asking Uncle Bill that evening while they were milking. Uncle Bill said he would like to help but that it would have to be during the day between milking; and that he would need help to get all the other farm chores done.

Graham also annoyed and alarmed Kylie by asking if Annabelle was coming with them to look for the gold. Kylie had been contemplating asking Bert but now instantly decided that he could not come; not if there was any chance of Annabelle coming as well!

The calf was still alive and feeding from the bottle when the children went to bed. That cheered Kylie. She was naturally excited anyway, at the thought of Christmas.

"Go to bed you children," Mrs Kirk said. "You still have to get up at four to do the milking."

"But Mum, that's too early. We might run into Santa Claus!" Graham replied in a teasing voice.

"Oh piffle! Now go to sleep," Mrs Kirk replied with a laugh.

They didn't meet Santa Claus, but, as always, Mrs Kirk had made sure that a pillowcase full of small presents was placed on the children's beds as soon as they were asleep. She also placed one on Gran's bed, much to the old lady's amusement.

When they rose at 4am to go and do the milking Graham started digging through the presents but was told it would have to wait. He muttered about life's injustices but got up and got dressed. But he did take a chocolate that had been one of the presents before going out to round up the cows. Uncle Bill and Kylie went to check on the calf.

The calf was still alive and that cheered Kylie enormously. She had feared it would be dead. *It will be a good Christmas now,* she told herself.

And it was. After breakfast they settled in the lounge room for photos and then the opening of presents. The presents were opened one at a time, Kylie fetching them from under the tree and handing them to the people they were for.

She was delighted with her own presents. Uncle Bill gave her a large 'Paint by numbers' painting of a farm, complete with little tubes of paint and brushes. Allison gave her soap and perfume in a set.

"That's because you pong so badly," Graham said. "It's a hint to bath more often."

Gran was shocked. "Graham! Don't be horrible to poor little Kylie."

Kylie just poked her tongue at him and opened her next present. This was a collection of books from her mother. Graham gave her a white T-shirt with parrots embroidered on the front. Margaret gave her a nice top and a set of ribbons. Her father had given her a necklace and matching bracelet; real jewellery, not little girls' play jewellery. Gran gave her a stationary set complete with pens, good quality letter paper and envelopes. Her oldest brother Alex just gave her chocolates.

Graham was also happy with his presents. Kylie gave him a set of six 1:50 000 scale army topographic maps for the area. "For you to use on your hikes," she explained.

Better still, his father had bought him a proper prismatic 'Silva' compass. Graham knew that the compass must have cost hundreds of dollars and was touched. "It's great!" he enthused. "It has both degrees and mils. I wish dad was here."

Margaret complemented the compass by giving him a new protractor; a square one that had the complete circle on it, and grid lines to help line it up on the map accurately. Uncle Bill gave him a set of secateurs.

"For cutting your way through the jungle; and you can practice by pruning the garden," Uncle Bill said.

"Thanks Uncle Bill. Have you got a pair too?"

"Yes, I have," Uncle Bill replied. "And better still I have gotten myself a Miner's Right and an 'Authority to Prospect'. So now we have the legal paperwork to go looking for gold."

Kylie and Graham were thrilled. "Oh show us please!" Kylie cried.

The documents had to be produced and examined before more presents were opened. Graham then went on opening his. Gran gave him a new dark green, long -sleeved shirt for bushwalking. His mother gave him a new pocket radio and Alex gave him socks and underpants. All in all it was a very useful set of presents. What warmed Graham's heart the most was the realization that the people who loved him had put a lot of thought into buying them.

"Well, we have everything we need now. So let's go and find that gold mine," he said.

"Christmas dinner first," Mrs Kirk said.

Chapter 12

LOOK!

As soon as the presents were opened the whole family went to Malanda to church. Graham was pleased to go as he particularly wanted to give thanks for having done so well on his Corporals Course. Kylie went in the hope of seeing Bert but none of the Reids were there. Nor did they appear to be at home, so there was no visit.

Christmas Dinner followed; the sort of dinner Kylie loved:- hot roast chicken and roast potatoes with peas and gravy; despite the summer heat. She ate till she could eat no more, although already being nagged by a conscience being driven by the 'thin' fashion of the age. Graham was less inhibited. In his own words he had a good 'pig out'.

Afterwards, Graham did the washing up and Kylie wiped. As they worked, Graham pointed out the window. "Heavy rain on its way."

"Good. That might cool it down," Kylie said. The temperature had climbed into the mid-thirties and the humidity had climbed to over 90% so that they were feeling very hot and sticky.

After lunch the rain began. There was a visit from the Griersons and later from another neighbour, but the children just said polite hellos and left the adults to talk. Graham studied his new maps and began to compare them with the old mining map and to make notes.

By milking time the rain had eased but the lanes were all muddy and slippery. Graham did not mind but walked cheerfully along using a broom handle as a walking stick. A check showed that the sick calf was much better and that brightened Christmas up even more for Kylie. The evening was spent quietly watching the TV. They all spoke to Captain Kirk and Alex on the radio telephone and wished them a merry Christmas and then it was time for bed. By then it was raining heavily again.

The rain was still drizzling down next morning when they went out to do the milking. They wrapped up in raincoats and old hats and sloshed out along the muddy lanes. Kylie slipped and fell over twice, much to her annoyance and to Graham's amusement.

After breakfast they changed and loaded into the car again, along with a bag of presents. An hour's drive took them to Mareeba where they called on their other grandparents, their father's mother and father. Graham liked the elder Kirks a lot but wasn't quite so keen on the horde of cousins who were staying there. Kylie really enjoyed visits to Mareeba and loved Grandma Kirk, who she thought was a very warm and understanding person. She also found the cousins fascinating.

The cousins were a rough and ready lot. They came from two cattle properties up in Cape York Peninsula. To Kylie they were a mob of real little bushies. Graham called them the 'country cousins' and said it in a mock 'Southern' accent to indicate they were hillbillies. Kylie actually had a delightful time playing with them, most being much younger than her and more than willing to play games.

The visit went on till well after lunch, another huge meal with roast pork and turkey. Then it was back to the farm for milking. By then Kylie was sad to leave and wished she could get to know these cousins better. As they drove back from Mareeba towards Atherton, they encountered rain again and drove through it all the way to the farm.

Milking was another cold and wet event, and the children were relieved to finish and to have hot showers and get into warm dry clothes. Another quiet evening followed. By this time Kylie was becoming tense and irritable as she wanted to get on with the search for the gold mine. She dropped off to sleep reading the old diary and puzzling over why the earlier searches had failed to find it.

During the night it rained heavily but by dawn the clouds had cleared away. Kylie went to check on the calf and found it was standing and feeding from her mother. That cheered her enormously and she went happily about feeding the other calves, singing, and humming to herself.

As it was Sunday, Mrs Kirk and Gran went to church again. Neither Kylie nor Graham wanted to go, pleading that they had just been two days before. This left them both at a bit of a loose end as Uncle Bill was working on an engine and needed no help. Kylie set herself up on the back veranda and began doing her 'paint by numbers' picture. Graham fidgeted, read a bit, then pulled on gum boots and clapped his old scout hat on his head.

"I'm just going to poke around a bit," he said as he paused to study Kylie's painting efforts.

"Don't get bitten by a snake," Kylie cautioned.

Graham just grunted and walked off, whistling cheerfully.

As she worked, Kylie pondered the puzzle of the old gold mine. More strongly than before the feeling was nagging at her that they did not have all the information. *Otherwise it would have been found by now,* she reasoned.

Unable to solve the riddle, she pushed the thoughts aside and settled to her painting. As she worked, she fantasised about meeting a wonderful man who would be kind and gentle and who would fall desperately in love with her. She tried to imagine Bert's face on the 'Mr Wonderful' image, but it did not seem to stick. As she painted, she also hummed or quietly sang. She was feeling very happy and content with life in general.

From time to time some outside activity would attract her attention. She would then gaze out over the fields and think, before resuming her art. On one occasion a flock of white cockatoos burst from the edge of the rainforest over beyond the milking shed. She watched them rise and circle, then shrugged and went on with her painting.

Half an hour later, just as she was trying to mix some green to the shade shown on the cover of the box, Graham came walking in. He stood and examined the picture critically for a moment. Kylie braced herself for disparaging remarks.

Instead, Graham said, "Kylie, come and see what I have found and tell me what you make of it."

Kylie asked what it was, but Graham shook his head and would not say. She had to clean her paint brush and follow him. They walked along the entrance drive to the road. Here Graham pointed across the road into the rainforest.

"In here."

That was even more mystifying, but Kylie dutifully followed him as he made his way into the tangle. She actually disliked the rainforest but had been into it a few times. Graham only went a few paces in, then stopped beside a large tree and pointed down.

On the leaf mould were a dozen cigarette butts. Kylie noted them but could not work out why they should interest Graham. "So what?" she asked.

Then it hit her, even as Graham said, "Someone has stood here for quite a while. They have had time to smoke all these cigarettes."

"Someone is watching the farm!" Kylie gasped. She felt her chest tighten with fear and she looked nervously around the dark forest.

"Yes, and he was here today," Graham replied.

"How do you know it was today?" Kylie asked. She knelt and picked up one of the butts to examine it.

"Because these are dry. We had heavy rain yesterday and last night and these are fresh," Graham replied.

"The cockatoos!" Kylie cried. "I saw them about half an hour ago."

Graham nodded, but said, "That was me. I crossed the road down beyond the milking shed and came up through the edge of the forest. But you are right. It was the cockatoos. I was down near the dam when I first noticed they were doing a lot of screeching. I didn't take any notice at first but they all took off and then settled further along after a while and I decided to take a look."

"Did you see anyone?" Kylie asked, looking anxiously around again.

"No, but I know how he got here and where he parks his car," he said.

"Parks? Do you think he has been here before?" Kylie asked.

"Yes. Look at this." Graham showed her a faint trail back into the jungle. The leaf mould had been trampled and several small vines had been cut. By bending down she could see where there were scuff marks on bark and on tree roots and logs. Moss had been scraped off in places. Graham led the way, pointing to the clues.

Twenty metres back the trail came out on an old, overgrown road. It was typical of such roads. Because the trees met overhead and blocked out most of the sunlight no new trees had grown up along most of the old road. Only a matt of deadfall covered it, and a few dead logs. Undergrowth from the sides made it much narrower than it had once been, but it was easy to walk along.

Graham pointed both ways along it. "Probably the original road, or maybe a timber snig track," he commented. "Watch that wait-a-while." He held the thin, almost invisible tendril, with its vicious barbed hooks, so Kylie could avoid it.

The old road slanted off roughly parallel to the modern road. It went up over the crest and then curved left to a point a hundred metres along the main road. As they walked quietly along Kylie kept glancing fearfully around, her heart beating rapidly. She also kept a wary eye open for wait-a-while tendrils.

"What if he is still here?" she whispered.

Graham shook his head. "He isn't. I heard him drive off, and I've looked," he replied.

"Oh Graham! That was silly. You could have run into trouble," Kylie scolded, concern for her brother fuelling anger.

Graham just shrugged. "I was alright. I am a good scout in the jungle. Anyway, I could just run away."

They came to an overgrown junction with wild ginger and conjuboy plants filling it. One road went left and downhill into the jungle. The other led right and curved out to sunlight. They walked twenty metres along this and the main road came into sight. Just back around the curve were distinct wheel tracks in the grass and leaf mould.

Graham pointed down. "He had a car parked here. And he's been here a few times, from the look of these wheel ruts," he explained.

It was a chilling thought and Kylie shivered and looked anxiously around again. "The men who want the treasure map," she said, voicing her suspicions.

"Have to be," Graham replied.

"But why?" Kylie asked.

"To keep tabs on what we are doing I suppose," Graham replied.

"What will we do?" Kylie asked.

"Nothing for the moment," Graham replied.

Kylie was shocked. "Oh but we must! We must tell mum and Uncle Bill."

Graham shook his head. "No, not yet. We don't have enough proof; and they will call the police and make a big fuss and then we won't be allowed to go anywhere. No searching for old gold mines."

"But... but... but what if the men come back?" Kylie replied. She could see what Graham was getting at but it wasn't in her nature to hide things from her mother.

"Peter, Stephen, and Roger will be here tomorrow. We can organize some secret observation of our own then. That will give us some facts to plan on," Graham replied.

Reluctantly Kylie agreed to this. Brother and sister then made their way out onto the road and walked slowly back along the road to the farm, discussing how they might find the old gold mine. It was a very thoughtful and anxious Kylie who spent the rest of the morning painting, her eyes being continually drawn to the wall of jungle. Graham set himself up on the veranda on the couch with a book, but he had binoculars handy and also a stout stick.

When Mrs Kirk and Gran returned Kylie felt quite ill at the thought of hiding anything from them, but she met Graham's eyes and he gave an emphatic shake to his head. One result was that lunch was a silent event and Kylie only picked at her food.

After lunch, Kylie resumed her painting while Graham went downstairs and laid out every item of his hiking clothes and gear and checked it. He then sat and studied the old maps and notes.

During milking Kylie felt quite sick. She badly wanted to tell Uncle Bill, if only to warn him, but managed to hold her tongue. Graham appeared quite happy and went about whistling and cracking silly jokes. That annoyed Kylie, as she experienced frequent flashbacks to the awful beating she had received and she knew she was scared.

"What if the men come tonight?" she asked Graham when they were alone after the milking.

"The dogs will warn us," Graham replied. "Anyway, I shall stay awake till late, just in case."

Kylie felt even more anxious and upset by teatime. She was so sick inside she could hardly eat. Her mother noticed this and asked if there was anything wrong.

"No mum. I am just a bit worried about tomorrow. I'm alright," Kylie replied.

Lying to her mother made her feel even worse and she was further annoyed by Graham's apparently relaxed attitude. *It's alright for him; he's a stupid male!* she thought angrily.

The result was that she had trouble getting to sleep. She lay awake for hours. At every sound, her heart would thump rapidly and she would break into a cold sweat. Graham checked on her several times and gave her a cheerful grin which annoyed her even more. In her mind's eye she could picture the two men creeping up on the house...

Monday dawned wet and misty. Bartle Frere was hidden in clouds and the grass was wet and the lanes muddy. As Kylie helped to bring in the cows in the half-light she could not help glancing continually at the wall of jungle beyond the milking shed. Graham saw her doing this and shook his head to indicate there was nothing to worry about.

After breakfast they set to work to arrange the bedding for their friends. This at least raised Kylie's spirits and she hummed happily as she worked. Morning tea was a cheerful affair and Mrs Kirk looked happier.

The girls were the first to arrive. Margaret and Allison travelled up from Cairns with Allison's dad; a dark-haired and grumpy man who tried to pretend he was happy. Luckily, he only stayed for a few minutes, pleading business commitments before driving off. It was instantly apparent to Kylie that Allison was not happy either, that she was only pretending.

"My mother has gone to Sydney because her sister is very ill," was all she said when asked. Somehow this did not ring true but Kylie did not want to probe.

She will tell me if she wants to.

Margaret was the opposite. She positively glowed with happiness and good health. She beamed at Graham and gave Gran a big hug and then handed her a small present. Gran was very touched, and Kylie felt a warm glow about her friend.

Now, if only that bone-headed brother of mine will return some of her affection, she thought.

Her own spirits lifted by the minute and the secret watcher in the woods was forgotten in the excitement of showing the girls where they were to sleep and in helping them unpack. There was also the thought of Peter. *Do I really like him?*

"Does Bert know you are coming?" Kylie asked Allison.

"Yes. He will come over this afternoon to say hello," Allison replied.

"Do your mum and dad know about him?" Kylie asked.

Allison shook her head. "No fear! They don't need to know yet."

That set Kylie's mind working. *Yet? Just how serious does Allison think this affair is?* she wondered. *Heavens, it is only a holiday romance. Oh dear, I hope she doesn't get hurt.*

The tooting of a car horn announced the arrival of the boys. All three had come in Mrs Bronsky's car. Kylie found that she was happy to see them, but noted that her heart did not go into wild palpitations at the sight of Peter. The car was unloaded and Graham took them all in to meet Gran and Uncle Bill.

Gran's face lit up. "Heavens! What an invasion!" she cried delightedly. "This is just what the place needs, a lot of young people to liven it up."

Morning tea was arranged while the boys lugged their gear down to the basement. Kylie was called on by her mother to help although she badly wanted to hear what Graham was saying to them downstairs. That he had said something was perfectly obvious to her as they all came up laughing and joking and pretending nothing unusual was going on.

Almost as soon as the cups and plates had been removed from the table the plot was revealed. The boys went downstairs in a huddle of whispers. Margaret tried to follow but was told to go away because they were changing. That made Kylie very suspicious. She went downstairs a few minutes later and found the four boys bending over a sketch map of the farm.

"What are you lot up to?" she asked.

"Nothing. Go away," Graham replied.

"If it has anything to do with the man watching us from across the road I will not. We have a right to know as well. We want to be in this too," Kylie replied.

"You are girls. This is dangerous stuff," Graham replied.

"Don't be a sexist pig Graham. We can help and still be quite safe," Kylie replied, her anger rising. Margaret and Allison had followed her down and now supported her.

Graham gave in. "okay. We were just trying to work out a plan to try to get a good look at this bloke, or at his car."

"What bloke?" Margaret asked.

Kylie described the watcher in the woods. Both Margaret and Allison made exclamations of fright and Allison's eyes widened with anxiety.

"Do you want to catch him?" Margaret asked.

"No, just get a good look at him, and at his car," Graham replied. "If it is the same men then the police can then lock them up or warn them off."

"Then we have to be involved," Kylie said. "You don't even know what they look like. You weren't here."

That was a hard argument for Graham to counter so, reluctantly, he let the girls join in the planning. It was a simple plan but needed a bit of preparation and time. Kylie was to go with the other girls and Stephen to circle around the open farm to the north side of the hill, so that they were hidden from the watcher or his car by the ground. They would circle around to the road beyond where the car was hidden, then lie under cover beside the road and watch. Half an hour was allowed for this move. After that time Graham, Peter and Roger were to walk out along the driveway, pretending to be going to the milking shed but were then to just walk straight into the jungle where the man was believed to be watching from.

"But what if he's there?" Margaret asked anxiously.

"Then he will have trouble explaining why," Graham replied.

"But what will you say if he asks what you are doing?" Allison asked.

"We don't have to explain anything. He is the one who is trespassing," Graham replied.

"But what if he's got a gun or something?" Margaret asked, her anxiety plain.

Graham shrugged. "He won't be game to use it, and anyway, he won't get all three of us. At least one will get away."

"Oh Graham!" Kylie cried.

She was appalled at the very idea. Equally she could see no way to stop the boys, other than telling Uncle Bill or her mother. Feeling sick at heart she went to get dressed in old clothes.

Chapter 13

SHARES?

As Kylie pulled on her boots, she felt sick in the stomach. The thought of the men being so close; and of the possible risk to Margaret and the boys made her feel she wanted to throw up. The attitude of the boys also exasperated her. All they could do was joke and grin. Graham had the light of battle in his eye and she knew he was enjoying the situation immensely.

When they were all ready, they gathered in the foyer. Graham gave some least minute instructions. While he was doing this Mrs Kirk appeared.

"What are you children doing?" she asked.

There was a moment of guilty silence. Kylie said, "Going for a walk," at the same moment that Graham said, "Playing a game."

Mrs Kirk looked suspicious but simply said, "Don't go far. Lunch is in an hour."

"Yes Mum."

Graham looked at Kylie. "Go on. We will see you in half an hour."

Kylie turned and led the way out through the side door through the garage. Stephen and Allison followed her. Kylie found her heart beating rapidly and she wiped sweaty hands on her trousers as she came to the fence. The group climbed over the fence and set off across the side of the hill beyond. As they walked, they kept looking back to check that the house was hiding them from the supposed location of the hidden watcher.

After a hundred metres the swell of the ground forced them up so that they were visible to anyone in the whole stretch of rainforest.

Kylie turned and led the way downslope to the right. "Don't look back. We will pretend we are going to Platypus Creek," she said.

The group tramped down across the open cow pasture and past a lone tree, to a gate leading into the lane that led around the hill. They went through the gate and turned left to follow the lane. Soon they were out of sight of the house and the rainforest.

"What if they are also watching from down at the creek?" Allison suggested, indicating the line of jungle along Platypus Creek to their right front.

Stephen shook his head, "There are only two of them. I can't see them doing that all day long. I reckon they would take turns."

The lane forked. The right fork led to the creek. The left fork went on around the hill to the main road. Several fields beyond the main road were also part of the farm and this lane led to them. When they came to the main gravel road Stephen stopped them while he had a good look along it in both directions. Satisfied no-one could see them he waved them across.

Kylie went last, closing the gate behind them. As she crossed the road, she looked left and noted with relief that the crest of the hill hid them from the rainforest. They went through another gate into the field beyond and set off across it. This field had waist high long grass and fear of snakes slowed them right down. Kylie was very glad she wore the high rubber gum boots.

The sun had come out by this time and they were all sweating. The long grass was full of butterflies which flew off as they were disturbed. Stephen now took the lead and led them across the side of the slope for three hundred paces before turning left and going uphill. This brought them to the fence beside the gravel road about fifty paces from the place where the car was possibly hidden.

"Find a good spot here," Stephen said. He took off his glasses and wiped them. "Bloody sweat!" he grumbled. The glasses were fogging up in the humid air.

The group made itself comfortable under a clump of small trees beside the road. They were hidden by a screen of long grass along the fence but made holes in this so they could clearly see the road and the rainforest on the other side.

"Ten minutes," Stephen observed. They settled down to wait.

While they waited, they talked quietly. Kylie did not really want to talk, partly because she was so worried, but also because she did not particularly like Stephen. When she was in his presence she experienced a feeling of unease, and she sensed that she did not trust him. She knew, from stories she had heard, that Stephen had been involved in a few dubious activities. She had also heard gossip which said he did things to girls.

The result was that Stephen talked mostly to Allison, who responded cheerfully enough, while Kylie alternately checked her wristwatch and studied the ants. From time to time she also eyed the long grass near her in case of snakes.

Suddenly a car engine burst into life just up the road.

"That's him!" Kylie cried. Her heart rate shot up dramatically and she moved into a crouching position. Almost immediately the engine note changed to a roar and a car burst out of the edge of the rainforest onto the road and turned towards them. It was an old dark green Ford with one man in it.

The car accelerated and was past them in a few seconds. Kylie stared at the driver and saw that he was a solid looking young man of about twenty with a big jaw and fair hair. *Oh dear! Is that one of the men?* she wondered. She bit her lip in anxiety and rose to try to get a better look, but the car sped away.

"Was that one of them?" Allison asked.

"I don't know. He might have been. They had stocking masks on when we saw them," Kylie replied. She stood and stared after the car as it vanished through the trees along the small creek at the bottom of the hill.

"I'll know that man if I ever see him again anyway," Allison replied.

"So will I," Kylie agreed. "Did you get the car's number Stephen?"

That had been Stephen's particular job and he nodded. "Yes. B. X. T. Four. Three. Five. A Ford Falcon, and an old bomb. There can't be too many of them around the Tablelands."

"Here come the others," Allison said.

From out of the rainforest appeared Graham, Margaret, Peter and Roger. The three climbed through the fence to meet them.

Graham called out as he walked towards them, "Did you see him?"

"Yes, but I didn't recognise him," Kylie replied.

"I think I did," Margaret replied. "I got a good look at him, and I think he is the one called 'Burg'."

"Carl Limburger?" Allison asked.

Margaret nodded. They discussed this possibility. Kylie explained that she wasn't sure because she did not see the man's body or his gait but Margaret replied that was why she thought it was him. "I only saw him from the back but he had the same solid build and way of walking as the fellow who bashed you Kylie."

Stephen took off his glasses and wiped them. "So what happened when you walked across the road?" Stephen asked.

Graham and Peter both laughed. Graham explained, "We walked out along the driveway talking and telling jokes and just went straight across the road and into the scrub. The bloke was there, and he obviously wasn't expecting that because he just gaped at us for a second, then turned and bolted."

Margaret chuckled. "He got all tangled up in a vine and tripped," she added. "Then he ran into a wait-a-while. That made him swear something horrible."

"Serves him right," Kylie said. She had an intense dislike of the two men.

Graham nodded. "Then he ran off along the old road. We called out but he ignored us and kept going as fast as he could. As soon as he got to his car he got in and drove off," Graham explained.

Peter said, "He certainly acted in a very suspicious manner."

Graham turned to Stephen. "You got his car number Steve?"

Stephen nodded. "Yes." He held up his notebook where he had jotted this down.

"So what do we do now?" Kylie asked.

"Phone the police and find out if Limburger or one of his friends owns the car," Margaret suggested.

Graham shook his head. "If we do that then the oldies might cancel our whole operation."

That was a sobering thought, but Kylie only considered it for a moment, then said, "We must tell them. Gran and Uncle Bill might be in danger."

Graham made a face and nodded. "You are right. Come on, let's do that now."

The group set off back along the road to the farm. Five minutes later they found Uncle Bill in the machinery shed and told him. Kylie acted as spokesperson, with some help from Graham.

The upshot was that they were half an hour late for lunch. Uncle Bill insisted that they show him everything and only then did he walk back to the farm with them. He looked very worried, and Kylie felt her hopes sinking. Mrs Kirk and Gran had to be told. Kylie and Graham did this while Uncle Bill telephoned the police.

Mrs Kirk was quite angry. "You should have told us yesterday. And as for walking into the jungle where he was! Why!... Why!... Words fail me! What if he had been armed and violent?"

"But he wasn't mum," Graham answered.

"But what if he had been? You silly boy! You did not see how violent he was when he was here. He bashed Kylie quite brutally. It makes me sick just to think of it," Mrs Kirk said.

"So what happens now?" Graham asked.

"You children stay inside until the police sort it out," Mrs Kirk said.

Kylie's hopes sank even more, and she bit her lip in disappointment.

Graham protested, "Oh Mum! Fair go! We can't all just sit here like prisoners. It's not fair." He gestured to the others. "They have all come up here to look for the gold mine. If we have to sit here, then they may as well go back to Cairns."

Mrs Kirk looked grim. "That may not be such a bad idea," she said. Kylie's heart sank even further, and she felt tears were close.

But Graham did not give up. He said, "Oh Mum, they aren't kidnappers. They are after the gold."

"Oh gold! Fiddle-faddle! I've heard about that gold all my life and none of those men who went looking for it could ever find it. What chance do you children think you have?"

That hurt. Kylie's eyes watered and she said, "So if you don't believe in it, why were you going to let us go looking for it?"

Mrs Kirk took a deep breath, then said, "Because I thought it would be a good way to keep you all busy during the holidays. I didn't think it was dangerous then, at least no more dangerous than the jungle is anyway."

"Oh Mum!" Kylie cried. A tear trickled out of each eye. "That isn't fair. Anyway, I think we have a better chance than all those people who looked earlier because we have more information. None of them ever had both the old diary and the letter."

"That's right mum," Graham agreed. "And we will still be safe. If we stay in a group, we will be alright."

At that stage Uncle Bill put down the phone and joined them. As he did, Peter spoke up, "Mrs Kirk, I think the fact that these men are still watching us is good news as it means there probably is a gold mine. Please, we would like to go on with the expedition."

Kylie nodded and wiped her tears. "Yes Mum, please! We really must find the gold so that Uncle Bill can save the farm."

"That's nice of you," Uncle Bill said, "but I will just keep my fair share."

Kylie shook her head. "No you won't. We will all just have a little bit each and the rest is for you," she insisted.

"I think we should get equal shares," Stephen put in.

"No!" Kylie insisted. "The whole idea is to save the farm. You can have my share anyway Uncle Bill."

Uncle Bill held up his hands for silence as they all started to talk at once. "Hold on! Don't count your chickens before they are hatched is an old farming saying. Let's find the gold first."

"Mum isn't going to let us go," Kylie said.

Uncle Bill looked at his sister. "I think they should sis. I have arranged things, so I can take them and I am looking forward to it. It will be a holiday for me if nothing else."

"But what about these men? It could be very dangerous," Mrs Kirk replied.

Uncle Bill shook his head. "They are a problem but first we have to find the gold. I think we should still go and look."

Mrs Kirk looked very anxious, but Gran now spoke up, "I think you should go, and the children should go with Bill. He hasn't had a break from the farm for a couple of years now and he needs it."

That made Mrs Kirk waver. Kylie agreed. "That's a good idea mum. We will all do extra work to help on the farm to make up for it. And I will stay here to help look after you and Gran. And you can have my share Uncle Bill."

"No, you can keep your share," Uncle Bill. "Let's find the gold first."

Gran spoke up again. "Kylie's right. You should agree who gets what now; to save any disagreements and bad blood later, just in case you do find something."

"So, let's sit down and discuss it," Uncle Bill said. He led them to the dining room and they all seated themselves on chairs.

When everyone was seated, he said, "I think everyone should get an equal share."

"That includes mum and Gran, even if they don't come," Kylie insisted.

The others nodded. Graham then said, "I think the 'Save the Farm' project should get a share."

The others all nodded at this. Kylie thought hard, determined to get as much as possible for the farm. "We are only talking about loose gold here aren't we? But what about the actual claim that Grandad Hector pegged? That must go to him surely?"

"But he's dead!" Stephen objected.

"So? So it goes to his descendants," Kylie replied.

"Oh, I suppose so," Stephen replied, seeing that the others agreed with Kylie.

Kylie turned to her mother. "So can we go and look please mum?"

Mrs Kirk gave a rueful smile and nodded. "Yes, alright, but it does depend on what the police advise."

"Yippee!" Kylie cried. She smiled and wanted to hug everyone. Mrs Kirk smiled again and said, "Now come and help me get lunch for this hungry horde."

After lunch Uncle Bill phoned the police again. The police reported that they had spoken to Burg and he had produced a witness, a man named Josh Dolan who insisted that Burg had been with him all morning helping repair his truck. The green car was traced to one that had been stolen in Townsville earlier in the week, but it could not be linked to either man. Donk also had an alibi, his employer saying he had been at work all morning.

That left them puzzled.

"Who else knows about this gold mine?" Peter asked.

"Half the bloody Tablelands!" Uncle Bill replied with a chuckle.

Kylie nodded. "Yes, the Reids certainly know about it."

"Maybe it is the Reids who are watching us?" Stephen suggested.

Allison drew breath sharply. "Oh it is not!" she replied heatedly.

Kylie supported her. "That is silly Stephen. They have as much information as us. Why would they possibly waste time watching us?"

Stephen shrugged. Peter asked, "What exactly do these Reids know?"

Kylie listed the copies of the diary, the old letter and the maps, plus notes from their own family expeditions. Peter listened then commented, "So they possibly know more than us. We had better get moving or they might find it before us."

The thought that the Reids might be rivals in the search came to Kylie as a shock although later she had to admit to herself there was no reason why it should. *After all their family has actually been out looking before.*

Uncle Bill stood up. "Well, let's get some work down and we can then get organized."

They all followed him out and were given various tasks to do which kept them busy till milking time. Allison was the exception. In mid-afternoon Bert drove over to see her. She dropped what she was doing and ran to meet him. Kylie thought they were going to embrace and kiss but they controlled themselves with Mrs Kirk present. As the others worked Bert sat and talked to Allison and she told him about the man and offered to show him where the man had parked his car.

Stephen glanced at Allison and Bert as they strolled off along the farm road. "They just want to get away for a bit of a smooch!" he commented.

Margaret looked annoyed. "You are just jealous," she said.

Stephen made a face, but Kylie knew she was right. As she watched Allison and Bert walk off hand in hand, she wondered if she felt jealous herself. She shook her head but then bit her lip and looked anxiously at Bert. *I wonder if the Reids are looking for the gold too?* She decided that they probably were. *So that makes them rivals and Bert is one of them.* Then another horrible thought came to her. *What if one of those men is back in the jungle watching?*

By then Bert and Allison had vanished into the jungle. Kylie voiced her suspicion. Graham just grinned and said, "Now you are the one who is jealous. You just want to go and see if they really are having a pash."

"Oh I am not!" Kylie insisted, but she blushed and knew it.

Half an hour Bert and Allison returned, Allison looking radiantly happy and walking with her arm very possessively around Bert's waist. Bert greeted them all cheerfully and then said farewell. "Have to get back for milking," he explained.

It was milking time on the farm as well. All helped here, Kylie gaining some amusement by watching Stephen getting his glasses splattered by cow poo while he was milking. That night they went over all the maps and notes again and arranged their plans for the next day.

As they went to bed Margaret said to Allison, "It's none of my business, but did Bert kiss you?"

Allison smiled and hugged her pillow. "Oh yes! And I kissed him back. Oh, he's such a hunk! I love him to bits."

"What did you talk about?" Margaret asked.

"We didn't talk all that much," Allison replied. Then she giggled and blushed.

Margaret was wide eyed with interest. So was Kylie but another thought came to her. She said, "Did you tell him all about the man watching us?"

"Yes, I did. He said he would come over and keep me safe if I wanted that," Allison replied, her eyes dancing.

"Please don't tell him our plans," Kylie said.

"Oh why ever not? He won't tell," Allison said.

Margaret giggled. "That's what all the boys say!" she said.

"Oh poo!" Allison replied. Then she giggled too.

Kylie shook her head. She wanted to say more but sensed it could lead to a disagreement so instead she said goodnight and snuggled down. The other two talked for a while longer about boys and love. Kylie listened with half her mind. The other half was taken up by thoughts of saving the farm by finding the gold.

Anyway, I will still give Uncle Bill my share, she vowed.

She tried to get to sleep, but found her mind too full of hopes and dreams. As well noises from downstairs kept disturbing them.

"What are those silly boys up to?" Margaret asked.

"Just being silly boys," Kylie replied. "Why don't you go down and shut them up?"

"Oh I couldn't. I'm only in my nightie!" Margaret answered in a slightly scandalized voice.

"They wouldn't mind," Allison commented.

Kylie laughed. "Go on. Graham has seen you in less than that."

Margaret cried out, "Oh Kylie! Don't keep dredging that up. We were only little then."

"It was only last year," Kylie reminded. "And you said Graham was very big."

The girls all giggled and that led to thumping on the floor. Graham's voice sounded, "You girls go to bed, and stop making so much racket. We are trying to sleep down here."

The patent untruth and injustice of this led to an outburst of denials and giggling which was only subdued by Uncle Bill's loud voice reminding them that they had to be up at four o'clock for milking.

Chapter 14

INTO THE JUNGLE

Tuesday, 29 December

As soon as the morning chores were done the group loaded gear into the cars and climbed in. Even with two vehicles it was a tight squeeze. Stephen and Peter went in the front of Uncle Bill's ute and the others in Mrs Kirk's car. Kylie made sure that Margaret ended up beside Graham. Gran sat in the front with her. Allison and Roger squashed in the back beside Graham. All were dressed for exploring the rainforest: long sleeved shirts, long trousers and strong footwear. Kylie wore an old green army shirt, jeans and gym boots.

It was nearly ten before the expedition got under way. By then Kylie was almost beside herself with impatience and excitement. It had seemed as though they would never get to go and search for the gold mine. *At last! We are off!* she thought as the cars started moving. She sat back and grinned at Margaret.

As they drove along Kylie gazed out at the scenery and dreamed vivid dreams of finding the gold and saving the farm. Their route took them back to the road junction at Lamins Hill and then down the Churinga Flat road. This was a gravel road which led past a couple of farms and through patches of rain forest and then through rain forest for several kilometres before coming out in an open clearing with more farms. The base of Bartle Frere loomed up only a few kilometres ahead, the upper slopes and top of the mountain hidden by thick clouds.

At a road junction they turned left onto a muddy side road and went along this for a bit before Uncle Bill stopped. Beside the road was the overgrown ruin of an old farmhouse. A mango tree grew next to a rusty water tank. They all climbed out. Uncle Bill pointed back and said, "If you want to climb Bartle Frere then you go right at that road junction back there. The road leads past the Churaana Bora Ground, and then to the base of the mountain."

"What is a Bora Ground?" Allison asked.

"A clearing where the Aborigines conducted ceremonies and dances and so on," Uncle Bill replied.

Allison looked around. "Are there Aborigines around here?"

Uncle Bill shook his head. "Haven't seen any for years," he replied.

Margaret stared up at the cloud-shrouded mountain. "Is there a road up Bartle Frere?" she asked.

Uncle Bill again shook his head. "No. Only a walking track. And I wouldn't go today. It takes all day and you want a clear day in winter or all you see from the top is cloud."

Kylie pointed to the old farmhouse. "Why did we stop here?"

"This is the old Pike farm where Grandad Hector lived," Uncle Bill replied.

That sparked Kylie's interest. She had somehow imagined the story had all happened at Gran's farm, even though she knew it had not. The ruined farmhouse had been built of timber on low stumps. The roof was corrugated iron. The house was now almost completely rotted and collapsed but it appeared it had once had a small veranda and only a couple of rooms. A tumbledown shed and a rotting outdoor dunny with a distinct lean stood in the waist high weeds which took up what had once been the yard.

"It isn't very big," Margaret said. "Weren't there a whole tribe of them?"

Gran laughed, "Yes there were, two adults and five children. You young people don't know what it was like in the 'good old days'," she said, the last tinged with sarcasm. "People were crowded more then. All us kids shared one big bed in one room and the parents the other room. It only had three rooms that I remember."

"But it's only a hut!" Allison exclaimed.

"Yes, it is. But that is how this country was settled," Gran replied. "They were tough people in those days, mentally as well as physically."

Kylie shook her head as she tried to imagine what it must have been like. "Who owns it now?" she asked.

"It belongs to that farm we passed back there," Uncle Bill replied.

"Do they own both farms?" Kylie asked.

Uncle Bill nodded. "Yes they do. In fact they probably own three or four of the old farms, same as we do."

"Why is that Uncle Bill?" Graham asked.

"Economics. You need a big enough area to run a couple of hundred head to make a dairy farm pay these days," Uncle Bill replied. "So lots of the small holdings have been amalgamated to make viable economic units."

Kylie understood what he was saying but was puzzled. "So how did they make a living in the old days?"

Again it was Gran who answered, "They lived a much simpler life than us. Their standard of living was much lower, and they didn't have the same expectations. They didn't have to pay for TVs and all those electronic gadgets you take for granted."

"It must have been awful," Allison observed.

Gran shook her head. "No, it wasn't. In fact they were probably much happier than us because theirs was a simpler world with clearer values. The only thing that was awful was the medical side. Lots of people died who wouldn't now, simply because the doctors didn't know enough. It was the little kiddies dying that was the worst." Gran's voice trailed away in sadness as she looked back through the tunnel of years.

"Can we have a look?" Kylie asked, as much to change the subject as anything. She did not want to think about little children dying.

Uncle Bill answered, "I wouldn't advise it. The place is sure to be a nest of snakes. They love old ruins. You kids be very careful and try not to walk on old sheets of corrugated iron. If you lift anything you look first and be ready to jump back fast."

That ended any desire to explore the ruin; although in truth they could see nearly as much from where they stood as they would if they went closer. It was obvious that no clues to help them find the gold mine would remain.

They climbed back into the vehicles and set off. The road dramatically deteriorated to two wheel tracks and then, at the edge of the rainforest, to a muddy track which was covered by a carpet of leaves and sticks and which had small bushes growing up along it. Mrs Kirk muttered a few times as the car squished through muddy puddles but the going was quite easy, so she continued to follow Uncle Bill's ute.

Graham followed their route on his map, moving his finger along the road marked on it. After about a kilometre and a half they came to an overgrown clearing with a road junction. Uncle Bill parked his ute and got out. Mrs Kirk pulled up nearby. Kylie was glad to get out.

Uncle Bill pointed to the other road, which was also partly overgrown. "That is the road to Windin Creek. There is a nice waterfall down there."

"Is it far?" Margaret asked.

"Two or three kilometres," Uncle Bill replied. "And I'd say the track is all overgrown now. I haven't been along it for a good few years."

After consulting the maps the group collected bags and gear containing food, water, first aid kits and odd items. The boys all wore their army webbing and Graham had a machete which he slashed at the overhanging growth with as they walked along. Uncle Bill led but all he used to cut a path were a pair of garden secateurs.

"This is what you want," he said to Graham. "Machetes make too much noise and they don't cut the vines very well. They won't cut wait-a-while at all. In fact they just make the bloody things jump about so that the other tendrils snag you."

Graham experimented with this when they came to the first wait-a-while plant which was blocking their path. He was quite familiar with wait-a-while so was careful. Even so, a mighty swipe with the machete failed to sever one of the thin tendrils. As Uncle Bill had said the whole bush then shook and all the dangling tendrils were flung about. One of these snagged Graham's back.

"Serves you right," Kylie said as Peter helped untangle him. Graham muttered and stubbornly would not admit he was wrong but after a while Kylie noticed that he quietly slid the machete back into its sheath and took out the new secateurs that Margaret had given him for Christmas.

The road wound along the top of a wide, gentle ridge. Thick rainforest hemmed them in and the trees met in an overhead tunnel. Because the road was no longer used or maintained it was blocked in places by fallen trees and by clumps of wait-a-while. Weeds and small trees grew up in the more open areas and the surface was a thick matt of deadfall.

The recent rain made the ground damp and there were muddy patches to be negotiated. Kylie soon found her feet were damp and she grimaced with dislike. As she walked, she looked around, admiring the incredible profusion of plant growth. The whole place was on massive riot of growing things and decaying vegetation.

Allison suddenly cried out. "Oh! Look at that butterfly!"

It was large, its wings a brilliant blue and edged with black. Kylie watched with fascination as it flitted off through the trees. On both sides of the track the trees grew so closely together that it was just possible to walk between them- or would have been if vines, ferns, and bushes had not taken up much of that space. Kylie decided that she could only see about fifty metres at most, and at times, much less than that. Ferns, palms, and other bushes blocked the view. Only a few of the trees were large. Many of these were festooned with lianas or strangler vines. Kylie knew a fair bit about the rainforest from school field trips and from earlier expeditions, so she studied it all with informed interest.

Graham was obviously thinking about their earlier expeditions too as he called back, "Hey Steve, don't get lost in this bit of rainforest."

The previous January, during a holiday trip to the Innisfail area, Stephen had spent a night alone in the rainforest after running into it to escape from some crooks. He snapped back, "I wasn't lost. I just had trouble seeing where I was going because of the rain."

Kylie glanced back at Stephen. She knew the story well. Stephen's problem had been heavy rain and humidity fogging up his glasses. She saw he was already starting to have problems that way now as they worked up a sweat. He did not look happy and was muttering as he walked along.

After about half an hour they stopped at what had once been a clearing. It was now overgrown with young trees, all of the same type and all the same height. Over to one side were some rusty old drums and steel objects. On another side was a litter of bottles and rusty cans.

Margaret pointed to where three large logs had been piled up one on top of the other against two trees. Earth had been pushed against one side of the logs. "What was that for?" she asked.

"A ramp for loading bulldozers," Uncle Bill replied.

"Did they use bulldozers to mine the gold?" Margaret asked.

"Sometimes, but these would have been for timber getters to use," Uncle Bill replied.

Margaret still looked puzzled, so Uncle Bill explained. "They used a bulldozer to push a track in to, or close to, a tree they wanted to get. They would then cut the tree down and the dozer would haul it out to a clearing where it could be lifted onto a timber jinker; that is a special trailer made to carry logs. The trucks then took them to a sawmill."

Graham added, "That is why there are so many side tracks running off in areas of rainforest that have been logged."

"I thought they just cut everything down," Allison said.

Uncle Bill shook his head. "No, not up here in the rainforest. They do that in the eucalypt forests down south. Clear felling it is called."

"Environmental vandalism I call it," Peter put in. "It absolutely devastates the wildlife; and all to make tissue paper we don't need."

Stephen snorted. "You can wipe your bum with your finger if you want," he commented with a grin.

"And you can bite yours!" Peter retorted. "You know what I mean. We waste a lot of paper and don't need to."

Kylie became impatient. "Come on. We came to find the gold mine, not discuss the timber industry."

Uncle Bill led them on along an overgrown track to the east. This time they had to go much slower and the secateurs came into use much more often. It became gloomy as clouds came over and there were a few spits of rain, but as they were all soaked by perspiration they ignored this.

After twenty minutes walking Uncle Bill pointed to a few sheets of rusty corrugated iron, the edges of which were protruding from the matt of leaves. "This is the 'Pride of Erin' mine."

Kylie looked around in dismay. All she could see were a few old rusty steel objects and some thick coils of rusty steel wire rope. She had imagined it would be like the old mines they had visited out in the open country: wooden poppet legs over the tops of the shafts except all overgrown with creepers. The only real sign that this had been a mine were a few low mounds of earth and a couple of depressions full of rotting deadfall which might have once been the entrance to mine shafts.

Graham made a face. "Not much left is there?" he commented.

"It's been over sixty years since the mine closed," Uncle Bill replied. "Nothing lasts long in this climate. The wood rots and the steel rusts."

"The bottles don't," Stephen said. He had found a few old bottles buried in the leaf mould and dug them up to see if they were valuable.

Kylie took out her notebook. "If this is the 'Erin' mine then this is where we start following the detailed instructions in the letter."

The others crowded around as she read them out. After reading through the list, she said, "Right, Number One says: 'From the Erin Mine go south'."

She turned and looked around. "Which way is that?" she asked. The sun was still hidden by the heavy overcast and she had no idea which way was which.

Graham took out his compass, which he had tied to the pocket of his new green shirt. "That way."

They all studied the jungle in the direction indicated. Peter scratched his head and said, "There would have been a track, but I can't see any sign of one."

They all moved across to search. Kylie thought she could detect a few changes in the vegetation which might indicate a track had once been there but there was certainly no clear path. She felt a sudden sinking of her hopes. She bit her lip.

Allison expressed her thoughts when she said, "This might be a little bit harder than we thought."

Mrs Kirk agreed, "I did warn you it would be. If it was that easy all those earlier expeditions would have found the gold."

As her eyes scanned the wall of jungle Kylie felt them water. She felt quite sharply cast down and began to feel she had been a fool to make her bold assertions about finding the gold. 'First catch your chicken,' Uncle Bill had said. The words seemed to mock her, and it was all she could do not to burst into tears.

Graham and Peter both scouted the edge of the overgrown clearing and after several minutes Graham called out. "I think this is a track. Even if it isn't we can still get through easily enough. How far do we have to go Kylie?"

Kylie looked at her notebook through misty eyes and read, "Cross the main stream, then it says: turn right at the 'Bright Smile'. That must be another mine, but it isn't on any of the maps we have."

Graham nodded and studied his map. Peter pointed to the map. "This must be the main stream, Christmas Creek."

"Christmas Creek. Yes, the old diary said that Grandad Hector came back along the Christmas Creek Track on his last trip," Kylie replied, feeling a glimmer of hope.

"How far is it?" Mrs Kirk asked.

Graham studied the map. "About two hundred metres. We can just push through that if we can't find a track. Come on, there must be some remains to show us where this other mine was."

With that he turned and set off into the jungle, secateurs in one hand and compass in the other. Her spirits lifting and her determination growing by the second Kylie followed.

Chapter 15

OLD MINES

As Graham had suggested, there were signs indicating the area had been mined- lots of signs- all over the place. Within twenty paces they found mounds of earth and items which indicated that a mine shaft had been dug there. The place was now overgrown with trees and covered by rotting leaf mould, but the mounds and leaf filled depressions were still obviously the result of man-made disturbance.

At first Kylie thought that this mine was just part of the 'Pride of Erin' mine but when they found a third mine after another fifty paces, then two more off to the side she began to worry. It soon became obvious that there had been many mines in the area.

"Well, it was a gold rush," Peter observed. "Anyway, these don't count. We have to cross Christmas Creek first. The 'Bright Smile' will be on the other bank."

If it was, they were unable to tell which one. Christmas Creek was a typical jungle stream: crystal clear water tumbling over moss covered rocks. It was only a few paces across and easily crossed. Margaret thought it was very pretty and Kylie agreed with her but was now so anxious to find the old gold mine that she had no time for the beauties of nature. They crossed by stepping from rock to rock and climbed up into the jungle on the other bank, to find the overgrown remains of another mine almost at once.

Peter indicated the mounds and dips. "The 'Bright Smile'?" he suggested.

Graham could only shrug and Uncle Bill did not know. Gran, who had been following slowly with Mrs Kirk shook her head.

"I can't remember. There was a creek near the 'Erin' mine but it is too long ago."

Gran looked very hot and sweaty. Mrs Kirk also looked less than happy. "Gran and I will sit here on the creek bank and wait for you," she said. "But if it starts to rain we will walk back to the car and I will drive it out to the old farm. I wouldn't like to get bogged in the jungle."

"Good idea," Uncle Bill said. "In fact you could walk slowly back out now. We will be out in two hours. I don't want to be away from the farm too much."

"Don't you and Gran get lost mum," Kylie said anxiously.

Mrs Kirk smiled. "We will be alright. You children are the ones who have to be careful. Now go on with your search and we will see you at three o'clock."

"Okay Mum," Graham said. He turned to Kylie. "Kylie, what do we do next?"

Kylie read the instructions, "Turn right and then we cross Nugget Creek."

"Which creek is Nugget Creek?" Peter asked. He took the map from Graham and looked at it.

"The next one we come to I suppose," Graham replied. He started off through the jungle beside the creek. Margaret made a face but followed him. Allison obviously wasn't enjoying herself either but kept going. Stephen came last, cursing as his glasses kept getting drips or condensation on them.

The creek went quite steeply uphill. Most of each bank was covered by thick rainforest through which they had to worm their way. Graham, Peter and Uncle Bill used their secateurs to snip vines and wait-a-while tendrils, but everyone still snagged their clothing or gear continually on tree trunks or thicker vines. Kylie kept losing her hat as the vegetation brushed it off. She found she was panting as though she had run a race and that feelings of irritation and claustrophobia were building up.

Graham treated it all as a game. He pushed and blundered through the rainforest, laughing, and joking. From time to time he would be held up by a clump of ferns or a vine and would try to break through by brute force.

"Ow! Bloody stuff! Ah! Made it!" he cried. Then he then tripped and stumbled on a few paces.

"Watch out for that wait-a-while!" Peter called.

"Aargh! Got me! Ouch! Bloody stuff!" Graham cried. He backed up and twisted. There was a ripping sound. "Ah! That's better. Bloody wait-a-while!"

"Slow down and use your secateurs," Peter said. "You don't have to barge through like Bessie the bloody Elephant!"

Kylie shook her head and smiled. In spite of cuts and scratches Graham was obviously enjoying himself immensely. Personally she found it unpleasant. So, obviously, did Margaret and Allison. Margaret quietly kept going and said nothing, but Allison began to grumble. This changed to shrieks when she discovered a leech on her arm.

"Oh! Oh! A leech! Oh! Oh get it off! Get it off!" she cried.

"Calm down!" Kylie said. "It's only a leech."

Allison jumped up and down while scraping at the leech. "Oh get it off! Oh I hate them! Get it off!" she screamed.

Graham was unimpressed. "Just pull it off. It hasn't latched on yet with its mouth."

Allison shook her head vigorously. "Oh I can't!"

Stephen moved over and took the leech off her sleeve. "Watch. Just roll it into a ball between your finger and thumb and flick it away." He demonstrated this. Allison shuddered and then began to search herself for more leeches; to rapidly discover two more. That caused another outburst. Once these had been removed, they all checked themselves. Kylie found one on her trousers and one on her boot. Margaret had one on her neck which she pulled off without any fuss, even though the resulting wound bled quite freely for a time.

Repellent was passed around and they wiped it on their exposed skin and around their collars and cuffs as well as around the bottoms of their trousers. That done they resumed the exploration.

After ten more minutes they reached a creek junction. Graham muttered as he studied his compass. "This creek goes almost west and the main creek goes northwest. If we keep going this way we will come back to the road we came in on."

"What do we do next?" Peter asked Kylie.

Kylie read the instructions, "Cross Nugget Creek. Turn left at Frank's Claim. Then it says go downhill to the mossy rocks."

"If this is Nugget Creek," Stephen commented as they made their way down to the water. The creek was un-named on any of the maps and was only a few paces wide. They stopped to wash their faces and to have a drink before climbing up through a thick belt of palm ferns into the jungle on the other side.

Graham turned left and began making his way along the creek bank. Kylie called out, "We turn left at Frank's Claim, not at the creek."

"Are you sure?" Graham questioned.

This led to another reading of the instructions which made Stephen gesture at the surrounding jungle disgustedly.

"So where is Frank's Claim?"

It wasn't marked on any of the maps either. Kylie shrugged, feeling unhappy and baffled. "Perhaps it's the next old mine we come to?"

They pushed on through the jungle with Christmas Creek close on their right. They began to climb fairly steeply. Fifteen minutes of pushing through the jungle brought them to some low mounds which might have once been old diggings.

"This might be Frank's Claim," Peter said. "Look around for more clues."

"Who was Frank?" Margaret asked as they searched the area slowly.

Kylie shrugged. "No idea. A friend of Grandad Hectors I suppose. I read that he got sick once and Grandad helped him."

Peter called out to them from further up the slope. "Come and look at this. It is definitely man-made."

They made their way up to look. Kylie saw that Peter was standing on a low mound with a shallow ditch on the uphill side of it. It appeared to have been dug right around the hillside as far as they could see in both directions.

"What is it?" Margaret asked.

Uncle Bill answered. "A contour drain, to carry water to the mines."

"What do you mean Uncle Bill?" Graham said. "There's plenty of water down there in the creek."

"I know. But if a mine was up on the side of a ridge the old diggers used to cut a drain from a point higher up the creek to take water right to the mine." He pointed off upstream. "Sometimes they dug these channels for kilometres. They even built wooden flumes to carry the water across gullies and valleys."

Allison shook her head. "I don't understand. What's a flume?"

"A timber gutter up on posts like a bridge," Uncle Bill answered.

"You mean like an ancient Roman aqueduct?" Graham asked.

"That's right," Uncle Bill confirmed.

Margaret frowned. "But why take it across another creek? Why not get the water from the closest creek?"

"They would have had to pump. That meant an engine, therefore fuel and so on," Uncle Bill explained. "So instead they just dug contour drains with a gentle fall to them so the water flowed easily along. When they came to a creek or dip, they built the flume at the same gradient as the ditch."

"Sounds like an awful lot of work," Stephen said. "Why didn't they lay a pipeline?"

"They did sometimes," Uncle Bill replied. "But pipes cost money. So they went for hard work instead."

Stephen obviously did not like that idea. Kylie shook her head in wonder. Once again, she was struck with admiration for the early pioneers who toiled so mightily under such conditions.

Graham said, "So, if this is Frank's Claim we turn left and go downhill to some mossy rocks."

"That doesn't make sense," Peter said. "Left is uphill."

That had them stumped. Kylie felt her hopes slump further. Once again, they crowded around to read the instructions. That left Kylie feeling even more puzzled.

"Well, the creek is just down there," Graham said. "So let's go and look anyway."

They made their way down to the creek and stopped.

"Plenty of mossy rocks," Stephen observed.

"Every creek is lined with them," Graham said. "Grandad Hector would have referred to a really obvious clump. Let's look around."

For the next half hour they ranged up and down the hillside and both creek banks searching for the rocks. Allison and Stephen soon gave up and sat on some smooth boulders in the bed of the creek. One by one the others drifted in to join them.

Kylie sat down unhappily and wiped her brow. She took off her backpack and took out a cordial bottle. As she drank her eyes roved the surrounding jungle. Ruefully she remembered her mother's warnings that it would not be easy to find the old gold mine.

Now I see why! she thought.

For a time they sat and discussed various interpretations of the instructions. That merely baffled them even more.

"Turn left means turn left, and downhill is not uphill," Peter said. Both he and Graham had searched the hardest and were a lather of sweat.

"The next instruction says to take the left fork to the second creek, then downstream fifty paces. Maybe we should have gone left back there at Nugget creek?" Kylie suggested.

"What about Frank's claim?" Stephen asked.

Kylie could only shrug. She was feeling very down about it all. "Let's look anyway," she suggested.

Peter supported her so they made their way back to the creek junction and then went along both banks of the other creek. A small creek only a pace wide came down the slope on their left to flow into it. They noted this and pushed on until they came to a second creek. It was no larger, merely a trickle.

"Now, do we go back down the main creek fifty paces?" Peter asked.

"We must. It is the only way we can go downhill," Graham said.

They did this. This brought them to an area of steep banks covered with wait-a-while on one side and ferns on the other. For the next ten minutes they searched the banks and the bed of the creek. Stephen crawled from rock to rock looking in the bed of the creek for any signs of gold.

"This is hopeless!" Allison cried as she disentangled herself from a vine. "I'm getting sick of this. Can we go home now?"

Kylie felt her emotions seethe. She felt hurt that Allison did not want to go on. She also felt embarrassed that it was her enthusiasm that had led them all to the search.

They stopped to have another rest and to re-read the instructions. Then Graham, Peter and Uncle Bill went on up the creek to see if there was a second creek on the right bank. Kylie and Margaret got up and went after them, with the others reluctantly following a few minutes later.

There was a second creek, another tiny gully all choked with fallen logs and weeds. Once again, they searched. As they did, it began to drizzle rain. Raincoats were donned but it did not take long for the grumbles of Allison and Stephen to take effect. Uncle Bill supported them. "It's nearly two now. Time we started back."

"We can't just give up!" Kylie cried. She was on the edge of tears.

Uncle Bill gave her a sympathetic look. "We won't. But that is enough for today. Now we know what we are up against we can plan better. We will have another look tomorrow."

"Which way back?" Graham asked.

"The way we came, except we search the other bank of Christmas Creek on the way," Uncle Bill said.

This plan was put into action. As they re-crossed Christmas Creek the rain increased in strength till it was a heavy downpour. Kylie found it cold and started to shiver. Stephen muttered and grumbled and tried to prevent drops splashing in under his hat onto his glasses. Graham and Peter both ignored the rain, not even deigning to don raincoats.

It took them longer then they expected to get back to the 'Pride of Erin' mine. By then Kylie was shivering and her skin was covered in goose bumps. The group's spirits were right down as they trudged back along the old road with the rain drops rattling down on them and the surrounding leaves.

It was with sighs of relief that Uncle Bill's ute came into view. They were loaded in the back and Uncle Bill drove slowly back along the road to the old farm. Several times the ute's wheels slipped and it almost bogged a few times. Kylie saw the open country come into sight with mixed emotions. She was glad to be out of the jungle but very downcast that they had not found the gold.

Mrs Kirk and Gran were waiting in their car. Mrs Kirk bundled them into the car, Graham and Peter staying in the ute with Uncle Bill. The rain became heavier and the road was soon awash. They drove slowly back, the car slithering from side to side on the slopes. It took twenty minutes to travel the few kilometres back to the farm.

As they drove in, they saw a white ute parked there.

"Bert!" Allison cried.

Bert was sitting on the front veranda and gave them all a big grin. "Where have you been?" he asked as they dashed from the car to the veranda.

"In the jungle looking for that old gold mine," Allison replied. She proceeded to describe their day to Bert.

Kylie heard her and felt a twinge of concern. As Mrs Kirk bundled them all in to have hot showers and to change, Kylie took the first opportunity she could to get Allison aside.

"Allie, please don't tell Bert what we have been doing. It's a secret."

"Oh it is not!" Allison snorted. "Anyway, they have looked for it before you, and you gave them copies of the old diary. So they must know as much as we do."

"Yes but..." Kylie replied. She did not want to argue and was prevented from saying more as Bert came in talking to the boys.

Wet boots were taken off on the veranda and the children were sent to the shower. Kylie made Allison go first. While she was in the shower Margaret came over to Kylie.

"Cheer up, Ky. We will find your old gold mine. The boys had a good day anyway."

"Graham and Peter certainly did. I don't know about Stephen though," Kylie replied.

Margaret sniffed. "Who cares? I don't like him much."

Kylie agreed, then said. "Sorry you got all cold and wet."

"That's alright. We expected to. It was different. I'm glad I didn't live in the good old days."

Until Allison came out the girls discussed what it must have been like for the early pioneers. Allison was quick as she knew that Bert had to leave soon. Margaret was next, then Kylie. She found the hot shower heavenly and her spirits rose as she warmed up. Regretfully she turned the hot water off and dried herself. Five minutes later, clad in warm, dry clothes, she joined the others in the lounge.

Allison was sitting there close to Bert. Peter and Stephen were also there. Kylie sat beside Margaret until her mother called her to help with afternoon tea. By the time this was ready Graham had joined them.

When all were seated Bert said, "I came over to ask you all if you wanted to come to a New Year party on Thursday night."

"I thought you came over to see Allison," Peter joked.

Allison poked her tongue at him and blushed. Bert laughed and agreed; "I did. I certainly didn't come over to see you blokes. Anyway, what about it?"

Mrs Kirk asked about the party, "Who will be there? Where? What adults are supervising?"

Bert assured her that his mother and father would be there and that there would be no problems with alcohol, "Or anything like that."

"Oh please Mrs Kirk!" Allison begged, her eyes alight with anticipation. Watching her Kylie experienced another twinge of jealousy, tempered by pleasure at Allison's obvious happiness.

"Yes, alright," Mrs Kirk agreed. "We will all go."

"Ripper!" Bert exclaimed.

He gripped both of Allison's hands and his eyes danced with delight, causing Kylie another bout of jealousy.

Soon after that, Bert drained his tea up and stood up. "Well, thanks for the tea. I must get back for milking. Good luck with your gold prospecting, and don't get lost."

That set the boys off. They snorted indignation at the idea of them becoming lost, but the idea struck a chill into Kylie. She now knew it would be all too easy to get disoriented in that tangle of ridges and greenery.

As Kylie stood watching Allison saying farewell to Bert, she said to Margaret, "I wish I had a boyfriend like that."

Margaret sighed. "I wish I had a boyfriend!" She turned her head to look wistfully towards where Graham and the other boys were laughing and joking.

Kylie put her arm around her friend. "You'll be alright. Don't worry."

Margaret gave her a grateful smile. Graham called to them, "You two coming to help with the milking?"

That got them moving. They changed back into their wet clothes and went out to help Uncle Bill and the contract milker, a wiry young man in his twenties named Larry. With that many people the work was done quickly and they were finished by 6pm. Another hot shower and change of clothes followed, then tea.

After tea they sat around and discussed the day's explorations. Kylie was worried that the others might not want to go out again. To her relief Graham and Peter were more determined than ever to search. Once again, they laid out all the maps and re-read the old diary and letter and puzzled over where they should look next.

Kylie went to bed feeling baffled but determined.

The next day was almost a repeat of the first except that Gran and Mrs Kirk stayed home. Gran was very tired and had caught a chill. That made Kylie both worry and feel very guilty. Mrs Kirk helped to drive them to the old farm at 9 o'clock, but then went home again. The rain had stopped but it was overcast and likely to rain again at any time. They travelled in the ute to the same parking spot as the day before. Once again, Kylie worried that the utility might bog in the soft, muddy road but it got there without any real trouble.

Allison and Stephen were again not really interested but went along. Graham, Peter and Uncle Bill led the way. They returned to the 'Pride of Erin' and resumed the search. This time they went right up both the creeks they had searched the day before until these petered out in shallow trickles. Several times Uncle Bill used his pan to look for traces of 'colour' in the sand of the creek bed, or the black loamy soil of the banks.

As on the previous day it began to rain after lunch. Leeches bothered them and they became wet, cold, and irritable. Kylie saw several scrub turkeys and some sort of rat but otherwise the rainforest seemed to be devoid of life. The rain had driven the birds to cover.

After following every creek and gully upstream of the start point along both banks they returned to the 'Pride of Erin'. It was 3pm by then and Allison was obviously not amused. "I'm getting a cold," she sniffled.

The group set off back along the old timber road towards the ute in silence. Rain drizzled down and dripped from every leaf and branch. Kylie flicked off another wet leaf and tried to stop the water trickling down the back of her neck. She was feeling very despondent, as well as baffled. It seemed that, no matter how they followed those instructions, they ended up in the wrong place.

Peter, who was walking just in front of her suddenly stopped. Before she could stop herself, Kylie ran into him.

"What! What?" she said. She peered around him to where Graham, who was leading, had crouched down to look at something on the track.

"What is it?" Peter asked.

"Cigarette. And it is still smouldering," Graham replied.

They crowded closer to look. Kylie crouched and peered at the cigarette. As Graham had said it was still smouldering. Even as she saw it a wisp of smoke came from it and she saw a raindrop hit what was obviously dry paper.

"So what?" Allison asked.

But Kylie knew; and so did the boys. Already they were peering around them, their eyes searching the gloom of the undergrowth.

"There is someone else here," Graham said.

He picked up the cigarette, snuffed it out and slid it into the plastic map case he had in his left hand. From the tone of his voice and the way he looked around Kylie knew he thought it was serious and that made her scalp tingle. A feeling of chill up her spine made her shiver.

Margaret voiced her thoughts, "Do you think we are being watched by those men?"

Graham nodded. "Yes, I do."

Chapter 16

BAFFLED

Kylie stared around in alarm. "Do you think he is watching us?"

"Possibly," Graham agreed. That got them all looking anxiously into the surrounding jungle.

"Let's look," Stephen suggested.

Uncle Bill shook his head. "No! Go back to the ute. It might be quite innocent. It might just be people who are birdwatching or studying orchids," he said.

Graham scoffed. "Birdwatching! In this weather!" he cried. He crouched to study the leaf mould for tracks.

Uncle Bill was adamant. "Back to the ute. Even if it is the same man watching us, there isn't much we can do about it. Now get going. Here comes the rain again."

With obvious reluctance Graham straightened up and continued walking. Kylie saw that Margaret was biting her knuckles and had anxiety written all over her face. She was aware that her own heart was thumping fast and she knew she was scared. *I hope we don't meet those men,* she thought. The idea that they might be lurking watching them sent shivers up her back and made the jungle look even more gloomy and forbidding than usual.

They walked faster now, the cold rain helping. Graham kept studying the track for footprints, but the thick matt of dead leaves and sticks did not yield any clear prints. Once he stopped and pointed to a boot print in a patch of mud. They studied it but they could not decide if it was one of their own or not. Kylie tried to imagine what a confrontation with the men might be like. The thought made her feel sick in the stomach. As she walked along, she kept looking into the jungle on either side of the track and glancing back over her shoulder.

Ten minutes later they reached the ute at the old road junction. The vehicle appeared untouched. Kylie felt a surge of relief. Graham and Peter quickly scouted around it.

"Wheel tracks," Graham said, pointing down.

Before Uncle Bill could forbid it, Graham and Peter had moved off along the other old track. Kylie walked over and looked. Two tyre marks showed plainly in the mud. With her heart thumping with anxiety she followed the boys.

Fifty paces on, just out of sight around the bend in the track, was a cream-coloured utility. It was locked and the back was empty. To Kylie's relief the driver was not there.

Uncle Bill looked very thoughtful. "Could be anyone. This isn't private property," he pointed out.

Graham extracted his notebook from a plastic bag and wrote down the utility's registration number.

Uncle Bill pointed back. "Right, let's get back to our vehicle and get going."

Graham and Peter obviously wanted to look around but obeyed. They returned to the ute and climbed aboard. Five minutes later they were back out at the derelict old farm. Mrs Kirk was waiting there. Ten minutes later they were back at the farm.

As soon as they stopped Graham said to Uncle Bill, "You must ring the police, quickly."

"I will," Uncle Bill replied. "But don't exaggerate the incident. We have no proof anyone was there watching us. They might just have been bushwalkers."

"Who was watching you?" Mrs Kirk asked.

As Uncle Bill explained, Kylie groaned inwardly. *Now mum will ban us from going to look for the old mine.* She was already depressed with their second failure and she was feeling baffled and irritated at their inability to find it.

Milking began immediately. They all went out and helped bring in the cows. With so many workers the job was done in one hour instead of usual two. The miserable conditions of drizzle, mud and manure helped to speed the work. Afterwards, Kylie and the girls went straight back to the farmhouse for hot showers and a change of clothes.

Half an hour later, just on dusk, Kylie heard the boy's voices outside on the driveway. She looked out and saw that they were walking down the track from the top of the hill.

"Where have you boys been?" she asked.

"Just checking that bloke isn't around," Graham replied.

The very idea sent a shiver of fear through Kylie. She told the boys to have their showers and get ready for tea, then stood on the front porch and stared at the wall of rainforest at the end of the driveway. In the drizzle it looked black and sinister. She shivered and shook her head, feeling even more depressed and baffled.

Before she knew it she was crying. She stood and gripped the corner post and stared miserably into the cold wind. It had been a horrible day really. *All my great plans to save the farm. Just silly pipe dreams,* she thought unhappily.

Margaret appeared beside her. Kylie tried to hide her tears and pretend she was alright, but Margaret had seen. She put her arm around her, and said, "It'll be alright, Ky. The boys and Uncle Bill will keep those horrible men away."

Kylie nodded, sniffled, wiped her face and nodded. "It isn't just them, although I am scared because of them," she replied.

"What do the men want do you think?" Margaret asked.

"They want the gold obviously. They will take it off us when we find it. If we find it," Kylie replied.

"Oh Ky! We will find it. We will!" Margaret cried. She hugged Kylie and looked anxiously at her. "Don't give up Kylie. It is early days yet, and we shouldn't let a bit of rain put us off. It certainly hasn't put the boys off. They are like pigs in mud."

The simile made Kylie smile. "Are you saying Graham is a pig?"

Margaret wrinkled her nose and then grinned. "No. Yes. He can be. But he and Peter are having a whale of a time. Anyone can see that. And they aren't ready to give up."

"Maybe not. But we don't seem to be having much luck. Every time we try the instructions don't make sense," Kylie replied.

"We must be missing some clue," Margaret replied. "Let's read them all again and see what it might be."

Somewhat cheered, and certainly warmed by Margaret's obvious concern and friendship, Kylie allowed herself to be led inside. The girls gathered in the lounge and began going over all the instructions again. After tea the others all joined them and there was a general discussion of the search.

Uncle Bill had phoned the police and he rejoined them to say that the police would investigate and would keep them informed.

"So we still don't know who this man is that is watching us?" Stephen said.

"No," Uncle Bill replied.

"He wants the gold obviously," Stephen added.

Kylie wished he wouldn't mention it because she could see it made her mother very worried. *She will ban the search if she thinks it is dangerous,* she worried.

And that was just what Mrs Kirk suggested. Graham objected strongly. "Fair go, Mum! Anyway, we have to find the gold first. He won't bother us until then and we will be able to trick him."

"Oh, yes? How?" Mrs Kirk asked, anxiety adding a sharp tone of sarcasm to her voice.

"We could take the dogs next time," Graham suggested.

Uncle Bill shook his head. "We could but you are not allowed to take dogs into a National Park."

"And you shouldn't take them out in the wet all day, they will get sick," Allison added.

"So will you children," Mrs Kirk said. "If it is raining tomorrow, I don't think you should go out."

"Aw Mum!" Graham cried. "It could rain for days. This is the wet season."

"So? You can look again in the dry season," Mrs Kirk replied.

"But that is months away!" Graham said. "Someone else might find the gold mine before us then."

"Might. But people have looked for half a century with no luck so I don't see how you can expect to just walk out and go to the spot," Mrs Kirk replied. "Now, supper time, then bed."

Bafflement was Kylie's dominant emotion as she went to bed that night. After supper she cleaned her teeth, then sat and read the diary and letter again and tried to work out where they were going wrong. It was certainly a puzzle.

Whichever way we go the instructions don't seem to make any sense, she thought. *What are we doing wrong? Are we starting at the wrong place?*

When the lights were out, she lay awake for what seemed like hours. Her mind kept turning over the events of the last few days and the clues, but no answer came. She also found that any odd noise outside made her heart begin to pound. Images of the men creeping through the darkness towards the house filled her with fear. Once the dogs barked at something and went dashing off, but they stopped after a minute and came back.

Then the rain began again; heavy, drenching rain which drummed on the roof. It all added to her misery and depression, and she began to quietly cry again. Nothing seemed to be going right!

When they went out at 4:30am to bring in the cows, the rain had stopped and there was a thick mist. Kylie found this spooky, and she kept looking nervously around in case the horrible men were creeping up. All the while she was hoping that they would be allowed to go searching again.

To Kylie's relief, the sun came out while they were having breakfast. The fog cleared away to show a clear sky. Bartle Frere stood up bold and clear and everything looked as though it had been scrubbed clean, even the sky. Seeing this Kylie asked her mother if they could go to search.

Mrs Kirk studied the sky and looked worried. After talking to Uncle Bill for a minute she said yes. "But don't forget that you have a late night tonight. And you children stay together."

Mrs Kirk did not say so but Kylie knew she meant because of the man or men who were watching them. The explorers happily prepared and were soon ready. As before Mrs Kirk helped ferry them to the edge of the jungle. As soon as they had been dropped off, she reminded them of the pick-up time. She also cautioned them again to be careful.

"You be careful too mum," Kylie said. "Will you be alright at the farm with Gran?"

Mrs Kirk smiled. "We've got Larry the milker and the dogs too. And I agree with you that the men will not bother us till we find the gold."

Being reminded of the men made Margaret and Allison both look anxious. Kylie felt scared but tried not to show it. As Mrs Kirk drove off and they climbed into the ute Graham said, "We could set a trap to catch this guy if we wanted to."

Uncle Bill shook his head. "We will do nothing of the sort. That could lead to violence or worse. We will mind our own business and just keep our eyes open."

Graham wasn't ready to give up that easily. "Well, we could at least have a couple of us hide to watch and we could see who he is."

Once again, Uncle Bill vetoed the idea. "No. We are staying together in one big group. That is the safest."

Graham had to be content with that. Kylie noted that he spent a lot of time studying the ground for tracks. When they arrived at the old road junction the boys scouted quickly along the other track but there was no vehicle there.

"He will follow us in," Peter suggested.

"That means he has been watching to see if we leave the farm!" Kylie said, her blood chilling at the idea.

"Probably," Peter agreed.

"Stop talking about them," Uncle Bill said. "You will just scare yourselves. Now, what is the plan today?"

They agreed that perhaps they were not going far enough beyond Christmas Creek after crossing it. "The letter says to turn right at the 'Bright Smile' and we have been turning right at the first diggings we come to. They may not be the 'Bright Smile'," Peter suggested.

They acted on this. They walked along the old track to the 'Pride of Erin', then made their way down to Christmas Creek. After crossing the creek they went on following what might have been an old track uphill. After twenty minutes of quite steep climbing through thick jungle, which got them all sweating, they came to another of the earth contour drains. They scouted this both ways till they found some old diggings two hundred metres to the left. From there they tried to follow the instructions.

Almost at once they were puzzled. "If we go right from here, we go uphill," Peter said. "But the instructions tell us to cross Nugget Creek."

"Maybe that is Nugget Creek down there," Margaret said, pointing down to their left.

Graham shook his head. "How could it be? The instructions say to turn right."

"Even so, there is no point in going right because that will just take us up over this hill and down to the creek we have already searched twice," Peter said.

"I vote we go down to the left," Stephen said.

After some argument this was agreed on but it was not a happy party that forced its way down through the tangle to the other creek. This was almost identical to Christmas Creek. Once again, they searched along both banks upstream. They found several old diggings but could not decide if any of them was Frank's Claim. By then they were hot and frustrated.

Peter shook his head. "If we keep on going upstream, we will come to Swipers Flat," he said after studying the map.

"That was an old goldfield, wasn't it?" Margaret asked.

"Yes, it was," Uncle Bill replied. "Part of the goldfield discovered by Christy Palmerston back in the eighteen eighties."

"Wasn't your Grandad's goldfield only found in the nineteen twenties?" Peter asked.

"Thirties," Kylie replied. She bit her lip and shook her head in annoyance. No matter what they did it just did not seem to fit.

After some discussion they sat on the rocks in the creek bed and had their lunch. Stephen then devoted himself to panning for shows of colour in the stream and along its banks.

"You'd better not let the National Parks and Wildlife Rangers catch you doing that," Uncle Bill commented.

Stephen made a derisive sound and gestured at the surrounding jungle rising up on all sides. "I can just see them suddenly bursting out of this!"

After lunch they continued to search; first upstream, then back down to where they had first struck the creek. That gave them no joy so they continued on down to where the creek joined Christmas Creek and turned left to follow it back up to where they had come down from the 'Pride of Erin'. By then Kylie's high hopes of the morning had again fallen to a feeling of miserable defeat.

Baffled and frustrated the group made its way back up to the 'Pride of Erin' and then back along the old road. On the way, Graham and Peter scouted carefully for any sign that they were being stalked by the men, but they found no definite sign that they were.

By 4pm they were back at the edge of the jungle. Mrs Kirk was waiting and they quickly sorted themselves into two vehicle loads and set off. Fifteen minutes later they were back at the farm. After a quick drink they went out to help bring in the cows. Kylie noted that the three boys made a detour to check the edge of the jungle. Somehow, she did not care.

We aren't going to find the goldmine, she thought sadly.

Two hours of hard work had all the cows milked and calves fed. The group then made their way up to the farmhouse to wash and change. As they came in Gran met them.

"How did it go, dearie?" she asked Kylie.

Kylie shook her head and did not want to trust herself to speak she felt so upset about their failure.

Gran patted her shoulder. "Never mind, dearie. Better luck next time. Oh, and there is a big envelope there for you from the Mines Department. It came in the mail."

Kylie felt her hopes rise. She went through to the lounge and took up the envelope. It was a brown government one and the marking on it said 'Department of Mines and Energy'.

"What is it?" Margaret asked.

"I sent away for some maps. This must be them," Kylie replied.

They were. On opening the envelope Kylie found three maps. Two were photocopies and the third was a complete map. All were black and white survey maps which showed the names and numbers of mining leases and mines. Kylie felt her hopes rise again as she quickly scanned them. There were many more names than on the few maps they had been using, and the locations were much more accurately marked against the creeks and main roads.

Mrs Kirk came to look then said, "Never mind looking at that now Kylie. Get showered and changed. Don't forget we are going to town for the New Year party in an hour."

Kylie reluctantly tore herself away from the maps and went to the shower. Allison had just finished so she was able to go in straight away. After that it was a rush to get dressed and ready for the party. She wore a white T-shirt and jeans and took extra care over her appearance.

Allison was bubbling with excitement and kept babbling on about Bert. Margaret was quiet but also happy. Kylie felt her own spirits rise. Mrs Kirk began calling them out.

As they went out, Kylie found the boys studying the new maps. Peter was bent over the largest map. He frowned and pointed.

"I hate to say this but there is another 'Erin' mine marked on this map."

"Where?" Kylie asked. They crowded around to look.

"Here. Down in the Mulgrave Valley. Only it is just the 'Erin', not the 'Pride of Erin'," Peter said.

Stephen swore and muttered, "I hope we haven't been wasting our time thrashing about in the wrong bit of jungle!"

A horrible feeling that this indeed might have been the case made Kylie feel sick in the stomach. She wanted to stay home and study the map and re-read the books and clues, but her mother firmly vetoed this.

"Nonsense! You are not staying here on your own. Now get in the car or we will be late."

Kylie grabbed up the maps and slid them back into the envelope.

"What are you doing with them?" Peter asked.

"Taking them with me. I'm not leaving them here. The men might break in and steal them," Kylie replied.

"Oh piffle!" Stephen snorted.

"Oh come on!" Allison cried. "We will be late."

Graham grunted. "Do Bert good to wait," he commented.

"He'll have to wait anyway, or he'll end up in jail," Stephen added.

Both Margaret and Kylie snapped back. "Don't be disgusting Stephen. It's not like that."

"Oh yeah? What is it like then?"

"True love," Margaret replied. She then glanced at Graham, who affected not to notice.

Mrs Kirk called from outside and Uncle Bill appeared with the door keys in his hand. "Come on kids, get going."

They climbed into the cars and were soon on their way. As they drove along, Kylie's mind was like a squirming mess of worms. Had they been using the wrong 'Erin' mine as their start point?

It would explain why none of the clues seemed to make sense, she thought. The more she thought about it the higher her hopes rose. *We will find the gold mine yet!*

Chapter 17

NEW YEAR

The party was at a house in Malanda. The house was low-set brick in a side street. The owners were a couple called Mathieson who had two teenage children of their own, a boy named Tom and a thirteen-year-old girl named Karina. Karina was a vivacious blue-eyed blonde. She wore a silky white blouse and a short, tight-fitting, yellow skirt. Kylie at once saw Margaret had competition. As soon as Graham set eyes on Karina, she had his interest.

Kylie muttered angrily under her breath. *Oh the bonehead! Can't he see that he is hurting Margaret?*

Graham began to talk to Karina in a bright, cheerful voice. Kylie noted the worried little smile on Margaret's face as she tried to pretend nothing was wrong. They said hello to the parents, then were introduced to a couple of other local teenagers. To Kylie's vexation, a hulking great lump of a youth named Barry grinned at her and began to monopolise her in conversation. She tried to tactfully put him off but failed.

Great moronic lout! she thought. But Barry wouldn't take hint. He grinned even more and sat close to tell her all about how he went pig hunting on weekends and on how good his dogs were. *He obviously thinks he is God's gift to girls,* she thought ruefully.

As she carried on a polite conversation in a neutral voice, Kylie noted that Bert and Allison were seated side by side holding hands. Peter and Stephen were yarning in the corner and Margaret sat beside Kylie in silence.

More teenagers arrived and the adults retired to the kitchen as the music was turned up. The newcomers included two more girls and three boys. None of the boys appealed to Kylie but one of them liked her and began competing with Barry for her attention, much to her amusement and Barry's obvious annoyance. Then Stephen moved over and started joking with Karina. Graham was clearly not amused but it gave Kylie a spurt of malicious pleasure.

The party seemed to have no form to it. Kylie found this boring. She was used to parties where there were games and activities. Here they all just seemed to sit or stand and talk. *Or rather shout,* she thought as the music was turned up even louder.

This brought Uncle Bill through from the kitchen to have the volume turned down again. Some of the new arrivals scowled and then left but more came in to replace them. Kylie found herself talking to a tall, good-looking youth who must have been 17 or 18 and who was clearly half drunk. She could smell the beer on his breath when he leaned close to her. She did not like that and tried to put him off by being unresponsive.

More youths arrived. They had a carton of beer. At that Kylie got up and went through into the kitchen to join the adults. Mrs Kirk raised her eyebrows.

"Anything wrong dear?"

"There's a horrible boy pestering me," Kylie replied. She did not want to dob about the alcohol.

Mrs Kirk smiled. "That is part of life, I'm afraid. A girl has to kiss a lot of toads before she finds a prince."

Kylie gave a wry smile. She had heard that bit of advice before. "His breath smells," she said.

At that moment, there was the sound of breaking glass followed by a chorus of yells and jeers from the lounge. The man who owned the house and Uncle Bill got up to investigate. They soon discovered the beer. There were raised voices for a while as they ordered the youths who were drinking to leave.

When they were gone, Kylie went back into the lounge and sat beside Peter. Margaret came over and joined them. Kylie noted that the good looking drunk was now gone but not Barry. He made a bee-line over to her and resumed his attempt to win on.

The party dragged on. Kylie became bored and then irritated and wished it would end. Finally she was rude to Barry, and he retired in a huff and tried to make a pass at Allison. Margaret nudged Kylie and giggled.

Kylie had to smile back. "Some hope, the stupid oaf," she said.

Bert was not amused either and he stood up, took Allison's hand and led her out to the front.

Margaret watched them. "Where are they going?" she whispered.

"To have a pash," Kylie replied.

She did not really know what that might be like, but she had a fair idea of what was involved. She tried to imagine this but found it off-putting. *I would have to be really in love,* she thought.

Margaret watched with interested eyes, and then said, "I wish I was going outside."

"There's Barry. He'll be in it," Kylie replied, knowing well what Margaret's response would be.

She was right. Margaret wrinkled her face up in disgust and said, "Oh yuk! Not with a creep like that. I meant with Graham."

Kylie smiled and patted her arm. "I know. I was just teasing. I'm bored. I wish they would do something else."

Luckily others felt the same. The suggestion was put that they walk down to the main street to see what was happening there.

"That is where everyone will be when midnight arrives," one of the local lads explained.

This meant getting the adults to agree. Kylie did the asking with Peter and Margaret. Mrs Kirk nodded. "Alright dear. But stay together and watch out for drunks. We will come down just before midnight."

After promising to all stay in a group they made their way out to the front. Outside it was much cooler, a sort of moist chill from the high humidity. Allison and Bert were there. They had obviously been kissing but were only sitting holding hands when the group came out the door.

"Come on," Kylie said. "We are all going down to the main street. And we promised mum to all stay together in a group."

"Spoil sport," Allison replied, but she grinned and got up to join them.

Bert also smiled and stood up too. He put his arm around Allison's shoulders and she put hers around his waist and snuggled her head onto his shoulder. They both looked very happy and once again Kylie felt jealous and left out.

She also noted that Margaret was trotting along beside Graham. It was so obvious to Kylie that she desperately wanted him to hold her hand that his obtuseness made her angry.

It was a cheerful and laughing group that turned the corner, to be greeted by a totally deserted main street. Nothing moved. There was not a person in sight. Not even a moving vehicle.

Stephen made a derisive snort. "Oh well, this has got to be where all the action is!" he said sarcastically.

"Not even a dog," Peter added with a laugh.

The only place where there was any sound was from the hotel at the corner. The group walked slowly along, the boys making smart remarks about the wild parties that were held in Malanda. They went slowly past the hotel and saw that it was full of people, all drinking and talking. A band was thumping away in a back room. Kylie peered in at the smoky and noisy interior of the bar and felt nothing but distaste.

At that moment Graham stopped and pointed to a vehicle parked among a row of cars and trucks outside the hotel.

"That ute. It's the one we saw in the jungle."

That got their attention. Peter bent to peer at the number plate.

"Are you sure?" Kylie asked, aware that her heart had begun to pound rapidly.

"Positive. Same colour, same registration number," Graham replied. Peter confirmed this. Kylie and Margaret both looked fearfully around.

"That means that the man who was watching us is here!" Kylie said.

"That's right," Peter agreed. "But I don't think he is watching us now. I reckon he's in town for the New Year celebrations."

"What is it?" Allison called. She and Bert had been dawdling behind, whispering sweet nothings to each other.

Kylie was about to explain when there was a burst of voices and noise from the door of the hotel. She looked around in alarm but it was only a group coming out. Then she caught her breath. One of the men was Cousin Victor. He and another man, a thin, weedy fellow in dirty lumberjack shirt and jeans, came walking across the footpath.

Victor saw them and stopped in surprise. He said, "G'day kids. G'day little brother. Having a good time?"

"You bet!" Bert said. The others made mumbled replies. Kylie was too stunned to speak.

Victor and the man walked to the ute. Kylie looked hard at the man in the light of the streetlights and thought he looked guilty, or at least anxious to be gone. He unlocked the door of the ute and climbed in. Victor stood leaning on the door talking to him as the group moved on.

For about twenty paces there was a sort of stunned silence before Graham turned to Bert. "Who's that bloke with Victor?"

Bert glanced back. "Oh him, that's Josh Doolan."

"How does Victor know him?" Graham continued.

Bert looked puzzled, aware that something had happened but not sure what. "They went to school together. Josh repairs our tractors, why?"

Graham shrugged. "Oh, nothing. Just wondered. Seen him about."

"Yeah, he lives here," Bert agreed.

Kylie met Graham's eye and he shook his head in warning. She then looked anxiously at Allison, who was looking very thoughtful. *What to do?* she wondered. *Should we say anything? How can we make sure Allison doesn't say anything?*

To Kylie it was an awful dilemma. It seemed very obvious to her that the whole mood of the group had dramatically changed, and she wondered if Bert had picked this up. It appeared he had not as he was again staring into Allison's eyes with loving adoration.

After another fifty paces the group stopped at a seat outside a cafe. While the others talked and joked Kylie wondered how to tactfully warn Allison not to say any more to Bert. Inside she was feeling guilty for having such horrible thoughts and doubts.

After a few minutes, Bert was drawn into some nonsense by the boys. Kylie at once took the opportunity to speak privately to Allison. "Allie, have you told Bert what we have been doing for the last three days?"

Allison looked worried and hurt. "Of course I have. He knew anyway. It wasn't a secret."

"Please don't tell him any more."

Margaret joined them. Allison was silent for a moment, then became angry. "Why not? We haven't found anything, and we won't!"

"Don't say anything about my new maps please," Kylie persisted.

"Why not? Don't you trust Bert?" Allison challenged.

Margaret answered. "He might tell Victor."

"So? He's his brother. Why shouldn't he?" Allison retorted angrily.

"Because... because he is talking to that man, that man in the ute back there," Kylie said. "He might say something to him."

"He won't!" Allison snapped.

Kylie saw that she was becoming distressed. She wondered what she could say to ease the situation, but Bert came walking back and she had no chance. Allison went to Bert and put her arms around him.

Bert looked at her with delight on his face. "Gee! That's nice," he said. "You should do that more often." Then he became aware she was upset. "What's wrong Allie?"

"Nothing," Allison sniffled into his shoulder. Bert looked at the others, but they could not say so he bent to comfort her.

Kylie was upset as well and wished the incident had not happened. She led Margaret to one side.

"What will we do?" Margaret asked.

Kylie shook her head. "There isn't much we can do. We will have to trust her. I don't want to spoil a friendship."

They left it at that. The boys knew something had happened but soon lost interest and forgot about it as they joked and sang. The group made its way back along the street on the other side of the road, ostensibly because they had already been along one side, but really to avoid the hotel. As they went back past it, Kylie looked anxiously across at the line of parked vehicles. From a distance she could see two men leaning on the back of a vehicle talking, but as they got closer she saw that they were two middle-aged farmers leaning on the tray of a truck. The ute was gone and there was no sign of Victor.

Soon afterwards, the adults arrived and other people began to appear. Several vehicles drove past. The noise from the hotel increased and people began to spill out of the bar onto the footpath. Singing and dancing began and loud music blared out. The teenagers joined in the shouted count-down to midnight. Screams of "Happy new year!" could be heard all over the town and people blew whistles, banged on pots and pans and tooted car horns.

Kylie tried to enter into the spirit of it all but had to fend off a hug and a kiss by Barry and by some other youth she had not even seen before. *Another year!* she thought. *And it is going to be a big one. I am starting Year 8.*

That was a sobering thought but when she noted Margaret still standing hopefully beside Graham another thought came to her. *Maybe he will start to take notice of Margaret if she is at High School too?*

Several times Graham had expressed fear of being accused of being a 'cradle snatcher' if he had a girl friend who was 'only a primary school kid' while he was in High School. Kylie thought this stupid as Margaret was only two years younger than Graham and she knew that it was considered perfectly normal for Year 12 boys to have Year 10 girlfriends.

This brooding was brought to an end by the adults wanting to go home. Kylie was ready to go and so was Margaret. Graham had given up on the local girls and the boys were just being silly. The only one who clearly wanted to stay was Allison. She appeared to have cheered up. She hugged Bert and they walked hand in hand at the rear all the way back to the house.

As they climbed into the cars, Allison hugged Bert and they had a passionate kiss. Uncle Bill called out in the end. "Righto kids, break it up. It isn't Christmas ya know. You can see him again tomorrow, Allie."

Stephen joined in, his voice tinged with jealous malice. "Yeah, let him come up for air!"

Allison poked her tongue at Stephen, gave Bert another kiss, then reluctantly climbed in beside Kylie.

Bert leaned on the car and looked in the window. "Will I see you tomorrow?" he asked Allison.

"If you want to," Allison said. She turned to Kylie. "We... we aren't going... going anywhere tomorrow, are we?"

"No," Kylie confirmed.

"Good," Bert said. He held Allison's hand till the car moved off.

It was a relatively silent group who returned to the farm. Most were now very tired, and Kylie was trying to decide how to let Allison know she was still her friend. In the end she decided the best policy was to act as though nothing had happened. To that end she began a light-hearted chatter about the people at the party, emphasizing Barry and his drunken mates to get the others laughing.

The plan seemed to work so that the girls went to bed without any more upsets. Kylie lay back and relaxed. Sleep claimed her within minutes.

Chapter 18

NEW PLANS

It had been decided, because of New Year, that there would be no exploration the next day. Kylie was glad of that. It gave her a chance to study the clues and to rethink their plans. She had been roused to help with the milking at 4am as usual and had gone to do this almost mechanically. The others helped and the job was done by 6:30am.

As they walked back up to the farmhouse, Graham pointed back at Bartle Frere. "Not a cloud in the sky. We should be going to explore."

Stephen yawned. "You can if you like. I'm going back to bed as soon as I've had breakfast."

The teenagers washed and made their way to the dining room. Kylie helped Margaret feed the dogs then joined the others. Breakfast was an almost silent meal. Kylie said little as she did not want to discuss what was on the top of her mind: what to do about Allison. To her relief no-one else said anything which could have caused a discussion.

Kylie tried to decide if there was an air of restraint among the others or not. *They are probably just tired,* she decided.

As soon as breakfast was over, the others all retired to their beds again. Kylie felt very tired but knew she would not sleep till she had studied the clues again. To save any problems she helped her mother wash up, then sat quietly until she was sure the others had gone back to sleep. Then she extracted the books, diary, letter, and maps.

The new map claimed her attention first and she scrutinized it carefully. Almost at once the name 'Erin Mine' stood out.

"The 'Erin Mine'," she muttered, rubbing the name with her finger. "And there is a 'Pride of Erin' mine and also a 'Hope of Erin' mine."

The 'Erin' was shown as being down close to the junction of the East and West Mulgrave, nearly ten kilometres from where they had been searching. She picked up Dempsey's book '*Old Mining Towns of North Queensland*' and leafed through it till she found the page she wanted. Then she settled to read.

Mulgrave Goldfield

In October 1879 alluvial gold was brought into Cairns from the Mulgrave River, a fast-flowing stream that tumbles down a corridor behind a spur of the Coast Range, just south of Cairns. Within weeks, 140 men were fighting the boiling, foaming water, searching for the golden treasure trapped in the crevices and potholes. At Upper Camp, poor alluvial deposits were soon depleted, but reefs were found lower down. Later, above Goldsborough, more reefs, worked between Tooheys and Butchers Creeks, were rich during their short lives. Fanningtown, later known as Goldsborough, was a lively place in its first few years with three hotels and several stores. Goldsborough was on the south bank of Tooheys Creek close to its junction with the river. About 500m up the south bank of the creek was the battery, and across the creek, the cemetery.

As she read this, Kylie became worried. 1879? She was sure she had read that the goldfield Grandad Hector had been working on was in the 1930s. She was also puzzled by the description of the place. She had been to Goldsborough on swims and picnics. A study of the map showed her that the place they called Goldsborough was in fact several kilometres downstream from the actual town site, which she now realised she had never visited.

There was the sound of footsteps and Graham came into the kitchen for a drink of water. He saw her and came over.

"What ya doin', sis?"

"Trying to work out where we should be looking. I was just reading about the gold rush in the Mulgrave Valley at Goldsborough." She showed him the passage and the locations of Toohey Creek and the old town. Graham took the book off her and sat down beside her to read.

Kylie was troubled by the lack of any reference to gold discoveries in the area of the two Mulgraves. She picked up her other book: '*Gold and Ghosts Volume 4*' and flicked it open at Chapter 6, which dealt with the Innisfail Mining District and which appeared, from the map, to cover the area she was interested in. While she was reading the Introduction, Peter came out and joined them.

Graham gave a few grunts while he read Dempsey. Then he held the book in front of her. "What about this, the Bartle Frere Goldfield?"

Kylie took it and read the section aloud. "The small Bartle Frere Field, found by Wilkie and Kraft in 1936 or 1937, is between the two heads of the Mulgrave- the North and South Mulgrave. Kraft's camp was on Krafts Creek at the foot of Coronation Hill. The gold was obtained from floaters- pieces of quartz lying about on the surface." She looked up. "The dates are wrong. Grandad found his gold in 1932. I checked with his diary, and the date on the letter confirms it."

"Maybe so," Graham said. "But there is a 'Krafts Camp' marked here on this old map and that is in the right area, just across the river from the 'Erin' mine on your Mines Department Map," Graham said. He held the map up for them both to see. Kylie noted the name 'Krafts Camp' on both maps and bit her lip. It was certainly exasperating. She bent back to reading 'Gold and Ghosts'.

"Here!" she cried happily, pointing to the page.

"Here what?" Stephen asked as he came in from the toilet.

Kylie held up the book. "It says here that: 'for at least fifty years rich alluvial gold was won from the river, but Bartle Frere was not 'officially' discovered until about 1931'. So it is the right area."

She passed the book over. Stephen took up Dempsey and read that. Peter and Graham both bent over the pages, Graham muttering while he read. Margaret appeared, yawning and rubbing her eyes. She plonked herself down beside Kylie.

Stephen held up the book and said, "I don't like the sound of this bit. It says: 'It can be described only as awful country. Everywhere, it is very steep, and normally rains every day, apart from a month or so in mid-winter'."

That caused a few wry faces. Graham shrugged. "Couldn't be much worse than the area we have been looking in."

"I wouldn't bet. That Top Camp is shown halfway up the side of Bartle Frere," Peter answered.

"The area we are looking at is in the bottom of the valley on the other side of the river," Kylie said.

"Could still be rough country. But are you sure it is the right area?" Peter asked.

"Yes, I am," Kylie replied. "Now some of the entries in Grandad's diary make more sense now. Listen to these. On the tenth of February he set out from the old farm to try a new area. He wrote: 'Walk all day. Camp on ridge.' Then the next day he said: 'Go down the track to the "Erin". Tough going in the wet.' Down to the 'Erin' you see. And he walked for two days."

Peter nodded and looked thoughtful. "Could be. You wouldn't say: 'went down to the 'Erin' when referring to the mine we went to."

"No," Kylie said. "But there's more. Listen. 'Twenty second of February. Frank needs to go to hospital. Help him pack and then take him down to Goldsborough'. Now I know where Goldsborough really is it makes sense. No-one from the goldfield up here would go all that way down the mountain. They would go to Malanda." To emphasise her point she indicated the places on the map. Then she went on, "He goes on to say: 'Spent the night there.' Then the next day he says he went back to Frank's camp and tidied up, then returned to his own camp. If the camp was up here, he would never do that in one day."

"Oh, he might," Graham said, estimating the distance.

Peter grunted. "Have to be bloody fit!" he commented.

"He probably was," Graham said.

"No he wasn't," Kylie said. "The next comment in his dairy says: 'very tired. Sick myself. Too ill to do any more today.' He didn't walk up the mountain."

"So where is the gold?" Stephen asked.

Kylie pointed to the map. "Somewhere up one of the creeks near here. See this claim, the 'Bright Smile'? It is mentioned in the diary, and in the letter. And there's one more clue here too. On the twenty ninth of February, after he found the gold, he set off home. He says: 'Post letter to Bert at the 'Erin'. Take the Christmas Creek Track but can hardly get up the hill. Spent the night in the scrub.' So he came up the mountain from somewhere down in the valley."

"That makes sense," Graham agreed. "Christmas Creek flows into the West Mulgrave."

"There isn't any track marked on the map," Stephen commented.

"I wouldn't put much score on that," Peter said. "What about all those ditches, flumes and so on we found? They weren't on the map either. Those old timers would have had tracks all over the place. You can bet they would have one connecting two goldfields."

They accepted this. Stephen said, "So what do we do now?"

Graham answered at once, "Organize an expedition to the Mulgrave Valley."

"We can't do that from here. There's no road," Peter said.

"Have to go in through Goldsborough and along past Kearneys Flats," Graham replied. "Along that road we followed on our Scout camp the year before last."

Peter nodded thoughtfully. "We may have to walk. I don't think you can drive cars in there."

"No. There was a locked gate wasn't there," Graham replied.

"Yes, and the road was badly eroded in places. It means a hike."

Graham visibly brightened at that. "Good idea."

Stephen frowned. "In this weather?" he asked.

"We can't afford to wait," Kylie said. "If we do then those men might beat us to it."

"How would they know where to go?" Peter asked.

Kylie wished she hadn't raised the subject, but now that she was pressed, she said, "From Cousin Victor."

Margaret looked surprised. "Do you think he is involved with them?"

Kylie pursed her lips and nodded her head. "It's possible."

"But how would he find out?" Margaret asked.

Stephen snorted and laughed sarcastically, then said, "From young Bert, via Allison."

"Oh she wouldn't tell!" Margaret defended.

"But she has!" Stephen cried.

"Well, she won't if we ask her not to," Kylie put in. She felt upset and saw that Margaret was looking anxious.

"I wouldn't bet," Graham said. There was a minute's uncomfortable silence.

"So what do we do about Allison?" Stephen asked.

"What do you mean?" Margaret asked.

Stephen made a face. "If she tells things to Bert then Victor might get to find out about them. How do we stop her doing that? I reckon we should cut her out."

Margaret was horrified. "Oh Stephen! That is horrible."

Stephen shrugged. "Maybe so, but it's a possibility."

The issue, once raised, had to be debated. Kylie felt quite upset about it but knew it had to be resolved. She said, "I think we have to trust Allison and just ask her not to give away our plans."

"But can she be trusted?" Stephen persisted. "She's a girl and her loyalty might be to her boyfriend."

"Don't be so sexist!" Kylie flared. "Just because she is a girl doesn't mean she can't keep a secret."

At that both Stephen and Graham snorted derisively.

"That will do," Peter said. "No need to argue. I agree with Kylie. Allison has been part of our team up to now and we can't suddenly just exclude her. She's a nice person and I think we must trust her."

"Well I don't!" Stephen snapped.

"We will take a vote on it," Peter replied. "Who is for Allie staying?"

Kylie put her hand up at once. So did Margaret and Peter. After a moment's hesitation, Graham did so as well. Stephen made a face and shrugged. "Let's hope you are right," he said.

"Okay, let's start planning," Peter said.

Margaret had been reading during this and she looked up and said, "I don't like this passage. It says that they all took up leases. 'Two thousand ounces went through the batteries. Every ounce was in floaters, the lot, and this right up near the top. But we never found the reef.' That sounds like we have a job ahead of us."

Kylie nodded. "We have, but we have Grandad's instructions."

Graham laughed. "We have been following them for three days!"

That caused the others to chuckle. Kylie remembered something she had read and skimmed through 'Gold and Ghosts'. "Listen to this. This is in 1931. 'At that time Messrs W. H. Kraft and J. Wilkie discovered alluvial gold in the gullies draining the hills on the Mulgrave side of Bartle Frere Mountain. Whilst working their find, the pair were constantly looking for its source and in 1935 discovered a white quartz reef crossing a gully in the area later designated as Lower Camp.' It goes on with more details, but obviously there are gold reefs there, and they aren't the ones found by Grandad Hector as they are on the other side of the river."

"So how do we get there?" Stephen asked.

At that moment Allison appeared, her face flushed from sleep. "Hi! What are you doing?" she asked.

There was a moment's uncomfortable silence, then Kylie answered. "We are planning our next expedition to try to find the gold," she replied.

"And you aren't to tell Bert," Stephen added.

Kylie was shocked at the bluntness of Stephen's statement. Allison looked a bit stunned and shook her head. "I won't," she replied.

Kylie intervened. "I asked Allie not to last night and she agreed. She won't, will you Allie?"

"No I won't," Allison replied. She looked embarrassed and annoyed. "I will ask Bert not to ask me about it."

"He might dump you then," Stephen said. "He is probably only taking you out so he can squeeze our secrets out of you."

Allison looked very hurt, and her eyes watered. "That's not true!" she cried. "He loves me."

Kylie was aghast at Stephen's cruelty and lack of tact. She snapped at him, "That was an awful thing to say Stephen. You are just jealous that Allison loves Bert."

"Aw crap!" Stephen retorted angrily. He flushed red and blinked angrily back through his glasses.

"No need to swear," Peter said. "Let's not have a fight. If Allison gives her word, I don't see a problem. So let's get on with some detailed planning. For example, how do we get to Kearneys Flat; and will we be allowed to go if we don't have an adult with us?"

That diverted the conversation. Graham took up the theme. "What if we ask Uncle Bill if he will come with us for a few days?"

"Can he get away from the farm for that long?" Margaret asked.

"Don't know. Let's ask him," Peter said.

The conversation settled down to details of when and how and all the clues had to be re-read and discussed. Throughout this Allison sat in silence. Later she spoke to Kylie alone.

"If there is a problem about trusting me, I won't come," she said.

Kylie shook her head. "Oh Allison, it is just that awful Stephen. He can be very cruel at times. I'd rather he didn't come. I want you to. You are my friend."

Allison looked doubtful. "Are you sure?"

"Of course I am," Kylie insisted.

Allison's eyes watered. "I... I'd like to come. I won't... won't have much to do when I go back to Cairns. My dad... my dad will be... busy," she said, her voice a choked whisper.

That confirmed the suspicion Kylie had that there was some serious family problem between Allison's father and mother, but she did not want to probe. She spontaneously hugged her instead and said, "Come with us. We'd love to have you along."

At that Allison burst into tears and clung to Kylie. Mrs Kirk came through from the kitchen and raised an eyebrow to Kylie who gave a slight shake of her head. After a few minutes Allison stopped crying and wiped her tears.

"Thanks," she sniffled. She blew her nose and wiped her tears. "I won't tell Bert. I promise."

Kylie nodded. "I know. Now come and help me feed the calves before that rain arrives."

Chapter 19

PREPARATIONS

For the remainder of the day the teenagers sat around the house talking, listening to music, and staring out the window at the rain. This had set in again as a torrential downpour.

Stephen looked out the window and shook his head. "It's a wonder that bloody mountain doesn't dissolve," he said, indicating Bartle Frere, which was dimly visible through the drifting curtains of 'liquid sunshine'.

"It is," Peter replied. "It is just taking a while to do it."

Kylie looked at her watch and stood up. "Who is coming out to help with the milking?" she asked.

There were groans and mumbles. Graham sat up. "Why don't we toss for it? It doesn't take six of us to bring in one herd. Two is enough."

This was voted a good idea. To Kylie's surprise Allison stood up and volunteered to go. To save any problems she then said she would go as well. The others accepted this.

"We will meet you down at the milking shed," Graham said.

"While you are waiting have a talk to Uncle Bill about our expedition to the Mulgrave," Kylie added.

Stephen stood up. "I'm going to phone my oldies and see if they can pick me up tomorrow. If we aren't going exploring again there are things I can do at home."

Privately Kylie thought that would be a good idea. She left them talking and went to put on her work clothes and raincoat. Allison did the same and the two friends went out into the rain. To her own surprise Kylie really enjoyed the next hour as they sloshed along the muddy lanes shooing the cows to the milking shed. Several times she laughed aloud and she smiled a lot.

"You are happy," Allison commented.

"Because we have worked out where the gold mine is, I suppose," Kylie replied.

"I'm glad," Allison said. "And Ky, thanks for sticking up for me back there. I was very hurt."

Kylie grunted and felt embarrassed. "That's alright. Forget it."

"I won't. But I won't say any more about it," Allison said.

The two girls walked along behind the cows in companionable silence, broken by an occasional 'shoo!' at some beast that wanted to stop to chew at the grass.

After milking and tea that evening, the group sat around the lounge room to discuss plans. Graham and Peter had explained the plan to Uncle Bill. He wanted to see all the evidence, so they went over it all again with Mrs Kirk and Gran present as well. At the end of the explanation Uncle Bill nodded thoughtfully and said, "That all makes sense. It is hopeful anyway."

"Can you come with us, Uncle Bill?" Graham asked.

Mrs Kirk spoke first. "What makes you think you are going at all? I think you should have asked me first. Your father and I have an interest in this too you know."

"Aw Mum, Dad will let us. He will think it is a good experience," Graham replied.

Mrs Kirk looked annoyed. "He might, but what about me?"

Kylie could see that Graham was liable to put her off-side with his usual bull-at-a-gate tactics so she spoke up, "We would very much like to do it mum. May we please?"

Mrs Kirk made a face. "And who are the adults who are going to be with you?"

"We don't need an adult with us mum," Graham put in. "We often go on hikes without any adult."

That was true but in this case cut no ice with Mrs Kirk. "This is a bit different, I think. You will be a long way from help if there is a problem and it is very rough country."

"Oh Mum! What could go wrong? Nothing is going to happen," Graham replied.

That did annoy her. "Rubbish! One of you could get hurt quite easily in that sort of environment. What if someone slips on wet rocks and breaks an arm or leg, or gets a whack on the head? No, you don't go if there are no adults."

"I would like to go," Uncle Bill said.

Mrs Kirk turned to him, a worried look on her face. "Bill, can you afford to take three or four days off just for a wild goose chase?"

"Yes. I will do what I have suggested and hire the contract milker again for a few days. I need the break, and I want to go."

That settled it. Mrs Kirk gave in and said yes. Kylie grinned with delight and bubbled with enthusiasm. That night she slept very soundly, sure that they would now succeed.

The next day followed a similar routine. They were up at 4am for milking followed by breakfast. The rain held off during this but clouds enveloped Bartle Frere and indicated more to come. Stephen packed up and they all sat and talked till his mother and father arrived. Morning tea followed.

While they were all sitting around having morning tea Stephen raised the question of whether he could join the others on their proposed expedition to the Mulgrave. That necessitated retelling the story of their search and of how they had now worked out where to go next.

In the middle of this they heard another car drive up and stop.

"I wonder who that is?" Mrs Kirk said. She stood and looked out. "Oh, it is only young Bert."

Kylie's heart rate shot up. Bert! "Oh Allison, stop him! We don't want him to hear all this."

Allison hurried out and the adults all looked mystified. "What is that all about?" Uncle Bill asked.

The teenagers squirmed uncomfortably. Kylie answered. "We don't want anyone to know our secret plans. We suspect that cousin Victor is looking for the gold too and Bert would tell him."

Mrs Kirk laughed. "Victor certainly is. His father and uncle searched for years and he has often talked about it."

"So we want our plans kept secret," Kylie replied. She turned to Mr and Mrs Bell. "Please don't talk about any of this please."

The Bells agreed not to and the issue of whether Stephen could join the expedition was resumed. Kylie rather hoped he wouldn't be allowed, but when they learned that Uncle Bill would be with them they gave their consent.

A few minutes later, Stephen left with his parents. As they drove off Allison and Bert came into view walking along the driveway hand in hand. A shower of rain caused them to run.

"Come in," Kylie said, giving Allison a meaningful glance. Allison gave an almost imperceptible shake of her head and Kylie relaxed.

"I can't stay long," Bert said as he seated himself in the lounge.

As he did, Kylie realised that all the maps lay open on the table. *Should I try to close them up?* she wondered. *Or will that be too obvious?*

Even as she tried to determine what to do Peter stepped forward and scooped the maps up into a bundle and walked out of the room with them. Bert did not appear to notice, being engaged in a conversation with Margaret about the party.

Mrs Kirk came in and asked Bert if he was staying for lunch. Bert shook his head. "I'd love to aunty, but I am expected back. I just wanted to see Allie. She tells me you are all going home in a few days."

"Yes, on Monday," Mrs Kirk confirmed.

Bert showed his disappointment. "Could Allison come for a drive or something tomorrow?"

Mrs Kirk shook her head. "Not on her own. She is too young. But you can all go somewhere as a group."

Bert looked at them hopefully. "What about that? What would you like to do?"

Graham shrugged and Kylie could not think of anything. Margaret pointed out the window to where the rain was still drizzling down. "It depends on the weather."

For a while they could not think of anything. It was Roger who suggested the plan they adopted. "There are steam trains which run from Atherton to Herberton on Sundays. I haven't done the trip yet. What about that?"

"When do they go?" Kylie asked. She wasn't fussed about the trains but any outing which helped Allison and Bert was a good idea.

Roger shook his head. "I can't remember exactly. The times are in the paper. I think it leaves Atherton at about ten a.m. and gets up to Herberton in time for lunch, then comes back to Atherton by about three."

"That sounds like a good idea," Kylie agreed. "We could be back in time for the afternoon milking. Can we do that mum?"

Mrs Kirk smiled and nodded. "I will see how much it costs. If it is too much, I will take it out of your pocket money."

Graham and Peter, who had returned, both enthusiastically agreed to the project. They were keen model railway buffs and were busy helping Roger to build a huge HO scale model railway under his house. The boys agreed it would be a good plan.

Bert then took his leave. Allison went out with him to say goodbye. Graham watched them talking close together. "I hope she doesn't let anything slip."

"She won't," Kylie insisted. "She has promised."

It was plain that the boys weren't entirely convinced but they let it go at that. The conversation returned to their proposed expedition. Bert drove off and Allison returned, her face aglow with happiness.

Lunch was served. Afterwards they were at a bit of a loose end because of the continuing rain. Most of them lay and read books or talked. Kylie, Allison, and Margaret helped Gran in the kitchen and learned to make pumpkin scones. The boys turned their noses up at this activity but ate the results happily enough.

The trip on the steam train was a big success. Straight after breakfast Bert arrived, driving a car. That allowed Uncle Bill to drive Gran to church. Mrs Kirk and Bert drove the teenagers to 'Platypus Station' on the southern outskirts of Atherton. Mrs Kirk then drove back to Malanda to go to church. The teenagers went on the train trip.

Kylie did not really enjoy the journey, but she did enjoy the outing. The carriages were open to the weather and there were a few showers of rain as the train puffed slowly and noisily along the swampy flats at Carrington, but once up on the mountain they were in a rain shadow and the weather was fine. The boys enjoyed themselves hugely, laughing and joking. Margaret sat and smiled at everything Graham said. Allison and Bert sat holding hands and whispering sweet nothings.

In Herberton it was cool and overcast. A few spits of rain fell but not enough to cause any problems. The group walked the streets, went to a cafe for food, then strolled back to the railway station. The boys all climbed onto the footplate of the locomotive, even Bert. Kylie stood next to the engine and was impressed by the heat and the apparent power of the smelly, steaming thing.

The return trip was uneventful. Mrs Kirk met them, and Bert helped to ferry them home. Allison and Bert were very quiet on the way back and there were a few tears when it came to the farewell at the farm.

"When will I see you again?" Bert asked. He looked very strained as well.

Kylie watched this and marvelled. *He must really be in love!*

Allison shook her head and wiped away a tear. "I don't know."

"Could I see you if I come down to Cairns?" Bert asked.

It must be love! Kylie decided. *If he is willing to drive all that way.*

"I suppose so," Allison replied. She now looked very unhappy.

"When? Next week?" Bert asked.

"No, not next week. We are going looking for the gold... er... Oh... er... We won't be there. We are going away," Allison concluded lamely.

"Allie!" Graham growled. Kylie groaned inwardly.

Bert appeared not to notice. Instead he asked again when he might see her. "Will you be away all week?"

Allison gave Kylie a guilty glance, then said, "We leave on Thursday."

"Then I will be down on Wednesday," Bert said. "I will convince mum there are important reasons for us to drive all the way to Cairns."

Allison was now bright pink. To Kylie she appeared to glow, mostly because of the obvious affection and adoration being lavished on her. Bert told her he loved her, ignoring the audience.

Soon after Bert drove off. Allison turned to the others looking very upset. "I'm sorry. I didn't mean to say anything." Then she burst into tears and fled inside.

Kylie and Margaret followed her in. They found Allison sobbing in the bedroom. Kylie put her arm around her and comforted her.

"Hush! Sssh! It's alright. It was a natural thing to do. Don't cry Allie."

Allison looked up, her face streaked by tears. "I'm sorry. But I do want to see Bert again. I really want to stay here with him."

Margaret and Kylie both hugged and patted her. It was obvious that Allison was very much in love, and also very upset. They calmed her after a while and the three girls went for a short walk along the road, leaving the boys playing a game in the lounge room.

The afternoon and evening seemed to speed past. The rain continued, making milking a miserable experience. Bedtime found them all tired and more than ready to sleep. Next morning they were up at 4am as usual for the milking. The rain still drizzled and it was cold and gloomy.

As they sat eating breakfast Uncle Bill thanked them for their help. He added, "You have been a great help. It has certainly made the milking easy. You kids can come any time you like if you work like that."

That pleased and embarrassed them. Kylie was already feeling fragile as she loved visiting the farm and now the parting was upon them. When they loaded the cars she found she was on the edge of tears. Roger's parents had driven up to collect him and Graham and Peter went with them. Allison and Margaret went with Kylie in Mrs Kirk's car.

There were tearful farewells. Kylie clung to Gran and wept. She had a secret fear that Gran would die before she saw her again, which did not make it any easier. She knew she had this fear on every visit but that did not help.

Gran patted her hair. "See you next time little baby," she said to her. Kylie nodded and sniffled and did not at all resent being called a little baby by Gran. Then they were in the cars and driving through the rain away from the farm.

As the car went down the long slope away from the farm, Allison looked out and said, "I loved that holiday, Kylie. You are very lucky to have such a wonderful Gran."

Margaret seconded this. "She is wonderful. She makes you feel so welcome and treats you just like one of the family."

That embarrassed Kylie and she said, "You only like it because of the boys."

Margaret laughed and Allison smiled. They then discussed boys as they drove along, till Mrs Kirk reminded them that some boys often only want one thing from a girl. That made Kylie blush and the three girls giggled and gave each other secret glances.

The road they followed did not go past the Reid's farm, which Kylie thought was just as well. That would just have made it harder emotionally. They drove north past North Johnston to the Gillies Highway and then east past Lake Eacham and Lake Barrine. Then it was down the 16 kilometres of winding road into the Mulgrave Valley.

As they went down, they came out under the low cloud and were able to see the whole length of the valley. That woke Kylie's interest in the gold mine. She looked out at the rain-shrouded valley below and wondered what it would be like. *We will definitely find that gold mine this time!* she vowed.

Allison was carsick after a while, and they were all glad to reach Little Mulgrave at the bottom of the valley. After that it was a quick half hour drive to Cairns.

In Cairns it was raining and overcast but that did not depress Kylie. It was nice to be home. They dropped Allison off first, with much discussion of times to meet the next day. Margaret was taken home next.

She obviously did not want to go. Not that she didn't love her parents. "I just want to be with Graham," she said.

Mrs Kirk laughed. "You are too young Margaret. Don't rush it. And you be careful, or you might see too much of him and then both of you might regret it."

Margaret blushed bright pink and Kylie laughed. "Yes Margaret, you are too big to have baths with boys now." That reference to the incident the previous year when she had been found in the bath with Graham made Margaret blush even more. She poked her tongue.

"See you tomorrow," she said and then she fled inside.

Then it was home. For Kylie that was wonderful. Her first action was to dump her belongings in her room, then she ran across the road to get the pets. 'Skip' the fox terrier was the first to meet her there. She jumped up and ran towards Kylie, barking excitedly. Kylie scooped the dog up and hugged her. The dog wriggled so much that Kylie could hardly hold her. There were snuffles and licks and much tail wagging and patting.

Mrs Marshall, the neighbour who had been minding the pets, came to see what all the noise was about and also gushed a welcome. She went and got the budgerigar cage and Kylie had to chirp and tweet at them for a few minutes, to the jealous annoyance of Skip.

Mrs Marshall handed the cage to her. "Here you are dearie. The cat is round the place somewhere. I saw him at breakfast time."

"Thanks Mrs Marshall. He will come home at teatime," Kylie replied. She wasn't worried about the cat. 'Claud' was not her favourite.

She returned home with Skip and the budgerigars. Skip repeated her welcoming performance for the others, then settled on the floor of the lounge as though all the world was now right. Unpacking and cleaning then began. Every single item of clothing worn in the jungle was placed in the washing machine and then in the tumble drier. Graham took the opportunity to lay out all his hiking kit on the concrete floor in the 'Ship Room', a large room under the house where he kept his models and where the boys played games.

The cat did appear at teatime as predicted. Kylie stroked him but Graham just ignored him. He didn't like the cat much. The evening was a quiet one. Kylie was glad to be home and found she felt very tired. Graham became absorbed in a book, then in working on a model of a battleship that he was building. Kylie was glad to go early to bed.

Tuesday was washing, cleaning, shopping, and chores. Kylie had to wash the dog and then the cat, clean the budgerigar cage, tidy and vacuum her room, water their father's orchids under the front of the house, and do a dozen other small tasks. Graham had to mow the lawn, trim the creeper from the side of the house, then prune a tree ('Good practice for cutting your way through the jungle,' Mrs Kirk said).

On Wednesday the friends all came over. They gathered on the front veranda to talk and listen to music. Margaret sat on Graham's bed reading while he worked on his model ship. Stephen, Roger, and Peter sat on chairs nearby studying the maps of the Mulgrave Valley and Kylie walked back and forth from her room to the front wondering if Allison was allowed to come.

When she had not arrived by 10am, Kylie went to telephone to see if she was allowed. To her relief, Allison answered the phone and said she was on her way. Twenty minutes later she was dropped off by her father. Kylie badly wanted to know how things were in Allison's family but was careful not to ask or hint.

No sooner had Allison seated herself beside Margaret than a car pulled up out the front. Kylie stood and looked out.

"Who is it?" Margaret asked.

"Bert," Kylie replied. "It must be love. He wasn't joking at all then."

Allison blushed and glowed. She stood and went to the door to greet him. Graham turned and said to Peter, "You'd better put those maps out of sight before he arrives. It's bad enough that he knows we are going. We don't want him to know where."

Peter scooped the maps into a bundle, folding them quickly. Graham had the topographic map on his desk, folded army-style with the part of the map he wanted on the outside. He tossed it to Peter. "Stick this with the others."

Peter missed the catch and dropped the map. He stood and bent to pick it up just as Bert came up the front steps. As quickly as he could Peter added the map to the bundle. These were placed in a cardboard folder. Peter walked over to put them out of sight as Bert greeted them. At that moment Skip woke from her slumbers under the table. Realizing that a stranger had arrived and mindful of her duty as a good guard dog she sprang out barking, running between Peter's legs as he did so.

Peter tripped. As he stumbled, he reached out to steady himself on the table. In doing so he lost his grip on the folder which fell to the floor. The maps spilled out of it at Bert's feet.

Bert helped steady him. "Hey, I don't mind Allie throwing herself at me," he said with a grin. He released Allison and bent to help Peter pick up the maps.

Oh no! Kylie thought. *Perhaps he won't notice where they are of.*

Bert obviously did. He straightened up with the old mining map in his hand. From the bed Kylie could see the pencil circle around the mines in the Mulgrave Valley and she could also see that Bert was staring at them. He gave a grin and handed the map to Peter. Peter was flustered and obviously angry with himself. Skip did not help by continuing to bark and by scattering the other maps more in her excitement.

Bert bent to ruffle Skip's ears. "Good dog! What's your name?" he asked. Kylie could see the topographic map lying right next to him. Peter scooped it up and hastily passed the bundle to Graham, who shoved them in a drawer.

"Her name is 'Skipper'," Kylie answered. "Good dog, Skip. Down girl! Down!"

"Yes, she is a good dog," Bert agreed with a smile.

Chapter 20

KEARNEYS FLATS

B ert appeared not to be interested. He turned to Graham and said, "I hear you have lots of model ships. Could I have a look at them?"

Graham nodded. Normally he was sensitive and defensive about his models, but they seemed a good way to divert things. "They are downstairs." He stood and led the way down the front stairs to the Ship Room.

As soon as Bert was out of hearing, Stephen said sarcastically, "Well done Pete! That gave the game away."

Peter flushed and replied defensively, "It wasn't my fault. Skip is the real villain, aren't you doggie?"

Skip, on hearing her name, looked up and wagged her tail. Peter bent and gave her a friendly pat. Kylie touched Peter's arm. "It doesn't matter. Bert may not have noticed."

Peter made a face. "I think he did. Let's hope we find the treasure before the opposition."

He turned and went down the stairs, followed by the others.

The 'Ship Room' took up nearly half the area under the high-set house. It measured ten metres by twelve and had a concrete floor and timber slats for walls. On the floor were dozens of 'scratch-built' models made from timber, balsa wood, cardboard and odds and ends. They were of 20th Century warships on a scale of 1:240. Also displayed on the floor were hundreds of tiny model tanks, trucks and aeroplanes, all made of balsa wood and cardboard.

Bert looked around in amazement. "What's all this then?" he asked.

Graham blushed and shrugged. "Just a game we play," he replied. He was embarrassed to be found to be still playing such games at his age. "A lot of the models belong to Peter and my brother Alex. It is something we did a few years ago and haven't done much of late."

"They look good models," Bert said, and knelt to study them.

Graham then felt constrained to show off his better models. While doing this Bert spied dozens of old sailing ship models stored on tables in the back corner. These had to be inspected next. After that they group went back upstairs and Bert said hello to Mrs Kirk. Morning tea followed.

After that, the girls and Bert went shopping leaving the boys to talk and plan. Kylie made sure that Bert and Allison were able to be on their own as much as possible.

"Are you buying food for your trip?" Bert asked.

That caused a moment's silence. Allison answered. "Yes, we are, and you aren't to tell anyone about it. Promise."

Bert laughed and gripped her hands. Kylie thought they looked so good together, a perfect match. *I hope it lasts,* she told herself.

Bert and Allison wandered off hand in hand after agreeing where and when to meet up. This allowed Margaret and Kylie to get on with their shopping. Mrs Kirk did the weekly grocery shopping at the same time. Afterwards they all met up at a coffee shop where Bert and Allison sat, deep in earnest conversation.

They drove back home and unpacked. Lunch followed, then the teenagers all went for a walk to the park and that allowed Allison and Bert to be alone for a bit more. All too soon, in Kylie's opinion, Bert had to say goodbye.

"If I don't go now, I won't be back in time for milking," he explained. He turned back to Allison. "When will I see you again?"

"Next week?" Allison suggested, half-turning towards Kylie for confirmation. Kylie nodded. She thought, but did not say: *If we haven't found the gold in a week we won't ever.*

Bert gave Allison a very tender and lingering kiss farewell. Both Kylie and Margaret watched with hungry interest while the boys made rude comments and 'yuk' noises. Bert just grinned and kissed Allison again, to her embarrassment and delight. Then he climbed into his car and drove off.

"Good!" Graham cried. "Now we can talk freely."

Kylie could have hit him as she could see that Allison was very fragile, her bottom lip trembling. The grouped settled to discussing arrangements for the following day. The boys still hadn't done their shopping for food, batteries and so on and they prepared to do this.

"Afternoon tea first," Roger suggested.

They took up this idea and trooped through to the kitchen. Mrs Kirk was there listening to the radio. She looked up as they came in and said,

"You children may not be going yet. If this rain keeps up the roads may be cut by flooding."

Kylie felt a stab of alarm. "Oh Mum, it hasn't rained much today."

"Maybe not, but I will be keeping a close eye on the weather. Now, when you boys are ready we will go and buy your food."

Shopping took the boys away for two hours. While they were gone the girls talked, played with the pets, and helped Kylie pack. When Mrs Kirk and the boys returned it was time for Allison and Margaret to go home. Mrs Kirk unloaded the boys and drove the girls home. Kylie noted that Allison was looking very fragile and on the edge of tears. As Allison climbed out of the car Kylie squeezed her hand.

"It will be alright Allie. You will see Bert next week."

Allison smiled, but it did not reach her eyes. "Yes, but I am wondering how we will see each other from then on. It is a long way from Malanda to here."

Kylie could only nod. She had wondered the same thing herself. All the old sayings such as 'love will find a way' ran through her mind, but so did something else she had heard one of the boys say once about a relationship between a boy in Cairns and a girl in Brisbane. 'GBI' they had called it- geographically bloody impossible. That was a depressing thought, but she did not voice it.

That evening there was no rain and that cheered her up. When she woke the next morning, it was sunny and clear. As soon as Kylie went to the kitchen for breakfast, she at once pointed this out to her mother.

Mrs Kirk shook her head. "Don't speak too soon. I've just been listening to the radio and there is a 'Low' in the Coral Sea. That could mean a lot of rain, or even a cyclone."

Graham looked up from his bowl of cereal. "That won't bother us mum. We will just keep listening to the radio and if things get bad we will drive home. It is only an hour from the Mulgrave to here."

Mrs Kirk frowned. "You may be walking in the rainforest so it could take hours more than that."

Graham shook his head. "Oh Mum, there will be plenty of time. They track cyclones very carefully with satellites and radar so we will get plenty of warning," he replied.

Mrs Kirk, as a ship captain's wife, was well aware of this, but she still wasn't happy. "I will talk to Bill when he arrives."

It was left at that until Uncle Bill arrived at 8:30 am. To the relief of the children he agreed with them. "We will keep tabs on any weather problems," he promised Mrs Kirk.

They loaded their gear into the cars, said goodbye to the puzzled pets once again, and drove off to collect the others. Peter's mother was also helping to ferry them to the Mulgrave valley and she had picked up Roger. Stephen went with Uncle Bill and Margaret and Allison went with Mrs Kirk.

All were ready and loaded by 9:30. The three cars set off in convoy. The first part of the drive- from Cairns to Gordonvale- Kylie did not enjoy. She never did- too much rush and heavy traffic. It wasn't till they turned off the Bruce Highway at Gordonvale onto the Gillies Highway that she relaxed and started to enjoy the drive. From then on, she stared out the window at the mountains which towered on either side. It was a pretty drive, particularly through the Mulgrave National Park.

At Petes Bridge they turned left off the highway and crossed the Mulgrave. Kylie noted that the river was fairly full but was flowing clear and wasn't obviously in flood. That was a relief as she had been worried, not just that her mother might veto the trip, but that they might not be able to ford the river to get to the area they wanted to search.

The road wound up over a high, wide ridge through sugar cane farms, then down to recross the Mulgrave again at The Fisheries. This bridge was a hundred metres long, a low concrete structure, and the river looked much higher and fuller here and Mrs Kirk frowned and muttered as the water was nearly lapping the bridge. After that the road ran through rainforest studded with houses until coming out on a wide flat covered with sugar cane. This was the area Kylie had always called 'Goldsborough' but she now knew that was wrong. Goldsborough was at the far end of the open cane farm area. Before reaching this they passed a line of houses, then turned left to cross the river for a third time.

Kylie looked out and up at the mountains which now towered up on either side. *You really know you are in a valley now,* she thought. She studied the steep slopes which rose a kilometre to the west and was surprised to see that they were not covered in rainforest as she had supposed, but in fairly open savannah woodland. A check of the range to the east showed it was thickly clad in jungle. *Must be a rain shadow or something,* she decided.

The river at the third bridge was an angry spate of white water and jagged rocks. That worried Kylie but her mother seemed to be busy driving on the narrow concrete bridge. The road then wound uphill, first through a belt of fairly thick eucalyptus forest, then into true rainforest again. The rainforest hemmed the road in all the way to Kearneys Flats.

They arrived at the National Park camping area. Uncle Bill was waiting there, his ute parked under some trees beside a toilet block. They pulled up and climbed out.

"You can't drive any further," Uncle Bill explained, after greetings. "There is a locked gate."

Graham nodded. "We know. We did a Scout hike through here a couple of years ago," he replied.

"You had better go to the toilet here," Uncle Bill added, looking at the girls. "After this it will be squatting in the bush."

"Oh yuk! Come on Kylie," Allison said.

Gear was unloaded and sorted. The adults talked and when Kylie came back from the toilet she overheard her mother saying, "Well, keep listening to the radio. I don't want you flooded in."

Uncle Bill nodded. "I've got a radio in my pack. We will be careful, don't worry."

There were farewells and packs and webbing were pulled on. Kylie was unpleasantly surprised at how heavy her pack was. It hadn't seemed that heavy when she had tried it at home. She returned a kiss to her mother and started walking. As she did, her spirits lifted even higher.

We are on the way. Now we will find the gold!

The boys were already twenty metres ahead, clad in a mixture of cadet and ex-army gear and laden with their army webbing and packs. Uncle Bill wore old overalls and had a very old army pack of the jute variety, with a blanket roll lashed to it. Kylie wore jeans and a long-sleeved blue shirt and cloth hat. Margaret was similarly clad except she wore an old jungle green shirt. Allison had a white shirt, which Kylie privately thought she would soon regret.

After a hundred paces they came to the gate. It was at the northern end of a large grassy clearing. They climbed over easily and continued on, out into the open.

"This is the actual Kearneys Flat," Graham explained. He had his map out and was following their progress almost step by step.

A sign pointing left said: KEARNEYS FALLS.

"Are we going to look at that?" Roger asked.

Graham shook his head. "No time. We have to walk all the way to the end of the valley. Anyway, we've been up it before."

"We haven't," Margaret replied, already puffing and perspiring.

"Never mind. We will come here for a picnic one day," Graham replied.

"Is that a promise?" Margaret asked, her face dimpling into a mischievous grin.

Graham snorted and started walking again. Kylie grinned at Margaret. *He likes her really. One day he will realise she is the girl for him,* she thought happily.

The road had deteriorated to a rough and rutted muddy track which led across the clearing. Out in the open, the sun struck them with particular force and they were soon all sweating. Kylie used her cloth hat to wipe perspiration off her face. She looked up at the mountains which now towered up on both sides. She noted that the slopes on her right were now also covered with thick rainforest.

That is where we are going, she mused. *Oh well!*

The road re-entered rainforest and that was immediate relief as it gave them shade. The road was still in poor condition, with lots of deadfall and sticks on the surface.

"This road doesn't get much use," Peter commented.

"No," Graham agreed. "In a few years they won't be able to get a vehicle along it at all."

Kylie pointed down the slope to their right. "There is the river down there."

The road ran along a hundred paces up from the river. They got glimpses of it from time to time but could hear it the whole time. The walk settled down to a plod as far as Kylie was concerned. Her shoulder muscles began to ache and chafing started under her arms and between her legs.

The group crossed a small creek which was flowing just enough to wet their ankles. Kylie managed to step from rock to rock but the boys just tramped through with their army boots.

Margaret looked along the small creek. "This is pretty," she called. She was puffing gamely along behind Kylie.

Kylie had to agree. There were ferns and reeds, moss, bright orange lichens, butterflies with blue wings and butterflies with yellow and black wings. She started to hope they would have a rest soon but knew the boys would pour scorn on the idea so hoisted her pack to a more comfortable position and plodded on.

They walked for the next two hours before stopping at another little creek for lunch. By then Kylie's shoulder muscles ached and she was developing blisters on both feet. Worse, she was starting to chafe under the armpits as the perspiration-soaked cloth of her shirt rubbed on her skin. Lunch for Kylie was two chicken sandwiches and a drink of cordial.

Margaret and Allison were both also looking quite worn and both let out loud groans when it was time to resume the march. However, they shouldered their packs and plodded along gamely. Graham, Peter and Stephen walked so fast they were often out of sight ahead, but Roger and Uncle Bill stayed with the girls. The road led on through thick rainforest and in places it was blocked by fallen trees. Undergrowth was now sprouting through the road surface.

From time to time they got glimpses of steep, jungle-clad slopes towering above them on both sides. Every time they did Kylie thought of the description she had read. *Truly awful country. It looks it,* she thought. It made her bite her lip with anxiety. With every kilometre the feeling grew in her that they were plunging deep into the heart of a true wilderness. *We are very isolated. I hope there aren't any accidents.*

They saw no other people and did not pass a single sign of human habitation. Only the road and an occasional overgrown clearing attested to the fact that people had once toiled here to win the gold and timber from the jungle.

"Bartle Frere," Graham called from the next bend.

He stood and pointed up. As she reached the bend and took in the view Kylie felt a chill of fear grip her heart. The massive bulk of the mountain seemed to tower up and fill half the sky. It blocked their path in the direction she was looking although she knew there was a low saddle between it and the Bellenden Ker Range to the east. As they walked on, she saw parts of this from time to time but mostly the thick vegetation restricted her vision along the road to about a hundred metres.

The road came down beside the river for a stretch and Kylie was dismayed to see a flood of white foam tumbling over rapids.

"How will we get across that?" she asked at their next stop.

"It should be only half that size once we get up past the junction of the East and West Mulgrave," Uncle Bill said. He had also been anxiously scrutinising the river. "If it is too deep then we will not try to cross."

That was a blow and Kylie fervently hoped the theory would be correct. In the event it was. After another half hour they came to where a concrete causeway led across. The causeway was covered by water which looked to be no more than knee deep.

"East Mulgrave," Graham said. "We are up above the junction. The main part of the old goldfield was up on that big ridge ahead of us."

Kylie lifted her eyes above the treetops on the other bank and shook her head. *Truly awful country alright!* she thought.

Uncle Bill insisted they rest. Packs were dropped while he took off his boots and tested the depth of water, and the strength of the current on the causeway. Kylie watched anxiously while he waded out into the swiftly flowing water.

To her relief, it only came up to Uncle Bill's calves and he easily crossed. However, when he returned, he said, "I will carry all the packs across. You kids take off your boots. If you slip in, then swim with the current downstream to the nearest bank."

Kylie stared at the tumbling water which foamed over rocks downstream of the causeway and knew she was scared. Margaret was also very worried. Uncle Bill insisted it was safe. "If it wasn't I wouldn't let you try," he explained.

"What if there is more rain and the river rises? We could be trapped," Stephen said. That idea sent a chill through Kylie as well.

Uncle Bill made a face and said, "That is why we must keep tabs on the weather. Now, give me your pack Kylie."

Half an hour later they were all on the other bank. Uncle Bill had held Kylie's hand as they waded across, which was not as bad as she had feared. Rather it was the unexpected coldness that caught her attention.

Uncle Bill chuckled at this. "It is flowing down off the highest mountain in Queensland," he reminded her.

On the other side they paused to have another drink before pulling on boots and packs. As she swung her pack on Kylie looked around at the jungle and the foaming river and felt a surge of excitement.

The real search begins now! she thought happily.

Chapter 21

BELOW BARTLE FRERE

From the causeway onwards the road deteriorated dramatically. It was deeply eroded, blocked by fallen trees, and overgrown wherever sunlight penetrated. Kylie shivered with apprehension.

We are right in the middle of the jungle now, she told herself. It seemed a very long way back to the nearest civilization. *I hope nothing goes wrong.*

Five hundred metres further on they came to a creek. Graham had been walking with his map in his hand. He pointed up the creek to the left. "Kraft Creek. There were diggings here."

Kylie looked around but could see no sign that the place had ever been anything but virgin jungle.

Peter shook his head. "You wouldn't think it," he commented.

"Where was the main gold field?" Margaret asked.

Graham again pointed up the creek. "Up this creek and on the ridge beyond it."

"Do we have to go up there?" Allison asked. She looked very tired and strained.

Graham shook his head. "No. The diggings we are interested in, the nineteen thirty ones are the other way, across the West Mulgrave; or at least I think so."

"Why do you say: 'think so'?" Allison asked.

"Because neither the old diary nor the letter actually mentions the Mulgrave," Graham replied. "All it says is: cross the main stream."

"Does it? I can't remember," Margaret said, looking at Kylie.

Kylie took out the copy of the old letter. The page was now soiled and crumpled and a bit hard to read.

As they crowded round to read it Uncle Bill said, "You'd better keep that sheet of paper in a plastic bag Kylie. We will look a bit silly if we have come all this way and it gets wet and disintegrates."

Kylie felt foolish for not having thought of that. She had carried it in a plastic bag up at Christmas Creek but had taken it out at home. When they had confirmed that the letter did in fact say 'cross the main stream', she took out a plastic bag and slid the letter into it.

"Where do we go now?" Stephen asked.

"We have to find the 'Erin' mine," Graham said.

"How do we do that?" Allison asked, gesturing at the wall of dense jungle hemming them in.

"From the Mine's Department map," Peter said. "Dig it out, Kylie."

Kylie dumped her pack and did so. They studied this. Peter pointed at a creek marked on it. "I reckon this creek is Kraft Creek, where we are now, so it should be just along the valley a few hundred metres."

The old road went on across the creek, heading south along the bank of Kraft Creek but it was even more overgrown and even harder to follow. They set off along it, having to push through vines and undergrowth which almost blocked it. A faint trail showed.

After a few dozen paces the road forked. Both branches were eroded and overgrown, but the one going west along the main valley seemed the clearest and showed signs of having been cleared at some time in the recent past. Graham pointed at the road going left along the creek.

"I reckon that is the road that went up Bartle Frere to the goldfield."

"Did it go all the way to the top?" Margaret asked.

Graham shook his head. "No, only up onto one of the lower ridges, to a place called Coronation Lookout on the spur between Kraft Creek and Babinda Creek."

"So which way do we go?" Allison asked.

"Right. The 'Erin' mine should be just along here a few hundred metres," Graham replied.

The group set off along the overgrown road. Graham pointed to places where vines or saplings had been cut. "Someone's been along here recently."

"I hope they haven't found our gold," Margaret commented.

"Probably just the local Scout troop," Peter said.

The going wasn't all that difficult, but it was very hot and humid and Kylie found herself sweating profusely again. By this time she was tired and sore and her shoulders and back ached. From the look of them Margaret and Allison were also feeling the same way. To Kylie's annoyance the boys seemed quite unaffected and pushed on at a pace she found hard to maintain.

After ten minutes walking Graham and Peter stopped. Kylie's eyes followed Graham's pointing finger to what appeared to be mounds of earth amidst the trees. The place had obviously once been a clearing as the vegetation was different from the surrounding rain forest. She saw four large logs piled one on top of the other.

Stephen saw it too and said: A ramp to load bulldozers on a truck, or to unload things."

Margaret pointed to a rusty object half hidden by creepers. "What's that?" she asked.

They looked. It was some sort of machine, all shrouded in vines and ferns. The group moved to cluster around it and Stephen dragged some of the vines off. "A motor, or a pump or something," he said.

"Pump," Uncle Bill said. He then pointed down and they saw a rusty pipeline half buried in the leaf mould. The pipeline led off to the north along what had obviously once been a road.

"I reckon this is the 'Erin' mine," Graham said.

Kylie felt her heart rate quicken. "Oh, I hope so," she said.

"So let's start searching," Stephen said.

Allison groaned. "Can't we stop for a rest? I'm sick of carrying this pack."

Uncle Bill supported her. Graham and Stephen both grumbled but Kylie did not care. Much as she was fired with the desire to find the gold she could see that Margaret and Allison both needed a rest. To ease the situation she sat on her pack and took out the letter again.

"From here we are supposed to go south, cross the main stream, then turn right at the mine called the 'Bright Smile'."

Graham frowned and looked at his map. "That can't be right. If we go south from here, we will be going uphill. The main stream is north of us."

That threw them. Kylie felt the same nagging sense of frustration that had dogged her all along. *Every time we seem to be getting somewhere it all ends up not making sense!*

She had to read the letter aloud again and they studied the map.

"Maybe the West Mulgrave isn't the main stream?" Peter suggested. They discussed this but could not think which creek might be the main stream otherwise.

Margaret was sitting beside Kylie. She leaned over to read over her shoulder. "What does it mean in the paragraph above where it says 'Just in case I don't make it follow these instructions using the method we used at school.' What does he mean by the method we used at school do you think?"

Peter let out an exclamation of delight. "Well done, Marg! What a mob of noddies we are for not noticing that."

"But what does it mean?" Allison asked in a puzzled voice.

"It is some sort of schoolboy secret code I reckon," Peter said.

They all looked at each other and Kylie felt a surge of hope.

Margaret frowned. "But what is the secret?" she asked.

"Be something simple," Stephen said.

Peter agreed. He nodded, then said, "What if they just reversed everything; 'go' means 'stop'; 'right' means 'left'; and so on?"

"We can try it. It is better than just blundering about the bloody jungle," Stephen answered. He took off his glasses and wiped them as condensation was fogging them up.

Graham stood up. "So let's go."

There were groans but the others moved. Packs were hoisted on. By the time Kylie was ready Graham and Peter had already vanished from sight along the old road. They followed, catching them up after a few minutes as they snipped their way through a tangle of wait-a-while where a tree had recently fallen down across the track.

Ten minutes of slow movement brought them to the West Mulgrave. They could hear it before they saw it and Kylie worried that it might be so much in flood that they could not cross it. To her relief she saw that it looked quite easy to cross. The river was about fifty metres wide and had several large piles of rocks in midstream but otherwise it was just knee deep and clear.

Boots were removed and slung around their necks. This time they linked hands and went across in a chain. There were a few anxious moments in the middle where a deep hole made it thigh deep for a few steps. The water was cold but refreshing. Kylie stubbed her toe once and nearly cried aloud at the pain but was able to hobble ashore.

As they sat to dry their feet Allison asked, "How much further?"

"Not far," Graham replied.

"Why don't we camp here?" Stephen asked.

They looked around. The jungle came right down to the water and there was no beach of any sort. Uncle Bill shook his head. "Too close. If there is a flood, we could get washed away. We will camp a bit further up the slope."

Boots were pulled on and they moved on, following the faint trail of the old road. Cuts and blazes still indicated that other people had been that way at some time in the last few months. The track led up a gentle slope. Once they were fifty metres from the river Uncle Bill stopped and indicated a small clearing they had reached.

"This will do for a campsite."

Allison looked around askance. "I don't like this much."

"If we find somewhere better, we can move later. It will do for now," Uncle Bill replied.

Kylie dumped her pack with a sigh of relief. "Do we set up camp?" she asked.

Graham looked at his watch. "It's only three o'clock. We could start looking."

Both Allison and Kylie groaned, and Margaret looked unhappy. Uncle Bill saved them. "We will have a break and set up camp. We've got plenty of time. There's no need to bust ourselves. This is my holiday don't forget."

They spent the next hour resting and setting up camp. The girls had a nylon tent which they erected in a small area scraped clear of sticks. Uncle Bill had a small canvas fly which he strung up between the trees. All the boys had army 'shelters individual', plastic sheets which were also tied between trees with nylon cord. When the shelters were up they sat around on packs and groundsheets to have afternoon tea.

Kylie took out the small hexamine stove Graham had given her to heat water. Margaret had a spirit stove and so did Allison. Uncle Bill went about things 'bushman' fashion, managing to light a fire using the damp sticks. He arranged a tripod of sticks to hold a billy of river water over the fire and brewed tea.

Stephen looked up from his cooking. "Are we allowed to camp here?" he asked. "Isn't this all 'World Heritage' National Park?"

Peter answered that one. "According to the map the river is the boundary of the National Park. This side of the river is private property."

Margaret looked anxious. "What if the owner doesn't want us here?" she asked.

Stephen scoffed and looked around at the jungle. "Owner! Here?"

Uncle Bill said, "In that case we will just move on, but as I have the right bits of paper to be allowed to prospect I think we should be alright."

The conversation turned to the jungle and what might lurk in it. Both Graham and Peter ridiculed the idea that there was anything more dangerous than a red-bellied black snake.

"What about cassowaries?" Margaret asked.

That caused a few nervous looks as they all had heard stories about the huge, flightless birds attacking people.

Peter shook his head. "Haven't seen any droppings," he said.

Graham took up the theme. "Anyway, if a cassowary appears you just lie down and make yourself look as small as possible."

"Why?" Allison asked.

"If you look big the cassowary thinks you are challenging it for its territory," Graham replied.

"You don't make thumping noises either," Peter added.

Stephen chortled. "You hear that Roger?" he said. "No farting."

"That will do!" Uncle Bill said, between the laughter.

"What I want to see," Peter said, "is a thylacine."

"A what?" Allison asked.

"Thylacine. A Tasmanian Tiger," Peter replied.

"This isn't Tasmania!" Stephen laughed. They all joined in with some good -natured ribbing, before the conversation moved on to thylacines and the last reported sightings in the North Queensland jungle.

After half an hour Graham said, "Never mind bloody extinct animals, what about this gold mine. We still have a couple of hours before dark. Let's look around."

Kylie saw the looks that crossed the faces of Allison and Margaret. She knew Margaret would not go against Graham's wishes, but it was equally obvious she was worn out. "No. I want to have a rest and a swim," she said.

Graham made a face, but the idea of a swim was popular and he was over-ruled. The group prepared for a swim. The girls crawled into their tent one after another to change while the males went behind trees. When all were ready, they trooped back down to the river.

Uncle Bill kept the boys under control and would not let them run on ahead, or go in till he was there. "No jumping or diving," he said. "I don't want to tell your mothers you will never walk again from spinal injuries."

The boys were first in, all clad in shorts or bathers. The girls were all shy and wore shirts over their bathers. Kylie knew it would be cold but it seemed much worse than it had been when they had crossed earlier. It took a real effort of willpower, helped by the boys splashing, to lower herself in.

One result was that they did not stay in long, but Kylie found it very invigorating and refreshing. Even Graham stopped grumbling about wasting time. A very pleasant twenty minutes was enjoyed.

As she lay in the water, Kylie looked up. Overhead was a clear blue sky but off to her right she could just make out the lower slopes of Bartle Frere. The massive bulk of the mountain dominated the valley and gave her a very closed-in feeling. Once again, she experienced and intense feeling of isolation. The obvious 'wilderness' nature of the place made her feel very lonely and far from help. She shivered and wondered whether it had been wise to come there. For the first time she wished they were already on their way home.

After a few more minutes they all climbed out and dried themselves. Kylie found she was shivering from the cold and her skin was covered in goose bumps. They made their way back up to their camp and changed back into clean, dry clothes. Graham again wanted to go off exploring, but Margaret suggested washing the clothes they had worn that day and Kylie and Allison both supported her. Uncle Bill also thought this a good idea, so they returned to the river.

As they rinsed the sweat-soaked clothes, Kylie wondered if it was the feeling of openness that they got at the river which had led her to wanting to return there. She certainly found the surrounding jungle and their campsite very claustrophobic.

By the time the washing was done it was time to cook tea. Already the afternoon sun had gone off the treetops. Being deep in a valley running North-South this was earlier than it would otherwise have been. The effect was to give them a long, gloomy twilight. This did nothing to lift Kylie's spirits. She was annoyed with herself for having such reactions.

We are so close to the gold mine I should be bubbling with joy, she told herself. However, she was unable to rid herself of a nagging sense of unease.

The group busied themselves making their camp more comfortable, cooking, and collecting firewood. The evening remained hot and humid.

There was no breeze and Kylie found she was perspiring even after the sun had gone down. They then sat around the fire and talked for the next couple of hours. Even that wasn't all that enjoyable. The available firewood was mostly damp and produced a very smoky fire. Even when the wood dried out properly it only burnt for a short while as it was all so rotten.

After reminiscing about various expeditions and adventures the group took itself to bed early. Kylie was glad of that as she felt very tired and her muscles were now stiff and sore. It was a real relief to take off her boots and massage her toes. The three girls squeezed into the small tent side by side and changed into pyjamas. After brushing their hair they lay talking quietly for a while longer. Margaret lay so she could see out, her attention focused on Graham as he unrolled his sleeping bag and prepared for bed.

"He's going to sleep in his clothes," Margaret whispered.

"What did you want him to sleep in, the nuddy?" Allison asked.

Margaret giggled and nodded. Kylie laughed and shook her head. "I don't know what you see in the big oaf."

"He's wonderful," Margaret sighed.

"You won't think so if he does something to you and gets you into trouble," Allison added.

The girls settled to whispering about boys and what they might really be like. Kylie was so tired that she took little part in this and soon drifted into a deep sleep, rousing from her slumbers a couple of times from bad dreams about snakes and centipedes.

Chapter 22

SEARCHING

Thursday dawned clear and hot. Even before the sun touched the upper slopes of Bartle Frere they were perspiring. Kylie noted this as she walked with Margaret down to the river to fill her water bottles. She was feeling much better, although stiff and chafed from the previous days march.

At least we don't have to carry our packs today, she told herself. *And we can get on with finding the gold mine.*

Her spirits lifted even more at the sight of the sparkling, clear water tumbling and gurgling around the boulders in the riverbed. It was a beautiful spot and it helped to lighten her sense of isolation.

When breakfast was over, they tidied the camp and prepared to explore.

"Are we going to just leave our camp?" Margaret asked as she buckled on her belt.

Graham shrugged. "Why not? Nobody is liable to come here," he replied.

Stephen looked up from doing up his pack. "There's been someone here recently," he pointed out.

"Not in the last week or so," Graham answered. "Anyway, you can stay and guard the camp if you like."

Peter shook his head. "Forget it. Anyone who comes here are only liable to be bushwalkers and they won't steal anything," he said. "Let's get going. I want to find this gold mine."

In high spirits they set off. Kylie carried the letter in her hand in a plastic bag and Graham had the maps. They walked on up the gentle slope along the overgrown track.

"We should come to the remains of the 'Bright Smile' mine after a few hundred metres," Graham said.

And they did. And it brought a bright smile to all their faces. There was no doubt it was an old mine as there were even mullock heaps and collapsed and rotting timbers over what had once obviously been a shaft.

A litter of rusty iron objects, empty bottles and vegetation changes all attested to it being an old mine site.

"The letter says to turn right at the 'Bright Smile'," Kylie said.

"So we do the opposite and go left," Peter added.

"Can anyone see where the track goes now?" Stephen asked.

They looked around and Uncle Bill pointed. "There is a fair sort of a track here."

Graham studied it and frowned. "It looks well used to the left."

A worrying thought crossed Kylie's mind and she voiced it, "Maybe somebody else is here searching for the old mine too?"

"It's possible," Uncle Bill agreed.

They bent to examine the ends of a bush which had been cut. Peter shook his head. "Even if it was this was cut weeks or months ago."

"So whoever cut it has made it easier for us. Let's keep going," Stephen urged.

The group set off along the track. It was easy walking, and they quickly covered several hundred metres before coming to a fair-sized creek which was gurgling merrily down towards the Mulgrave. They stopped on the bank to have a drink and wash perspiration off their faces.

"Do we cross this?" Stephen asked.

"The letter says: 'cross Nugget Creek'," Kylie replied.

"It might, but if we turn left when it says right does that mean don't cross when it says cross?" Stephen asked.

That was a worry and they debated it for ten minutes. Finally Peter said, "Even if we don't cross, I can't see where we should then go. There is no obvious track along this bank, but I can see where this old road we have been following goes on up the other bank."

That was true so they decided to continue on. The creek was easy to cross by stepping from stone to stone and they plunged back into the jungle. The track went up a low rise then across a large flat area. The jungle was, if anything, thicker than ever.

After only a few hundred paces they came to another old mine. At least they thought it was. It wasn't nearly as clear as the previous one; just a few low mounds of earth among the trees and a large tree stump. For a couple of minutes they looked around. Kylie gulped a big drink of water and wiped sweat from her forehead.

"If this is Frank's Claim then we turn right here," she said.

"Turn right! But there isn't any track. The track continues on up the valley," Stephen said.

That was obviously true. The track they were on was quite clear. Graham and Peter began scouting around for signs of another track. Kylie joined them. Graham shook his head and looked worried. He pointed and said, "This might be a track, but it was never a road."

Peter nodded. "It looks like a track. I suppose your grandad never had a proper road to his camp."

"It would have only been a foot track," Kylie agreed.

"And there wouldn't have been much more than a few bushes cut from his camp to the 'Jeweller's Shop'," Graham added.

"And that was over half a century ago," Peter added gloomily.

However, it was all they had to go on. After some argument they set out along the faint trail. At least it led in the right direction, which was uphill along the spine of a gentle ridge. Now they moved even slower. Graham and Peter both took frequent compass bearings and noted paces and directions in their notebooks. The 'track' was very hard to follow and only an occasional old blaze mark on trees indicated they were possibly going the right way.

"We are now looking for moss covered rocks," Kylie reminded them.

In this they were both disappointed and baffled. There were numerous small rocks protruding from the jungle floor and all had moss growing on them, but none was large enough to stand out as any sort of a landmark. The searchers became hot, sweaty and irritated.

After a time they lost the 'track' and came to a standstill. There were no rocks in sight and nothing to indicate which way to go. Downhill on both sides they could hear the murmur of creeks. This led to an argument about where to go next.

Kylie favoured the creek to the east of them, on their right, as the old letter said 'take the left fork'. To her that meant take the right fork in the track. She wiped her brow and had a big drink, then insisted they go that way. As there was no track they had to push and cut through the jungle. This was not too difficult, except when they had to detour around several large 'wait-a-whiles'.

Fifteen minutes of this had them down at the creek. Graham looked up and down it, shaking his head. "This is the same creek we crossed lower down," he said.

"I know that," Kylie snapped angrily. "So let's look for moss covered rocks."

To do this they split up. Kylie, Margaret, Allison, and Uncle Bill went downstream and the boys upstream. They had to scramble along the bank or step from rock to rock. The rocks were slippery and they all slipped several times. Kylie nearly sprained her ankle doing this. When Margaret fell heavily and bruised her bum, Kylie began to worry that one of them might get hurt so badly they had to be carried out on a stretcher. It was a daunting prospect.

Kylie began to regret having urged them to come on the expedition. As time went by she also began to doubt that they would find anything. They searched every clump of rocks and every side gully for hours, becoming sweaty and scratched in the process. Tempers began to fray and their enthusiasm flagged.

Feeling quite dispirited the group sat around on boulders in the creek bed to eat lunch. Mosquitoes and leeches assisted in the process of lowering their spirits still further. Several arguments flared about whether they were interpreting the instructions correctly.

Uncle Bill defused these by pointing out they could try both methods. Lunch was mostly eaten in silence. Afterwards they went on upstream in a group. At each small tributary they stopped and a couple explored it for as far as it went. As before, this was a slow and frustrating job with much wrestling with vines and thick vegetation. Kylie began to hate the sight of the rainforest, and the claustrophobic feelings it engendered.

They gave it up in disgust at 4pm. By then they were all tired and dirty. It had been a very hot day and the sweat had caused damp clothing to chafe tender flesh. Kylie had dirt and dead leaves down the back of her shirt, further irritating her. Allison was obviously chafed under her shirt and looking very pale and drawn.

"That's enough for the day," Uncle Bill said. "Let's get back to camp."

Now the careful compass bearings and paces noted by Graham and Peter came to their aid. They could have made their way down the creek but they were sick of slipping and sliding over the wet rocks by then. Instead, they retraced their steps through the jungle. After a time, Graham, who had an eye for such things, saw a tree he recognised, and then one of the old blazes. After that they were able to retrace their steps with no difficulty.

At 4:45pm they were back at the old mine they had decided was 'Frank's Claim'. They stopped here for a drink and to remove leeches.

Just as they turned left to start the walk back to their camp Stephen cried out and put his hand to his ear. "What was that noise?" he asked.

They all stopped to listen. Faintly but distinctly Kylie heard a thud off to the west in the jungle. "I can hear it. What is it?" she asked.

"Someone chopping wood with an axe I reckon," Uncle Bill said.

They all stared in the direction the faint sounds were coming from. Kylie felt twinges of alarm. Who could it be?

Allison said, "I hope it isn't those horrible men again."

Margaret let out a little cry. "Oh Allie! Don't say that."

"I doubt it," Kylie said, although she had a sinking feeling in the pit of her stomach. Who else could it be?

"They don't know we are here," Graham said.

"I wouldn't bet on it," Stephen said. "Bert knew we were going to the Mulgrave. He could have told them."

"Oh don't be horrible!" Allison cried. "Why would he?"

Stephen shrugged but before he could answer Uncle Bill cut in, "None of that please."

Graham started walking towards the sound. "I'm going to have a look."

Again Margaret let out a little cry. "Oh no Graham. Don't!"

"But we should know who else is in the area," Graham replied. "I'll be careful."

Uncle Bill held up his hand. "I agree. We should be aware of who is around, but we will all go. We don't need to sneak around. We have every right to be here."

So they all set off towards the mysterious sounds of chopping, Graham and Peter leading, then Uncle Bill, Stephen, Kylie, Margaret, and Allison. Kylie felt quite sick with worry. She did not really want to go, but agreed it was important to know who else was in the area.

Particularly if it is those horrible men, she told herself.

Travel was easy. They just walked west along the cleared track which became more and more obvious as they went. After several hundred metres it was a well used trail clear of all vegetation.

Stephen sniffed. "Smoke," he commented.

Kylie realised she could smell it. Then she saw it drifting in the trees.

The sound of chopping became louder and clearer all the time. Much as Kylie did not want to go she found herself borne along by the event.

After less than five minutes walking they came to a clearing in the rainforest. On the right was a huge pile of sand and gravel with a wheelbarrow resting upside down on the side of it. Just beyond, against the side of a low hill, was the bare earth and black entrance to a mine. Timber props held up the roof and the whole thing looked very primitive. *Like one of those mines in an old photograph,* Kylie thought.

The reason was immediately apparent. On the other side of the small clearing was a camp. In front of it, chopping wood with an axe, was a white-haired old man. He wore gumboots, filthy old trousers held up by braces and a dirty, mud-stained shirt of indeterminate colour. His face was mostly hidden by a white beard and his hair was straggling and unkempt. A battered felt hat topped off his ensemble.

The man's camp consisted of a corrugated iron roof on bush saplings, open on two sides and with a tent at the far corner. Under the roof were a fireplace, table, chair and stacks of boxes and piles of gear. A smoky fire smouldered in the fireplace, the smoke drifting slowly across the clearing to hang in the still air.

The group came to a standstill on the edge of the clearing. The old man raised his axe and split a billet of timber with an expert swing. As he bent to reposition the wood, he noticed them. For a moment he showed surprise. Then he lowered the axe and straightened up.

"Good dayee to yer," he called.

Uncle Bill took the lead. He walked forward replying to the greeting. The teenagers followed. They stopped a few paces from the old man, who looked them over.

Uncle Bill put out his hand. "Bill Feltham. I've got a dairy farm up near Lamins Hill."

The old man took his hand, looked him squarely in the eye and nodded. As they shook hands he replied, "Blair Donaldson. I'm a gold miner. Or at least I would be if I could find any of the damned stuff. I guess I'm really just a fossicker."

Uncle Bill introduced the teenagers. "These are all nephews, nieces and assorted friends. They come from Cairns." He gave their names. The old prospector nodded. "Aye, I know Captain Kirk. I sailed with him once, as a deckhand that was." He paused and stared into what would have been the distance if there hadn't been a wall of jungle in the way. "Be a good ten years ago, when I were a bit younger."

"I hope we didn't frighten you," Kylie said.

The old man shook his head. "Not at all missie. Mind you, I don't get many visitors here. In fact you are the first I have ever had in two years."

"Do you live here?" Margaret asked.

The old prospector nodded. "Aye. This is my home, such as it is. Ah! Now here's me forgettin' me manners and you my guests. Come and have a cuppa. The water should be nearly boiled."

Kylie did not want to but no-one else made any objection, so they were ushered over to the shelter. They seated themselves on various boxes, bundles and blocks of wood.

"We can't stay long," Uncle Bill said. "We need to get back to our camp before dark."

"Oh aye. And where is that?" the old prospector asked as he stoked up his fire.

Uncle Bill told him. Kylie noted Graham and Peter staring around at the details of the camp with fascinated interest. She had expected it to be very dirty but noted with relief that it was actually quite tidy and clean. The old prospector's clothes were covered in grime but that was from the day's work she decided. This impression was reinforced by the sight of washing hanging on a line at the side of the shelter.

"Are you Scottish?" Margaret asked.

The old prospector gave a wry grin. "Aye, but I'd have hoped I might be called an Aussie after living here all these years."

Margaret blushed. "Oh! I'm sorry. I didn't mean that. It was just your accent."

The old prospector smiled. "It's alright lassie. It's a hard thing to shake off, an accent. Mind you, I can talk like a proper Aussie when I try." He paused for a second, then said in a broad Australian accent, "G'day mate. Strewth, stone the bloody crows!"

It sounded so funny to Kylie she burst out laughing, then hastily stopped lest she offend the old prospector. However, he grinned at her. "Yer see, dinkum Aussie eh?"

That caused them all to smile. The old prospector then explained, "I was born in Aberdeen and came out here as a wee bairn just after the second war. But the accent has stuck with me all these years."

"Are you really a gold miner?" Kylie asked.

Again the old prospector gave his wry smile. "I am that. Or I try to be. Mind you I worked at a lot of jobs over the years. Spent most of my life working in an office checking lists of figures though. Now I'm glad to spend my days a bit closer to nature."

"Have you found any gold?" Kylie asked.

The old prospector made another face. "I find a bit now and then; enough to pay my way. But this is terrible hard country to prospect in."

"We know," Graham added, earning a frown from Kylie.

The old prospector did not appear to notice this exchange but went on, "I spent five years fossicking around the Hodgkinson, if you know where that is."

"Out near Mt Mulligan," Graham replied.

"That's right. Then I came here two years ago to try my luck."

"Don't you get lonely?" Margaret asked.

"Not really. I go home every week or so and that gives me a good dose of people."

"Do you live near here?" Kylie asked.

"No. Like you, in Cairns," the old prospector answered. Again he smiled. "I've a tribe of kids and grandkids you know and they keep me busy."

The old prospector did not mention a wife and Kylie did not like to ask. *I like him*, she decided.

The conversation became general and they discussed mutual acquaintances. After a while, the old prospector asked, "If you don't mind me asking, what brings you to this part of the world?"

That caused an awkward silence. Kylie thought fast but decided there was no point in trying to keep secret what they were doing.

"We are looking for gold too," she said.

The old prospector's face split into a grin. "Well, good luck to ye then. Have ye found any?"

They shook their heads and the old prospector grinned again. "Ah well, don't give up. Keep looking for a year or two and ye might find a bit."

That made them all pull faces again. "One day is enough!" Allison grumbled.

"So what made you all come to this neck of the woods then?" the old prospector asked. "I mean most people would go to one of the more famous goldfields like Charters Towers or the Palmer River."

That caused another awkward silence. Kylie met Uncle Bill's eyes and he nodded. She said, "We are looking for a gold mine my great grandfather discovered."

The old prospector's eyes lit up with interest. "Oh aye. And what would be the name of his mine?"

Again Kylie hesitated but then decided that there was no point in not telling the old man. She said, "He called it 'The Jeweller's Shop'."

The old prospector nodded slowly and then said, "Aye. I've heard of that. That is what brought me to this place."

Chapter 23

NUGGET CREEK

For a moment there was an awkward silence. Kylie was appalled and amazed. She blurted out, "How did you know about the 'Jeweller's Shop'?"

The old prospector raised his eyebrows, then said, "Everyone knows about the famous 'Jeweller's Shop'. Every fossicker I have ever spoken to has wanted to find it. It is an item of local folklore."

Kylie made a face and felt silly. "I thought it was a family secret."

At that Uncle Bill laughed. "Some secret! Everywhere we go we find people who know about it and are looking too."

"You said a family secret?" the old prospector suggested.

Kylie nodded. "Great Grandad found it back in 1931."

Again the old prospector raised his eyebrows. "So you should know where it is. Didn't he tell you?"

Kylie's mind raced. *Should I answer that question? What can I say?* Her eyes met Uncle Bill's and he nodded and answered for her.

"He did. He left a diary and a letter, but we have only recently found both of them and they don't seem to be much help."

The old prospector was clearly interested. He said, "Well, I wish you luck. I've been searching for two years for it and have covered just about every square yard of this blasted jungle and not a sign of it. Just an occasional bit of colour in a creek. I've given up and now I'm working over this old claim."

Kylie felt her hopes sink. Two years! If this man had been looking that long what chance did they have, and in only a few days! She felt foolish and depressed.

The old prospector asked, "It's none of my business of course but why don't your clues help you find it?"

Uncle Bill held out his hand to Kylie and she reluctantly passed him the old letter. He did not give it to the old prospector but read a bit from it, then continued, "It's finding the right place to start. Once we follow the instructions things start to go haywire. We've just spent hours thrashing around in the jungle up Nugget Creek there and none of the instructions made much sense." As he spoke, he pointed back to where they had spent the last few hours.

The old prospector raised one eyebrow and half turned to glance in the direction Uncle Bill had indicated. He shook his head. "That isn't Nugget Creek. That is Reward Creek."

"Are you sure?" Uncle Bill asked.

"Positive," the old prospector replied.

Kylie felt her heart beat more rapidly as the implications of what the old prospector had said sank in. She said, "So where is Nugget Creek?"

The old prospector pointed the other way. "Next creek to the west. Along that track there."

Graham took out his map and looked at it, a puzzled look on his face. "But... but how could it be? This map must be wrong."

"Do you mind if I look at it?" the old prospector asked.

Graham shrugged and handed it to him. The old prospector studied it for a minute. "It's okay, just not complete. There were a lot more mines and claims than are shown here."

"But it is the official Mines Department map," Kylie said.

The old prospector smiled. "I'm sure it is. Lots of men came and did some digging without bothering with the formalities of registering a claim. It saved paying a lot of government charges and taxes you see."

Margaret opened her mouth in scandalized surprise. "But that would be breaking the law!" she said.

The old prospector met her eyes and smiled. "Yes. But it was during the Great Depression this gold rush. Men were desperate and their families starving."

Margaret nodded and blushed. Kylie pointed to the map. "So where did we go wrong? If that creek there isn't Nugget Creek, what is it?"

The old prospector looked at where she was pointing and shook his head. "That is Reward Creek."

"But you said Nugget Creek was the next creek to the west," Kylie said, staring at the tiny black lines which indicated creeks on the map.

"No. I don't think all the creeks are marked on that map," the old prospector said. "It is the next creek. Look, you start there at the 'Erin' mine, which was the main mine in the area, then cross the Mulgrave to this point, which is here, then turn left to go west."

"But we started at the 'Erin' and that took us to that creek back there," Kylie replied in a puzzled voice.

The old prospector looked in the direction she had pointed and shook his head. "Couldn't be. The 'Erin' is just across the river from here." He pointed to a track just beside the shelter. It led south into the jungle.

"But... but if that isn't the 'Erin' mine where we started from, what is it?" Kylie asked.

"That would have been the 'Shamrock'," the old prospector replied. He smiled and met her eyes.

He's a very nice old man, Kylie thought. While they talked, he had been stoking the fire and now he paused to lift off the billy. Tea leaves were added to it and he spent a minute chatting while he set up three metal pannikins.

"Sugar? Sorry but the only milk I've got is condensed," he explained.

Kylie was almost busting with impatience, wanting to ask more questions but she held her tongue until the tea was made. The old prospector passed the cups to Uncle Bill, Peter, and Margaret. "Sorry. I only have three cups. I don't get many visitors and I left the best China at home," he explained with a chuckle. He seated himself again and said to Uncle Bill, "Bill Feltham you said? It was Hec Pike who found the 'Jeweller's Shop' wasn't it?"

Uncle Bill nodded. "That's right. He was my grandad. Mum was Grace Pike. She married Stan Feltham. It was a sad story. He made the find but was very sick at the time, some sort of fever. He managed to walk home, back up onto the Tablelands there, and then died. Before he left he wrote this letter and wrote the story in his diary."

The old prospector nodded and his eyes gleamed with interest. Uncle Bill went on, "We've got a copy of the diary here. I'll read it to you."

Uncle Bill read from the copy of the last few pages of the diary. The others sat and listened. Kylie wasn't sure if she wanted Uncle Bill to give so much information to a stranger but conceded that, if they couldn't find it themselves, it didn't matter.

When Uncle Bill finished the old prospector nodded thoughtfully and said, "That's a real sad tale that. The puir woman; left with three bairns and one of them only a baby."

Kylie added, "He badly wanted her to have her share of the gold. That's why he wrote to his brother Herbert."

"So if Herbert got the letter with the instructions how come he didn't find the gold?" the old prospector asked.

"Because he didn't have the diary to tell him where," Kylie explained. "We only found it among some old papers just before Christmas."

Graham added, "Even then we spent a week looking in the wrong place. We didn't read it carefully enough and spent days thrashing around in the jungle up at the headwaters of Christmas Creek."

They all groaned and laughed and embellished this part of the tale. Kylie explained, "That was because he mentioned going along the Christmas Creek track in the diary." She went on to explain how they had worked out that they were searching in the wrong place. "So we concluded it had to be down here in the Mulgrave valley," she concluded.

The old prospector nodded again. "Aye. That was where the rumours I had heard put it."

Peter now asked, "So, if the mine we started from is the 'Shamrock' and if, as you say, the 'Erin' is just across the river from here, what is the mine we found on the other side of the creek you call Reward Creek?"

"The 'Just Reward'," replied the old prospector.

"We thought it was the 'Bright Smile'," Peter replied.

The old prospector shook his head. "Nope. This is the 'Bright Smile' right here." He pointed to the tunnel entrance in the slope.

"Are you sure?" Graham asked.

The old prospector gave him a hard look, then nodded. "Of course I'm sure. I measured it off from the survey pegs and I've got the lease from the mining warden."

Uncle Bill said, "I know this isn't any of my business so don't answer if you don't want to, but have you found any gold?"

The old prospector made a face. "A bit. About enough to cover me rations and some whisky. I keep hoping though. If I don't find more soon though I'll have to give up and go back to the blasted old people's home and put up with that witch of a matron."

"What sort of gold have you found?" Graham asked.

"Mostly only a few specks of colour in the wash. I also found some tiny nuggets," the old prospector replied. He stood up and reached up onto a shelf against the back wall. In a small glass jar he had about a dozen tiny pieces of gold. Most were only the size of grains of sand, but one was as big as a pea. The teenagers examined them with great interest.

"Found the big one in Nugget Creek," the old prospector said. "I reckon there's more, but I can't find the seam that it and these other floaters come from."

"It could be the 'Jeweller's Shop'," Graham suggested.

"Might be. I'll look up the creek again when the wet season is over," the old prospector agreed.

Kylie felt her hopes surge. The sight of real gold from Nugget Creek fired her imagination. She said, "You wouldn't know where 'Frank's Claim' was would you?"

The old prospector shook his head. "Don't know of any place named that. Did it have any other name?"

They did not know. Peter said, "We thought it was the old diggings just back along this track, just this side of Reward Creek."

"That was the 'Golden Hope'," the old prospector replied.

During this exchange Kylie's mind had been furiously busy. She felt a wild surge of optimism and said, "So now we know where to start. Let's go and look."

"Steady on," Uncle Bill said. "It's getting late."

Peter checked his watch. "It's only half past five."

"And it will be dark by seven," Uncle Bill replied. "We need to get back to camp to cook before it gets dark."

"Oh please Uncle Bill! Just for a little while," Kylie pleaded.

Uncle Bill relented. "Half an hour. No more." He stood up and drained the last of his tea, then handed the cup back. "Thanks Mr Donaldson. That was nice."

Kylie took back her letter of instructions and read them. Then she asked the old prospector if there was another old mine just across the other side of Nugget Creek.

The old prospector nodded. "Aye. There is. Wasn't ever much though I don't reckon. Just a few mounds and some empty bottles in the scrub."

"Are there any tracks leading up beside Nugget Creek?" Graham asked.

The old prospector nodded again. "Yep. There's a few. Some are still in pretty good condition. I've been using them meself."

"Thanks very much," Graham replied. The others added their thanks and then prepared to start walking. The old prospector smiled and waved. "Guid luck ter ye. Hope ye find plenty of gold."

The group hurried on west along the track which led off the other side of the small clearing. The track was well used and easy to move along. Within two minutes they had reached Nugget Creek. By then the sun had gone off the treetops although the sky overhead was still bright blue. Nugget Creek was larger than the previous creek, being at least five metres wide and flowing quite well. It was a typical jungle stream with alternating sandy stretches and rocky rapids and pools. The water was crystal clear and refreshingly cool.

Kylie paused to refill her water bottle and to wash her face. All the while her excitement had been increasing. *At last we are starting to get somewhere,* she thought happily.

The foot track went on up the other bank. Fifty paces on it abruptly forked beside a mound which might have been artificial.

"Frank's Claim?" Graham suggested, indicating the mound.

"Should be," Peter agreed. "What do we do now Ky?"

Kylie checked the instructions. "Turn left at Frank's Claim, which means turn right, then go downhill to the mossy rocks. That means go uphill." She looked at the track going right. It certainly went uphill. The sight of that made her excitement mount. "That way," she said.

"Let's go," Graham said.

"Ten minutes more," Uncle Bill cautioned.

"Come on!" Kylie cried.

She hurried after Graham. The others followed, and this time there was a track. It was cleared and easy to walk along. Gnarled scars on the bark of the larger trees marked old blaze marks but the vegetation had not reclaimed it and the old prospector had obviously kept it open as well. They were able to make good progress. The slope was quite gentle and the jungle fairly open. They went steadily uphill for at least five hundred metres. The ridge then began to narrow and become steeper, and Kylie soon found she was panting.

"Mossy rocks!" Graham cried.

Kylie's heart leapt. Yes! She could see them. Slap in the centre of the ridge was a huge pile of boulders and they were all covered with moss and lichen. The track went around the rocks on their right-hand side. It had obviously once been bench cut and was still easy to follow.

"Time to turn back," Uncle Bill called from the back. He was puffing along with Allison and Roger.

"Oh Uncle Bill! We are nearly there," Graham cried.

"It is ten to six. We go back," Uncle Bill replied firmly. "The gold mine has waited seventy years or so. It can wait another few hours."

"Oh Uncle Bill!" Kylie pleaded.

"No. Back we go. We can get here in half an hour tomorrow, now we know the way."

"Can we just find the next track junction please?" Graham asked.

"No. It is getting late, and I don't feel like trying to grope my way home through the jungle in the dark. Back we go."

Reluctantly they turned back. Kylie felt sharply disappointed but had to concede that Uncle Bill was right. It was already quite gloomy, and she certainly did not want to find herself blundering about the rainforest in the dark.

In ten minutes they were back and Nugget Creek. Two minutes later they reached the old prospector's camp. He was cooking at his fire. He gave them a cheerful wave as they went past.

"Any luck?" he called.

"It seemed to be right," Uncle Bill replied.

"See you tomorrow then," the old prospector answered.

They hurried on along the track to Reward Creek. Now Kylie became worried that they would not make it back to camp in daylight but in only a few minutes they were across Reward Creek and at what they now knew was the 'Golden Hope'.

"I love the names they chose for these old mines," Margaret commented as they passed the overgrown site.

"So do I. They are really imaginative," Kylie agreed.

Five minutes later they reached their camp. It was still light but Uncle Bill said, "Down to the river for a quick wash and fill your water bottles while it is still light. Take your torches though as it will get dark quickly. I will get the fire going while you do that."

They did as they were bid. Kylie snatched up her torch and her towel and toilet bag. The girls went down as a group, in the wake of the boys. Out in the open at the river it was still quite light, but evening was clearly upon them. The boys went downstream a short distance until they were out of sight. Soon after the sound of splashing and swimming came to the girls as they crouched beside the water.

"The boys must be having a swim," Margaret said.

"I didn't see them change into bathers," Allison commented.

"They didn't. They will be swimming in the nuddy," Kylie replied.

"Lucky them," Allison said. She looked in that direction.

Margaret giggled. "You can join them if you want to. I'm sure they wouldn't mind," she said.

"You'd know!" Kylie replied with a grin. "Didn't you and Graham go skinny dipping once at Kamerunga?"

Margaret blushed and snorted. "We were only little then."

"I'd love a swim," Allison said. She looked upstream. There were several pools but Kylie shook her head. "Better wait till morning. It is getting dark fast."

That was true. The jungle already looked almost grey and inside it appeared black. Regretfully the girls washed their faces and then filled water bottles. As they stood up Kylie called out, "You boys better get out. It will be dark soon."

Allison added, "If you don't get out we will send Margaret down to get you."

Margaret was deliciously scandalized. "Allie! Don't say that. They will think I am awful."

To add to her embarrassment Stephen's voice came back to them, "Send her down. She can scrub Graham's back for him."

"Don't be rude Stephen Bell!" Kylie called. "Just hurry up."

The girls set off back for their camp. As soon as they entered the rainforest, they had to turn on their torches it was now so dark. They walked in single file back to where the welcoming glow of a fire marked the camp. Uncle Bill was seated beside it adding twigs. He was listening to his pocket radio. The reception was poor, with lots of crackling, but Kylie could hear music.

As the girls arrived Uncle Bill looked up from the fire. "Bad news girls. That 'low' in the Coral Sea has turned into a cyclone. We will have to head home tomorrow."

Chapter 24

THE RIGHT FORK

Cyclone! Must go home tomorrow! Kylie's mind tried to grapple with this as her emotions reeled and plummeted. *Every time we seem to be getting somewhere we run into problems!*

She sat down beside the fire and said, "Uncle Bill we can't go home. We are so close."

Uncle Bill shook his head. "We are going home. It is better to be safe than sorry. The cyclone will only last a few days and then we can come back and continue the search."

"But someone else might find the gold first!" Margaret cried.

Uncle Bill gave a thin smile. "Not during a cyclone they won't. These creeks will all be raging torrents then. No-one could get here, even if they knew where to look."

"What about that old prospector?" Allison asked. "He must have a fair idea where to look now."

This time Uncle Bill laughed. "If he finds the gold before we do then good luck to him. If he has been searching for two years, then he deserves to win."

Kylie sat and stared at the fire. She felt terribly downcast and frustrated. She tried to think of an argument that Uncle Bill might accept but couldn't. The noisy return of the boys led to the argument being resumed. Graham in particular was angry and insisted they keep searching. It was to no avail. Uncle Bill was adamant.

The group then sat around the fire to cook their tea. They were all tired and the low spirits led to a few snaps of bad temper. As they sat eating, they listened to the news on the pocket radio. At the end was the weather forecast and then the official Cyclone Warning. Kylie listened to this anxiously, worrying about her father and brother Alex.

They are out at sea there somewhere.

"I hope Dad and Alex are alright," she said.

Graham made a face. "They'll be okay. Only the good die young."

"Graham! Don't be horrible," Kylie replied.

"Stop worrying, sis. I think they are up near Thursday Island somewhere. This cyclone is only halfway up the Cape," Graham replied.

"Where is it?" Margaret asked.

"The radio said it was a Category One cyclone and that it was about five hundred kilometres northeast of Cairns," Uncle Bill replied.

"Five hundred kilometres. That'll take days to get here," Graham said.

"Depends how big it is and how fast it goes," Uncle Bill replied.

"If it's only a Category One then it can't be very big. That is the weakest category of cyclone," Graham replied.

"It could be up to a hundred kilometres across," Uncle Bill cautioned.

"That shouldn't affect us here," Graham insisted. "The mountains should break the force of the wind."

Uncle Bill shook his head. "It isn't the wind I am worrying about. It is the rain. Cyclones bring flood rains remember, and we could easily get trapped here. Besides, the mountains could have the effect of funnelling the winds, increasing their force."

They all knew this was true and it was a sobering thought. The argument was dropped and the topic of conversation switched to the old prospector. Kylie took little part, feeling too tired and depressed, except to say, "I thought he was a nice old man. I hope he finds some gold."

All were tired so it was early to bed. Kylie tried to cheer up and to join in the chatter with the other girls, but she found it hard going. Later, when their torches were turned out, she lay and went over the events of the last few days in her mind.

The boys were awake at the first hint of dawn. Kylie heard them talking quietly and she looked out of the tent. Graham and Peter were busy heating water on their stoves. They were fully dressed and looked ready to go. A check of her watch showed that it was only ten past six. Pulling on her boots Kylie crawled out to join them.

"Morning, Ky," Graham said. Peter said the same and favoured her with a pleasant smile.

"What are you doing?" she asked, noting that the sketch map lay open beside them.

"We want to go and have a quick look before we have to leave," Graham said.

"You'd better not go without asking Uncle Bill," Kylie cautioned. "He would be ever so angry."

From the way the boys glanced at Uncle Bill's swag she divined that such had in fact been their intention. She shook her head. "Don't please Graham. It will cause a lot of ill-will. We can wait."

Graham made a face but had the grace to look abashed. Peter was also plainly embarrassed. Reluctantly Graham nodded. "Okay. But I am still going to ask him."

From Uncle Bill's swag came the muffled question, "Ask who what?"

The teenagers gave a guilty start. Uncle Bill rolled over and looked at them. Then he sat up and rubbed sleep from his eyes. "I suppose you kids want to rush off and look for this gold mine."

"Yes, we do," Graham answered. "Please Uncle Bill. The cyclone is hundreds of kilometres away still and it hasn't even begun to rain yet. A few hours won't matter."

Uncle Bill muttered something then picked up his pocket radio and turned it on. "Let's have some facts to work on," he said. Then he stood up. "While we wait for the seven o'clock news let's have a wash and some breakfast."

The sound of talking had woken the others. With mumbles and grumbles at the early hour they all appeared. Kylie collected her towel, toilet gear and water bottle then said to the other girls, "Come on. Now is the time for that swim."

Allison wasn't keen but Margaret cheerfully agreed. The two girls then jollied Allison to join them. They made their way down to the river, passing Uncle Bill who had already been down to wash his face and fill his billy.

At the riverbank Kylie looked up. There wasn't a breath of a breeze and the air was humid and still. The river gurgled cheerfully down over the rocks. Birds chirped and, except for a bit of high-level cirrus, the sky appeared to be completely normal. The water felt cool and fresh. The girls separated to have their wash as they were very self-conscious about their bodies. Margaret selected the first pool upstream while Kylie went fifty paces further on before she was satisfied. She found a nice pool behind a large boulder. Allison made her way another twenty paces past that.

Satisfied the boys would not accidentally see her, Kylie stripped off and gingerly lowered herself into the cold water. It took an effort of will power to wet herself, but once she was in she felt very refreshed and her spirits rapidly improved. Several times she saw Allison's head and once she even caught a glimpse of her standing naked on a rock in the morning sunlight.

Heavens Allie is well developed for her age, she thought admiringly.

At that moment, Allison turned her head and saw her. She waved and then dived into a deep pool out of sight. Kylie finished her toilet and stood to dry herself. While she did this a flock of white cockatoos suddenly erupted from the trees a hundred paces upstream. The birds wheeled overhead, screeching and chattering.

Kylie watched them, wondering what had caused them to suddenly take fright. As she watched she saw Allison, still nude, climb out of the water to stand on a rock. She stared upstream, her womanly shape making a delightful picture against the green of the jungle.

Allison shrugged and went out of sight behind a boulder. Kylie finished drying herself and dressed. Then she sat in the first beam of the morning sun to brush her hair. As she did, a fully dressed Allison came back, hopping from rock to rock to join her.

"You shouldn't run around in the nuddy like that, Allie. You scared all the birds," Kylie said. Allison laughed and sat down beside her.

"That was really nice. I felt so free and relaxed," she said.

"You looked lovely," Kylie added. "I'll bet Bert would have loved to see you like that."

Allison tinged pink. "He might, one day. If he is nice."

"Allie!"

The conversation turned to boys and what they liked. Kylie had a fair idea about this, from overhearing her two older brothers, and Allison was quite fascinated to hear. Margaret joined them. She looked very fresh and happy.

"Come on you two. The boys are calling. They want us to help weaken Uncle Bill's resolve."

"How do you know?" Allison asked.

"Graham told me," Margaret replied. Suddenly she went bright pink. Kylie smiled and voiced her suspicions. "Did Graham come down to the river while you were swimming?"

"Yes, he did," Margaret replied. "But I stayed in the water so he wouldn't have seen much."

"Much! Margaret! You naughty little girl. You will get into trouble one day," Kylie replied, but she wasn't shocked and secretly thought that it would be great if Graham did love her.

"Did any of the other boys come down?" Allison asked.

"Yes, but they stayed near the track and didn't see me," Margaret replied.

"So how did Graham find you?" Allison asked.

Once again, Margaret blushed furiously. "He saw me when I stood up to see who it was."

Kylie laughed as she pictured the scene. Allison smiled too but then asked, "Those boys didn't come creeping along the bank to peep at us did they."

Margaret looked shocked. "No. Oh no! They wouldn't do that. They aren't like that."

"All men are like that," Allison replied.

"Stephen might," Kylie added. "But the others wouldn't sneak."

Allison nodded. "I hope not. For a moment I thought it might have been the boys who scared those cockatoos."

"Oh Allie!" Kylie was shocked. "They wouldn't. Anyway those birds were on the other bank."

Still discussing the boys the girls made their way back up to the camp. All the boys were there and they were busy arguing with Uncle Bill while they cooked breakfast. The girls had missed the news, but Graham soon gave them the details of the latest official Cyclone Warning.

"It is now a Category Two cyclone and is moving south but it is a long way off," Graham explained.

"Where is it?" Kylie asked.

"About a hundred kilometres east of Cooktown," Graham answered. "It is still three hundred and fifty kilometres northeast of here."

Uncle Bill added, "So it has moved one hundred and fifty kilometres overnight. That is over ten kilometres per hour."

"That's not a very strong wind," Allison said.

For a second they all looked at her, not understanding what she had said. Then it dawned. Peter explained, "That is the speed of movement of the whole system. As a Category Two cyclone it will have wind speeds of around one hundred and fifty kilometres per hour."

Allison bit her lip. "Sorry. I didn't understand. I've never been in a cyclone."

"We have," Graham replied, "and it is no fun."

"So home we go. Let's eat and get packed up," Uncle Bill said.

"Oh Uncle Bill. Can't we just search for a few hours? It will be hours before the cyclone has any effect on this area, even if it is more than a hundred 'K's across," Graham replied.

"At ten kilometres per hour that means it won't be hitting this area till late this afternoon," Peter added. "We can walk back to the cars in about three hours."

Graham took this up. "That's right. We could spare the morning to have a look and still be safely out by three or four o'clock."

"Not if the cyclone speeds up," Uncle Bill said. "They do you know. Speeds of fifteen and even twenty kilometres per hour are common when they get moving. And the weather people said it was liable to intensify."

"Oh please Uncle Bill! Just a couple of hours," Graham pleaded.

"The girls could start walking out now and we could catch them up," Stephen added.

"Oh poo to you, you sexist pig," Kylie snapped. She hated it when boys suggested that girls were weaker.

Uncle Bill wasn't impressed either. "The party stays together. We all go or nobody goes."

From the tone of his voice Kylie sensed that Uncle Bill was wavering. She puzzled over how to turn the argument. Suddenly the radio gave another repeat of the last Cyclone Warning. As they listened an awful thought came to her.

"I wonder if the old prospector knows there is a cyclone coming?"

That set them thinking. "I didn't see a radio," Roger said.

"We must warn him at least," Graham added.

Uncle Bill let out a big sigh. "Yes, we must. Okay. Get packed up and we will go, but only for three hours. We are leaving here by ten o'clock at the latest."

"Oh Uncle Bill! Thank you!" Kylie cried.

After that it was twenty minutes of frantic preparation. Breakfasts were wolfed down and washing up was only perfunctory. The tent was taken down and camping gear packed. The packs were then lined up beside the track.

As they did, this light rain began to spatter on the leaves. Kylie looked up and bit her lip. She could not see the sky but from the way the light had suddenly reduced she knew it must be from clouds coming over. For a moment she feared that Uncle Bill would cancel the expedition but apart from looking up and frowning he said nothing.

At 7:40am they set off. Uncle Bill took his pocket radio and insisted they all carry a spare meal and raincoat. The boys set off at such a speed the girls had to almost run to keep up. Uncle Bill called on them to slow down but this had little effect. The group hurried along the track. No time was wasted on sightseeing or navigation. They just walked quickly past the 'Golden Hope', crossed Reward Creek, and hurried past the turnoff to the track they had searched the previous morning. As they walked the drizzle stopped, easing one worry.

By 7:55 they were at the old prospector's camp. He was busy cooking his breakfast. As the group walked across to the shelter, he raised a hand in greeting. He was removing a 'damper' from the fire.

"Morning all. Would you like some damper?" he asked.

"No thanks. We've just had breakfast," Uncle Bill replied. "We came to warn you that there is a cyclone out in the Coral Sea and it is headed this way."

The old prospector nodded thoughtfully. "Oh aye. Cyclone, eh? I suppose I'd better pack up and get out of here. When is it due?"

Uncle Bill took out his pocket radio. "Tonight or tomorrow I'd say. We should get another cyclone warning at eight."

He turned the radio on and adjusted it. The reception was very poor, with lots of static, but they were able to hear the news report. The cyclone warning was very detailed and even gave the latitude and longitude of the storm's eye.

"Pity we don't have one of them grid maps with the lat and long on it," the old prospector commented. "We could plot its position more accurately then."

As they listened, he broke off a piece of the damper. It looked very well cooked and was a crisp golden brown on the outside. He opened a bottle of syrup and used a teaspoon to drip some onto the damper.

He held this out to Kylie. "Try this lassie. Have ye ever had damper before?"

Kylie wasn't really hungry but out of good manners took the piece. "Only one we cooked at Guides," she replied. "And it wasn't a success."

She took a mouthful while the old prospector broke off another piece which he passed to Margaret. To Kylie's surprise the damper was hardly more solid than ordinary bread. It had none of the heavy doughiness she associated with such bush cooking.

"This is really good!" she said. "Thank you."

The old prospector smiled his appreciation. He passed another piece of syrup coated damper to a hesitant Allison. Kylie noted her reluctance and said, "Go on Allie. It is really good."

Margaret wiped syrup from her chin and agreed. "It is too. You are very good cook Mr Donaldson."

"Thank you missie." The old prospector said. He broke off another piece and held it up towards the boys. "Anyone?"

Graham and Peter shook their heads but Roger accepted. The old prospector tore off another piece and dripped syrup on it. "Anyone else? Oh, by the way, did your friends find you?"

For a minute the comment did not register. When it did Kylie felt a sharp stab of concern. "Friends?"

The old prospector nodded. "Three men. They came here yesterday just after you had left. They told me they were your friends and were supposed to join you."

"What were these three men like?" Kylie asked. The others all looked worried as the same thoughts crossed their minds.

"All young fellas about twenty. One solid, square faced sort of chap, a big fair-headed chap with real pale blue eyes; and a thin, dark haired chap with acne," the old prospector replied.

"Those men!" Margaret hissed, her face creased with worry.

The old prospector looked sharply at her. "Not your friends, eh? I thought it was a bit odd that they weren't with you. Who are they?"

Margaret acted as spokesperson. She told the story of the two men and how they had bashed Kylie, then secretly watched the farm. While Margaret talked Kylie's brain felt as though it was squirming with maggots.

Three men he said, and one of them about twenty with a squarish face. The only person she could think of who fitted that description was Victor. *Surely, he wouldn't be associated with those thugs?* It was an awful thought.

The same idea had obviously occurred to the others. Stephen said, "I'll bet that is the men we saw, and your cousin Victor."

Allison was appalled and shook her head. "Oh no! He wouldn't be with those horrible men."

"Victor was with one of them on New Year's night," Peter pointed out.

"But Bert's not like that! He wouldn't associate with people like that," Allison cried.

"How do you know?" Stephen said. "How well do you really know him? He was probably just leading you on to see if he could squeeze information out of you Allison."

Kylie was appalled at Stephen's cruel comment. She saw that Allison was very upset. She choked back tears as she cried "No!"

Kylie leapt to Bert's defence, "You are just jealous Stephen."

"Am not!" Stephen replied with a sneer that was nearly as hurtful.

"That will do!" Uncle Bill snapped. He turned to the old prospector. "Which way did these men come from?"

The old prospector pointed down the track beside his shelter. "From the 'Erin', across the Mulgrave. They went on the way you people just came from."

At that Kylie felt quite sick. "They didn't come to our camp," she said.

"They might have watched us," Graham said.

That was another sickening and worrying thought and it brought another, equally upsetting. Allison voiced it. "The cockatoos!"

The girls looked at each other in horror. Kylie shook her head but replied, "Oh I hope not!"

"What cockatoos?" Graham asked.

"When we were swimming this morning," Kylie replied. "A flock of cockatoos suddenly took fright and flew away."

Stephen laughed. "That's because they saw you without any clothes on," he said.

"That's enough of that," Uncle Bill said. "Mr Donaldson, did you see these men after that?"

"Nope, not a sign. I assumed they joined you at your camp," the old prospector replied.

Uncle Bill looked thoughtful and rubbed his jaw. Then he said to the old prospector, "Would you please not tell those people where we have gone if you see them again?"

"Aye, if they're the villains ye say then I'll not say a word," the old prospector replied.

Peter interrupted then. "Can we get going please? It is ten past eight already."

The group stood up and thanked the old prospector. He called good luck and waved as they set off. They went the same way as the previous afternoon, west across Nugget Creek to what they assumed was Franks Claim, then right up the track which went up the spine of the low ridge. They walked mostly in silence, but all the while Kylie's mind was turning over ugly thoughts about the three men who were stalking them.

As they reached the mossy rocks, it began to drizzle again. Uncle Bill looked up and muttered. Without pausing Graham led the way on along the track below the rocks. The track had been bench cut into the side of the slope but was only wide enough for one person to walk along. The ridge became steeper and the jungle on it thicker. A hundred paces past the rocks the track curved back up onto the crest of the ridge.

At this point the track forked. That cheered Kylie enormously. *That is what should happen,* she thought, her spirits lifting slightly.

They stopped briefly at the junction while the instructions and map were checked. As they did, a gust of wind shook the treetops and heavy drops showered down. Kylie noted that Uncle Bill looked worried and checked the time. 8:30am. She bit her lip.

We will have to start back in about an hour. She felt a sharp stab of concern. *To be so close to success and to run out of time!*

"Come on!" she said. "Hurry up! We are running out of time."

Graham nodded, folded his map away and set off along the right fork.

Chapter 25

TO THE LETTER

The track went down around the right side of the ridge. It was easy to follow, with hardly any undergrowth. Only an occasional rotting log blocked the path. Down to the right Kylie began to get glimpses of Nugget Creek. With every step her hopes rose. She kept glancing at the copy of the letter which she clutched in her left hand.

Only two more things to do: second creek and upstream fifty paces, she thought.

Graham still led, snipping an occasional vine or wait-a-while. He had his map in his other hand and Peter had the photocopy of the old diary in his. A fierce sense of urgency gripped them all. This was added to by concern over the weather. As they walked along the drizzle became heavier. Kylie found she had to shake drops off the plastic bag in which she had placed the letter to be able to read it in the wet.

After several minutes' walk they came to a flat area on a small spur. Graham stopped and they looked around.

"What is it?" Kylie asked.

"I reckon this was Grandad Hector's campsite," Graham replied.

Kylie studied the place. It looked big enough for a tent. Peter agreed with this. "This area has been levelled. It isn't natural."

"Here's the fireplace," Graham said. He walked over and knelt at some stones which showed through the leaf mould. Carefully he lifted the leaves aside to expose a circle of stones. At the sight of the blackened earth and stones Kylie felt her chest tighten up with emotion.

This where my great grandfather cooked his meals just before he died, she thought.

It was the most tangible thing yet to link her to that long dead ancestor. Somehow it was much more moving than the old diary or the letter or even the photos.

As they stood there, a heavy shower of rain swept across the valley. "Time to move," Uncle Bill said, glancing at his watch again.

The track led on around the side of the spur and into a small re-entrant. The creek was only a pace wide and was a mere trickle. "Great Grandad's water supply," Graham commented as they stepped across it.

"That is the first creek. We go on to the second creek," Kylie said. Now she began to feel really excited.

After the creek the track deteriorated. It was still plain to follow but was not cut out of the hillside. Soon after the creek the track went around the end of a small spur. At this point it passed over sharp rocks and there was a very steep drop down through jungle to Nugget Creek. Kylie could clearly see the creek about ten metres below.

After scrambling over the rocks the track went downwards to the bed of the creek. It then went along beside the water, weaving through the trees. By this time it was no longer an identifiable track and only an occasional old blaze mark on the bigger trees indicated they were still on it. The vegetation along the creek bank was much thicker and they had to stop to cut away several clumps of wait-a-while.

These delays made Kylie fret with impatience as she was very aware that time was slipping quickly away. 9am came and went and they still had not reached the second creek. Worse still the overcast had thickened up to make it quite gloomy and the drizzle was turning into steady rain.

At ten past nine they reached another creek. This flowed downhill from the left along a large re-entrant. The creek was nearly as large as Nugget Creek. Its bed was choked with rocks and large boulders and ferns and wait-a-while grew thickly on the banks.

"Second Creek," Graham said. "The instructions say go downstream for fifty paces, so we must go upstream." He gestured to Nugget Creek which was only five paces on their right.

"Let's hope our reading of the clues is right," Peter said. "And that it doesn't mean the first creek or the third."

Kylie shook her head. She was now so excited that she was feeling slightly giddy and nauseous. She pushed past the boys and began walking up the second creek, counting her paces as she went. The others all followed, several of them also counting paces.

This was hard to do because the creek bed was so irregular they had to step or jump from rock to rock. Graham simply walked in the water, ignoring the resulting wet boots. Stephen tried to go along the bank, but the vegetation was too thick. After thirty paces the creek levelled out and flowed along a straight section with a mostly sandy bed. The sides of the re-entrant closed in and became steeper, so that rough, rocky slopes went almost straight up from the bed. On the left the rocky cliff even overhung the creek bed. Further up the creek were a small waterfall and some small rock pools.

As she went Kylie's eyes were flicking rapidly around, searching eagerly for any sign of gold. In reality she wasn't quite sure what she was looking for but knew that quartz was the rock that generally carried gold. It was now quite dark and she looked anxiously for any glimpse of white on the dark rocky slopes.

"Fifty. It should be just around here somewhere," she said. She looked at the rocky slope on her left. It was some sort of layered rock with lots of overhanging shelves. Ferns and moss festooned it, making everything look black and green. There was nothing obvious to be seen. The others joined her and began to eagerly search the bed and both banks.

Kylie felt a wave of sharp disappointment, coupled by nagging urgency as she noted it was 9:20. "Ten minutes," she muttered. "Oh where is it?"

The others obviously felt the same as they began turning over stones, sifting sand and digging up the leaf mould on the banks. Kylie moved closer to the rock wall beside her and scanned it carefully. Was that a band of white? She put up her hand and rubbed at a film of moss on the rock face.

The green slime came away easily and exposed a clear band of quartz. A dyke, she knew it was called, where a volcanic igneous rock had forced its way up through a crack in another layer of rock. And what was that? She bent closer and felt her heart skip a beat.

Is it? Surely it can't be that easy? she thought.

Her fingers rubbed the rock face, touching the dull, yellowish metal that was embedded in the quartz. She shook her head in disbelief and hesitated, not wanting to make a fool of herself. She looked and saw more streaks and tiny nodules of yellow metal with the same dull gleam. Biting her lip she used a sharp stone to scratch at one of the protruding nodules.

Gold!

Without a shadow of doubt. As soon as she scratched the tarnished surface and exposed the metal, she saw it gleam brightly.

"Gold!" she cried. "I've found it!"

The others raced and splashed across to join her. She felt so excited that she was giddy. Her heart pounded and she had trouble focusing her eyes. With an effort she shook her head and bent to study the rock face.

She now saw that the whole seam of quartz for several metres was studded with small nuggets the size of a pea and that there were streaks of gold in the rock which looked for all the world like caramel topping swirled into white ice cream.

Uncle Bill touched the rock face further along and muttered to himself, then said, "Gold alright. Just look at it all. This must be it, the famous 'Jeweller's Shop'."

The others were now searching every square metre of the rock face in either direction. After a minute, Graham let out an exclamation, "Look! This rock has been chipped away."

The others crowded round to look. Uncle Bill ran his fingers over the rough edges of another vein of quartz. "This might be where Grandad Hector broke off his samples."

Kylie bent closer to look. That vein seemed to have even more gold in it than the one she had found. She shook her head in disbelief and gently touched a large nugget almost the size of a hen's egg which was protruding from the rock.

Stephen clambered up onto a ledge to look higher up the rock face. Margaret let out a little cry and bent to pick something up.

"Look what I found!"

On the palm of her hand was a nugget the size of a marble that had been lying in a crevice. They all stared at it in wonder and it was passed from hand to hand. Kylie marvelled at how heavy the nugget was. It was gold for sure. Her last doubts were dispelled. She began to laugh and cry at the same time.

"Oh we've done it! We've found the gold mine!" she cried.

She embraced Margaret and then they were all shouting and dancing. Graham even hugged Margaret in the excitement. Peter jigged up and down and it was him slipping and falling into the creek that calmed them down.

"Are you alright Peter?" Kylie asked as Peter struggled to his feet.

Peter nodded and grinned. "Yes."

"You are all wet," Margaret said.

Peter laughed. "Who cares? We are getting wet anyway." He gestured at the sky. Rain was now falling steadily and they were getting soaked anyway.

Margaret held the nugget out to Uncle Bill. "Here you are Uncle Bill, your first gold."

Uncle Bill smiled and shook his head. "You keep it. You found it. There is plenty more."

"But it's yours," Margaret insisted.

Again Uncle Bill shook his head. "No it isn't. No-one has pegged and registered a claim yet. Please keep it, Margaret."

Margaret murmured her thanks. Graham said, "Quick Uncle Bill, mark out your claim before anyone else does."

Uncle Bill laughed. "And who else is going to rush in and try to beat us to it? We are in the middle of nowhere, remember."

Stephen was still up on the rock ledge above them. He knelt on hands and knees and peered into the crevices.

"What are you looking for, Steve?" Peter asked.

"Wasn't there some reference about your great grandad collecting some samples in glass jars and storing them somewhere?" Stephen replied.

"Yes, there was," Kylie replied.

She quickly read the letter, but the reference wasn't there. Peter found it, on the last page of the photocopy of the old diary. "Here it is. Grandad Hector says: 'Fill a dozen jars with gold but too weak to carry them so hide them under the rock overhang'."

"That's what I thought," Stephen replied. He bent and peered under the rock ledge above the one he was clinging to.

"Careful Stephen, don't slip," Margaret cautioned. Stephen ignored her and groped in under the ferns and tree roots which covered the crevices.

Suddenly he let out a gasp, "Ah! Yes!"

Before their astonished eyes he produced a piece of rotten hessian, then a glass jar with a rusty lid still screwed on. Kylie could only gape, her heart pounding rapidly with excitement. As Stephen held the jar up, she could see it was full of gold.

He passed it down to Graham who let out a cry of amazement. "Strewth! You should feel how heavy this is."

The jar was passed around. 'Finest Pickles' it said in raised letters on the glass Kylie noted as she took her turn to hold it. She realised instantly why Great Grandad Hector had not taken the bottles. It really was heavy. She could get her fingers a bit over halfway round the jar but, small as it was, it was nearly too heavy for her to hold up. She had read about the mass of gold but was not at all prepared for the experience.

"Are there any more?" Peter asked Stephen.

Stephen knelt and groped in under the rocks. "Yes. Here, someone give me a hand."

The first glass jar was placed gently on a flat rock over to one side. Stephen then passed down more jars, all full of gold. Kylie saw that most of the gold was either flakes or tiny grains not much bigger than sand or sugar granules. Some jars had small nuggets in them and a few had shards of quartz with gold thick in it.

"There should be a dozen," Roger reminded as more jars were passed down and lined up.

Graham shook his head. "Eleven. Great Grandad Hector took one back with him remember," he said.

Another jar was passed down. Kylie counted them. Eight so far. Roger stood on tiptoe to peer into the crevice. "We want them all," he said.

"Don't be greedy Roger," Uncle Bill replied. "That is enough for one each."

"Oh we can't take any of this," Roger said. "This is your gold, to save the farm. After all, your grandad found it."

"We will all share," Uncle Bill replied. "You helped find it so you all must get some." He reached up and took another jar from Stephen. "Ten. Anyway, from the feel of these jars just one of them will pay the farm's debts."

"Do you really mean that Uncle Bill," Kylie asked.

Uncle Bill placed the jar carefully beside the others, then nodded and said, "Gold is fourteen hundred US dollars an ounce at the moment. I'd guess that one of these jars has several pounds in it. Say five pounds. That is er.. fourteen ounces to the pound... er."

Peter did the sum for him. "That would be seventy ounces. At fourteen hundred dollars per ounce, then one jar is worth... um... umm... worth... Holy Moses! Worth ninety-eight thousand dollars."

Kylie whistled in astonishment and stared at the line of jars. "Ninety-eight thousand dollars! Just for one of them. Would that be enough to save the farm Uncle Bill?"

"Not quite. Two of them would clear the debt nicely though," Uncle Bill replied.

"You can have mine," Kylie offered.

Uncle Bill shook his head. "As I said, we will share. You can have your fair share."

"Ninety-eight thousand dollars. What ever would I do with that sort of money?" Kylie said. Her mind boggled at the prospect.

"Put it in the bank," Uncle Bill replied. "It would be a nice nest egg to help buy a house when you get married."

"Or to help pay university fees and so on," Peter added.

"So what are all eleven worth?" Allison asked.

"Ten. We haven't found the last one. Is there any sign of it Steve?" Peter said.

Stephen shook his head. "No. The bag was all rotted away. It might have washed out in a flood."

"Or an animal dislodged it," Roger suggested.

"I'll have another look," Stephen said. He bent and groped under the rocks further along the ledge.

"Watch out you don't grab a snake or something," Graham cautioned.

By this time Peter had done the sum for eleven jars. "They are worth about one million and seventy-eight thousand dollars."

Kylie was struck speechless for a second, then gasped, "Over a million dollars! Just here in these jars! Incredible."

"And it's all ours," Uncle Bill said.

Even as he said this, a voice called out loudly from down the creek, "Wrong! It is ours."

They all spun to look in that direction. Kylie stared in horror. Two masked men stood there. Both wore black balaclavas and had guns. Even though their faces were covered she was sure it was the two thugs who had beaten her and Gran. The sight filled her with cold shock.

"Back off!" snarled one of the men. He gestured with a shotgun.

Burg, Kylie thought, noting the pale blue eyes.

Uncle Bill placed a restraining hand on Graham's sleeve. "Do as he says. Money isn't worth getting hurt over."

Terrible fears instantly gripped Kylie: that one of the boys might be shot and killed; or badly hurt; that the crooks might take one of the girls as a hostage; that the men might murder them all to stop them talking. She felt her heart pounding with anxiety.

The other man, thin with dark eyes, stepped forward and placed his rifle down on a rock. He then swung a haversack off his shoulders and picked up the jars one by one and placed them in the haversack.

"Go easy with them, Donk," the man with the shotgun said as two of the jars clinked noisily together.

Margaret recovered first. "Those are ours you thief. Leave them alone," she cried indignantly.

The man with the shotgun pointed it at her. *I wish she hadn't said that,* Kylie thought. Even as she thought this Graham stepped across in front of Margaret and Uncle Bill also moved to shield her. The man sneered and snarled, "Shut yer mouth moll. It is ours now. So find yourselves some more."

Donk had packed all the jars into his haversack by this. He swung it back on and picked up his rifle. Kylie saw him lick his lips.

He's nervous, she thought.

Donk said, "I got them Burg. Come on, let's get out of here."

"Get goin'. I'll follow. I..." Burg began.

However, at that moment Allison slipped on the wet rock she was standing on. She splashed into knee deep water towards him. The shotgun was instantly levelled on her, and Kylie's heart leapt into her mouth. She saw Burg's eyes flicker, then his mouth twist into a cruel grin.

"Well, well! If it isn't the pretty one who likes to swim in the nude. Maybe you should come with us, sweetie. We could teach you a thing or two."

Kylie felt her blood run cold as the fearful implications of what Burg was suggesting sank in. Suddenly the situation had taken on a whole new, and very ugly and sordid, twist.

Allison regained her footing and backed away. She gasped in fear and shock as the implications of what the man had said sank in. In a hoarse whisper she asked, "Were you watching?"

Burg gave an evil grin and nodded. "Yeah, an' it was real pretty. Except we was a bit too far away to see properly. So maybe you could show us close up like?"

"No!" cried Allison fearfully. She moved backwards.

Uncle Bill stepped forward. "Leave the girls alone. You will be in enough trouble as it is. They haven't done anything to you."

Burg pointed the shotgun at Uncle Bill and glared. For a second Kylie thought he was going to shoot, and she was swamped by dread.

It was Donk who saved the situation. "Leave them, Burg. For God's sake, you've done enough already. Let's get out of here." He turned and began making his way down the creek.

Burg twisted his lips in a grimace of frustration but apparently gave up his evil designs on Allison as he snarled, "You people stay here for one hour and don't try to follow us. If we see you then you just might meet a bit of lead coming the other way."

To emphasise this Burg fired the shotgun over their heads. The bang was so loud, and so unexpected, that Kylie let out a scream. So did the other girls. The boys all flinched and Roger looked very pale.

Burg turned and followed Donk back down the creek. The friends stood in a stunned group and watched them until they vanished from sight.

Graham spoke first, "Oh quick! We must get after them. They are getting away with all the gold!"

Chapter 26

TOO LATE

Uncle Bill held up his hand. "No. We stay here till they are gone."

"But Uncle Bill!" Graham cried. "They are getting away with the gold."

"Let them. I don't care. I don't want any of you hurt," Uncle Bill replied.

Stephen, who was still clinging to the ledge above them, added, "Anyway, they didn't get all the gold. Look."

He was holding the eleventh jar and grinning. That started them all talking. Kylie moved to Allison, who had started to cry. Margaret joined her.

"Those disgusting, horrible men!" Allison whispered. "Watching me swimming. They were going to... going to..." She could not finish.

Kylie hugged her. "I know. It's alright now, Allie. They have gone."

As they talked the rain began to fall more heavily. The sound of the drops hitting the leaves was so loud they had to raise their voices to be heard over it. Graham was still fuming over the crooks getting the gold.

"They can't have gone far," he persisted. "We could follow them and at least see what type of vehicle they are driving so we can tell the police."

"No," Uncle Bill replied firmly.

"But they are getting away with all the gold!" Graham cried. "We can't just sit here and do nothing!"

"No we can't," Uncle Bill agreed. "We won't. They haven't got all the gold at all. Most of it is still here in the ground, so we will use the time to mark out our claims."

"What a good idea!" Kylie cried. She got up and helped Allison to her feet.

"Who gets what?" Stephen asked.

"Uncle Bill gets this rock face," Kylie replied.

There was no disagreement about that, but a lot of discussion about where, if anywhere, the quartz reef might run. The upshot was that Kylie was given the next claim uphill, then Graham, as being blood relatives.

A second run of three was given to Peter, Roger and Stephen upstream of that. Allison was given the one across the creek where the rocks vanished underground again, and Margaret opted for a section on the downstream side of the rock face.

Half an hour was spent cutting and placing marker pegs to 'stake' their claims. Uncle Bill had the correct pieces of paper to put on each peg. These were filled out with some difficulty as the heavy rain persisted. Peter and Roger held their raincoats to make a roof to keep the paper dry while Uncle Bill wrote. The papers were then placed in plastic 'snap lock' bags and wired to the marker pegs or trees.

As they worked, Uncle Bill kept looking anxiously up at the treetops. "I don't like this rain," he muttered. "We had better get moving or we could get cut off by floods."

"This creek has risen already," Graham observed.

Kylie saw that he was right. Where it had been only ankle deep it was now knee deep and flowing more swiftly. Rocks that had been exposed were now covered.

Uncle Bill looked at his watch and bit his lip. "It has been over half an hour. Those men must surely be well out of the area by now. Let's go."

It was 10:30 by then and raining heavily. Kylie was glad to be moving as she was feeling cold. They splashed their way down the creek, slipping and sliding on the rocks or wading along the sandy stretches.

"Doesn't make any difference," Graham said. "We are soaked anyway."

They reached the junction of the two creeks and found the end of the track. That was easier going and Kylie was thankful to be out of the water. Graham and Peter now led, scouting ahead the way they had been taught to do in the army cadets. Uncle Bill, Roger and Stephen came next; Stephen having great difficulty as his glasses kept getting wet, despite his hat.

A couple of minutes walking had them up on the steep spur where the track went around above the small cliff. From then on things got easier as the track became better and better. Hector's camp was passed and they walked quickly on around the side of the ridge. Within five minutes they were at the moss-covered rocks.

"I can see now why these rocks have moss on them," Roger commented.

Stephen gave a short laugh, then said, "What I'm wondering is how those crooks knew where to come."

Kylie had thought the same thing but did not want to voice it.

Roger did. "They must have just followed us," he suggested. "That wouldn't have been hard. We cut a clear enough track."

"But all the way from Kearneys Flat?" Stephen replied. "How did they know to come to the Mulgrave Valley?"

"Just guessed I suppose," Roger replied.

"I'll bet Bert told them," Stephen suggested.

"Oh he did not!" Allison cried unhappily. "He promised he wouldn't. And he's not one of the gang!"

"You hope," Stephen replied sarcastically.

"He's not!" Allison cried in anguish.

"Stephen, stop it!" Kylie cried. "It doesn't matter how they found us. They did."

The boys in front had heard the argument and stopped. Uncle Bill frowned. "We have enough problems without bickering among ourselves, so please be quiet."

Stephen muttered sullenly and took off his glasses to try to dry them with his damp handkerchief. Kylie glared daggers at him, her anger stoked by the realization that it was a wasted effort as he could not see how hurtful his comments were.

The group continued walking and was soon at Franks Claim. As they walked several strong wind gusts shook the treetops violently.

"That cyclone must be getting closer," Peter commented.

"Listen to your radio Uncle Bill," Roger suggested.

Uncle Bill shook his head. "When we get back to the old prospector's camp. We should be there in time for the news at eleven."

Nugget Creek was their next problem. The rain had already raised its level and it was flowing swiftly. There was no chance of crossing dry. As they were all soaked this did not matter, but safety was an issue. Kylie also began to worry that they would have trouble walking far with their packs. Wet clothes would chafe and wet feet would blister more easily.

One by one they crossed the creek, holding hands and helping each other across the deepest part, which was now thigh deep. The water was cold and even though it was only a few paces Kylie found it scary.

"I didn't like that," she said as they stood dripping on the far side.

"No, if the Mulgrave is like that it will be very dangerous to cross," Uncle Bill said. "I'm afraid we may have left it too late."

They started to move off. However, they had not gone ten paces before Graham suddenly ducked down and urgently signalled to take cover. A spasm of sickening fear coursed through Kylie. She moved over behind a tree and waved to Margaret and Allison to do the same.

Someone was running along the track towards them. She could hear the squelching thud of his footfalls before he came into view. *Oh, I hope it isn't one of the crooks*, she thought anxiously.

The runner burst into view around the bend in the track. Kylie gaped in astonishment.

Bert!

Bert saw them at the same moment and slowed down. A look of relief crossed his face. He looked quite exhausted and was red in the face. For a minute he was too winded to speak. It was obvious he had run a long way. When Allison saw him, she raced forward to embrace him. He smiled with relief and hugged her.

The others crowded around. "What's going on?" Graham asked. "What are you doing here, Bert?"

"Looking for you to warn you," Bert replied. He was still panting and his chest heaved between words. "Those crooks are in this area looking for you."

"We know," Graham replied. "We have met them."

A look of pain crossed Bert's face. "Oh. I'd hoped to get here first. They are following you. What did they do?"

"Robbed us," Graham said angrily.

Bert looked miserable. "Sorry. I thought they would just wait till you had found the gold mine, then try to muscle in on the claim, try to register it before you could. Did they take much?"

"About a million dollars' worth of gold," Peter answered.

"Gold! A million... Gold! Did you find it then, the 'Jewellers Shop'?"

"Yes, we did," Uncle Bill replied. "And we've staked our claims."

"But... but where did the gold come from?" Bert asked.

"Grandad Hector collected a dozen jars of the stuff and hid it there," Uncle Bill replied. "We found it. Or rather, Stephen did."

"Great! But they took it? How?" Bert asked.

The robbery was described. Bert looked very unhappy. "I think it was my fault. When I went home last Wednesday mum asked when I was going to Cairns again to see Allie and I said: 'Not for a week, they are going on another expedition to look for the gold mine'. I realised then what I was doing and clammed up, so I didn't tell her where you were going."

"You knew, though?" Graham queried.

Bert made a wry smile. "It was pretty obvious. When you dropped the maps of the Mulgrave it was plain that it was not just a cunning ploy to fool me."

"Was Victor there when you were talking to your mum?" Kylie asked. She did not want to ask but knew she had to. She saw a look of pain cross Allison's face as she did.

Bert bit his lip and nodded. "Yes, he was. I think he is with these crooks. Did you see him?"

"No we didn't," Kylie replied. That set her thinking. Where was Victor?

Peter said, "That old prospector said that there were three men looking for us this morning. He was probably the third man."

Bert pointed back along the track. "Is that the old bloke back there in the mine?"

"Yes."

"I just spoke to him. He said that three men came this way," Bert said.

"So Victor stayed out of sight while his cronies did the robbery," Stephen suggested.

"No. The old guy said that he only saw two men come back," Bert replied. He looked very upset and worried. "I'm sorry. It is all my fault!"

"Time for that later. Let's get out of here," Uncle Bill said. "We must get across the river before the rain floods it."

Bert shook his head. "Too late. I came across half an hour ago and nearly got washed away. It was rising fast then. I don't like your chances."

"We must try anyway," Uncle Bill said. He set off along the track at a fast walk.

As they walked, Graham asked Bert, "Did you see the two crooks?"

Bert shook his head. "No. I think I came in along another track. The old prospector pointed down a different one from the one I followed. I came past your camp."

"A line of packs in a little clearing?" Graham queried.

Bert nodded. "That's right." He paused to look up as a strong gust shook the treetops above them. "I hope we aren't stuck here. That cyclone is getting closer fast. Mum was real upset when I defied her to drive down here. I don't feel good about it at all."

"What happened?" Allison asked.

Kylie strained her ears to hear above the wind and rain.

"At breakfast I asked mum where Victor was. He wasn't at home yesterday either and didn't come home last night. She said he had gone pig shooting or something with a couple of his mates. The moment she told me who they were I knew what they were up to."

"So you weren't with them?" Peter called back over his shoulder.

"No. I was at home. I only found out this morning. I left home straight away and drove down to that picnic area about ten kilometres back."

"When did you get there?" Graham asked.

"I left home about eight o'clock. So it must have been about nine. I ran from there," Bert replied.

"You must be bloody fit!" Graham replied.

"Not really. I did a lot of jogging and fast walking. I was worried about Allie." He gave her a smile and she blushed with pleasure and smiled back. Kylie grinned and felt a warm glow for them.

By then they were at the old prospector's camp. He was busy rigging canvas sides to the two open sides of his shelter. The wind had stopped again but the rain was still pouring down. The clearing was all slush and mud. At the entrance to the mine a small diesel pump was puttering, spewing water out into a drain.

"In ye come. I wondered when ye'd be back," the old prospector replied. He looked at Bert. "I see ye found yer friends."

Bert nodded. "Yes thanks."

Graham asked, "Did you see those three men come back this way?"

The old prospector nodded and gestured towards the track leading off beside his shelter. "Aye. 'bout half an hour ago. I were workin' on me pump over there and they didn't see me. They went that way, 'cept there weren't three, only two. I presumed the other fella was with you."

"No he isn't," Uncle Bill replied. He looked very worried.

"They robbed us!" Margaret added indignantly.

"Robbed ye! Aye, they were a mean looking pair of cusses, particularly that big blond brute," the old prospector replied.

"Did they go across the river?" Graham asked.

"Don't know," the old prospector replied.

"We must look," Graham replied.

Uncle Bill tried to restrain him but Graham shook his head and started walking down the side track. "We have to know. If they are still on this side of the river we have a double problem."

Uncle Bill nodded sadly, then agreed. "Yes. And we must cross the river as quickly as we can too, or we will be cut off as well. Come on. See you later Mr Donaldson."

"Oh aye. Ye'll be back then will you?" the old prospector asked.

"You bet. We've all staked claims," Uncle Bill replied.

"Have ye now! Now don't tell me that ye have gone and found the famous 'Jewellers Shop'," the old prospector asked, his bewhiskered face alive with interest.

"We have. Tell you about it after this cyclone," Uncle Bill replied. "Come on kids."

Peter and Uncle Bill both went off after Graham along the track. The others followed, wishing the old man well as they did.

"What about our packs?" Roger asked.

"Leave them," Uncle Bill replied. "We can get them after the cyclone. They will only slow us down anyway."

It was only a hundred metres to the river. Well before they reached it they could hear the rush of floodwaters. When they were still well inside the jungle, they encountered flowing water. It took some scouting to find a place where they could get a clear view of the river, and even then they had to wade out through waist deep water among the trees and vines.

One glance at the foaming water was enough. They were too late.

Kylie stared at the river in frightened amazement. Gone was the enchanting stream of the morning gurgling slowly from pool to pool. In its place was a raging, foaming torrent a hundred metres wide. Large boulders protruded from the welter of foam, but Kylie could not see any way to get across.

"It must have been raining heavily up in the headwaters during the night," Uncle Bill said.

"What do we do?" Margaret asked. She looked frightened and was shivering with cold, her arms covered with goose bumps.

"Go back and camp till the river goes down," Uncle Bill replied.

He looked so unhappy Kylie's heart went out to him. *Poor Uncle Bill. He will be in trouble for not getting us out in time and all the parents will be so worried.*

Graham set off, splashing through the flooded jungle. "I'll check that those men are gone," he called. "I don't fancy sharing a camp with them."

He had not gone ten metres before he let out a cry and gestured for the others of join him. He pointed out through a gap in the trees as they splashed over. "The men. They didn't make it in time."

Kylie peered through the foliage and gasped. Out in mid-stream, perched on top of a huge pile of rocks, were the two men. They were staring around them at the rushing water and did not look happy. Both had removed their balaclavas and Kylie saw that she had been right; it was Burg and Donk. Donk still wore his haversack but neither now appeared to be armed.

"They are trapped," Peter observed.

"Good!" Margaret added.

A horrible thought came to Kylie. "If the river rises more, then they could be washed off and drowned."

"Serves them right," was Stephen's comment.

"They could swim for it," Graham suggested.

Uncle Bill shook his head, "They wouldn't have a hope. No-one could swim in that and live. You would be tumbled over and over by the turbulence. You would whack your head against a rock and be knocked unconscious. Then you would drown."

"We must do something to save them," Kylie said, appalled at the thought of the two men being killed.

"What can we do?" Stephen said. "We have to save ourselves."

"We could try to get a rope to them," Graham suggested.

"Where are you going to get a rope a hundred metres long?" Peter asked.

"From the old prospector?" Graham replied.

"I wonder where Vic is?" Bert said.

Kylie had forgotten Victor but now she felt a stab of anxiety. Where was he? Was he waiting on the other bank?

Bert waded and swam forward to the edge of the trees and clambered onto a boulder where the men could see him. He waved his arms and shouted. "Hoy! Hello! Hey you blokes!"

Kylie saw the two men's heads turn. Bert yelled at the top of his voice, "Where is Vic?"

Burg put his hand to his ear to indicate he could not hear but Donk pointed back to their bank. Bert yelled again, asking if Victor was on the other bank.

"No," Donk yelled back.

Again he pointed back and called. Kylie could not hear him properly because of the sound of rushing water but she understood that Victor was somewhere on their bank.

"Save us!" wailed Donk.

Bert came splashing back after again trying to get a clear answer. He looked very strained. "Vic is somewhere on this bank. I don't like this. I hope they haven't done anything to him."

Chapter 27

VICTOR

"Where is Victor? We must find him," Bert said. He looked around in a distracted way.

"Ask those crooks again," Peter suggested.

Bert shook his head. "They won't tell me. I've tried that. I'm worried they have done something to him."

"Murdered him you mean?" Stephen blurted out, voicing all their fears and causing Bert to compress his lips into a grim line. He nodded unhappily.

"But why?" Margaret queried.

"So they wouldn't have to share the loot probably," Stephen said.

Kylie did not like the trend of the conversation. She said, "Let's think positive to begin with. Victor might be at our camp."

"Or lost in the jungle," Stephen added gloomily.

"Let's go to our camp," Uncle Bill said. "We need to go there anyway. You kids need some food and dry clothes."

They made their way back to the old prospector's camp. Here they paused while Bert and Uncle Bill checked the old prospector's story. He was adamant that three men had gone west along the track towards Nugget Creek but that only two had returned. "As I said, I thought one of them had stayed with you, like this young fella did."

"We are cut off by the floods," Uncle Bill said. "What do you recommend we do? Where is the safest place in a cyclone?"

The old prospector grinned. "Somewhere else! Another hundred kilometres inland. But search me. I ain't never been through a cyclone in the jungle afore. I guess here's as good as anywhere if you care to join me."

Uncle Bill nodded. "Thanks. The cyclone may not come here at all but we need to be ready. We will go and get our packs and then have lunch."

It was still raining steadily and the wind was gusting again. The group walked rapidly east to Reward Creek and stopped in surprise. The creek was flowing deep and swift. However, they were still able to cross by jumping from rock to rock and climbing along a tree trunk which grew out at an angle.

Ten minutes later they were at their camp. To Kylie's intense disappointment Victor was not there. They walked on down to the river to check if he was there, and on the off-chance that it might be possible to cross there. Victor was not there either, and they could not get within twenty metres of the edge of the jungle. Swirling floodwaters had swamped the forest.

"There aren't crocodiles in this river are there?" Margaret asked.

Kylie looked at the dark, swirling waters, with their surface load of floating debris and shuddered. "No," she replied shortly. *We've got enough to worry about without conjuring up more horrors,* she thought.

The group returned to their camp and picked up their packs. These were swung on and they made their way back to Reward Creek. Uncle Bill would not let them cross with their packs. He had Graham and Peter cross and then swung the packs across one at a time himself. Then the teenagers went across one at a time, held by Uncle Bill and then passed to Peter and Graham.

The group returned to the old prospector's camp in torrential rain. They found him busy digging his storm drains deeper. All were ushered inside but that made it very cramped. Still, it was a real relief to be out of the rain and under cover. The old prospector kept digging. Kylie watched him as he carefully dug mud from the drain and piled it inside the tent.

"It's not the drain that's important," the old prospector explained. "It's the dam inside. The drain is just a borrow pit to get the soil from. The drain fills up in a few minutes. The dam is what stops the surface flow from running into your tent. So it must be inside the tent so that the floor doesn't fill up and you can maintain it. Would ye mind fixing that bit over there?"

He indicated a section of the dam which was low enough for water to start seeping over the top. Graham and Roger both moved to kneel and pat the mud into a higher, more solid dyke.

"That's good boys. Now, let's re-arrange this so we are all a bit more comfortable," the old prospector said. They were moved to sit around the outside of the shelter, leaving the centre clear and also the entrance to the tent and near the fireplace. The old prospector had stacked up cords of firewood on cross pieces, which kept it out of the mud and dry. They sat on the firewood, on old boxes, or on their packs.

The old prospector pointed to his tent. "You'd better all get out of them wet clothes before you get a chill," he said.

Uncle Bill shook his head. "No, we are going out again as soon as we have had a feed. We have to find Victor."

"Who's Victor?" the old prospector asked.

"My brother," Bert said. "I am Bert Reid. Victor was with those two men."

"Oh aye. Then ye'd best look for him. It wouldn't do for him to be out in this weather all night," the old prospector replied. He placed a billy on the fire and added sticks to build up the flames.

Kylie sat on her pack and followed the lead of Uncle Bill and Graham, both of whom took out their stoves. "Hot food," Uncle Bill said. "You need to keep up your body core temperature, and your morale."

Kylie wasn't really hungry. Indeed she felt sick at heart with anxiety over the approaching storm and with worry over what had become of Victor. However, she made herself heat a tin of sausages and vegetables and ate this. Once she started spooning the warm food in her appetite returned and she quickly downed the lot. By then the billy was boiled and she gratefully accepted a cup of hot, sweet tea to which she added condensed milk.

"At least we have enough cups this time," she said as the old prospector poured the hot water into her cup.

During the meal Uncle Bill took out his radio and set it up. Reception was even worse and all they could glean was that the cyclone was still heading their way and was intensifying. The news that it was expected to develop into a Category 3 by evening was sobering to all of them.

At length Uncle Bill drained his cup. "Time we went. It is half past twelve. If the cyclone is coming, we want to find Victor and be back here as quickly as we can. I think you girls should stay here."

Kylie shook her head. "No. I want to look. We can all help."

Uncle Bill looked doubtful, so Kylie persisted. "Please, Uncle Bill. We don't want to be left here with those horrible men just down there at the river. They might manage to get ashore."

That made Margaret gasp with concern. Graham said, "Should we keep watch on them?"

"Not a bad idea. What if two of you do that. You can keep on checking up on the camp in case Victor wanders in. Who would like to stay?"

No-one volunteered so Uncle Bill said, "Stephen, you and Roger stay. That way you can keep those glasses of yours dry most of the time. If the men come ashore, or if Victor arrives, then come along the track to our find to tell us. We will be along there somewhere."

There was a bustle of preparation. Raincoats were donned and Uncle Bill took a haversack containing his First Aid kit, radio, food, and water. As soon as all were ready, they made their way outside. Even the old prospector joined them, a piece of old tarpaulin draped over his head and shoulders.

They set off back along the track to the Jeweller's Shop. As they walked Graham and Peter studied the ground carefully for any sign of tracks or broken vegetation off to the side. The others followed, scanning the jungle on either side as they walked slowly along. The rain persisted but varied from heavy showers to solid drizzle.

In spite of the raincoats they were all soon soaked again but at least the raincoats helped to keep them warm. Kylie was amazed at how cold she was. *This is the tropics! We are only seventeen degrees from the Equator.*

Nugget Creek held them up nearly half an hour. It was badly swollen and they had to search up and down its banks to find the safest point to cross. The water was waist deep where they did this but a log and some rocks just upstream of that point broke the force of the current and gave them a back eddy which helped. They were already so wet that wading and floundering in the cold water made no real difference.

After that it was slow scouting and searching. They made their way to Franks Claim and looked carefully along two other old tracks which radiated out from it. The one to the west had been used by the old prospector and was fairly obvious so they followed it for several hundred metres to another old mine. After that it petered out and they gave it up.

They were looking for footprints in the mud but there was so much dead fall that the spongy surface barely registered that they had all walked on it. Nor was there any sign of the vegetation being disturbed. Feeling even more worried they turned and set off back the way they had come.

At Franks Claim they turned up the track towards the 'Jewellers Shop'. They slowly searched up this until they reached the moss-covered rocks. All the while the rain poured down and wind gusts shook the treetops. Once the wind caused a large dead branch to fall nearby. That made them all look fearfully at each other, and Kylie felt particularly sorry for Uncle Bill, knowing he would be blaming himself for getting them into the situation.

At the track junction near the moss-covered rocks they stopped to consider their next move.

"We had better follow this track that goes to the left," Uncle Bill. "Someone has been along it recently."

"I have," the old prospector answered. "It goes up to an old mine halfway up the mountain, a quartz blow I thought looked promising."

"Victor may have followed it so let's go that way," Bert said.

"Why don't we split up?" Graham suggested. "We would cover more ground that way."

"No!" Uncle Bill replied emphatically. "We have already left two at the camp and we are not going to get scattered all over the bloody jungle in this weather."

The fact that Uncle Bill swore gave Kylie a clue to the strain he was under. *Poor Uncle Bill,* she sympathized.

The group set off up the other track. This was steeper and much less clearly defined than the other one. It went up the spine of the ridge, winding through thick jungle and around more clumps of rocks. These slowed them down. As Uncle Bill insisted, they carefully search all around them, just in case Victor had slipped and lay injured among the boulders.

The ridge grew steeper and steeper and they began to get glimpses out through the trees. These showed grey curtains of rain and dark looming mountains across the valley and behind them. Kylie knew one of the mountains must be Bartle Frere, but she was becoming both disoriented and distressed. She was also aware that she and Margaret were both shivering with cold. Allison appeared fine, but then she was walking with Bert and they exchanged frequent loving glances.

The higher up the mountainside they climbed the worse the wind became. It drove the rain hard at them and shook the trees wildly. Leaves whipped past and several times they heard trees or branches fall nearby. A gap in the canopy showed that the sky was solid overcast. It was dark enough to be late evening rather than mid-afternoon.

The climb got them all puffing and tested sore muscles and will-power but at least the effort warmed them a little. The rain poured down without a break, seeping in under their collars.

It was 2pm when they reached the old mine. It was a sad disappointment. The scars of old earthworks showed where tents had been pitched and a collapsed and overgrown tunnel entrance indicated the actual mine, but it was a cold, wet and windy place and there was no sign of Victor.

For a few minutes the group stood in shivering silence, looking around. Kylie felt sick at heart and had begun to quietly pray. Bert was now visibly upset.

"Where else can he be?" he cried. His face showed that he was undergoing mental anguish and was close to tears.

"In the jungle somewhere?" Peter suggested.

"But where? Why? Why would he leave the track?" Bert shouted.

"Maybe he was running away from those men?" Graham suggested.

Bert shook his head. "That doesn't make sense. They were supposed to be mates."

"Thieves falling out, when they realised how much money was involved?" Peter said. "Gold makes people terribly greedy, so I've heard."

"But he wasn't there when the two men robbed us," Kylie said.

"Maybe they snuck up and watched, then had an argument about what to do?" Graham suggested.

They considered this for a moment. Kylie said, "Which would mean they must have been quite close to where we found the gold."

Uncle Bill looked sick. His face appeared haggard, and he nodded. "We are a bunch of fools. We should have thought of that earlier. We are wasting time. Let's get down to the 'Jewellers Shop'."

The thought that they had wasted several hours did not appeal to any of them. It was enough to make Kylie choke up with emotion. Led by Graham they set off back down the mountain side, going as fast as safety would allow, and some times too fast as they all slipped several times.

It was 2:30 by the time they reached the track junction near the moss-covered rocks again. Without pause they took the track to the 'Jewellers Shop'. As they walked along it the old prospector commented. "It ain't my business I know but is your gold mine, the famous 'Jewellers Shop', down this track?"

"Yes," Uncle Bill replied.

"Drat! I searched this way a dozen times. Went up every creek too. Ah well, good luck ter ye."

"You can have some too," Kylie said.

"Thanks lassie, but I'll do me own finding," the old prospector replied with a smile. "Lookin's most of the fun do ye see?"

Kylie nodded. She wasn't really interested in gold at that moment. It was enough to know that the farm had been saved.

They walked quickly along in the driving rain, a mostly silent single file. Within a few minutes they had reached Hector's campsite. There was a pause while they looked around. Graham even looked over the slope near the tent. Nothing. Sick at heart they continued on.

The small creek near the camp was now a foaming flume that they had to jump across. Progress slowed as the track deteriorated. As it passed out around the end of the spur they went even slower. Down below Kylie could see that Nugget Creek was now racing along, swirling and foaming over the rocks in its bed.

Suddenly Graham stopped. He bent to look at a bush, then pointed. Without a word he stepped off the track and made his way down the steep slope. It was so dangerous he had to move from tree to tree. Peter pointed down as the others came up. To Kylie it seemed as though her heart had stopped. She did not want to hope in case it was a false alarm. There was a scuff mark on the bark of a tree and the leaf mould had been disturbed.

"Here he is!" Graham cried. He was five metres below them now, right on the lip of the steep drop down to the creek.

"Oh thank God!" Kylie cried, only to have her heart seize up with anxiety as Peter called, "Is he alive?"

Chapter 28

CRISIS

"Vic!" Bert cried. He scrambled down the slope towards him.

"Steady! Slow down!" Peter called, reaching out to stop Bert sliding down the cliff. It wasn't a big drop, only about ten metres, but it was enough.

Graham held up his hand as Bert slithered from tree to tree to join him. "No more! Stay back up there."

Kylie had moved a few steps down the slope from the track, but she now stopped, her heart in her mouth as she watched Graham bend and place his fingers on Victor's neck. She could only just see the top of Victor's head and saw that he was wedged against a tree, right on the top of the drop.

Bert knelt beside Victor, his face a mask of anxiety. Graham nodded and called out, "He's alive!"

"Thank God!" Kylie cried. She was moved to hug Allison who was looking very drawn.

Bert and Graham knelt and did some more checking. Kylie could not hear what they were saying but saw them nodding in agreement. Graham straightened up and called up to them, "We must get him out of here quickly. His pulse is very weak and he is extremely cold. Form a line down to here and grab hold of each other and we will drag him up."

Under Graham's direction they did so. Bert was sent back up the slope and Peter took his place because, like Graham, he was wearing army webbing and that gave a good strong handhold. The line then ran Bert, Uncle Bill, the old prospector, Kylie, Allison, and Margaret.

"Grab hold of each other," Graham called. "No, not by the hands. Grab their clothes."

"By the belt," Peter supplemented.

They did this. Bert shook his head and muttered unhappily. Kylie did not like this procedure. She called down, "Can't we lower him down?"

"No. Too steep."

"Won't we cause more injuries doing this?" she called back.

Graham shook his head. "Don't think so. Anyway, exposure is more of a problem. He doesn't appear to have any bones broken."

Still not happy but seeing no option Kylie gripped the old prospector's leather belt and the small tree beside her. When they were all linked up she watched Graham bend down and take hold of Victor's coat at the shoulders. Graham had his back to them and was only prevented from pitching forward over the edge by Peter gripping his webbing at the back.

"Okay, heave! Walk away up the track," Graham yelled.

They tried but most slipped and had to change their grip and better position their feet. Kylie found the wet bark of the tree much more slippery than she had imagined and had to wipe her hand. Her hand still slipped so she curled her arm around the tree. The group resumed its uphill move, muscles straining and fingers cramping. They heaved and struggled. Kylie moved uphill enough to put the side of her foot against the tree and to reach up to another sapling. That helped. To her relief she saw that Victor had been dragged up over the lip of the rocks.

After that it was easier. Graham urged them to keep walking backwards as he dragged Victor over the deadfall and rocks. Within a minute Victor was lying on the track. They stopped pulling and crowded round to look. Kylie was appalled. Victor had obviously been bashed hard in the face and on the temple. A dark, purple and black bruise marked his right cheek. Worse, and more worrying, was a huge greenish lump on his left forehead. He was breathing but that was barely discernible.

"He's very cold. We must get him to shelter quickly," Graham said.

"We need a stretcher," Peter said.

"We can make one," Graham answered. He looked around, then shook his head. "We need tools; an axe or a machete."

"I've got them at my camp," the old prospector said.

"Come on then. You others wait here," Graham said. Without waiting to see if he was obeyed, he dropped his webbing and set off at a fast walk. The others stood in a shivering huddle.

Peter now took charge. "We can cover him from the rain. Give me hand." He peeled off his raincoat and held it over Victor's face. Kylie also took off hers and she and Margaret held it while Bert and Allison held Peter's. Peter and Uncle Bill crouched and carefully checked Victor for other injuries. They gently felt along his limbs and neck.

"Can't find anything broken," Peter said. "I think it is just his head."

"He's had a big whack," Uncle Bill said, indicating the greenish lump.

A wave of nausea almost overcame Kylie as she looked at Victor. His face was pinched and pale and his breathing was barely noticeable.

"Murder!" Bert cried angrily. "Those bastards tried to murder him. They hit him on the head and tossed him over the edge."

Uncle Bill nodded grimly. "Yes, they probably did."

"Burg," Kylie added. "I'll bet it was him." She was sick to the bottom of her heart with horror and dread. It was obvious that Victor was in a bad way and that he might still die if he did not receive proper medical treatment quickly. She bit her lip and tried to hold back the tears. Her worst fears were being realised: a serious injury as far from the car as they could possibly be, and cut off by a flooded river!

The next half hour was one of anxiety and impatience. Several times either Bert or Allison muttered, "Oh where are they?" This nettled Kylie a bit as she knew that Graham would be taking foolish risks to go as fast as possible. Through all of this the rain poured down and the wind in the trees grew stronger.

"We were supposed to be back at the cars by now," Margaret said quietly at one stage. Kylie could only nod unhappily.

After what seemed an age, Graham and the old prospector returned. Both were carrying stout poles and Graham wore a pack and had a bundle of basic webbing.

"Steve's and Roger's," he explained as he dropped it all.

"Where are they?" Margaret asked.

"Tying a rope across Nugget Creek," Graham answered. "Okay Pete, let's get to work." Graham and Peter went to work quickly, buckling their own basic webbing up and then placing the four sets of webbing in a line. They then slid the poles through the belts and straps.

"What are you doing?" Bert asked.

"Making an improvised stretcher," Graham replied. Bert looked doubtful but Kylie knew exactly what the boy's meant. She had seen this done as a demonstration during the cadet unit's annual 'Passing-Out' Parade the previous November. While they did this Kylie was appalled at how cold Victor's skin felt and it was a real relief to know they had at least got him into some sort of shelter.

"Shouldn't we tie a couple of sticks across to keep the poles from closing in and squashing him," Uncle Bill queried.

Peter shook his head. "No need. This will work fine. We do it at cadets," he explained.

Graham pointed. "Okay people, all on this side. Now slide your arms in underneath him. When I say lift, lift him up and Pete, you and Uncle Bill slide the stretcher underneath from the other side."

The stretcher did not look much but to Kylie it was a huge step forward. A minute of group effort directed by Graham had Victor lying on it. Graham pointed to his pack.

"Get the shelter and sleeping bag out. Try to keep the bag dry."

Margaret extracted the sleeping bag while Kylie, Bert and Allison held the plastic shelter over them. The sleeping bag was unzipped and wrapped around Victor. The plastic shelter was then draped over him. Peter pulled the plastic up to shield his face but Bert bent and pulled it back, so his face was partly exposed. Kylie knew why: it made him look too much like a corpse. The thought made her shudder.

Peter now took charge. "Okay, now the hard part begins," he said. He instructed them to group themselves around the stretcher. "As soon as someone feels they need a break then get someone else to take over. Don't try to tough it out. Keep changing every few paces if you have to. Now, hands on... prepare to lift... lift!"

Kylie took the left back corner. Instantly she realised what Peter was talking about. She knew he and Graham had been trained to make bush stretchers in the cadets and they had obviously had practice at carrying them. Peter gave the orders and nobody queried them. He and Graham went at the front on either side. Margaret and Uncle Bill went on each side. The old prospector went ahead of them to cut and push vines out of the way and to relieve them. Bert took the other back corner with Allison to help him.

It was much harder than Kylie had ever imagined it could be. Her hands kept slipping on the wet timber and her fingers seemed to cramp up within seconds. The stretcher was just too wide for the foot track and they kept having to stop to manoeuvre through gaps between trees or to cut vines. At these places people had to let go one at a time to step around trees. They then resumed their place on the stretcher.

"You can see why we need eight people to carry a stretcher," Peter commented.

Kylie could only agree. Within one minute, she knew she could not last more than a few seconds. She called to Peter and he told them all to stop and lower the stretcher. Then they all moved clockwise one place.

"Both hands on the stretcher if you can," Peter said. "It spreads the load better and you are less likely to lose your grip and drop the patient."

The stretcher was then lifted and the group struggled on down the narrow, muddy track with it. They managed to cover about fifty paces before Margaret and Allison called for relief. The old prospector then took over from Graham who went ahead. Another fifty paces were covered. By then Kylie had been scratched by wait-a-while and could feel her shoulder and arm muscles beginning to protest.

As before, the stretcher kept snagging in bushes and vines and after another couple of minutes they had to give up and rest. The stretcher was lowered to the track and Bert moved to try to shield Victor's face from the rain. Kylie saw that Victor was now shivering violently and that made her feel even more distressed.

They tried again, Uncle Bill taking the lead and Graham taking Kylie's place. She led the way, finding it a huge relief. But she also felt guilty, as though she wasn't doing her fair share. They covered another hundred paces in five minutes. By then they were all sweating and shaking from the strain.

"Time for a real rest. Prepare to lower. Lower!" Peter ordered.

"We aren't getting anywhere!" Margaret cried.

Peter shook his head. "Yes, we are. We can't give up now. We must keep going," he said. "It isn't far to Franks Claim now."

They rested for a few more minutes. Then 4:30 passed. The rain became even heavier. Kylie bit her lip with anxiety and tried not to meet Bert's anxious eyes.

"Let's go. Hands on," Peter ordered.

They bent and picked the stretcher up. The slow, shuffling movement resumed. The track was awash by surface run-off by then and they were all trying to wipe rain from their faces to keep their eyes clear. The movement began to take on nightmare qualities.

Suddenly Uncle Bill stumbled. His foot slipped in the mud. He let out a cry of alarm and tried to regain his balance but caught his foot against a tree root. With a cry of pain he fell, knocking Bert aside as he did. The stretcher coming down heavily on top of them. Victor was rolled out and let out a ghastly moan which made Kylie's blood run cold.

"Are you alright, Uncle Bill?" Graham asked as Uncle Bill muttered and grimaced. They lifted the empty stretcher off him.

"Think I've sprained my ankle. I'll be alright," Uncle Bill said. He stood up and shook his head angrily. "Come on, let's get Victor back on the stretcher."

They lifted Victor back on and Uncle Bill moved to lift his corner again. It was immediately apparent that he was hurt more badly than he wanted them to admit. However, he gamely carried the stretcher another fifty paces before calling on Graham to take over. By then Margaret and Allison were visibly weakening and were only able to last twenty or thirty paces before calling for help.

Allison ended up dropping her corner. It slipped from her hands, but Margaret was able to save it from a fall. Peter told them to lower the stretcher. They then stood disconsolately in the rain with heads bowed and chests heaving.

"This is no good," Graham said angrily. "The bloody track is too narrow. Pete, get your toggle rope."

Under Graham's direction Peter took the strong three-metre-long nylon rope off his webbing. Graham did likewise, then tied the ends to the handles of the stretcher. "I saw this in a movie about World War One," he explained. He then wriggled in between the stretcher poles and placed the rope over his shoulder like a yoke. Peter did the same at the back.

"Help us up. All hands on. Prepare to lift... lift!" Graham cried. Uncle Bill and Margaret steadied Graham as he stood up, his face going red from the strain. Bert and Kylie helped Peter up. As soon as the two boys were steady on their feet Graham began walking. "Hold the sides of the stretcher and steady us so we don't slip," he instructed.

It was immediately apparent that this was a better method, but Kylie could also see that it was a terrible strain on the two boys. However, they stuck it for a hundred paces and reached Franks Claim. That was a relief. Uncle Bill moved to take over the front, but Graham refused as Uncle Bill had been limping. Bert took over from Peter and they turned left and headed for Nugget Creek.

They almost made it to Nugget Creek in one lift but by then Graham was gasping, his laboured breathing audible even at the rear. They had another rest and then pressed on to the creek.

Seeing it was another shock but also a boost to morale. *Not far now,*

Kylie told herself to try to keep her spirits up. The creek was a real spate now and rocks which had earlier been exposed were now covered. Stephen and Roger waited on the far bank and had a rope tied across.

There was a delay while they debated how to get across. In the end they passed all the loose items across first. Uncle Bill insisted that no-one be in the yokes while they crossed. "You must be able to get free if you slip," he said.

It wasn't far but was just too great a distance to pass the stretcher. Graham, Peter and Uncle Bill edged into the fast-flowing rapids and wedged themselves against rocks with their arms hooked around the rope tied across. The stretcher was then passed slowly from hand to hand. To Kylie this was a real heart-in-mouth operation as she could see that if they dropped Victor in he would be instantly swept away and drowned.

Her relief when Roger and Stephen reached forward to grasp the front handles was intense. They eased the stretcher across and the old prospector took over while Roger moved into the water. Then the stretcher was across and they could all heave a sigh of relief.

"You girls now," Graham ordered.

They gripped each other and were passed from hand to hand. Kylie found this frightening as she was completely swept off her feet the moment she entered the rapids. Only Peter's strong grip stopped her from being washed head over heels downstream. He passed her to Graham, then to Roger, then to Stephen, who hauled her up the bank.

Margaret, Allison, and Bert followed.

"Oh I'm glad that is over," Margaret cried thankfully.

Only then did Kylie realise that they had another crisis on their hands, and one which was potentially fatal.

Uncle Bill had lost his footing and slipped into deeper water. He clawed frantically at a rock and managed to stop himself from being swept away but the look of agony on his face told Kylie he was in real trouble. He was in the middle of the creek and to her horror she saw that the force of the water was pushing him over so that it surged and foamed up over his shoulders.

"Help! Help!" Uncle Bill cried. "My foot is stuck!"

Graham acted at once. He yelled, "Grab me, Pete!"

As soon as Peter had a grip on his waistband Graham stepped forward into the foam, bracing his boots against rocks under the water.

He reached out for Uncle Bill's desperately clawing hand. In a second he had hold of it. Kylie clutched her hand to her heart and held her breath. With a heave Graham pulled Uncle Bill up so that his head was again clear of the water.

There was a desperate struggle for a few seconds. Roger splashed in to help, grabbing Peter around the waist to steady him. Graham was able to reach down and grab Uncle Bill's shirt. Graham reached down so that his head was under water, allowing him to get his arms under Uncle Bill's. With a convulsive heave he hauled Uncle Bill up. Suddenly Uncle Bill came free. His legs were instantly swept downstream and he trailed in the racing water, his boots throwing up showers of spray.

For another minute they struggled. Bert went into the water and reached out to help. His clawing fingers closed on Uncle Bill's leg and a moment later he was ashore. Peter and Roger hauled Graham ashore. Kylie and Margaret both went to help. For a moment they just stood with water draining off them.

"Phew! That was close," Graham said. He grinned and hugged Margaret close. She sighed with relief and then scolded him, "That was a foolish thing to do! You could have been drowned."

Graham grinned. "Uncle Bill doesn't think so. Now, come on, let's get Vic to the shelter."

That effectively defused the emotion and they quickly organized themselves. Uncle Bill was clearly in pain as it was the same leg he had injured earlier. He was helped up by Margaret and he leaned on her while hopping off along the track. Roger, Stephen and the old prospector took over the front of the stretcher and the others shared the rear. That made things much easier. As well the track was better to move along.

This time they made good progress and arrived at the old prospector's camp after a few minutes. The stretcher was eased into the tent and Bert and the old prospector got rapidly to work. They peeled the wet sleeping bag and plastic off and passed it out, then stripped Victor and towelled him dry. He was lifted onto the old prospector's folding camp bed. Blankets were then wrapped around him and he was made comfortable.

"You kids had better get into some dry clothes too," Uncle Bill said. He was seated on a box and was unlacing his boot.

Allison looked around, "Where can we change?"

Bert grinned at her, "Here if you like."

Allison went bright pink but returned the smile. Kylie at once said, "You boys go outside while the girls change."

"What! Chucked out into the storm like poor little homeless children!" Peter cried in mock horror.

Graham stood up. "Come on, let's go and have a look at those men. Are they still there, Roger?"

"They were an hour ago," Roger replied. The boys went outside and sloshed off down the muddy track towards the river. Uncle Bill limped into the tent and pulled the flaps across.

The girls quickly found their packs, dug out towels and dry clothes, then stood with their backs to each other while they stripped and dried themselves. Kylie found it a real relief to pull on the dry clothes, although she got mud on her feet and trousers.

When they were changed, they went into the tent to see how Victor was. Bert, Uncle Bill, and the old prospector went out to change. Soon after that the boys came back.

"Were the men still there?" Kylie asked.

"Yes, clinging to the top of a big rock," Graham replied. "They aren't going anywhere in a hurry."

"Unless they get washed off by the flood," Roger added.

"I hope they are," Stephen said.

Kylie was horrified at this callous comment but had to admit she did not like the men. *Still, they don't deserve to die,* she thought.

"I think they've lost their guns," Peter added.

"Good!" Kylie replied. That was something.

"Can we get changed now?" Roger asked. "I'm freezing."

The girls were sent into the tent and the flap lowered again. While they waited in the tent, Kylie thought hard about what they should do next. It was obvious that Victor needed proper medical attention.

By the time the boys had changed it had become quite gloomy. The old prospector lit a pressure lantern and then rekindled his fire.

"Good cup of tea is what we all want," he said.

"What do we do now?" Margaret asked.

"Get Vic to hospital," Bert said.

Uncle Bill shook his head, "Not in this." He gestured to the twilight outside where the wind and rain were increasing in force.

"But he needs a doctor!" Bert cried. "He might die otherwise."

Chapter 29

NIGHT

"If we try to go anywhere in these conditions then we could kill someone," Uncle Bill replied. "We will have to wait till morning."

That was an appalling idea, but they all agreed it was sensible. Bert bit his lip but swallowed and nodded.

"A good feed is what we all need now, and a good hot cup of tea," the old prospector added.

He had heated water by this time and they lined up to make hot drinks. Kylie opted for Milo with sugar and condensed milk. As she sipped this Uncle Bill switched on his radio and they listened to the latest cyclone report.

This was no comfort. The cyclone had intensified to Category Three, which meant it could have wind gusts of several hundred kilometres per hour. It was now closer, being only about 200 kilometres away, to the north-northeast of Cairns.

"It's coming our way," Graham said gloomily.

"We are in the edge of it now," Peter commented.

Allison looked anxiously at the canvas walls as they shook to a wind gust. "How big are they?"

"Cyclones can be several hundred kilometres in diameter," Uncle Bill explained. "They vary, but they can hit half North Queensland in one go."

"They aren't like tornados which only last a few hours or minutes and only devastate a small strip," Stephen added.

Allison did not look happy with this information. Kylie shook her head and wished that the boys would stop talking about cyclones. She was scared and knew it. In her heart she felt sick with apprehension, both for herself and her friends, but particularly for Victor.

Hot food was prepared and they sat and ate, mostly in silence. Outside the wind started to whine in the treetops and the rain drummed even harder on the roof, making it difficult to carry on a normal conversation. By the time the evening meal had been eaten it was fully dark.

There was nothing to do then but prepare for the night. "You will all sleep fully dressed and with your raincoats and boots on," Uncle Bill said.

"But my boots are wet," Allison commented in surprise.

"Too bad. Try to dry them at the fire now. But if we have an emergency in the night, you can't go running around in bare feet," Uncle Bill replied.

They all saw the sense in that and set to work stoking up the fire to dry socks and footwear. Graham also draped his sopping sleeping bag over a line above the fire to try to dry it out. More hot drinks were prepared, and they sat in an anxious huddle listening as the sounds of nature's fury outside grew audibly stronger. The canvas sides began to slat and flap, and the iron roof started to groan and shake.

Every few minutes there would be a strong gust which caused them all to glance anxiously at the source of the sound. After an hour of this Margaret suddenly burst into tears and cried out.

"Oh I'm sacred! I wish it would end!"

Kylie was about to move over to comfort her when Graham reached out and put his arm around her. Margaret thankfully snuggled into his embrace and that made Kylie feel much better as well. Time crept past very slowly. Bert sat at the front of the tent where he could see Victor's face and he checked him every few minutes. Kylie half expected him to report that he had died each time he did this and she steeled herself to face the worst.

And it did get worse. They tried to listen to the next hourly advice on the radio, but atmospheric interference defeated them. A thunderstorm was building up and the sound of thunder crept closer. After a while the camp was being lit up by lightning flashes every few seconds. The wind and rain increased in fury and so did their fear.

Uncle Bill had them all get into their sleeping bags and try to rest. The old prospector packed away all of his cooking utensils and other belongings and asked them to do the same. He then went outside to re-peg the tent which had begun to shake and flap alarmingly. He added guy ropes to the surrounding trees.

There weren't enough sleeping bags. Allison shared hers with Bert and Margaret and Graham wrapped themselves in hers. Kylie snuggled up between them and Peter. Uncle Bill wrapped his around him but stayed seated on the box listening to the radio and watching.

The storm increased in strength as the hours dragged on. Water began to flow across the floor and they were soon soaked. Attempts to stem the flow were futile and they soon gave up and huddled in their wet bedding, trying to keep as warm as they could. Several times the rending sounds of trees or branches crashing down out in the jungle made them all start up in fright.

Allison began to whimper and beg the storm to stop. Bert patted and stroked her, in between checking on his brother. Kylie nodded with approval when she saw Graham hug Margaret closer and then pat her gently.

Suddenly the canvas front ripped from top to bottom. The canvas flapped wildly, thundering and cracking. The lantern was sent flying and Kylie heard the tinkle of breaking glass. They were plunged into darkness, broken by the lightning flashes and a dull glow from the fire. This soon died away as rain lashed in. Graham and Peter tried to restrain the wildly flogging canvas but both got battered and flicked by it and were driven back. Uncle Bill shouted at them to give it up and to keep away.

Now the cyclone became truly terrifying. In the flashes of lightning Kylie could see the trees across the clearing threshing and twisting as though being shaken by a demented giant. Surface water several centimetres deep began flowing through the shelter. It was cold and she felt so scared she could only pray for it all to stop.

Roger put it in perspective when he shouted in answer to Graham's comment about the roof starting to come off, "Could be worse. I'm glad I'm not out in the middle of the river trying to cling to a wet rock."

The thought of the probable plight, and possible fate, of the two men made Kylie feel very upset. She tried to push the image out of her mind but it kept returning. They would be so cold their fingers would cramp and their grip could fail. She kept praying and shaking her head.

Another savage gust shook the shelter. *I don't believe this!* she thought. *It is getting stronger!*

There were several very close lightning strikes. There was no time lapse between the flash and the thunder, which came as heart stopping cracks so loud Kylie cried out in fear. The rain began to fluctuate in intensity, one moment a torrential downpour and the next just drizzle. The wind was shifting too, blowing stronger than ever and changing direction to blow more from the south.

"That cyclone must be moving south," Peter yelled to Graham. Kylie thought about this, trying to remember what she had been taught at school. Cyclones in the southern hemisphere rotated in a clockwise direction. That meant that, if the wind was coming from the south then the cyclone had to be out to the east of them somewhere.

"That is good news, isn't it?" she cried.

"Yes, it means it is heading parallel to the coast and not directly towards us," Peter answered.

"Don't forget these mountains will be channelling and deflecting the wind," Graham said. "We can't tell much from the wind direction here."

Kylie was about to speak but was interrupted by an odd groaning noise. For a second she thought it was Victor crying out, but then she realised it was much louder than that and outside. She opened her mouth to ask what it was just as another fierce gust shook the shelter.

"Look out!" Peter yelled.

But look out for what? Kylie could not see and all she or the others could do was cringe in fear as a massive splintering and crashing noise sounded above the storm. Suddenly, the roof burst apart and she was struck hard on the shoulder. Sheet iron struck her on the head and she felt wet leaves all over her face.

A tree! She knew instantly what had happened. A tree had been blown down and had crashed onto the shelter. She felt panic surge, even as the sheet of iron was whipped away by the wind. She got a terrified glimpse of it whirling through the air in the next flash of lightning. This also revealed that half the shelter had been crushed and that the other half, and the tent, were covered by a mass of threshing leaves and branches.

Faint shouts of fear and wails of distress reached her ears above the raging of the storm. *Oh no! Who is hurt?* she thought. For a moment she struggled frantically to disentangle herself from her sleeping bag and from the branches and pieces of timber which lay on her. *I don't think I'm hurt,* she thought, more worried about her brother and her friends than herself.

She managed to get to her feet. A flash of lightning revealed Peter and Stephen both groping their way to their feet amidst the wreckage. It also showed that the trunk of a massive tree lay across the clearing and onto the tent.

"Oh no! Victor!" Kylie cried.

She began to pull at the branches and pieces of wreckage. The wind snatched at things and she was struck hard on the arm and something whipped her face, making it go numb. To her great relief, Graham and Margaret both emerged from the tangle of leaves and branches.

"Bert! Allie!" Kylie screamed.

A cry of distress answered her. Kylie tore at the wreckage and branches frantically, heedless of the rain lashing her. She found Uncle Bill beside her.

"Bert and Allie are just under here," she yelled.

Uncle Bill nodded and directed the boys to help. Without lights it was very hard as the lightning flashes were infrequent and left them temporarily night blind. Kylie's groping hand encountered someone. To her relief, the person's hand grabbed hers. They were alive! It was Allison and she was soon pulled clear.

"Bert! Bert!" she screamed hysterically.

"I'm alright," Bert yelled from under the leaves and iron. "Help me get Vic clear."

Uncle Bill grouped them to clear the debris. They dragged away small branches, getting scratched and whipped in the process as the branches were flailing around in the wind. Kylie saw Graham and Peter both wrestle with larger branches and snap them off. She found it hard to see and even harder to think as the rain and wind battered her.

It took ten minutes to get Victor clear. The trunk of the tree had crashed across the tent and landed on his legs. Only the thick lower branches had saved him from being crushed. The branches had splintered and snapped but in doing so had stopped the massive trunk from smashing hard into the tent.

As she helped to drag Victor clear, another horrible thought came to Kylie. *The old prospector! Where is he?* She bent and crawled into the leaves and under the remains of the tent. She found herself crawling in slush and cold mud. Her hands touched clothing and flesh.

"He's here!" she yelled.

With trembling hands she felt along his body, fearing the worst. This was rapidly confirmed. The tree had landed on the old prospector. When she felt the rough bark pressing down on the man's stomach and chest Kylie let out a sob of anguish.

Oh no! He's been crushed!

"Is he alive?" Graham shouted from near her.

Kylie crawled further under and pressed her fingertips to the old prospector's throat. For a moment she could feel nothing but then she detected a faint pulse.

"Yes, but he's trapped," Kylie yelled. She felt around and realised that the old man had mud and water cascading around his head and shoulders. *He will drown,* she thought anxiously.

The others worked with urgent haste to clear the leaves and branches from around them. Kylie carefully felt the old prospector's head and neck and decided that he was not injured there. To save him from the mud and water she gently raised his head and slipped her left forearm under it. With her other hand she began scooping a ditch to divert the surface flow.

When they had cleared the wreckage and rubbish away, they found that the old prospector was solidly trapped beneath the log. His lower chest, stomach and upper legs were under the trunk. Uncle Bill leaned down and checked the old prospector's breathing and airway. Kylie could just detect movement in the old man's chest and she heard him snuffle and groan a few times.

"We must get him out," Uncle Bill said. "I think his ribs may be broken and if he is bleeding into his lungs he will drown in his own blood unless we can turn him over."

What a ghastly thought! Kylie felt even worse. She felt so helpless and very scared. The storm seemed to be getting worse and she realised she was shivering with cold. *If I'm cold, then the old prospector must be freezing. We must get him free!* she thought.

But how? Graham asked the same question. "We can't lift this tree, that is for sure," he shouted above the wind.

"Dig him out. Come on, dig like crazy," Uncle Bill yelled.

That set them all to work, digging with whatever was to hand, mostly with bare hands. Kylie was directed to keep holding the old prospector's head up as they dug because the holes instantly filled with water. She knew she was shaking, but somehow she concentrated on her task, even though her muscles began to cramp and she felt her left arm go numb.

In fact, by the time they had dug right under the log on both sides of the old prospector she felt numb in mind and body from the ceaseless battering of the wind. She began to doubt if she could last and continually prayed for the strength to carry on.

It took what seemed for ever, but was actually took about an hour (so Peter later told her), to dig away enough mud to free the old man. He was then slid out and Roger and Stephen set to work by the light of pocket torches taken from their webbing to examine his injuries.

"He's in a bad way," Roger said. "I think he has broken both thighs and he definitely has internal injuries."

"We'd better get him into some sort of shelter, or he will die of exposure and shock," Stephen added.

Shelter! But where? They cast around for ideas and finally decided that the wrecked shelter was still their best option. Stephen suggested the mine tunnel, but a flash of lightning showed that it was mostly collapsed and was flooded, the small pump underwater.

It took time to clear a space in what was left of the shelter. Only one canvas wall and part of one sheet iron wall remained and they did not really block the driving rain. Canvas and the remains of the tent were tied and stretched taut to make some sort of a roof and the two injured men were moved into the shelter. The others then huddled into what cover they could find.

Exhaustion began to tell on Kylie. She found herself shivering and dizzy. She snuggled into some wet bedding along with Peter and Roger and they clung to each other. The strike of a lightning bolt close to them made them all cry out in fear and clutch at each other. The sound of another tree crashing down added to their terror. The whole experience became a living nightmare.

Through it all Kylie worried. She could not stop thinking about Victor and the old prospector. Even thoughts of the two horrible men gave her pause for pity. Their ordeal, clinging to a rock in mid-river, surrounded by the raging floodwaters and flailed by the elements must be truly horrific.

Perhaps they have been washed away by now? she wondered in a sick daze.

The storm went on and on, hour after hour. Rain and wind, wind and rain. It buffeted and battered at her until her senses went numb and her body felt like on huge soggy bruise. From time-to-time Bert or Uncle Bill would check the two injured men but it was obvious that nothing more could be done in the dark.

"They both need proper medical treatment urgently or they will die," was Roger's gloomy prognosis.

Chapter 30

WE MUST TRY!

At some point in time, Kylie became aware that she could see more than just the dim black outlines of those around her. With growing relief she realised that it was starting to get light. A check of her watch showed it was nearly 6am. She realised that it was darker than it would normally be at that time because of the clouds and rain. The storm continued unabated. She could only marvel in numbed shock that anything could go on so long, so fiercely.

With an effort she wiped rain from her face and looked around. She met the vacant and haggard looks of Roger and Allison. Allison looked absolutely stunned. Kylie could never remember feeling so exhausted and wrung out in all her life. She found it was an effort to even think, much less do anything.

But someone was moving. It was Bert. He sat up from checking Victor. Kylie could not see Victor because he was under the rough shelter.

"How is he?" she managed to croak. She was amazed to find that her throat felt dry and all choked up. *In all this rain!*

Bert looked awful. His eyes were sunk into his face which was grey and lined. His hair was plastered all over his head by mud and rain. *I suppose I look the same,* Kylie thought.

"He's still alive," Bert called, "but he's having difficulty breathing. We must get him to a doctor."

"And the old prospector," Kylie added. "How is he?"

"Haven't checked," Bert admitted.

While they talked, some of the others began to stir. Kylie tried to sit and found that all her muscles were stiff. She felt so numb she could barely move. It took an effort even to lift an arm to wipe her face. With a groan she got to her knees and crawled across to the shelter. In the process she bumped Graham and Roger who both stirred. As she crawled past, she met Peter's eyes. He lay in the wreckage looking utterly exhausted.

Kylie crawled in under the remains of the tent with Bert to check the old prospector. To her relief he was still breathing, but it was in rapid, short pants which she thought indicated pains in the chest. Victor, on the other hand, was breathing with a harsh snoring sound which she found even more worrying.

Serious head injury? she wondered. Both casualties looked ghastly in the grey light.

When she emerged from the tent, Kylie saw the others sitting up and moving slowly. It had been a relief to be in under the canvas for even a couple of minutes as the wind and rain were still slashing at them.

"How are they?" Uncle Bill asked.

"Alive, but they need a doctor and proper treatment fast," Kylie replied. She shivered and put her arms around herself.

"I don't think there is much we can do while this cyclone lasts," Uncle Bill replied.

"Oh we must! We must try!" Kylie cried. She was sickened by the thought of the two men slowly dying. She knew she had to do something, if only for the sake of her own conscience and sanity.

"It has rained all night," Peter said. "The river will be still in flood. We can't get out."

Graham had stretched himself, waking Margaret in the process. He suddenly stood up. "The river! I wonder if those crooks are still there?"

"Let's have a look," Peter suggested.

"I think you kids should stay under cover," Uncle Bill said. "We don't want any more accidents." He indicated the driving rain and the trees, which were still whipping and flailing in the wind which still howled and raged around them.

Graham shrugged as he stood up. "Can't be worse than here. This isn't much of a shelter."

Uncle Bill looked around and nodded. "You are right. Let's try to rig up something better now we can see."

Graham persisted in his plan. "In a minute. I will just check the river. We have to know if we can cross or not." He pulled the sodden sleeping bag around Margaret then turned and picked his way through the wreckage.

As Graham started walking, Peter stood up and followed him. Kylie was seized by an urgent need to know what had become the men. Had they been washed away in the night? She also stood up and sloshed down the track after the boys. Uncle Bill said not to go but she ignored him.

Once in the jungle the wind was much less but the rain still dribbled and gushed down everything. The track was covered with loose branches and leaves and there was a tree across it but they climbed over this without any trouble and made their way on down the slope. It was at once obvious that the river was even higher. They could hear the roar of the water above the howl of the wind. The floodwaters were even further up into the forest than before.

Graham just waded in. Kylie was so wet she didn't hesitate and followed, only to get a shock. The water was icy cold and took her breath away. But having started she wasn't going to turn back. The trio made their way from tree to tree into deeper and deeper water. It was still quite gloomy in the rainforest.

Graham stopped and pointed, then continued on. Kylie looked and let out a gasp. A huge python at least five metres long was coiled up a tree which was leaning over at an angle.

"Been driven out of his hiding place by the floodwaters," Peter commented. The boys just ignored the huge snake and went on wading. Kylie edged past the great reptile and followed.

Five minutes later they were at a place where they could see out onto the river. In the grey half-light it looked fearsome, a surging mass of white streaked water. Logs and leaves racing past gave the sense of its speed and power.

"They are still there," Graham called. "Or at least one of them is."

Kylie moved to join him. She could just see a dark shape huddled on the very top of a large boulder. Only a metre of the rock was still above the level of the racing floodwaters.

"They are both there," Peter added.

A black blob which was the other man's head, was just visible on the other side of the rock.

"If that river comes up much more, then those two are goners," Graham commented.

The idea made Kylie feel sick. She had never experienced a situation where she could witness another person's death and it was not something she wanted to do. She shivered violently.

"Let's go back and do something," she said.

They made their way back to the clearing. On arrival they found Uncle Bill huddled under cover with his radio held to his ear.

"Any news?" Graham called.

Uncle Bill held up his hand for silence and they waited till he put the radio down and said, "According to the latest reports the cyclone is now about one hundred kilometres northeast of Cairns and moving south at about ten kilometres per hour. It is east of Cape Tribulation. Worse still it is now a Category Four cyclone."

"You mean it hasn't arrived yet?" Allison asked incredulously.

Uncle Bill nodded. "That's right. At the rate it is moving it will be another ten hours before it gets here, if it comes this way."

"Ten hours!" Allison cried. "I can't stand another ten hours of this!"

"It will be more than ten," Graham said. "Once it arrives it takes just as long to leave."

Kylie did the calculation in her head. It was just after seven. That meant that the cyclone could arrive at around five that afternoon and would not be over until the next morning. She was appalled. "That means nearly another twenty-four hours! Another night like that! Victor and the old prospector won't last that long. They must get medical treatment," she cried.

Uncle Bill shrugged and looked defeated. Allison began to sob. Bert moved to put his arms around her. Kylie became very agitated. "We must do something!"

"What can we do? We can't possibly cross the river," Stephen said.

"Can't we go down along this bank until we come to the road?" Kylie queried. She remembered that the road in to Kearneys Flats crossed several bridges but wasn't sure of the layout. She just felt impelled to do something.

Graham bit his lip and dug into his map pocket. "I think there are a few big creeks to cross. They will be flooded too," he said. He took out his map, still luckily dry in its plastic bag. For a minute he studied it, continually brushing rain drops off the plastic. Peter moved over to look as well.

Graham frowned and then said, "We might be able to go the other way, but there is no road."

Kylie felt a surge of hope. "What do you mean by the other way?"

Graham held the map for her to see. "Up the mountain and along this ridge back to Lamins Hill."

"To the farm?" Kylie asked, her heart fluttering with hope.

Graham nodded. "There is a ridge which runs all the way back from here to Lamins Hill. It doesn't have any creeks across it."

"Don't be ridiculous!" Uncle Bill snapped. "Nobody could get up over these mountains. It's impossible!"

"I don't see why," Graham replied. "During the gold rushes the main track from Goldsborough to the Tablelands ran along that ridge. I marked it on my map."

"Show me," Kylie said. She moved over and wiped rain from her face to peer at the map.

Uncle Bill shook his head. "That was donkey's years ago. The track would be all overgrown by now."

"It won't be any worse than the tracks we have been exploring during the last week or so," Graham replied.

"But it would take days," Uncle Bill said.

"No it wouldn't," Graham replied.

Kylie agreed. "I read in Grandad Hector's diary that he walked from down here to the farm."

Peter said, "That's right. I've got it here." He took out the photocopy in its plastic bag and read it. "It took him two days though. He spent the night on the track."

Kylie took the diary copy to read, then said, "But he was so sick he died the next day."

"That's right," Graham agreed. "We can do better than that. We've climbed mountains that big in one day on hikes."

"How far is it?" Kylie asked.

Graham bent to his map and quickly did the calculation. "About fourteen kilometres. And about seven hundred metres up. That should take us about... er... about... nine or ten hours at most, even if we have to cut our way through the jungle."

"It will take longer than that," Uncle Bill said. "How far is it around along the ridges?"

"That is the actual distance," Graham replied. "It is only ten kilometres in a straight line."

"You'd never do it," Uncle Bill said. "You'd end up getting lost in the jungle."

Kylie glanced at Graham and noted a stubborn, angry look. "Whatever happens we won't get lost!" he snapped. "We are very good navigators."

Uncle Bill looked distressed. "But you can't walk through the jungle in a cyclone!"

"It can't be any worse than sitting here," Kylie replied.

Margaret now spoke. "I'd rather be up and walking instead of sitting here freezing to death."

Kylie glanced at her and saw she was shivering and looked blue in the face. She felt frozen herself. As well Margaret's simile of 'freezing to death' made her sickeningly aware of what must be happening to Victor and the old prospector.

She said, "We have to try. We can't just sit here and let Victor and the old prospector die."

Once again, Uncle Bill looked upset. "But how will I ever face your grandmother if anything happens to you? What will I tell your mother?"

At that Kylie sensed that Uncle Bill was weakening and she kept up the pressure. "If we start now, we could be there by five o'clock this afternoon."

"What good will that do?" Uncle Bill said.

Graham answered that. "They could come and get Victor and the old prospector with a helicopter."

"In this!" Uncle Bill cried, gesturing to the driving rain and low cloud.

Graham shrugged. "We have to try."

Kylie agreed. "We must Uncle Bill. We can't just sit here."

Uncle Bill gestured to his leg. "But I'll never get up over those mountains with this ankle of mine."

"We can make it," Graham insisted. "You stay here to look after Victor and the old prospector. Pete and I will be okay."

Uncle Bill shook his head. "No. Not just two of you. If one of you gets hurt you couldn't just leave the injured person alone in the jungle. There must be at least four of you."

Kylie knew then they had won. "I'll go," she offered, even though she doubted if she had the strength for the ordeal.

"So will I," said Peter, Stephen, Roger, Bert and Margaret simultaneously.

Uncle Bill again shook his head. "Bert, you'd better stay here in case Victor regains consciousness and needs you. I will need someone strong here anyway, to help rebuild the shelter."

Bert looked worried and upset. He bit his lip and nodded. "Alright."

Allison moved closer to him. "I'll stay with you Bert. I don't think I could make it over those mountains. I would just hold everyone up."

"That's very sensible Allison," Uncle Bill said. He looked at Stephen who was blinking myopically in the rain, his glasses in his pocket. "I reckon you should stay too Steve. Without your glasses in this rain you could injure yourself and hold them up."

Stephen looked unhappy but nodded. Uncle Bill looked at Margaret. "What about you young Marg? Do you think you can make it?"

Margaret looked anxiously at Graham and nodded. "I can do it."

Uncle Bill looked doubtful. He also glanced at Roger but, to Kylie's relief, did not suggest he stay. She knew that would have hurt Roger's feelings.

"I still reckon it should be just Pete and me," Graham said. "The others aren't as fit and will slow us down."

"No," Uncle Bill replied. "A group or nobody."

"Alright. Then let's get organized and get going then," Graham said.

Kylie felt her spirits rise. With a groan she got to her knees and began searching through the wreckage and fluttering leaves for her belt and water bottle. Graham and Peter lifted Victor and dragged out their webbing.

"Have something to eat before you go," Uncle Bill said.

Graham shook his head. "We will never get a stove going in this. We will eat cold food while we walk."

Uncle Bill accepted this and said to Stephen, "Steve, let's see if we can find a better spot to put up some sort of shelter."

"In the jungle there," Graham said, pointing. "In behind the buttress roots on that big tree."

Kylie pulled her jacket tight around her and buckled on her belt. She dug out a packet of jellybeans and a chocolate from her pack and slipped them into her pocket. She was scared now, but relieved they were up and doing.

Stephen and Bert set to work clearing a space in behind the base of a massive tree. That made Kylie look anxiously at the trunk of the huge tree which had fallen on them. "What if it blows over?" she asked.

"Safer right next to it than further away," Stephen replied. "You don't get that whiplash effect. okay Bert, you rig the shelter while I try to get a fire going."

Kylie left them and joined the others who were standing in a group in the driving rain. Uncle Bill stood with them, looking haggard and miserable. "I still don't like this," he said. "You are sure you can do it without getting lost?"

Graham answered. "Yes, Uncle Bill. Okay, if everyone is ready let's get going. The sooner we leave the sooner we arrive."

"Good luck," Uncle Bill said.

Peter grinned and replied, "We depend on skill, Uncle Bill. Cheer up. It will be okay. You just look after those two." He indicated the collapsed shelter.

Fired now by a burning urge to save the two injured men Kylie said goodbye and urged Graham to start walking. He turned and set off along the track towards Nugget Creek.

"Why are we going this way?" she asked. "Shouldn't we be going uphill?"

"Yes, we should," Graham replied, "but if we can get across Nugget Creek and go up the track to that old mine half way up the mountain we will save a lot of time."

Kylie saw the sense in that. It would just be a walk along the track they had already cleared. She wiped rain from her face and wished she had been able to find her hat.

None of them had hats but all wore raincoats or jackets. Even so it was bitterly cold and they shivered as they walked. The rain lashed by the wind was the worst. It kept getting in their eyes. Wet leaves were continually blown against them, sticking to their skin and causing them to squint and shield their eyes. They also had to climb over several trees that had been blown down and lay across the track. This was difficult and unpleasant as the bark was wet and slippery.

Nugget Creek was the first real obstacle. It was a raging torrent and a moment's glance was enough to show that they could not safely cross. Graham shrugged and took out his secateurs. "Oh well, nothing for it but a bit of good old jungle bashing."

"I think the cyclone is doing that for us," Peter said cheerfully. He managed a smile for Kylie and took out his own secateurs. "You navigate Graham, and I will go first," he said.

The climb up the mountain began. Just on 8am, Kylie noted.

Chapter 31

THE RIDGE

The climb up the ridge was the hardest thing Kylie had ever done in her life. She knew, even as they began the ordeal, that the experience would be fixed in her mind indelibly. It wasn't just the steepness of the slope; or the stiff pace Graham set, which soon had them all gasping; it was the storm. That really made it a grim and frightening event.

After the first few hundred metres, which rose gradually, the ridge went steeply up into the racing clouds and driving rain. At the angle they were climbing the wind howled in from behind them so that there was no way they could get into any sort of a lee. They had to drag themselves up the slope exposed to the full fury of the storm.

As they got up above the level of the tree canopy in the bottom of the valley the wind increased dramatically in strength. The trees shook and flailed, and leaves and sticks whirled and slashed around them. Kylie quickly began to doubt if it was possible to go on safely. During one of their frequent halts she voiced this.

Graham shook his head impatiently and yelled back, "Of course it's not bloody safe! But what other option is there? I'm not going to just sit and wait till two people die."

Put like that Kylie could only nod and agree. It was how she had felt. Now, confronted by the reality, she was truly terrified. They resumed their upward movement. Surface runoff gushed back down the slope and the rain continued unabated as a torrential downpour which wet everything. It made the trees slippery to grip and everyone in the group had dozens of stumbles and slips. And every ten or twenty paces they encountered a tree that had been blown over and had to clamber over it.

Graham went as fast as he could, and he and Peter soon drew ahead. After a while the pair stopped and looked back. "Hurry up!" Graham shouted.

Anger flared in Kylie. "No! You slow down a bit and help us. We must stay together," she screamed, her voice barely audible as it was snatched away by the howling wind.

For a moment brother and sister glared at each other. It was Margaret who came between them.

"Where are we on the map? Have we come far?"

Graham turned his back on the wind, crouched down then took out his map and showed her. "About here. We have come one kilometre and climbed a couple of hundred metres." The wind was so strong he had to grip the folded map tightly.

Kylie was going to say, 'Is that all?' but she bit it back. Inside she was dismayed. She already felt worn out. *That means thirteen kilometres more and hundreds of metres to climb,* she thought. Her doubts increased.

To her credit, Margaret only nodded, although she looked very pale and drawn. She was so white her freckles stood out starkly. When Graham resumed climbing, she went behind him and Kylie followed her. Roger came last, gamely puffing up the hill.

As they got higher up the slope, the jungle gave way to more open bush which was easier to negotiate. However, the slope became ever steeper. Kylie found it a real effort to push herself up. She found her heart thudding rapidly and her breath came in hot gasps. After a time, her legs felt like lead and she felt dizzy. The only positive thing she could think of was that she wasn't as cold.

Most were so unfit they had to stop every hundred paces. During the halts they huddled behind rocks or trees and shivered in the wind. The rain felt like ice. Kylie saw that Roger was really gasping and she wondered if they had made a real mistake.

Maybe Graham and Peter should go on alone? she wondered.

At one point they got a view out along the valley. Kylie found it both awe-inspiring and terrifying. The mountains were shrouded in racing cloud and driving rain. The river could be clearly seen through gaps in the showers. It showed up as a white and caramel streak through the grey-green jungle.

Peter gestured back along the valley. "I wonder if those two blokes are still clinging to their rock?" he said.

Graham shrugged. "Who cares? Serves the bastards right," he said.

Kylie found herself torn emotionally over that. Part of her agreed with her brother's callous comment, but mostly she just felt a feeling of sick dread.

They resumed their upward struggle. The slope became so steep that they had to haul themselves from tree to tree. Their hands and boots slipped continually, and it seemed they went up only one step for every two they took. Behind her Kylie could hear Roger's gasping breath even above the howl of the wind. She glanced back to see how he was getting on. At that moment, he was hauling himself up over a rock and she distinctly saw a look of genuine agony cross his face. However, he managed a sickly grin as he stood panting on top, clinging to a tree for support.

On upwards they struggled. They had to climb over or around dozens of fallen trees and half a dozen times a tree or branch fell near them, causing hearts to palpitate in fright. The wind became ever stronger and seemed to press them down. They had to cling on as they climbed. At one point Kylie got a clear view across the re-entrant on the left. The whole of the mountainside appeared to be shimmering. She realised it was from millions of leaves and branches flickering and twisting in the wind.

The view puzzled her and she thought that the forest looked different. *Bare. I can see more branches and tree trunks,* she decided. Then she realised that the wind was stripping the trees of their leaves. The whole spectacle was so dramatic it helped ease the gnawing fear that was chewing at her insides.

They continued climbing in slow, painful stages, halting to recover their breath frequently. At 9:30 they stopped in the shelter of several large boulders and Kylie was amazed what a relief it was to be out of the wind and rain, even temporarily. By then she was feeling battered, dazed and chilled.

It took a real effort of will power to force themselves out of that safe haven back into the tempest. Soon after that they almost lost Roger. There was a rending crack, then a tree came crashing down. It all happened too fast for Kylie to even jump aside. She found herself surrounded by leaves and a branch whipped her face and shoulder savagely. Roger went down under the tangle.

For a ghastly moment Kylie thought they would have another serious casualty to care for, and in the worst possible place. However, Roger struggled to his knees and shook his head. He rubbed at his shoulder and left arm and looked badly frightened.

"Are you alright?" Kylie yelled in his ear.

Roger nodded. "I think so. Just a bit bruised."

"You've hurt your face," she said. Blood showed on his left cheek. Roger put a hand to it and looked at the blood, even as the driving rain washed it away.

"Hit my face on a rock. I'm alright," Roger insisted.

They continued on upwards. Kylie found her knees and leg muscles complaining and cramping. But she had gotten her 'second wind' by then and settled down to a steady plod which kept her moving slowly upwards. She was able to keep up.

At 10am they entered the cloud. From then on all they could see was the area a few metres around them. Cloud and rain hid everything else. The ridge became steeper and narrower and that allowed the wind to swirl and eddy in vicious cross-currents which made it difficult to stand. The wind also whipped branches into their faces and made it even more dangerous and unpleasant. Several times thin branches whipped across Kylie's eyes, leaving her blinking in pain, fearful she had suffered permanent eye damage. Luckily the pain went away and the blurriness cleared after a few frightening minutes.

Peter found some more rocks for them to rest behind and they huddled together, relieved to be out of the savage wind for even a few seconds. Kylie pressed herself back against the wet rock and marvelled at the sheer speed and savagery of the wind. Leaves, branches, and sand were all flying past, abrading their skin and getting in their clothes, mouth and eyes.

They had a drink and Peter insisted they all eat some chocolate. "You need the energy," he shouted. "And keep eating jellybeans, one every few minutes. The sugar will give you raw energy to boost you up the hill."

"Just fatten me up and make it harder than ever," Roger moaned. He looked grey and drawn.

"Rot!" Peter replied. "Sugar is a carbohydrate, not a fat." He proceeded to lecture Roger on the food groups.

Kylie stopped this by asking, "How much further? We must be nearly at the top surely?"

Graham studied his map, nearly having it plucked from his grasp by a sudden swirl of wind. "I think we are."

Margaret was slumped against him. She shook her head. "I hope so. I don't think I can go on much further."

That was a worry. Kylie began to wonder how they might cope if someone broke down or was injured. They were now in just about the most inaccessible place in all of North Queensland.

Maybe Uncle Bill was right? she thought unhappily.

Graham took Margaret's hand and hauled her to her feet, then went on up the slope, holding her hand and helping her. The sight of that sent a warm feeling through Kylie. Otherwise she was just feeling absolutely exhausted and numb from the constant battering. With a groan she hoisted herself up and followed.

After that came several false crests. At each one their hopes rose that they were on top of the main ridge. The disappointments were all the sharper when they found they weren't. Kylie cheered herself up by noting that the vegetation was changing to Sheoak forest and short grass studded with grass trees. She knew these grew on the higher slopes.

Suddenly they were there. They found the ground plummeting away in front of them with the main ridge running of to right and left as far as they could see in the swirling clouds. Through a gap in the clouds they glimpsed another large valley with another jungle covered slope beyond.

"Butchers Creek," Graham cried, pointing down to the thread of white which seamed the jungle at the bottom of the valley. "Come on. We only have to follow this ridge now for about twelve kilometres."

Kylie was dismayed. So was Margaret. She said, "Are you saying we have only come two kilometres?"

Graham nodded, then shouted, "Yes, but that is the worst part over. From now on it is just along the top of this ridge."

"Have a rest first," Kylie insisted.

They made their way thankfully over the slope into the lee of the ridge and slumped on the wet grass. Graham would not let them sit for more than a couple of minutes, however.

"We must keep moving. It is ten thirty already and we must make it before dark."

"I don't think I can!" Margaret wailed. "I'm getting cramps."

"All the more reason to keep moving," Graham said. "If your muscles go cold, they will stiffen up. Come on."

He urged them up and got them moving. Kylie stumbled numbly along behind Margaret as they set off along the ridge. There might have been a track once but there was no real sign of one now so they just walked on the downwind side of the slope, the wind and rain slashing and swirling just over their heads. What now frightened Kylie the most was the way all the trees were bending over their heads, their tops and branches flailing in the wind. Already dozens of trees had been blown over and almost all of them lay across their route, necessitating frequent and very wearing detours.

The vegetation changed back to rainforest and that withstood the force of the storm better, even if it was harder to move through. The trend of the ridge was still upwards, with steep little knolls that slowed and wore them down. Kylie tried to keep her spirits up by telling herself they were getting closer to the farm with every step. Graham encouraged Margaret.

"We are up about six hundred metres. We are nearly at the level of the Tablelands."

That was heartening. The jungle however baffled them for a while. From time to time they followed gaps which might have been an old track but much of the time it was just a slow plod with the boys at the front snipping vines and wait-a-while. The only good thing was that the jungle gave some protection from the driving wind.

Graham had his compass out now and was counting paces. Kylie could see his lips moving and the look of intense concentration on his face. She knew that if they took a wrong turn on one of the many knolls, they could waste a lot of time and energy retracing their steps. Twice this happened and once they tried to get back on the right spur by cutting across the top of a jungle choked re-entrant. This wasted ten minutes each time and reduced Graham to fury. Several times he lost his temper and struggled like a mad thing to force a passage through the ensnaring saplings and vines.

Wait-a-while brought this outburst to an abrupt end, with much swearing and the sound of ripping cloth. Blood trickled from numerous scratches, but Graham ignored this. Peter snipped him free. They resumed their slow movement, but it infuriated all of them. Every second it seemed that one or the other of them was being snagged by a vine or branch which caught in their clothing or webbing.

"Bloody stuff!" Graham shouted. "I can see why all those pygmies run around the jungle naked."

Peter laughed aloud. "You can if you like, but personally I don't fancy getting my important bits jagged on the wait-a-while."

Graham managed a grin. "No by Jove. And I suppose the leeches wouldn't be much fun."

Kylie hadn't thought about leeches but now discovered several on her. She pulled these off in disgust. The rain seemed to get even heavier, drenching everything. The slow move along the ridge went on. They had to slog up onto a fair-sized knoll and arrived panting on top. By then Kylie's hands were white and crinkled. She felt wet and chilled right through. Her jellybeans had gone soggy and mushy in the packet, so she shovelled the sticky mass into her mouth rather than waste it.

Roger puffed up to join them, then stopped, leaning on a tree and had a drink. Within seconds he threw up, the water and mucous being whirled away by the wind.

"You okay, Roger?" she asked.

Roger raised miserable eyes to hers. "No, but I'll make it."

"You've got a big bruise on your face," Kylie observed.

"So have you," Roger replied. Kylie put her hand to her face, but it just felt numb. She knew it was being hit repeatedly by branches and leaves. She wiped rain off and had a drink herself.

The ridge changed direction almost at right angles at that point and ran westwards. Graham showed them on the map where he thought they were. Now, as they walked, the wind and rain struck them on the left side. Kylie was appalled at the sound of the wind tearing at the foliage. The trees threshed and waved wildly from time to time as sharp gusts eddied around from a different direction. A huge tree fell close beside them with a rending, heart-stopping crash.

For the next hour they struggled on down into a saddle and up over another knoll. After that they got off course and went down the wrong spur. As the slope got steeper and steeper Graham looked more and more anxious. Finally he admitted he had made a mistake and they turned and retraced their steps back to the top and waited while he scouted to find the start of the right ridge. He returned after five minutes and they set off, Peter still cutting the track and Graham navigating with map and compass in hand.

They turned to southwest for a few hundred metres and even went into a small area where they were down behind a knoll and out of the direct force of the wind for a few metres. But not out of the rain. This still deluged them and flowed ankle deep in places down the spur. On top they found another pile of boulders and slumped thankfully in their shelter.

It was 12 o'clock. Kylie was appalled. "We have been going for over four hours and have only come four kilometres!" she said, as Graham showed them where he thought they were. That meant ten to go.

At this rate we will take at least ten more hours! It will be dark long before then, Kylie thought in dismay. It was a disheartening thought.

Graham wasn't discouraged. "We are over the worst of it now. Getting up the mountain was the hard bit. If we don't miss the ridge, we should be able to do about two 'Ks' per hour."

His prediction turned out to be right. After ten minutes rest he urged them on. They clambered out of the rocks and into a shallow saddle. Almost at once Peter said. "This used to be a clearing. There's an old track."

It was. Kylie felt her hopes surge and tried to rein them in. She did not want to get them too high and then have them dashed. Peter went much faster now. Kylie saw that they were actually following an old road. It had once been graded and had distinct edges. In places the old road was almost clear and they could walk as fast as their tired legs and heaving chests would allow them. In other places small trees and ferns had grown up which they had to push or cut through. Time after time a mass of wait-a-while blocked their path and hundreds of dead logs and freshly blow down trees lay across the road. Some they clambered over and others they had to crawl under or detour around.

After a time Kylie stopped worrying about leeches, or being wet, or of thorns scratching her. She just concentrated on putting one foot in front of another. Margaret passed her some chocolate, but it made no impact on her taste buds. She just ate it mechanically. At one point Graham helped Margaret over a log and she slumped down the other side into his arms. He held her for a second and then said, "You are a real game little trier aren't you."

Margaret gave him a weak little smile and could only nod. To Kylie it appeared that she was ready to collapse. That was how she felt herself. What both encouraged and annoyed her was that both Graham and Peter kept joking and making stupid comments to each other. It occurred to Kylie that the boys saw the event as an adventure which they were enjoying.

Stupid men! she thought in exasperation.

They slogged on. The old road wound up and down and changed from West to southwest and back again as it followed the ridge top. Graham kept looking at the map and nodding with satisfaction. An hour went by and they stopped for a brief rest. Peter and Graham kept getting further and further ahead and had to wait for Kylie and the others to catch up. At times the two boys got right out of sight. By then Kylie was so exhausted she was starting to break into tears.

Perversely she was also thirsty as she had drunk her water bottle dry. She had to drink rainwater and that helped. They moved on at 1:30pm. By then Kylie was almost staggering and was starting to lose interest in the reason for the effort. She found herself walking with Margaret and Roger, both of whom looked utterly exhausted. The storm continued unabated but by this time they barely noticed it. It had gone on so long they accepted it as a form of normality.

Kylie staggered and panted up another slope, her breath coming in gasps and her boots slipping on the greasy wet leaf mould. At the top she found herself in a muddy clearing. The two boys were waiting. For a moment it did not register but then she cried aloud with relief. "A road!"

Graham waited till Margaret and Roger had joined them, then pointed to his map. "I reckon we are here at the end of this road, at Hill Seven One Six. Pete and I are going to dump our gear and run. You follow us at your best pace."

Kylie nodded. Now they were on a road she felt safe, so splitting the group did not seem to matter. "How far to the farm?" she asked.

"About four 'Ks'," Graham replied, "but you should come to the Anderson's farm before that. Come on Pete, let's get going."

"Carry our webbing please," Peter asked as he swung his off.

"Okay," Kylie replied.

"And don't eat all my chocolate," Peter added as he set off after Graham at a jogging trot.

Chapter 32

BLOODY SCARY!

Kylie watched with a feeling of intense relief as Graham and Peter jogged out of sight. "Only four kilometres to go. They should cover that in an hour," she said.

"Or even less," Roger added. "We should be able to do it in that time."

Margaret hitched up Graham's webbing and peered into the rain. "Then let's go. The sooner this is over the better," she said.

They began plodding along the gravel road. This turned out to be difficult to do. The rain was still driving in and Kylie realised it was blowing almost directly into their faces. The water was running down rills in the road surface in gushing flows. On both the downslopes and upslopes they found themselves slipping continually. It was annoying and very hard on their overstrained muscles. And there were trees across the road they had to climb over or detour around.

The road sloped down for a few hundred metres then ran level for the next half kilometre. Dense rainforest hemmed them in on both sides. By now Kylie was sick of rainforest and just wanted to be out of it. She found it hard to push herself to keep plodding and on the next upslope she came to a shivering, shuddering standstill.

The others stopped with her, but the rain was so heavy and so cold the halt did not seem to give any relief. With a groan she forced herself to continue. The road wound up and around the side of a hill and then went down to a small clearing. This was only two hundred metres across and all overgrown with lantana and molasses grass, but it was still a welcome change from the jungle.

The overgrown ruins of a hut stood beside the road under a mango tree. For a minute they stood and contemplated it but it did not offer any shelter. The rain was still slatting in almost horizontally. Hunching her coat closer around her neck Kylie resumed her slow plod. She knew she was close to the end of her endurance and could see that both Margaret and Roger were also looking exhausted.

On the flat the road became knee deep mud in deep ruts which caused them to slip and stumble. After two hundred metres of sloshing misery they re-entered the jungle and the road went up another slope. Margaret muttered a miserable 'Oh no!' as she set herself to climb it. The road was greasy and water gushed down it. Kylie tried walking on the leaf mould at the side but found that just as hard as she had to climb around trees and dodge wait-a-while and vines.

The road climbed for over a kilometre. It wasn't steep, just a continual, steady, upward slog through a dark tunnel of rain forest. Kylie began to think she would not make it and found that when she stopped to wait for the others her legs were trembling uncontrollably. It took the three children five rest stops and thirty minutes to get to the crest.

Here they rested again for a few minutes. Margaret began to cry and was visibly shivering.

"Come on, not far now," Kylie encouraged. She was wishing she hadn't taken Peter's webbing now as it felt very heavy and she contemplated leaving it to collect later. Instead she had a drink from one of the water bottles, then rummaged around in the basic pouches and found half a chocolate. She broke off a row of squares and offered one to Margaret.

Margaret shook her head. "I don't want it thanks."

"It's Graham's," Kylie gently teased. "Go on, eat it. It will give you a boost of energy."

Margaret managed a weak smile, then burst into tears. Kylie held her for a minute, then made her eat the chocolate. The group resumed slow walking down a long, gentle downslope. A check showed Kylie that it was nearly 3pm.

The boys should be at the farm by now, she reasoned.

Every time they rounded a bend, she was filled with the hope that she would see places she knew and was cast down each time this did not happen. Everything looked grey and gloomy and wet. The wind and rain flogged at them still and she began to get upset. *If only it would stop!*

"Stop rain! Stop!" she shouted in distress.

The road turned sharply to the right and Kylie saw a circle of light ahead. The road ran out of the tunnel of jungle into open country. She gave a little cry of relief and felt her hopes rise again.

It was the end of the jungle. As they emerged from the tunnel of trees they could see for kilometres out over rain sodden cow pastures. Kylie cried with relief. *Not far now!*

They sloshed on along the muddy road. Out in the open the wind and rain slashed at them with icy fury, and they had to shield their eyes to be able to see. When gusts struck them, they staggered and twice Kylie lost her balance and fell in the mud. The other two were also blown off their feet a couple of times.

To add to the discomfort, cold water trickled into the necks and fronts of their jackets, adding to their misery. By now all were shaking continually, and Kylie knew in her heart that the situation was deadly serious.

We must get to shelter soon, or we will die of exposure, she thought.

Even as she did Margaret let out a cry as she slipped on the muddy road. She went down with a splash in a large puddle. Instead of getting up immediately she just lay there and began to cry. Kylie walked on a few paces, then stopped. Roger bent down and put out his hands.

"Up you get Margaret," he said.

"No. Go on without me. I can't walk any more," Margaret wailed.

"You can and you bloody well will!" Roger snapped angrily. "I am not leaving you here so either get up and walk or I will bloody well drag you."

Margaret stared up at him from wide, misery laden eyes but reached up and took his hand. With an effort that had them both slipping and sliding on the greasy clay she got to her knees, then to her feet. Roger put his arm around her waist and helped steady her. Kylie moved and held her up from the other side.

"Not far now," she said. "The farm is only about a kilometre. We can walk that in ten minutes."

Margaret nodded dumbly and set her trembling legs into motion. The group set themselves at the slope and plodded slowly up it, straight into fresh showers of driving rain.

Now walking truly became a test of character and endurance. Each step seemed to require an intense effort. Even breathing was hard with the rain striking their faces. They bowed their heads and plodded slowly on. Five minutes went by, then ten. Every time Kylie glanced up she did not know whether to be disheartened or not. The muddy road seemed to stretch on gently upwards for ever.

Through a driving mist of rain and low cloud she saw a copse of three trees. *Those trees. They are at the bottom end of the farm, down near the creek,* she thought. It took a moment for the realization to sink in but then she felt a new surge of hope and energy. "Nearly there! We are at the farm. Come on, it is only up this hill."

Somehow, they struggled up it. It took ten minutes to go three hundred metres and they were gasping and shaking at the end of it but then they all cried out with relief. There, just ahead, was the turn-off and signpost. They stopped there for a minute to get their breath back, partially shielded from the savagery of the wind by the wall of jungle just beyond.

Margaret eased herself out of their grip and set herself to walk the last few hundred steps. Kylie heaved a sigh of relief and made her own shaking legs follow. Those last few hundred metres were amongst the worst. The teenagers groaned and plodded painfully up over the low rise between the hilltop and the jungle, then went down the slope beyond like shuffling zombies.

The shed! Kylie thought as the dark shape came into view through the rain.

The trio tottered down to the turn-off and almost crawled up the driveway to the house. As the house came into view Kylie felt elated and very lightheaded. The world seemed to spin and swirl.

Just the cloud, she told herself, seeing the low cloud streaming and shredding over the top of the jungle on her right.

Then the front door flew open and out raced Mrs Grierson, followed by Gran. It was all Kylie could do to make herself take those twenty steps to the door. All she could think of then was the two boys.

"Peter. Graham. Did they get here?" she managed to gasp as Gran seized her with surprisingly strong arms.

Gran nodded. "Yes, they did. About half an hour ago. They have both gone with Mr Grierson to get help. Now you children just come inside and don't worry about anything."

They were divested of sodden webbing, belts, jackets and shoes on the porch, then helped inside. Now that they had arrived their own muscles seemed to give up. Kylie felt an intense sensation of relief as they passed out of the flailing wind and rain into the shelter of the house. Roger was allowed to slump onto the lounge room carpet and a blanket rugged around him. The two girls were half-carried to the two bathrooms. Mrs Grierson picked a sobbing Margaret up and carried her downstairs while Gran helped Kylie into the upstairs bathroom.

She found her fingers were too numb and that she was shaking too much to unbutton her clothes, but Gran deftly stripped her. A hot bath had been run in anticipation and Kylie was eased into it. At first she experienced a burning sensation and the water felt much too hot but Gran assured her it was only as warm as a baby's bath.

"Tested it with me elbow dearie. It's just that you are so cold. You'll soon thaw out. Now, are you alright for a minute? I want to go out and get young Roger a hot drink and I don't want you to drown while I'm doing that."

Kylie assured her she was alright, although in truth she felt like just slumping down. Gran hurried out to help warm Roger up as well and Kylie gently splashed the warm water over her chest and face. After a while the warmth began to penetrate, causing more sharp pains. These persisted for a few more minutes but after that it was bliss. She slid down so that only the top of her face was out and thought it was the most heavenly sensation she had ever experienced.

By then Gran was back and she soon made her sit up, then stand up and towel herself vigorously. A thick, flannel dressing gown was wrapped around her and Gran led her out to the back bedroom. Kylie was astounded to find that her legs would not work properly, her muscles trembling violently. She was immediately tucked in bed and hot water bottles added. Gran bustled off and returned with a cup of warm Milo. That was also bliss. While Kylie sipped it Gran hurried off to get Roger into the bath. Kylie managed a feeble smile at hearing Roger's protests as Gran treated him like a little boy.

Soon afterwards Margaret was carried up and placed in the bed beside Kylie. Mrs Grierson brought Margaret a hot Milo as well.

"Can we ring mum please Mrs Grierson and let her know we are alright?" Kylie asked.

Mrs Grierson shook her head. "Sorry dearie. The phone lines are down. We still have electricity but from the way this cyclone is building up I think we will lose that soon too. Don't worry. Mr Grierson will arrange for them to be told by the police when he gets to Malanda."

"Is the cyclone coming here?" Margaret asked, casting a fearful glance at the window as she did. Kylie now realised that the house was shuddering from the blasts of the wind and rain.

Mrs Grierson again shook her head. "We don't think so. The last report at three put it about fifty kilometres out to sea from Deeral. That is at least seventy kilometres from here with three mountain ranges in between. It is moving slowly south. I think we are safe."

Kylie finished her cup of Milo and snuggled down into the flannel sheets. A gnawing worry made her ask, "Do you think they will be in time to rescue Victor and the others?"

Mrs Grierson made various comforting answers but did not really answer. Instead she went and brought them both second cups of hot drink. Kylie gulped it down, then snuggled under the quilt. A profound sense of warm well-being made her relax. Exhaustion took over and she slipped into a deep sleep.

* * *

Later she got the rest of the story from Graham. His opening line, which he repeated a dozen times was, "It was bloody scary!"

At about the time Kylie was slipping into sleep Graham was standing with a group of police and the crew of a rescue helicopter from the Emergency Services Department at Mareeba Airport. When he and Peter had arrived at the farm and found that the telephone wasn't working, he had quickly told Gran the story, then he and Peter had run on to the Grierson's.

Mr Grierson had driven his wife over to the farm to help Gran get ready for the girls. He had wanted to drive back to get the girls and Roger, but Graham had insisted that time was vital if they were to get a helicopter to rescue the others before it got dark. Mr Grierson had accepted this and drove them to Malanda. It had been a frightening ride as the wind was so strong up on the open ridges that he had found it almost impossible to keep the vehicle on the road. Numerous stretches of flooded road slowed them and the driving rain kept their speed down to a crawl. Twice a fallen tree blocked the road, but Mr Grierson had a chain saw and a winch and was able to clear a path.

In Malanda it had taken a few minutes to convince the police but then they had acted quickly. Using their radio communications they had contacted the Emergency Services. Mr Grierson had been sent with Peter to inform the Reids of what was happening while Graham had gone in a police vehicle to Atherton, then to Mareeba. The police had wanted to put him into hospital, but he had insisted he had to show the pilot of the rescue helicopter where to go. They had accepted this but pumped a few hot drinks into him.

The helicopter had been at Charters Towers, 300 kilometres to the south and well clear of the cyclone, but, by the time he had been driven to Mareeba, it had flown to there. Mareeba had been selected as the nearest airport where it was reasonably safe. That was because it was sheltered by the Lamb Range; and in the right-rear quadrant of the cyclone, where the wind and rain were least. Even so the wind was gusting to fifty kilometres per hour.

While the helicopter was refuelled Graham had shown the pilot where the others were on a map. He described the site and the pilot had looked grim and thoughtful.

"This is going to be bloody difficult," the pilot observed.

"Do you think it is too dangerous?" a police inspector asked.

"Possibly. First, we need to find a safe route to the area. We will have to play it by ear from there," the pilot replied. "What really worries me is actually finding these people in all this rain."

"I can help you," Graham had said. "I could show you exactly where to go."

"Hospital for you lad," the Inspector had said.

Graham shook his head. "Not till they are safe," he had replied.

The pilot had looked hard at him. "Did you really walk up over those mountains in this weather this morning?"

Graham nodded. "Yes, five of us. I navigated. I am a very good navigator. I can take you straight to the place."

"Do you feel up to it?" the pilot asked. "I don't want you dying on me from hyperthermia."

"I'm fine for a bit longer," Graham replied. "I'm very fit."

"I can believe it," the pilot answered. He turned to the doctor in the crew. "Do you think it is a fair risk, Doc?"

The doctor nodded. "He's warmed up already and should just be exhausted. If what he says about the injuries to these other people is right, then every minute counts. I can look after him."

The pilot nodded. "Okay son, you come with us if you are willing, but I have to warn you it will be bloody dangerous."

Graham managed a grin. "Couldn't be worse than what I've just been through."

The pilot then turned to his co-pilot and they bent over the map to plot the best route. Both looked very worried. The police had reported that the cloud level over the Atherton Tablelands was down to ground level, even though at Mareeba it was several hundred feet.

"This is going to be bloody hairy," the pilot muttered. "We will have to fly so low we never lose sight of the ground and risk hitting a powerline. It will take pin-point navigation."

Graham had been listening and fretting with worry. Now he leaned forward and pointed to the map. "Why not go this way, up through the valley at Davies Creek and across the saddle into the Little Mulgrave? That means you wouldn't have to go over the Tablelands and might be able to keep under the cloud all the way."

The pilot studied the suggestion. "Yes, I think that is a good idea. We will do that. Come on! Let's get this show on the road."

Graham was given another hot drink, sent to the toilet, then led out to the helicopter and strapped in. By then the engine was going and the ground crew were untying it. Graham was seated beside the port door and had a headset fitted so he could communicate with the pilot. The door was slid shut and they were off.

Graham was already nervous, and this turned to genuine apprehension as the helicopter lifted off and began to toss and pitch in the turbulent air. The helicopter turned left and headed east along the main power line towards Cairns until they came to Davies Creek. Graham looked down with a mixture of fear and fascination. He was very interested in the ground they were flying over as he had hiked over some of it in the past.

Going through the pass between Lambs Head and Mt Tiptree was hair-raising. The wind was channelled by the mountains and the ridges caused savage cross-currents and severe turbulence. Graham clung on but knew it was really the seat belt that held him as he was too weak to have done it all himself. His stomach he could not hold onto and one second it was in his mouth and the next in his abdomen. He had been through storms at sea in his father's ships and prided himself on never being sea-sick but this certainly put him to the test.

The sudden appearance of a massive rock face amidst the swirling clouds caused Graham to flinch in fear, even as he registered what he was looking at. *Kahlpahlim Rock,* he thought. *I must climb it one day.* That had been an ambition of his for several years now. As the dark, looming bulk of the huge rock outcrop slid out of sight behind them another of similar size, but more broken and rugged, appeared: Lambs Head.

Through the earphones Graham heard the pilot and co-pilot debating whether to turn back as the turbulence got worse. The co-pilot said they must be encountering head winds of about a hundred knots.

A hundred knots! he thought. *That is about two hundred kilometres per hour!*

Looking through the windows was terrifying as the mountains seemed to roll and pitch up and down and several times the helicopter dropped like a stone until it was just above the treetops. It was obvious even to Graham that the pilot was having trouble controlling the machine. The crewman seated opposite Graham was looking pasty faced and grim and the doctor looked genuinely worried.

Then they were through. The valley widened and Graham knew they were in the valley of the Little Mulgrave. The bumping and sickening swoops eased, although they did not end. The helicopter began to encounter rain showers. Overhead, Graham could see thick grey clouds swirling past well below the level of the mountain tops. Below him, he saw sodden cane fields sliding by. The sugar cane was being blown in swirling patterns and much of it looked to be flattened.

We are making better time now, he thought.

He knew they were flying closer to the cyclone all the time and were obviously well into the zone of destructive winds around it. It was a sobering thought to be told that the 'eye' of the cyclone was about a hundred kilometres and two mountain ranges away.

"It is about fifty kilometres out to the east of Babinda," the pilot explained.

Graham plotted that on his mental map and realised that there would be ferocious winds blowing in through the gap between the Bellenden Ker Range and Mt Bartle Frere.

We are flying straight into that. Maybe it will be too dangerous? he thought. A vicious lurch changed that thought to: *Maybe we are going to crash?*

Chapter 33

THIS IS YOURS

As the helicopter shuddered and swooped in the turbulence, Graham found he was nauseous and felt icy cold, yet was sweating. Fear of crashing and death began to dominate his thoughts. The pilot was obviously very worried now as he kept asking the co-pilot for wind speeds and for checks on their position. Rain enveloped the machine and the treetops below became a grey blur.

"Do you know where we are?"

It took a repetition of this before Graham realised the pilot was speaking to him. He clutched his map and stared out the window. For a moment he was mystified, then a fleeting glimpse of white foam and the Goldsborough bridge gave him their position. He pressed the switch on his headphones.

"Yes. We are passing over Goldsborough. Follow the river if you can, so that I can see it. The river should do a sharp turn to the left just ahead."

"Roger that," the pilot replied. "That is what we thought. Thanks."

The helicopter flew on into even heavier rain and the buffeting from the wind became continuous. Graham began to feel worn out from holding on and his leg muscles started to cramp painfully. The helicopter turned left and followed the river for a minute before turning right again, to fly on southwards.

Graham peered down through the rain and strained his eyes to pick out places he could recognise. He was hoping to see the Kearneys Flats picnic area and was rewarded by a brief glimpse of flooded lawn, buildings and a white utility under a tree. The ute was just above the level of the swirling brown floodwaters.

Uncle Bill's car. I hope it doesn't get washed away.

He reported his sighting to the pilot, who thanked him. They flew low over the clearing to the south of the picnic area and Graham briefly glimpsed the white spray of Kearneys Falls out on the jungle covered mountainside on his left. Now he was anxiously following every twist and turn of the river, sliding his thumb along the map to keep track of which bend it was they were passing over. The pilot flew so that he could just see the river and road most of the time.

The wind was really strong now and Graham knew they were only a few kilometres south of the saddle and directly in line with it. The rain and turbulence became truly frightening.

The earphones crackled. "I think we'd better give this up or it will be us needing rescuing," the co-pilot said.

Graham felt the same way but was also conscious of sharp disappointment. He said, "We are nearly there. As soon as we reach the causeway near the junction of the two Mulgraves turn right. We should get in behind the big ridge coming down from Bartle Frere then."

The pilot answered, "I can see the junction, but that ridge might not give us any shelter. It might cause quite unpredictable turbulence and cross-winds instead."

"Please try," Graham pleaded. He was terrified now but did not want to give up that close.

"Only if everyone in the crew agrees," the pilot replied.

He then called each by name and asked them. To Graham's relief they all agreed to try.

Soon after that, they turned West and flew low up the West Mulgrave just above the level of the trees. To Graham's intense relief, the buffeting did ease although he realised the helicopter was flying crab-wise up the river. Now he peered anxiously down, searching for detailed landmarks.

"Can you open the door so I can see better?" he asked.

"Other side," the crewman answered. He unclipped Graham and helped him across. Once Graham was seated and buckled in again the crewman slid open the leeward door. Graham gripped a hand-hold and leaned his head out. The crewman did likewise.

The sight of the boiling, foaming river below was truly awe-inspiring. It was just one long mass of brown turbulence and white foam. Graham wiped rain from his face and tried to ignore the icy wind lashing at him. Where was the old prospector's camp? Where were the tracks? All he could see were treetops swirling and thrashing about in the wind. The whole jungle looked a tangle of downed trees and bare trunks.

Panic began to seize Graham. *Have we flown too far up the river?* he wondered. They passed slowly over a flooded creek which gushed down the mountain side.

"Is that Nugget Creek?" In his anxiety Graham spoke aloud. He looked desperately around, feeling the double pressure of his boast and the fear that, if he could not find the place, then four people might die. He lifted his eyes to take in the cloud swirling and streaming low overhead.

That gave him a clue. *Which ridge did we go up?* He stared at the rain lashed grey shape of the mountain side. *That one? No, the one to the west of it. So that creek ahead must be Nugget Creek.*

Into the intercom he said, "Don't go past the next creek. The old prospector's clearing should be just below us somewhere."

Even as he said this, he had a brief glimpse of bare mud through the treetops, then of a huge tree lying across the clearing. In the flailing treetops it was just that one glimpse.

"There it is! Directly below us now," he shouted.

The crewman leaned out and looked down. "Got it. Strewth! It isn't very big. We aren't landing in that."

The pilot answered. "No. Has to be a winch job. Now, let's find these two men who are marooned in mid-river."

"Can't we get Victor and the old prospector first?" Graham asked.

"No, they are safer, so they can wait a few minutes," the pilot replied.

"But these two are just thugs who bashed Victor and took our gold," Graham replied. He was worried that they might have difficulty in finding the clearing again if they left it.

"Sorry, son. We rescue them first. Where are they?"

"Just in the river south of the clearing," Graham replied. "But please don't lose this place."

"Don't fret son, we won't. We've put the co-ordinates into our GPS," the pilot replied. Graham understood how a GPS, a Global Positioning System, worked from satellite radio cross-bearings but did not want to trust such invisible technology.

The pilot took the helicopter round in a circle upwind. As they did, the wind snatched at it, shaking it and tossing it up and down so that they almost hit the trees. Graham cried out in fright and broke out into a cold sweat again.

For several minutes they searched slowly along the river. Graham scanned all the exposed rocks in mid-stream and was appalled at how foam and even logs were washing over some of them. There was no sign of the two men. A sick feeling settled in his stomach.

"Is that them?" the crewman asked. He pointed down.

Graham stared as the helicopter came to a hover at tree top height. Was that black shape a leg? The crewman obviously thought so.

"I'll go down chief," he said. "I'll have to clip them on one at a time and bring them up."

"Make it snappy, George. I don't want to try hovering here too long," the pilot replied. Graham agreed with that as the wind was still buffeting the helicopter savagely.

The crewman clipped on a harness attached to the winch and stepped out onto the skids. The doctor moved to operate the winch and the crewman was lowered down, spinning, and swinging in circles. It made Graham feel sick just to watch and he marvelled at the man's courage.

If that wire breaks, he will fall into the river! It was plain no-one could survive in that flood for more than a few seconds.

The crewman landed on the rock, thanks to some very skilful work by the pilot. Graham saw movement and realised it was the men, both of them. Even as he registered this, he saw the crewman bend down and clip a harness around one of the men. As soon as the crewman gave the thumbs up signal the doctor set the winch going and the pilot wound the helicopter higher.

It seemed to take ages to winch them up but when the men arrived Graham helped grab their clothing and pull them into the cabin. As soon as they had a good grip the crewman unclipped the man (it was Burg Graham saw. He had somehow known it would be!). The doctor at once placed Burg in a seat and clipped him in. Burg just slumped forward and for a second Graham thought he was dead but then he realised the man was just comatose from the battering and exposure.

The crewman was lowered again. This time he had much more difficulty as the wind caused the helicopter to buck and slew around and he was swung in several wide circles, even dragging his feet in the raging floodwaters for a few seconds before being placed on the rock. Within seconds he had grabbed Donk and clipped the harness on him. His arm went out and Graham shouted, "Thumbs up!"

The doctor was watching and set the winch going instantly. Once again, it seemed to take a long time to winch them up but was in fact only about a minute. As the two men came into view, Graham saw that Donk was slumped unconscious, and that he still wore his haversack.

"The gold," Graham said as he reached out.

He grabbed the haversack and used it to haul the two men in. As soon as they were inside the doctor hauled the haversack off and dropped it on the floor. Even above the wind Graham heard the thud and tinkle. Graham snatched at it to stop it sliding out the door and into the river.

The doctor looked astonished. "Holy mackerel! That was heavy. What the devil is in it?"

"Our gold," Graham cried.

He hugged the haversack to his lap. Donk was strapped in and the doctor set to work on the two men.

"Right, let's get these other people," the pilot said.

The helicopter turned and slewed around in the turbulence, then slid across the treetops. It took a few minutes of anxious searching before the clearing was sighted. Graham described the layout and what to expect. This time the crewman unclipped a metal frame stretcher from the landing skids and went down with that. Graham leaned out and watched anxiously as the crewman went down past the wildly thrashing treetops into the clearing. Rain still flogged in and he knew he was getting soaked but did not care. All he could think about was his friends below.

The crewman unclipped himself when he reached the ground. Graham saw him move towards the wreckage of the old prospector's shelter. At the same moment a blur of white across the clearing caught Graham's eye. It was Bert, staring up at the helicopter. The crewman saw him and sloshed across to him. Graham heaved a sigh of relief.

The stretcher was unclipped and carried off into the jungle. All the while Graham was aware that the pilot was wrestling with the controls and that the helicopter was buffeting up and down so that the treetops appeared to rise and fall.

Several minutes of anxious waiting went by, the helicopter hovering with difficulty. Graham could hear the pilot talking to the crewman on a radio but could not hear the crewman's answers.

Then a group appeared in the driving rain below, bent over and crouched against the fury of the storm. They were carrying the stretcher and Graham recognised Bert, Allison, Stephen and Uncle Bill. At that he relaxed a fraction. At least they were safe.

The stretcher was clipped on and winched up, the crewman riding with it to steady it. As it reached the level of the cabin the doctor reached out and swung one end in. It was hauled in and then slid lengthwise, to be secured on the floor at their feet. On it was Victor. Graham saw that he had a ghastly wax-like look and had blue lips and forehead.

As the crewman went down again with a second stretcher Graham asked, "Is he still alive?"

The doctor reached down to check. He nodded. "Yes, but only just."

At that Graham began to shake and then cry. He was barely able to help pull the next stretcher in the door. Strapped to it was the old prospector, his soaked hair matted over his face and beard. Then, to Graham's consternation the crewman seated himself, unclipped and secured his winch harness and slid the door shut.

"What about the others?" Graham cried in dismay.

The crewman turned his face to him and said nothing for a moment. Graham realised he looked exhausted and battered. The man said, "They are alright. We can't take any more without overloading dangerously. We are going to get these people to hospital first, then come back."

Graham accepted this. He looked down as the doctor knelt to examine the old prospector and was relieved to see him nod. The old prospector was alive as well.

The engine note changed abruptly and the helicopter spun round, then raced over the treetops, climbing rapidly as it did. Graham glanced out and noted they were now racing north along the Mulgrave valley. Satisfied they were now at a safe height he concentrated on what the doctor and crewman were doing.

Now reaction set in and he found himself shivering and cramping. After a while he sat back and closed his eyes. Almost at once exhaustion and relief took over and his consciousness swam. Once he opened his eyes and found himself staring into the sullen and baleful eyes of Burg, but it was Burg who broke the contact and stared out the window.

Going through the gap from the Little Mulgrave to Davies Creek was a bit hairy. Graham opened his eyes in fright as the helicopter was tossed around. "Nearly three hundred knots!" the pilot informed them. "We've got a bit of a tail wind."

On the north side of the mountains the flying conditions dramatically improved. There were only occasional showers of rain and the wind died noticeably. They flew fast just under the clouds.

Within minutes Graham recognised Mareeba below. The helicopter settled in an open area beside the hospital. To Graham's relief there were uniformed police there. As soon as the helicopter had settled, these ran forward with the hospital staff. The door was slid open and the crewman unbuckled Burg.

When Burg saw the police he snarled hate at Graham. The crewman sneered at him. "You should be thanking him, not cursing him. The kid saved your life."

Burg was taken off, then Donk taken out and placed on a stretcher to be wheeled off. Victor and the old prospector followed. Graham went to unclip his seatbelt and found his hands trembling too much. The crewman did it for him and the doctor took the haversack and helped him out. More white clad orderlies and nurses were waiting and before Graham realised what was happening, or could protest, they had lifted him onto another stretcher and started wheeling him into the hospital as well.

"Don't lose our gold," he called to the doctor.

The doctor laughed and assured him it was safe. As he was wheeled into the building Graham began to really relax, satisfied he had done all he could.

"Please ring Gran and check that Kylie and Margaret are safe," he asked.

He was taken into a ward, stripped of his sodden boots and clothes and taken to the bath. The wonderful process of recovery began. As he was doing that he heard the helicopter start up and lift off. "Is it going back to rescue my friends?" he asked.

"Yes, now relax," the nurse replied. Graham did and was wheeled off to a hot bath. He was just being tucked into a deliciously warm bed when the report came through that the others had also been rescued by the helicopter. "Another half hour and it would have been too dark," the nurse told him. "Then your friends would have had to spend the night there."

A second night! Graham thought. *That would have been the death of them.* "What about my sister and Margaret and Roger?"

"The police have reported they are safe at your grandmother's farm," the nurse replied.

That was what Graham had hoped to hear. At that he let go and slipped into oblivion.

* * *

A week later, Graham stood in the same hospital ward in Mareeba. With him were Peter, Stephen, Roger, Kylie and Margaret. They stood beside the bed in which the old prospector lay. Uncle Bill and Mrs Kirk came in to join them, followed by Bert and Allison.

The old prospector smiled up at them. "It's guid ter see ye," he said. "I hear ye walked over the mountains in the cyclone to get help?"

"Five of us," Graham replied. "It wasn't that hard. Even Kylie managed it."

Kylie glared at him and Margaret frowned her disapproval. She said, "We couldn't just leave you to die."

The old prospector nodded. "You are two very brave lassies. Never mind these hulking louts. Now, tell me the tale in detail, all I've got so far is a gabbled outline."

"You tell it, Graham," Kylie said.

Graham recounted events after the tree fell on the shelter, with Margaret and Kylie adding details that he left out.

When Graham finished the old prospector nodded. "And how is Victor now?"

Bert answered, "He is still in hospital in Cairns. They had to operate to lift part of the skull which had been depressed and fractured. The doctors said he would not have lasted more than another few hours. We got him to hospital just in time."

The old prospector nodded and looked at Graham. "I hear that ye guided the helicopter through the storm to rescue us."

Graham flushed with embarrassment. "Yes, and those two men."

"Oh aye. And where are they now?"

Like Graham, the two men had only been kept in hospital overnight and then had been taken into custody. "They broke their bail conditions about keeping away from the girls," he explained.

"Good. Justice might be done. And I hear that ye got yer gold back," the old prospector said.

"Yes we did," Uncle Bill answered. "And it's all been banked and things are fine."

That made Kylie feel very good. She explained, "The farm has been saved. Uncle Bill was able to pay his debts."

"He'll be more than able to pay his debts if he's found the famous 'Jewellers Shop'," the old prospector commented.

Uncle Bill laughed. "They all will. We have registered all the claims and I am in the process of negotiating with a mining company to do the actual mining. I'd rather stick to cows."

"Sensible fellow," the old prospector replied. "Ye could end up like me otherwise."

"We have all combined our leases and are going equal shares," Kylie said. "And we all agreed you should have a share too."

The old prospector turned to her and smiled. For a moment his eyes went moist. "That's real kind of ye, but ye've no need."

"We insist," Kylie said. "You helped, and you are our friend."

The old prospector struggled with emotion at that. Stephen suddenly snapped his fingers and dug into the bag he was carrying. "That reminds me," he said. He held out his hand. "This is yours I think."

In his hand was a gleaming gold nugget the size of a large potato. For a moment they were all stunned speechless by the size and beauty of it. The old prospector reverently took it in his hands and fondled it. He looked quizzically at Stephen.

"Mine ye say?"

Stephen nodded. "Yes. It was stuck in the roots of that tree which blew down on your camp. There were more too, but I didn't have time to get them."

"Well bless my soul!" the old prospector said. "And me digging for months in the wrong place and it was right under me feet!"

At that he began to laugh loudly. After a moment, the others joined in. Graham gave Margaret a smile (which she thought was worth more than a gold nugget any day), and Bert and Allison kissed passionately.

Enjoy more C.R. Cummings stories

The Air Cadets

The Navy Cadets

The Army Cadets

www.ingramcontent.com/pod-product-compliance
Lightning Source LLC
Chambersburg PA
CBHW031602240626
47153CB00002B/604